31 Dream Street

LISA JEWELL

First published in Great Britain 2007
by
Michael Joseph,
an imprint of Penguin Books Ltd

Published in Large Print 2007 by ISIS Publishing Ltd.,
7 Centremead, Osney Mead, Oxford OX2 0ES
by arrangement with
Penguin Books Ltd

British Library Cataloguing in Publication Data
Jewell, Lisa
31 Dream Street. – Large print ed.
1. People with social disabilities – England – London – Fiction
2. Landlord and tenant – England – London – Fiction
3. Large type books
I. Title II. Thirty-one Dream Street
823.9'2 [F]

ISBN 978–0–7531–7958–1 (hb)
ISBN 978–0–7531–7959–8 (pb)

Printed and bound in Great Britain by
T. J. International Ltd., Padstow, Cornwall

Dedicated to Kay, my beautiful mother.
1944–2005

The simplest questions are the most profound.
Where were you born?
Where is your home?
Where are you going?
What are you doing?
Think about these once in awhile, and watch your answers change.

Richard Bach, *Illusions: The Adventures of a Reluctant Messiah*, 1977

Acknowledgements

Thank you to my friends on the Board. I forgot to thank you last time, so you go first this time, to make up for it. I have no idea how other writers manage without having a place like ours to go when things get tough (or lonely, or silly, or annoying). I'm grateful to all of you.

Thank you to Sarah B, for, amongst many other things, seeing that Leo really needed to be Leah and to Judith for your wisdom, counsel, loyalty and top-notch editing skills.

Thank you to Mari, Liz, Rob, John, James, Naomi and everyone at Penguin who works so hard to make my books eye-catching, legible and widely available. And a special thank you to Louise Moore, for everything you have achieved for me over the past five years. Thank you for your vision, your belief and your friendship.

But mainly, after a year during which at some points it was hard to believe that I actually had to write a book on top of everything else, thank you to my sisters, my father and my husband for being there. I couldn't have done it without any of you.

Prologue

Leah peered through the gap between her curtains at the house across the road.

Detached from its neighbours by both its position and its appearance, 31 Silversmith Road was an eccentric building which stood alone. It rose three storeys and had been built a hundred and fifty years earlier by a pair of retired silversmiths who'd chosen the location for its sweeping views towards the Hertfordshire countryside. To fully enjoy the view they'd commissioned an ornate wrought-iron veranda which wrapped itself round the entire ground floor. Nowadays anyone sitting on the veranda would enjoy a view of nothing more inspiring than the terrace of characterless Victorian cottages opposite and beyond that the upper floors of three brutal tower blocks, sprouting from the wilds of Enfield.

The silversmiths, an unconventional pair, had chosen to decorate the exterior of their home with brightly coloured tiles picked up from their travels around the bazaars and flea markets of the world. On either side of the front door were richly coloured tiled panels depicting peacocks, which lent the house its unofficial local name of the Peacock House. In fact, when describing to people exactly where in East Finchley she lived, Leah would often say — you know, just opposite the Peacock House.

It looked more intriguing at night when it was lit up from the inside. It reminded Leah of a ceramic lamp she'd had in her bedroom as a child which was shaped like a mushroom with windows and doors cut out and little ceramic people who lived inside. She'd often fantasized about living inside that little mushroom-shaped house, all snug and cosy and safe from the elements. The Peacock House made her feel the same way. It was so inviting with its stained glass and its ornate tiles, its hanging lanterns and gables and plasterwork lions with chipped noses.

As she watched, the front door opened, and the Girl with the Guitar emerged. She and Amitabh had nicknames for all the people in the Peacock House. As well as the Girl with the Guitar, there was Old Skinny Guy, Young Skinny Guy, the Teenager, the Air Hostess and Sybil (so-called because she changed her image so frequently and so dramatically that Leah and Amitabh were convinced she must have a multiple personality disorder). The Girl with the Guitar stopped at the bottom of the front steps and lit a cigarette. Then she pushed a shank of black hair behind her ear, slung her guitar case over her shoulder and headed left, towards the High Road, the tips of her stiletto-heeled boots issuing a sharp metallic clack as she went.

Young Skinny Guy watched her, as he did every night, from his window on the second floor. His face was illuminated, as ever, by the light from his computer monitor and his expression, as ever, was one of quiet, lovelorn resignation. He was a strange-looking fellow, not unattractive, but seemingly intent on making the worst of himself. His hair was an unrestrained mass of curls, verging on an Afro, and he had equally exuberant muttonchop sideburns which sprouted from each side of his face like angel wings. He rarely left the company of his PC and Leah had seen him leave the house probably only five times since she'd moved to Silversmith Road.

Leah had no idea who any of the people over the road were. She didn't know their names or their relationships. She had no idea who owned the house or what the set-up was. Was it divided into bed-sits? Was it a house share? Or some kind of strange interbred family? She'd lived opposite the Peacock House for nearly three years, yet she'd never had a conversation with anyone who lived there. Never even exchanged nods or smiles. Leah was a curious person by nature. She liked to know what was what, who was who, how everything worked and fitted together. But she was also a Londoner who played by the rules regarding personal space and keeping yourself to yourself. So she sat and she watched and she wondered and she waited because she knew that one day, somehow, she'd find a way to answer all her questions.

Fifteen Years Earlier

1 August 1990

Toby,

Jemma and I are leaving for Cape Town tomorrow morning. I'm sorry we'll miss your wedding next week, but I'm sure you understand.

I am enclosing a set of keys. I have bought you and Karen a house as a wedding gift. Peter got it at auction. I haven't seen it, but Peter assures me it was a good buy. In need of some TLC, but structurally sound. Which is just as well, as this house also represents your inheritance. I thought it best you have something now as I will be abroad for the foreseeable future and, once Jemma and I start our new family, things will get complicated in terms of who gets what. Much simpler this way.

Property is the thing, Toby. You're on the ladder now. I can see big things happening with the London property market. Make the most of it.

Peter says there's one snag. A sitting tenant. I'm sure he'll be able to advise you on how to get him out. I've enclosed Peter's card, if you need him.

I wish you and Karen all the best for Saturday. Jemma and I will raise a glass of champagne to you both as the sun sets over Camps Bay.

Nothing much else to say except good luck, I suppose.

Best,
Reggie/Dad

In August 1990, Reggie Dobbs came to the bitter conclusion that raising his only son had been a complete waste of his time, his money and his sperm. He still recoiled at the memory of what bearing this gigantic heffalump of a boy had done to his first wife's young, firm body and had never forgiven him for it. The enormous infant had continued to grow at a disgusting rate, six foot three at thirteen and thin as a streak of piss, useless at sports, covered in spots, not a pretty sight. Toby had inherited his model mother's height, but sadly not her looks. It was unnerving, craning your neck to look up into the ineffectual gaze of your gigantic son, looming over you like an overgrown bird of prey.

They'd sent him away to school at five years old and tried to make more babies, but none had come. And then Angela had died and Reggie had been stuck with this one son, a giant, a waste of space who claimed to be a "poet". Reggie said, "Poet?! You look more like a teapot in that ridiculous hat!" But somehow, by some incredible stroke of luck, this strange boy of his had found himself a woman — a woman who was prepared to marry him. Not a beautiful girl, but then Toby should be grateful for what he could get.

He wanted to give them something, as he wasn't going to be a part of their lives, so he'd sat down with his accountant and concluded that his son was worth £75,000; £3,000 for every year of his life. He gave this money to his property broker and told him to get the best he could for it at auction.

And then he and his third wife slipped into the first-class cabin of a 747 and flew to Cape Town, where another property broker was waiting for them with the keys to a penthouse apartment overlooking the Atlantic. Reggie didn't leave Toby a forwarding address or a telephone number. He just disappeared.

Reggie wondered about Toby from time to time, especially after the kids arrived. He wondered if Toby and Karen had had children, if he was a grandfather yet; he wondered if Toby was happy, if he'd managed to make a living out of writing his wretched poetry or if he'd grown up and taken responsibility for himself. He doubted it very much. But mostly he didn't think about Toby at all. Mostly Reggie just drank vodka, ate rich food, avoided his family and wondered when he was going to die.

2 September 1990

Dear Toby,

This isn't working. Marriage isn't what I thought it would be. I expected more, not just you and me and a smelly old man rattling around inside a big, damp old house without a penny between us. I think I've realized that I don't love you enough to live in penury with you. I thought I did, but I don't. I'm sorry that I didn't realize this earlier, but I think it took something dramatic like getting married to clear my head of my silly, over-romanticized view of you.

You're a good man, Toby, but you're not enough for me. Please don't hate me,

Karen xx

A ROOM OF YOUR OWN?

Finchley-based poet, unexpectedly alone
in rambling Victorian mansion, has four big
bedrooms to fill. Shared kitchen and bathrooms.
Rent negotiable, but reasonable.
Preference given to artists and performers.
Please write to tell me why you should live here.

November 1990

Dear Lonely Poet,

My name is Ruby Lewis, I am sixteen years old and I'm a singer. My mum threw me out last week because her ugly husband kept hitting me. Which was my fault, apparently. I'm staying with this man at the moment. He's thirty-two and he thinks I'm twenty. I don't really like him, but he lives in Camden which is really cool. Anyway — I'd really like to come and live in your house because it sounds really cool and because you sound really cool and because I can't afford to pay proper rent. One day I'm going to be the most famous singer in the world and then I'll buy you a Lamborghini to pay you back. Please let me live with you. You won't regret it.

Lots of love,
Ruby xxxx

April 2002

Dear Sir,

My name is Joanne Fish and I am an actress. I am thirty-one years old, single and currently living in New Cross. I do not have much experience of sharing houses, but I was attracted to your advert because I am currently at an interesting and unexpected juncture in my life — a crossroads. Your advert struck me like a neon sign on a long and circuitous journey. I realize you will have received a thousand responses to your advert and that the onus is on me to make myself appear more interesting and needful than the other nine hundred and ninety-nine, so I will try my best.

I have had an interesting life. I have lived abroad and in various corners of this country, including Luton (!) and the Isle of Man. I have had many jobs, from the sublime to the ridiculous. I once spent a summer sticking eyes on balls of fluff in a factory that produced promotional "bugs". I also once spent a summer helping a famous actress rehearse for a role whilst she was suffering from a mild case of amnesia. I am not what I would call a particularly gregarious person, but I do like the company of other people and that is why your home appeals to me so much. My flat is very well insulated and living alone I sometimes miss the noise of existence.

I am currently researching a role for a film that is due to begin filming at the end of the year. It is a small role but pivotal and the director is very well known. Unfortunately the project is top secret so I can't divulge any more information than that. It does mean that I will not be earning a regular salary until filming commences (although I will take on occasional temporary work) so the possibility of being able to pay rent on an ad hoc, flexible basis could not have come at a more opportune moment.

I am also clean, tidy, reliable, polite and non-smoking.

I look forward to hearing from you.

Yours, in good faith,
Joanne Elizabeth Fish

February 2004

Dear Sir/Madam,

I have to admit I don't usually read the Private Eye but someone left it in the toilets at work so I thought I'd have a flick through and your advert caught my eye. Not for myself, you see, I'm a married man with three kids and a house in Hainault, but for my friend, Con.

Con works with me at Condé Nast. He's an assistant in the post room here, been working here for about a year now. He's a nice lad, a bit of a loner, but reliable to a fault. He's never had a day off. He's young, eighteen I think, and what's happened is that his mum's done a runner, buggered off to Turkey and left him alone. His grandmother raised him and then after she died the mum came back and promised him the world, rented some luxury flat for the pair of them and then two months later she buggered off again. Poor kid couldn't afford the rent on his own so he moved out, about a week ago. He was staying with a girlfriend for a while, I think, but then she kicked him out too. I don't know where he's living now but I can't help noticing he's not looking as sharp as he usually does. And he's getting that smell, you know, that sort of grime smell. I reckon he's sleeping rough. He gets the papers, looks at the ads for rooms but he can't afford anything decent, not on what he earns here. I've tried to persuade him to come home with me but he's too proud, and, if I'm honest, we haven't really got the room for him anyway.

I know your advert says you want creative people and Con's not exactly that, but he is young and just starting out and this could be the moment in his life which makes or breaks him. When I was his age I got in with a bad crowd, lots of popping pills, taking speed, fighting, that kind of thing. Lucky for me I met Chrissie and fell in love. She showed me a better way to be, you know? She saved me.

Maybe you could save Con.

Hoping for your kindest and fullest consideration.

Yours faithfully,
Nigel Cadwallader

September 2004

Dear Toby,

It was lovely to meet you the other night. I just wanted to say thank you again, for what you've done for my Con. It fears me to think what might have happened to him if you hadn't taken him in and given him a room. You are a very good man.

The reason why I'm writing is that I'm in a bit of a bind. I won't go into too much detail, but suffice it to say that I'm going to be homeless too, not to mention unemployed, unless I find somewhere to live. Con said that he's happy for me to share his room, but he said I should write to you, officially, as you like to do things properly, which I totally respect. So, would it be OK if I shared with Con for a while? I'll pay you rent and it will only be for a few weeks, just until I get myself settled back in the country and get myself a job.

I really need to be near Con now, after what happened to him when I left the country. I feel so guilty and I've got so much to make up for. If you would allow me to spend some time with him in your beautiful house, I'd be forever in your debt.

Yours faithfully,
Melinda McNulty

CHAPTER ONE

Early mornings were the only time that Toby felt that his house belonged to him. Everyone was still sleeping. There was no imminent possibility of a key in the door, of footsteps down the stairs, of voices carrying through walls. It was just him, in his pyjamas, sieving flour into a bowl, tap, tap, tap, against the palm of his hand.

Toby made bread every morning. It was a ritual, something that Karen had done every day when they were together. The first morning after she left he'd come downstairs and immediately started pounding dough, desperate to re-create the scent of his failed marriage. He didn't even eat it any more, just left it on a cooling tray every day for his tenants to enjoy.

Toby had slept badly and his usual sense of melancholy was now overlaid by a thick blanket of tiredness. It was three days into the New Year and life had already fallen flaccidly back into place. He was still trapped in this mausoleum of a house, still surrounded by people he didn't know and didn't want to know. He was still married to a woman whom he hadn't seen since he was twenty-five. He was still an unpublished poet and he was still penniless.

A pile of bills sat on his desk upstairs, unopened and unpaid. Next to the pile of bills was a pile of rejection letters from publishers and literary agents. And next to that was a letter from a local estate agent informing him that there were people queuing down the street, apparently, to buy a house like his and enclosing examples of houses the agent had sold recently for unseemly amounts of money. While Toby was grateful to them for alerting him to this fact, it was really of no possible use to him. Toby's house was full of people who had no intention of leaving and he had no intention of making them.

Toby finished making his dough and pressed it into a loaf tin, which he then slid into the Aga. He could hear the tinny drone of someone's radio alarm switching itself on upstairs and he headed quickly back towards his room, before he inadvertently crossed paths with anyone. He glanced at things as he passed through the house. A pair of Con's trainers sat under the coffee table in the TV room, with his socks curled up inside them like sleeping dogs. There was a copy of *Now* magazine on the arm of the sofa and a mug half full of blotchy tea on the floor. Ruby's black lacy cardigan was hanging from the back of the armchair and Joanne's Clarins face powder sat in a little plastic pot on the coffee table next to Ruby's cereal bowl. A small plastic Christmas tree with multicoloured fibre-optic tips twinkled forlornly in the early morning gloom. A pair of Ruby's pointy boots lay by the door, one upright, the other on its side, as if it had fallen over drunk. Toby picked up one of the boots and stared at it longingly.

This was his world, had been for years. A world of other people's possessions, rhythms, dramas, smells and habits. His presence left no imprint on the dynamics of his home. It was as if he didn't exist. What would it be like to live alone, he wondered, to come home and find everything as he'd left it? To never have to take someone else's unwashed saucepan out of the kitchen sink to pour himself a glass of water, never to be woken up by the sound of someone else's snoring or someone else's lovemaking? To know people only as they presented themselves to the world, not to see the ragged, domestic underbelly of strangers any more. Would he feel more substantial? Would he feel more alive?

He climbed the two flights of stairs to his room, three at a time, and closed the door silently behind him.

CHAPTER TWO

Ruby watched Con leaving for work from her bedroom window. He moved with the slightly lolloping gait of a teenage boy in trainers. His dark hair was slick with product and his jeans hung somewhere short of his waist but not quite below his buttocks. He was a lovely-looking boy, clear-skinned, well proportioned with startling indigo eyes. But Ruby didn't find him attractive. She didn't appreciate younger men. She liked older men. Not *old* men, just men who were slightly used, a little creased, like second-hand books. In the same way that you might look at a small child and try to envisage their adult face, she liked to look at a mature man and imagine the young man who'd once inhabited his features.

"What are you staring at out there?"

Ruby turned and smiled at the man in her bed. Paul Fox. Her slightly creased forty-five-year-old lover.

"Nothing," she teased.

She sat on the edge of her bed. One of Paul's feet was poking from the bottom of the duvet. She picked up his big toe between her thumb and forefinger, put it between her front teeth and bit down on it, hard.

"Ow." He pulled his leg back under the duvet. "What was that for?"

"That," she said, "was for ignoring me last night."

"What?" His brow furrowed.

"You *know* what. Eliza walked in and suddenly it was as if you didn't know me any more."

"Oh, Christ. Ruby — she's my *girlfriend*."

"Yeah, I know. But it's still not very nice, is it?" Ruby and Paul's relationship had always been an informal mix of occasional business and no-strings pleasure. He got her the odd support slot for one of his acts, they got together once or twice a week for sex or drinking or both, and he paid her what he jokingly referred to as a "salary", a small monthly cheque, just to keep her ticking over, just to keep her in tampons and vodka, because he could afford to and because he wanted to. It was easy-come, easy-go, a bit of reciprocal fun that had worked for both of them for the past five years. Ruby didn't expect anything more from Paul. But at the same time she couldn't help feeling a bit gutted that Paul had failed to fall in love with her throughout their five-year relationship. And she couldn't help feeling a bit cheated that six months ago Paul had fallen in love with a forty-two-year-old earth mother from Ladbroke Grove with two kids, her own business and a vineyard in Tuscany.

"Look," sighed Paul, sitting up in bed, "I had no idea she was going to show up last night. She said she couldn't get a babysitter —"

"Sorry?"

"She'd originally said she was coming to see the band and then her babysitter let her down and —"

"And you invited me instead."

"Well, yes."

"Fucking charming."

"Jesus, Ruby —"

"Jesus-Ruby-what? I'm sick of this. This whole thing is fucked."

"Ruby. Come on."

"No. I will not come on. You and I. We used to be equals. We used to be the same. But ever since you met Eliza it's like I'm just some bit of crap who follows you around plugging the gaps in your life."

"That is *so* not true."

"And don't talk like that. Like some American teenager. You're forty-five years old. You sound *ridiculous*." Ruby winced inwardly as the words left her mouth. She was being a bitch, but she couldn't help it.

She glanced at herself in the mirror. Ruby had an image of herself that she carried around in her head. It was an image of a smoky brunette with black eyes and creamy skin and a look about her as if she'd just had sex or was thinking about having sex. Generally speaking the mirror reflected back exactly what she expected to see. Every now and then it didn't. This was one of those moments. Her make-up was smudged under her eyes. Sometimes when her make-up was smudged under her eyes it made her look sexy and dangerous. Right now it made her look tired and vaguely deranged. Her hair was dull and dirty — she should have washed it yesterday, but just couldn't be bothered — and she had a big spot on her chin. She wondered what Eliza looked like first thing in the morning and then realized that it didn't matter what Eliza looked like first thing in the morning because Paul was in love with her and to him she would look beautiful no matter what.

There was a knock at the door. Ruby breathed a sigh of relief and pulled her dressing gown together.

"*Ruby. It's me, Toby.*"

She sighed and opened the door.

"Hi. Sorry, I was just, er — oh, hi, Paul." He peered over her shoulder and threw Paul a stiff smile.

Paul put up a hand and cracked an equally stiff smile. He looked silly, arranged between Ruby's marabou-trimmed cushions and fake leopard-skin throws with his big hairy chest and his mop of greying hair. Silly and like he didn't belong here. He looked, Ruby suddenly and overwhelmingly realized, like a silly handsome man having a silly adulterous affair. She gulped silently.

"Yes, I was just wondering about the rent. Just wondering if maybe you could give me a cheque today. It's just, there are some bills, and if I don't send a cheque by the end of the week, then, er, well, there'll be no hot water. Or heating. That's all."

"Fine," sighed Ruby, "fine. I'll give you a cheque tonight."

"Yes, well, you did say that last week, and you didn't. I haven't had any rent off you since the end of November, and even then it wasn't the full amount and —"

"Toby. I'll give you a cheque. Tonight. OK?"

"Right. OK. Do you promise?"

"I promise."

"Good. Right, then. See you. *See you, Paul.*"

"See you, Toby."

Ruby closed the door, and turned and smiled at Paul. He peeled back the cover and smiled at her invitingly.

"Sorry, mate." She flipped the duvet back over his naked body and picked up an elastic band from her dressing table. She pulled her hair back into a topknot with it. "I'm not in the mood."

Paul threw her an injured look. "Not even a quickie?" he said.

"No. Not even a quickie." She winked at him, softening the bluntness of her rejection. She wasn't in the mood for another scene. She knew there was a Big Conversation waiting to happen, but she didn't want to have it now. Right now she just wanted to have a shower. Right now she just wanted to feel clean.

CHAPTER THREE

Con pulled the glossy brochure out of the envelope and flicked through it impatiently, his eyes taking in the images a second at a time. Blue skies, palm trees, creamy beaches. But this wasn't a travel brochure. This was a brochure for the Right Path Flight School in Durban, South Africa. Con gazed at crop-haired men in icy white shirts and epaulettes, sitting in tiny cockpits lined with a thousand buttons and lights, knobs and levers, and felt a thrill of excitement. Then, before anyone could ask him what he was looking at, he slid the brochure back into the envelope and headed for the eighth floor.

The *Vogue* fashion department looked like a normal office. It had desks and computers and printers and wastepaper bins. It had a suspended ceiling and fluorescent lighting and phones ringing and fax machines chirruping. It looked like a normal office, but it absolutely wasn't.

Con partly relished the point in the day when he was called upon to push his trolley through the *Vogue* fashion department and partly dreaded it. He liked looking at the girls, rail-thin, delicate as wisps of smoke with their serious clothes and their perfect skin. He liked the way they sat behind their desks, slender legs knitted together like vines, tap-tapping at their keyboards with lean fingers. He liked their flat, pointy shoes and their strange accessories, the scarves and rings and tiny cardigans, so different to the girls he knew from home. And he liked the way they talked, their husky Marlboro Light voices and the peculiar shapes they made out of ordinary words. They appeared to him like people from dreams — half-formed, semi-opaque, not quite human. They fascinated him. And they repulsed him. It annoyed him that they existed so separately to him. It wound him up that he could move through them with his trolley, invisible, even to the ugly ones. They passed him their packages and parcels; they asked him stupid questions about costs and timings; they addressed him only via pieces of paper.

In his world, outside the gilded gates of the Condé Nast building, Con was a player. He met his friends in the pub on a Friday night and girls, *good-looking* girls, shimmied around him, glanced against him, willed him to pay them attention. Here he was just the post boy.

One of these wraith-like girls approached him now, her hand clutching a large white Jiffy bag. She had fine blonde hair, the colour of rice paper, and pale waxy skin. She was wearing a biscuit-coloured suede waistcoat with a shaggy trim over a grey lace top. Her eyes were icy blue. Con had never seen her before.

"Erm," she started, handing him the envelope, "this has to go recorded. Will it get there by Friday?"

Con took the package from her hand and examined it. It was addressed to someone in South London. "Yeah," he said, "should be OK."

"Excellent," she said. And then, miraculously, she smiled. Not one of the smiles that these well-brought-up girls usually served him with, not the practised co-ordination of facial muscles to force the mouth into an upturned crescent, but a proper burst of sunshine. "Thank you," she said, still smiling. "Sorry . . . what's your name?"

Con felt a flush of surprise rise from his midriff towards his temples. He hesitated for a second, not entirely sure of the answer to that question. "Connor," he said eventually. "Con."

"Con," she repeated, cocking her head slightly to one side. "I'm Daisy."

Daisy, he thought. Perfect. That's what she looked like. A colourless, uncomplicated flower, tiny and well formed. "That's nice," he said, feeling the heat of his embarrassment starting to fade.

"Thank you," she smiled again. Her teeth were slightly crooked, but very white. "My sisters are called Mimosa and Camellia. I must have been a very plain baby."

Con laughed. He noticed a girl sitting at the desk nearest to him look up at the sound of his laughter. Her face registered a situation she didn't quite comprehend. She looked away again.

Daisy said, "It's my first day today. I'm in charge of letters and things so you'll probably find me bugging you about stuff."

Con shook his head. "That's OK," he said.

"Good," she said. And then she went back to her desk.

Con dropped the white Jiffy bag onto his trolley and pushed it towards the doors at the far end. As he passed Daisy's desk she looked up at him and grinned. She mouthed the word "Bye" and waved at him. He waved back, his heart leaping around in his chest like a wild salmon.

As the door closed behind him and he found himself in the corridor outside, he breathed out and leaned against the wall. He tried to decipher what had just happened from the mixed messages his head and his heart were sending each other, but none of it made any sense. He had a curious feeling that something significant had just happened, that his life had reached a mini-roundabout, that suddenly he had options. And all because a beautiful girl called Daisy had smiled at him.

He pulled himself upright at the sound of the lift pinging and wheeled his trolley quickly towards the features department.

CHAPTER FOUR

It had snowed the night before, and Silversmith Road was gleaming with ice, so when Leah left her house on Thursday morning and saw Old Skinny Guy lying face-down on the pavement, his arms and legs spread out as if he were making angels in the snow, her immediate assumption was that he'd slipped and fallen.

Leah saw Old Skinny Guy leave his house most mornings. He had a very set routine. At eight o'clock he started to leave the house. It took him approximately three minutes to make his way down the front steps, leaning heavily on a gnarled mahogany cane as he went. At the bottom of the steps he would stop for a while, his hand resting on the head of a plaster lion. He would then remove from the pocket of his grey tweed overcoat (worn through all four seasons) a voluminous white handkerchief and rub it vigorously back and forth across the end of his nose. No matter the weather or the time of year, the old man always had a streaming nose. He would then fold the enormous handkerchief back into a triangle, tuck it into his overcoat pocket and begin his ritual inspection of the pavement outside his house. Any stray sheets of newspaper or cigarette butts were dispatched into the gutter with a firm thwack of his walking stick, then he would be on his way.

"Hello," she made her way tentatively across the slushy road. "Hello. Are you OK?"

Old Skinny Guy failed to respond in any way. Leah leaned down and shouted into his ear. "Are you OK? Do you need any help?" The man lay motionless and Leah began to suspect that there might be something seriously wrong. She picked up his hand and felt around the ribs and nodules of his wrist for a pulse. Something juddered beneath the tips of her fingers like a truck going over a speed bump. Leah couldn't tell if it was the clunk of the old man's blood or some kind of subcutaneous carbuncle. She let his hand drop and glanced at the front door of the old man's house.

She clambered up from her knees. "I'm going to get someone," she shouted. "I won't be long."

She hurried towards the Peacock House and banged loudly against the front door. A figure appeared through the mottled stained glass of the front door and then he was there, in front of her, Young Skinny Guy, all sideburns and hair and enquiring, slightly panicky facial expressions.

"Yes?" he said.

"Er, the old man," she began, "he's there," she pointed behind her. "I think he might be dead."

"Oh, Jesus." He peered over his shoulder at the prone figure on the pavement. "Oh, shit. Let me . . . God. I need shoes." He glanced down at a pair of unfeasibly long and bony feet. "Hang on. Just a sec.

Hold on." He turned to go, but then spun round again. "Have you called an ambulance?"

"No." Leah shook her head.

"Right. Maybe that's the thing to do. I reckon. Right. Shoes. Back in a tick."

She was in the middle of trying to explain exactly what was wrong with the old man to a woman with a northern accent who'd answered the phone quickly enough to restore Leah's faith in the emergency services, when Young Skinny Guy lolloped back down the hallway wearing a pair of gumboots. He followed her down the front steps and out onto the pavement. "He's just sort of flat on his face," Leah said to the operator. "I'm not sure if he's breathing or not." She glanced at the skinny guy who was crouched over the old man with his ear to his mouth. He shrugged.

"No," continued Leah, "we're not sure. He's very old."

"Ninety-seven," said the skinny guy, picking up the old man's wrist and feeling around for a pulse. "He's ninety-seven."

"Jesus," she said to the operator, "he's ninety-seven."

Gus Veldtman was pronounced dead half an hour later and taken away to Barnet General Hospital, where it would later be ascertained that he had died of a massive heart attack. Leah and the skinny guy stood together on the pavement and watched the ambulance as it pulled away. There was something stultifyingly tragic about the silence as the ambulance headed slowly towards the

High Road without sirens or flashing lights. There was no hurry. Being dead wasn't an emergency.

"Well," said Leah, looking at her watch, "I guess I'd better get on."

"Off to work?"

"Yes," she nodded, "I run a shop, up on the Broadway."

"Oh, really," he said, "what sort of shop?"

"It's a gift shop," she smiled, "a very *pink* gift shop."

"I see," he nodded, "I see."

"So. Is there anything else I can do?" she said hopelessly.

"No." He ran the palm of his hand across his face. "No. That's it now, really, isn't it? I'll call his relatives. They'll sort out the rest of it, I suppose. Just got to sort of get on with things, I guess." He shrugged and tucked his hands into his pockets. "But thanks . . . sorry, what *is* your name?"

"Leah."

"Leah." He nodded. "I'm Toby, by the way." He offered her a hand the size of a baseball mitt to shake.

"Toby," she repeated, thinking that of all the possible names she'd ever considered for Young Skinny Guy, Toby was absolutely not one of them. "Funny," she said, "I've been living across the road from you for nearly three years and I finally get to talk to you because someone dies." She shrugged. "That's London for you, I guess."

Toby nodded his agreement.

"So, who was he? Gus? I always thought maybe he was your grandfather."

Toby laughed, nervously. "You did?"

"Yes. But I'm assuming from your reaction to . . ." — she gestured at the spot on the pavement where he'd died — "that I was wrong."

"No. Gus wasn't my grandfather. Gus was my sitting tenant."

"Ah," she said, "I see. So it's *your* house?"

"Yes," he nodded. "It is."

"And the other people who live here — they're . . . ?"

"My non-sitting tenants." Toby was starting to look somewhat strained by the conversation.

"I'm sorry," said Leah. "The last thing you need right now is me asking you loads of questions. It's just — I'm such a nosy person and I've been wondering about your house for years, wondering who you all were and how you all knew each other and . . . well, anyway. I'll let you get on. And if there's anything you need, you know where I live. Please — just ask."

Toby smiled. "Thank you. I will. And Leah?"

"Yes?"

"Thank you, so much."

"What for?"

"For being here. Thank you."

He turned then and ascended the steps to his big, peculiar house. Leah turned, too, heading towards the bus stop. Looking back at the cold patch of pavement where old Gus had taken his final breaths, she caught a brief glimpse through the front door of the Peacock House. She saw someone glide from one room to another, like a ghost. The door slammed shut and she snapped out of her reverie. It was time to go to work.

CHAPTER FIVE

Toby pushed open the door to Gus's bedroom. He'd been into Gus's bedroom on only two previous occasions — once to check that he was alive when he hadn't appeared for breakfast one morning (he'd tripped over his shoes and twisted his ankle) and another time to check that he was alive when he hadn't appeared for dinner one night (he'd accidentally taken a sleeping pill instead of a headache pill and had been asleep in his overcoat and shoes since teatime).

The room was papered with a terrible striped flock in burgundy and cream, and hung with ugly oil paintings lit by brass light fittings. The curtains were slightly flouncy in blue floral chintz and the carpet was a flattened rose-coloured shag pile. A brass chandelier hung from the central ceiling rose. Only one bulb still worked. The double bed sagged in the middle like a hammock and was dressed in burgundy sheets and a thick layer of woolly blankets. The room smelled, not as you might expect, of oldness, or of loneliness, but of malted milk and elderly cat.

The malted milk could be explained by the fact that Gus ate a whole packet of the biscuits every day. The elderly cat couldn't really be explained at all.

Toby walked towards Gus's desk. It was positioned in the window and looked out over the back garden and the asphalt roof of the bathroom below. Gus had a proper old-fashioned typewriter. Toby couldn't remember the last time he'd seen a typewriter. He also had piles of books and paperwork and a collection of old tin snuff boxes in a glass box. There was a manuscript on the desk. It was obviously very old and was covered in faded pencil marks and ink amendments. Gus's clothes hung in a burr-veneered 1920s wardrobe from heavy wire hangers which jangled together like wind chimes when Toby tugged at a pair of trousers.

And there, at the bottom of the wardrobe, lay a red plastic tray filled with cat litter. A solitary cat poo poked out of the grey nuggets — it was fresh. On the other side of the wardrobe was a green saucer filled with brown pellets, a small bowl full of water and a huge bag of Science Diet.

"What you doing?"

Toby jumped and clutched his heart.

"Shit."

It was Ruby. She was eating a banana.

"Sorry. I thought you'd heard me come in."

"Look at this," he said, pointing inside the cupboard.

She peered in over his shoulder. "*What!*" she grimaced.

"I know. And it's fresh. Did you know he had a cat?"

She shrugged. "News to me. Where is it?"

They both glanced around the room in unison. Ruby finished her banana and dropped the skin nonchalantly into Gus's wastepaper bin. Toby noted the action and filed it away as yet another reason why he should stop being in love with her. He now had about thirty to forty reasons why he should stop being in love with Ruby Lewis.

She'd slept with more than fifty men.

And at least one woman.

She left her toenail clippings on the bathroom floor.

She called her female friends "honey" and "sweets".

She always slammed the front door when she got in at night, even though Toby had asked her not to, politely, about a hundred and fifty times.

She swore too much.

She smoked too much.

She never gave anyone their telephone messages.

She rarely paid her rent.

She was the centre of her own universe.

She believed in God (when it suited her).

She left used cotton buds and cotton-wool balls covered in old make-up on the shelf in the bathroom.

She called him "Tobes".

She flirted with everyone, all the time.

She had a yellow stain on one of her front teeth.

She read magazines with exclamation marks in the titles and insisted on regaling him with titbits of gossip about so-called celebrities he'd never heard of.

She did only one wash a month and would then drape and festoon every radiator in the house with the entire contents of her wardrobe, leaving Toby in the position of having to stare at her (surprisingly unpretty) knickers while he ate his dinner.

She thought classical music was boring.

She thought literary classics were boring.

She thought Radio Four was boring.

She thought staying in was boring.

And she thought, more pertinently, that Toby was boring.

She told him all the time, "God, Tobes, you're *sooo* boring," whenever he tried to broach a subject that was in any way serious or important or even slightly domestic in nature.

She laughed at his clothes and his hair and cupped his bottom, occasionally, through his jeans to tease him about his lack of padding in the buttock department.

She was awful, really, in so many ways. An awful girl. But, God, so beautiful and, God, so amazingly talented.

"Under the bed?" she suggested.

"What?" Toby snapped out of his reverie.

"Maybe that's where his cat lives."

"Oh. Right. Yes."

She fell suddenly to her hands and knees, and adopted a position that put Toby in mind of one he'd seen on the Internet last night. He glanced at her denim-clad behind as it swung from side to side like a search-light.

"Oh, my God. I don't believe it."

"What?"

"*Hello*," she whispered to something under the bed. "*Don't be shy. It's OK.*"

Toby stopped staring at her bottom and joined her on his hands and knees.

"Look," she pointed into the corner. "Over there."

Toby blinked and a pair of eyes blinked back at him. "Oh, my God."

They managed to coax the little creature out by shaking its food bowl and making lots of silly noises.

"That's the smallest cat I've ever seen in my life," said Ruby, watching it crunch delicately on nuggets of Science Diet.

It looked like a slightly insane illustration of a cat. It had a gigantic head and a tiny body and stringy black fur. It looked like it might be even older than Gus. Toby's natural instinct was to pet the poor animal in some way, but there was something about the dandruffy look of its coat and the way its bones stuck out of its flesh that put him off.

"I can't believe he kept a cat in here all these years," said Ruby. "Why did he keep it secret?"

"Lord knows," said Toby. "Maybe the old landlord didn't allow animals in the house. Maybe he thought I'd make him get rid of it."

"Tragic, isn't it? Like a little runt or something."

"Terrible-looking creature." Toby tutted and shook his head.

"Oh, but quite cute in a funny sort of way, don't you think?"

"Not really." Toby stood up and stretched his legs. "What the hell are we going to do with it?"

"I don't want it," said Ruby, recoiling slightly.

"Neither do I."

"We'll have to get rid of it."

"What — kill it?"

"*No!*" Ruby looked at him aghast. "Give it to a home. Or something."

"Oh, God," Toby sighed as yet another job added itself to the list of Things He Had To Do Because Gus Had Died. He'd already spent an hour on the phone this morning trying to track down Gus's great-niece, who'd moved, it seemed, about ten times since Gus had last spoken to her. He'd then somehow found himself offering to host a "small drinks party" after Gus's funeral the following week which would be hideous, absolutely hideous. Next, he had to find a new tenant for Gus's room, which would probably necessitate a full redecoration as he doubted that anyone under the age of sixty would have the slightest interest in the 1970s boarding-house look Gus had created in here. And now he had to do something about this odd little cat that Gus had been hiding in his room for possibly fifteen years.

Ruby got to her feet and sauntered towards a chest of drawers. "I wonder what sort of stuff he's got," she said, idly pulling open a drawer.

"Ruby!" Toby chastised. "You can't go through his stuff."

"Why not? He's dead. Oh, my God. Jesus — look at these!" She spun round, clutching a piece of bright orange paisley cotton.

"What is that?" said Toby.

"Gus's pants!" she beamed. "I mean, where do you even buy things like this?" She held them up to the light and examined them.

Toby glanced around the room again. His heart lurched. "I can't believe he's dead."

"Me neither." Ruby put the pants back and closed the drawer . . .

"Ninety-seven years," sighed Toby. "He's taken ninety-seven years of life to the grave with him. All those experiences, all those emotions. People he loved, places he's seen — gone." He clicked his fingers and let his head drop into his chest. "I wish I'd talked to him more. Wish I'd let him pass on his stories to me. I could have kept them for him. You know."

"Oh, stop being so maudlin." Ruby poked him in the thigh with the toe of her shoe. "He was a miserable old bastard. He didn't want to share his stories with anyone. I used to try talking to him all the time. Got nothing. I tell you what you need," she stretched and yawned. "A stiff drink."

"But it's not even five o'clock."

"Yes. But by the time I've made the drinks and brought them back it will be. And besides, it's dark out. It's as good as night-time. Rum and Coke? Gin and tonic? Something stronger? I've got a bottle of schnapps?"

Toby stared up at Ruby, his face pulling itself automatically into an expression of disapproval. But he let it go. He couldn't be bothered playing the fusty old stick, not today. "A glass of red wine would be lovely," he said, letting a small smile soften his face.

"Good boy." She beamed at him.

She left the room then and Toby watched her go. Ruby Lewis. The love of his life.

The little cat scurried back under the bed at the sound of a slamming door downstairs and Toby got to his feet. He went to the window and stared out across the rooftops. The snow on the ground had melted, but it still clung to the roofs and treetops like sheets of royal icing. It would be gone by tomorrow morning, though, disappeared down drainholes and gullies, taking the memories of a snowy January day with it. London snow was like life: here today, gone tomorrow. What was the point of it all?

Ruby returned, clutching a bottle of Cava and two long-stemmed glasses.

"I found this in the fridge," she said. "I think it's Melinda's."

"Oh, my God, she'll go mental."

"Yes," Ruby winked. "I know. But it just seemed fitting." She popped the cork and poured them a glass each. "To Gus," she said, holding her glass aloft. "A funny old bastard, but he always left the seat down and he never left a skid mark."

"To Gus," said Toby. "And to the future. May it be as bright as Gus's underpants."

CHAPTER SIX

In bed that night, Leah lay awake for longer than usual. Her head was full of Gus and Toby and peacocks and cold pavements. How did a person end up living in a house full of strangers, without a wife, without a family? How did a person end up so totally alone? And if she were to die at ninety-seven, she mused, she wouldn't even have a great-niece to claim responsibility for her remains. Her brother, Dominic, was gay and unless something radical happened to his brain chemistry there was no chance of any procreation there. No nieces or nephews to have kids and keep her in relatives in her old age. It was all down to her.

She glanced across at Amitabh's slumbering form. As usual, he had kicked off the duvet and was lying flat on his back, little squeaks and whistles escaping from his nostrils. Leah manoeuvred herself onto her elbow and looked at him properly. She stared at the line of his nose and the contours of his forehead. She touched his thick hair with the palm of her hand. And then, she couldn't resist it, she leaned over and brushed his lovely cheek with her lips.

"Jesus!" he jumped. "What! What is it?!"

"Nothing," said Leah, springing away from him. "Nothing. I was just kissing you, that's all."

"Why?"

"Because . . . I don't know. I just wanted to."

"Jesus. It's nearly two. Why are you awake?"

She shrugged. "I can't sleep. It's that man. That Gus. I can't stop thinking about him."

"Oh, God." Amitabh sighed and pulled the duvet back over himself.

"How do you do it?" she said. "I mean, you must see it every day. Old people, dying, alone. Doesn't it, I don't know, doesn't it . . . *get to you*?" Amitabh was a nurse in a geriatric ward. He knew about these things.

"Oh, God. Leah. Not now. Please."

"But is it better or worse if they're alone? Does it seem sadder if there are loads of relatives and grandkids and things, or is it worse if there's nobody there at all?"

"Let's have this conversation in the morning, shall we?" He reached out and squeezed her wrist perfunctorily.

"I don't want to end up all on my own," she said. "I really don't want to."

"It's OK. You're a nice person. You won't be on your own."

"Yes, but being nice isn't any guarantee that you'll get married and have kids and that all your friends won't die before you, is it?"

"It helps," he said.

"Hmmmm." Leah sank back into the bed and pulled the duvet over her chest. Within ten seconds Amitabh's breathing had grown heavy. Ten seconds later he was fast asleep. Leah looked at him again and suddenly knew what she had to do. It was obvious. She'd never felt more certain of anything in her life.

"Am. Amitabh," she shook him gently by the shoulder. "Am."

"Oh, God! What?" He turned over and stared at her accusingly.

"I love you."

He raised an eyebrow at her.

"No. I mean, I really love you. And I want to be with you for ever. You know. Until I die. I want to marry you."

"*What!*"

"I want to marry you."

"No, you don't."

"Yes. I do. Will you marry me?"

"Oh, my God. You're being serious, aren't you?"

"Uh-huh."

"Jesus," his face softened, "Leah. It's so late. I can't . . ."

"It's OK," she said, brushing his hair away from his face. "You don't need to answer now. Sleep on it. Think about it."

"Is this to do with that old man? Are you having some kind of crisis?"

"No," she said. "Honestly. No. It's just made me think, that's all. About what's important. About what I want. And I want you. For ever."

"Let's talk about it in the morning," he said.

"Yes," she said, "let's."

CHAPTER SEVEN

Wallace Beaton was a dusty-looking man in a grey suit and a bottle-green tie. He sat behind a desk the size of a dining table and turned paperwork with long, dry fingers. "Mr Veldtman has left instructions that you be the sole beneficiary of his estate."

"Estate?"

"Yes. Mr Veldtman has bequeathed you all his personal possessions which are, I assume, in your property?"

Toby gulped and thought sadly of the ugly pre-war furniture and the snuff-box collection. "Yes. That's right."

"And guardianship of his cat."

"Oh, God. Really?"

"Yes. With the strict instruction that it must stay with you. Until it dies. Or you die."

Toby gulped again. "And if I die?"

"Then it should be sent to live with Mr Veldtman's great-niece in Guernsey. Right. Next." He pulled out another sheaf of paper and cleared his throat. "Mr Veldtman has a, er . . . novel in print."

"He does?"

"Yes. Published in Dutch in 1930. And reprinted twelve times since. Mr Veldtman has a royalty account with a firm of agents in the Hague. He has instructed that his literary estate be bequeathed to you and any payments be paid directly into your bank account."

"Wow, really?"

"Yes. But to put that into perspective, Mr Veldtman's royalty payment for the past six months was £5.26."

"Oh. OK. But that's still quite cool, isn't it? Having a literary estate."

"Yes," Wallace Beaton smiled wryly. "It is quite cool."

"And, er, is that it?"

Wallace Beaton shrugged his shoulders. "Yes."

"Right. It's just that when I spoke to Gus's great-niece on the phone last week she intimated to me that Gus might have had some stocks and shares and such?"

"Really?"

"Yes. She said he was quite a player on the stock market in his younger days."

"Well, there's no evidence of that here," he waved his long fingers over the paperwork piled on his desk. "Perhaps he sold them. Or perhaps," he said, with a twinkle in his eye, "he kept it all underneath his mattress?"

Toby yanked up the corner of Gus's mattress and felt around underneath. He found nothing at the near side of the bed so he climbed onto the mattress and pulled back the further corners.

He saw something then, slotted into the back of the bedstead. A blue book with a scuffed canvas cover. It looked like a notebook, or possibly a diary. He leaned across the bed and pulled it out. It was a thick book, crammed with bits of paper. There was a gold logo embossed on the front that said "Regal" in fancy lettering.

Toby sat down and opened the book. It smelled of wet leaves and damp lino. On the front page, in predictably spidery handwriting, were the words "Property of Augustus Veldtman". Toby flicked through the book to determine what kind of journal it was and soon realized that what he had in his hands was, basically, the inside of Gus Veldtman's head: lyrics, poetry, shopping lists, accounts, letters, diary entries, thoughts, quotes, bills and scripts. There were till receipts from ten years ago, marked with little notations — next to the listing for a packet of Waitrose Honey Roast Ham were the words "pleasant enough". The label from a cheese-and-pickle sandwich had been detached and placed in his diary with the words: "Made me sick. Write to manufacturers to demand compensation."

There were lists of pills he'd taken, books he'd read, meals he'd eaten. There were bus tickets and doctor's prescriptions and postcards from someone called Michael who lived in Germany ("I think of you often, my friend, especially at this time of year.").

Most of the contents of the book were mundane and repetitive, but every few pages there'd be something peculiar that caught Toby's eye. One page was empty except for a random thought, framed with quotation marks:

"There are two toothbrushes in the beaker in the bathroom today. They are resting side by side and look like they are copulating."

Another, less concise page contained a detailed description of the condition in which he'd found the kitchen one morning:

"Towering mountains of filthy plates that put me in mind of the leaning tower of Pisa having been defecated upon by a flock of poisoned geese, surfaces encrusted with scabs of putrid food, a slick upon the kitchen floor which, for all I know, might have been a spillage of raw human effluence. I am sickened to know that people can live this way."

Another passage described an encounter with Ruby in the hallway:

"She appraised me as a stallion might appraise a mule, before returning to her room where another of her feckless men lay in wait. Within minutes my ears were once again assaulted by the painful sounds of her frantic mating."

There was also much talk about a person called Boris.

"Boris continues to ignore me. He thinks this game will bring him my attentions, but he is wrong."

"It is the fault of Boris. He is a selfish and ill-mannered individual. I hope he shall die before too long."

"Boris and I enjoyed an hour of fresh air today in the garden. He sat on my feet and we admired the triumphant blue fists of hyacinth bursting through the chill February sod."

It wasn't until Toby read the passage: "Boris seems to have developed a digestive complaint. His faeces are loose and foul-smelling. I have been compelled to replace his litter five times today," that he realized that Gus had been referring to his cat.

Toby pulled back the corner of the mattress and peered through the wooden slats. Boris looked up at him. "Hello, Boris," said Toby. The cat glanced away awkwardly. "Gus tells me you're selfish and ill-mannered." The cat turned away and curled itself into a ball. "And maybe he's right."

And that was when he saw it. A black fabric bag wedged between the bed salts. Attached to it, by an elastic band, was an envelope addressed to him. He opened it and pulled out a letter, typewritten on thin, crackly paper:

My Dear Toby,

Well, finally I am gone. I sincerely hope that my death didn't cause you too much inconvenience, that I didn't drag on with some incessant disease or terrible plague. If I did, then I apologize. I chose to be alone and, if that choice resulted in you being responsible for me in any way that you found tedious or bothersome, then I do apologize.

I have bequeathed to you my meagre possessions and my meagre cat. Do what you wish with the former, but please be kind to the latter. And of course there is my literary "estate" — ha! — for what it is worth. Additionally, and more importantly, I have fulfilled the cliché of the elderly person who does not trust anyone else to look after their money and hoarded my life's savings underneath my mattress. I am not sure of the exact amount, but it is a substantial sum. I would like you to have it, but on one condition. And THIS IS VERY IMPORTANT. You are a good man, but misguided. These people in your house do not appreciate you or your generosity. They are holding you back. My greatest fear for you, Toby, is that you will end up like me, alone, misunderstood, unappreciated, and I fear this could happen all too easily. Please, Toby, use my money to make your life everything it could be. Sell your house; lose your shackles. The house is just bricks and mortar. Repair them, then repair your soul.

I do not believe in an afterlife so I will have to trust you to fulfil my instructions. But you are the most trustworthy man I have ever known, so I feel confident that you will do so.

God bless you.

Your friend,
Augustus Veldtman

* * *

Toby breathed in and out slowly, trying to calm his racing heart. And then he picked up the bag, pulled open the drawstrings and peered inside. He saw a flash of red and shut it again. Red — wasn't that the colour of a fifty-pound note?

He opened it again and pulled out a note. It *was* a fifty, crisp and glossy and mint. He pulled out another one. And another one. He poured the contents of the bag onto the bed. It was a sea of red. No tens, no twenties, no fives. Just fifties. He clapped his hands across his mouth, so that he wouldn't scream or squeal or shriek. "Calm down," he soothed himself. "Just — calm down." He took a deep breath and began counting. Five minutes later he stopped.

£62,550.

Sixty-two thousand five hundred and fifty pounds.

Slowly and methodically he piled the notes back into the bag, stuffed the bag up his jumper and, with the stealth and light-footedness of an alley cat, he made his way back to his bedroom.

CHAPTER EIGHT

Amitabh didn't mess about when he got home from work the following night. No sooner had he unwrapped himself from his winter layers than he'd sat Leah down on the sofa, turned off the TV, picked up her hands and said, "Leah, I love you. But I'm not going to marry you."

She sighed. "I knew it."

"I'm really sorry."

She dragged her hands through her hair and sighed again. She couldn't think of anything to say.

"It's not your fault."

"Right."

"It's just, I couldn't do that to my parents."

"What?"

"It would kill them, completely."

Leah stared at him in confusion. Amitabh's parents *loved* her. Amitabh's parents thought she was delightful.

Amitabh paused and sighed. "Look." he said, "I'm thirty now. It's all well and good mucking about in your twenties . . ."

"Mucking about?" Leah felt her stomach muscles knitting themselves into a knot.

"God, no, not mucking about. I didn't mean it like that. It's just, you and I. This . . ." He gestured around the room. "This can never be . . ."

"Jesus Christ, Am — what are you saying?" Her heart was pumping adrenalin through her body on an industrial scale.

"I'm saying, I can't marry you. Not now. Not ever. My parents can accept you as a girlfriend, but never as a wife."

Leah could hear the words, but couldn't make sense of them. "What?" she said. "Because I'm white?"

"Yes, because you're white. Because you're Christian. Because you aren't professional. Because your brother's gay. Because you drink. Because you swear."

"Oh, my God."

"I thought you knew this. I thought you accepted it."

"No," she said numbly. "No, I didn't."

"So what did you think?"

"I don't know," she said. "I didn't think. I thought they liked me."

"They *do* like you."

"So why . . .?"

"It's the way things are, Leah. That's all."

"So what if we didn't get married? Couldn't we just carry on the way we are?"

Amitabh stared at the ceiling and exhaled. "It's not as simple as that."

"Why not? If the only problem here is that your parents don't want you to marry an English girl, then don't marry me."

"But I'll have to marry *someone*."

"Why?"

"To have a family. I have to have a family."

"You don't need to be married to have a family."

"Yes" — he stopped and sighed — "I do."

Leah gulped then as everything finally made sense. "So are you saying that the past three years have just been . . . *a phase*?"

"No. Of course not. I just didn't think it through. I was young. I thought I had all the time in the world. I didn't think that you and I would last so long . . ."

Leah stared at him, at this *stranger* with whom she'd shared the past three years of her life. It was as if he'd suddenly announced that he was a bigamist or a terrorist or a secret agent. She'd read stories over the years about inter-racial couples who'd found themselves in this position; she'd seen them on the *Kilroy* show and she'd felt so smug, thinking that that would never happen to her and Amitabh because his parents loved her and approved of them as a couple. And beyond their first couple of meetings, she'd barely even noticed that Amitabh was Indian, to be perfectly honest.

"Are we going to split up?"

He nodded. Shrugged. Nodded again. "I think so," he said.

Leah started to cry.

12 January 2005

Toby,

It has been a long time. I'm sorry not to have been in touch but that's the way life goes. Jemma and I are divorcing. She is to stay in Cape Town with the boys (we have two sons, 12 and 9) and I am moving to Johannesburg. I have some business to attend to in London at the end of March and will be staying in my flat in Chelsea for a couple of weeks.

I would like to see you again. I am interested to see what became of you, after your less-than-promising start in life. And what became of the house I bought you all those years ago. If you'd had any sense you'd have taken advantage of the property market and moved up the ladder considerably. Peter tells me the house should be worth more than half a million in the current market, in a finished state, so that should be sufficient to subsidize your "poetry"! I've watched the book pages of the *Times* over the years, waiting for a mention of your name, but, alas, have seen nothing!

Anyway — I look forward to hearing a full report of your life. I haven't given up on the possibility that you might still have made me proud. I believe you will be forty soon, the age at which a man knows whether or not he will be able to call himself a success when the grim reaper comes to call.

I will be in touch, via Peter.

Best,
Reggie (Dad)

CHAPTER NINE

It was almost impossible for Toby to ascertain what all the disparate members of his household were up to at any given point of the day, so finding a moment when the house was empty so he could invite an estate agent in for a valuation was a challenge.

But a few days after his father's letter arrived in the post he found himself unexpectedly in possession of the knowledge that Ruby was at rehearsals, Joanne and Con were at work and Melinda was ensconced in a salon in Crouch End having her highlights done.

The agent who arrived at his house five minutes later was called Walter. He had a moustache. "Well, I must say that this is a very exciting opportunity," were his first words upon entering the house and shaking Toby's hand. "It's not often that a property like this comes on to the market." He wiped a slick of sweat off his forehead with the back of a hairy hand and wrote something in an A5 notebook. "Oh yes," he said, gazing round the entrance hall. "Oh, yes, yes, yes. Quite magnificent. So, you are the owner, Mr Dobbs?"

"Yes, that's right."

"And you've owned the house for how long?"

"Fifteen years. Almost." Toby gulped. The combination of Walter's suit, moustache and notebook made him feel like he was being interrogated by a detective from a 1970s TV drama.

Walter nodded approvingly.

"I must warn you," said Toby, sensing that Walter was getting too excited, too soon, "I haven't maintained the house particularly well. It's in need of a fair bit of TLC."

"Ah, well, let's see it, then."

Toby led him through the house. Due to the short notice, he hadn't had a chance to tidy or clean, and random items were strewn carelessly about the place: shoes, mugs, papers, hairbrushes, empty jiffy bags, CDs, old toast, a plant that was halfway through being repotted on a sheet of newspaper on the dining-room table, the combined detritus of five people's separate existences.

"It's a bit messy, I'm afraid. I live with quite a few people and they're all out."

"Oh, so you don't live alone?"

"No. I live with some friends."

"I see. No family, children?"

"No," he said. "just us grown-ups." He laughed nervously.

Walter didn't say much as they moved round the house, just scratched notes into his notebook and made the occasional approving noise. Toby felt guilty as he opened the doors of his tenants' rooms for Walter to peruse. He never, under any circumstances, went into his tenants' rooms. He tried his hardest not to look at anything.

Ruby's room, predictably, was the messiest. The windows were hung with silky lace-trimmed shawls and dusty strings of fairy lights. The floor was covered in clothes, books and CDs. Her bed was unmade and overloaded with cushions and discarded underwear. A full ashtray sat on her dressing table, surrounded by scruffy cosmetics and piles of jewellery. It looked like the bedroom of a student, of someone who'd just left home and didn't know how to look after themselves. It smelled of forgotten sex and cigarettes.

Con and Melinda's room was bare and minimal. Melinda's bed was made with a neat crisp duvet and two fat pillows; Con's mattress on the floor was unmade and messy. A wooden panel to the left of the window had been decorated with the word "Clarabel" and a small black painting of a pretty girl wearing a hat and smoking a cigarette. Clarabel was a manic-depressive performance artist who'd lived here for six months in 1996 and left to marry a Russian gymnast and move to St Petersburg. It was strange to see her avant-garde and mildly disturbing self-portrait staring out at him from the midst of Con and Melinda's bland possessions.

"How many bathrooms do you have?" said Walter, heading towards Joanne's room.

"Two," said Toby. "One on each floor."

"Good," he said. "Any en suite?"

"No. I'm afraid not."

Toby pushed down on the handle to Joanne's door and realized with some surprise that it was locked. "Ah," he said, turning to face Walter. "Erm, it seems it's locked."

Walter nodded.

"Joanne — very private girl," Toby offered, pointlessly.

Upstairs, Toby showed Walter his own overstuffed room and Gus's garishly decorated room, apologizing for the smell of elderly cat and explaining that the cat's owner had recently passed away. By the time he led Walter into the back garden and noticed for the first time the pile of compost that had been sitting on the lawn since the end of last summer and the weeds sprouting forth from every conceivable — and inconceivable — crack and crevice and the old bicycle tyres, the rusty treadmill and the aged fridge stained an unappetizing brown, Toby was feeling thoroughly depressed. There was so much to apologize for, so much to excuse. He couldn't imagine that Walter would be prepared to put his house on the market for fifty pounds, let alone five hundred thousand pounds.

He offered him a cup of tea and sat down with him at the kitchen table.

"Well," began Walter, "it's a beautiful house."

"Do you think so?"

"Oh, undoubtedly. But, as you say, there are some maintenance issues. Not to mention some decorative issues and some lifestyle issues."

"Lifestyle?"

"Yes. Because here's the bottom line. I could put this property on the market for you tomorrow, as it is, and probably, if we could find a buyer or, more likely, a developer prepared to put in the work, to see beyond the aesthetic problems, we would probably be looking at something in the region of seven hundred and fifty thousand pounds."

Toby stopped breathing.

"*But*. If you were able to reconfigure the house, to replace the kitchen, the bathrooms, do some basic work in the garden and, more importantly, *remove your housemates* and give the place the feel of a *proper* family home, we could be asking for considerably more."

"How much more?"

"Oh, I would say that this house, redecorated, modernized, made fit for a family to move straight into, I could put it on the market for around nine hundred thousand pounds. Maybe even a million."

"*No?*" Toby blinked. "Surely not that much."

"Oh, yes, definitely. Maybe more depending on the quality of the renovation."

"Jesus Christ." Toby breathed in deeply and tugged at his sideburns.

"This house is unique, Mr Dobbs. There's nothing else like it in the area. People will pay a premium for unique."

"So, if I were to put it on the market now, what do you think would happen?"

"I would expect to sell it to a developer. Maybe to be developed into two or three apartments. Or to a family with a fondness for home improvements."

"And if I were to make the improvements myself and evict my tenants . . . I mean, *friends*?"

"Then you could command a much higher asking price and make a much bigger profit."

"And what would you do, if you were me?"

"Well, if I had the cash at my disposal, I would go down the latter route. Most definitely."

"You would?"

Walter nodded, emphatically. "Without a doubt. But you'd need to get cracking on it. The market's precarious right now. Get your tenants out, get your builders in, get the house on the market. Maximize your profit."

"Right," said Toby, staring through the kitchen window at the wilderness of the back garden and feeling a sense of unbridled panic galloping through his insides. "Right. Then, that's what I'll do."

Toby did something he'd never done before after Walter left. He made a list.

Suddenly there was so much to consider, so much to do, and he thought that setting it down in writing might somehow make it easier to control.

Things To Do

1. Buy new sofas
2. Get hair cut
3. Buy new socks
4. Look at kitchens
5. Look at bathrooms

6. Get builder in to quote on works
7. Get plumber in to quote on works
8. Get decorator in to quote on works
9. Get tenants to move out
10. Sell house
11. Move to Cornwall (?)
12. Get a publishing deal (?)
13. Get divorced
14. Stop being in love with Ruby
15. Find someone proper to be in love with
16. **START LIVING**

CHAPTER TEN

Leah found it hard to believe that she'd ended up working somewhere called the Pink Hummingbird. She'd thought it was a joke at first when the woman at the agency had mentioned it to her.

"The what?"

"Yes," she'd said, "I know. You'll understand when you see it."

It was the most violently, unremittingly feminine shop in London. It had a sugar-pink façade and windows strung with feather-shaded fairy lights. It sold things that only girls would ever want to buy, such as gem-encrusted picture frames and writing paper scented with eau de toilette. The ceiling was dripping with bejewelled chandeliers and whitewashed bamboo birdcages. The walls were hung with Venetian glass mirrors and soft velvet hats in shades of plum and passion fruit. It sold underwear constructed from pure gossamer and presented in tissue-lined sateen boxes with rosebuds on the lid. And soft plush cats dressed in fur coats and heels. And birthdays cards handmade using diamanté and sequins. And cushions made from pastel-tinted Mongolian sheepskins. And pens decorated with lilac glitter and wisps of marabou.

It was sugar-coated decadence on a sickly scale.

Leah wasn't really a pink sort of girl. Leah liked wearing chunky footwear and hard-wearing jeans. She wore the minimum of make-up and no perfume. Her only concession to femininity was her hair, which she wore long and wavy, and her fingernails which she kept manicured and shiny. She didn't really need make-up. She had one of those scrubbed land-girl kind of faces that looked better with just a touch of eyeliner and a pinch of the cheeks. Maybe that was why Ruth had offered her the job. Maybe she hadn't glanced down and seen the chunky-heeled boots and the hint of old mud clinging to the hem of her only smart trousers. Maybe she hadn't noticed that Leah was wearing a T-shirt with a logo on it. Maybe she'd just taken in the cute face and the girlie hair and decided that Leah was a Pink Hummingbird in the making.

Whatever the reason, she'd offered her the job. Leah had been managing Ruth's shop for five years now, ever since Ruth had relocated herself to LA and opened Pink Hummingbird II in Beverly Hills. Leah quite liked working here. It was a sweet-smelling antidote to the scruffiness of the rest of her life. It was nice to walk in here in the mornings, stepping from the grey of the pavement outside into this fragrant pink grotto.

But if someone had told her ten years ago that one day she'd be thirty-five years old, unmarried, non-home-owning and managing a gift shop in Muswell Hill she'd have kicked them in the shin. But here she was selling overpriced gewgaws to girls and grannies and clinging — she could feel it as keenly as an oncoming train today — to the sheer rock face of an existential crisis, by the tips of her shiny fingernails.

The doorbell of the Pink Hummingbird sounded at three o'clock, just as Leah had opened a new copy of *heat* and was about to tuck into a tortellini salad. She jammed the plastic tub under the cash desk and glanced at the door.

It was Toby.

He was wearing a cream cable-knit turtleneck jumper with narrow black jeans and a red scarf. On his head was a grey ribbed woollen hat. His shoes were enormous and shiny, but he somehow managed to pull the whole look off, even with his abundant and unfashionable sideburns. She smiled when she saw him; she couldn't help herself.

"Hello," he said, peering at her from beneath the Chinese-print paper parasol she'd been hiding behind.

She peered back at him. "Hello."

"It's me," he said, apologetically, "Toby."

She nodded and smiled. "Yes, I know."

"So," he said, nervous eyes taking in the shop, "this is where you work?"

"Yup. Uh-huh. This is my . . . pink and fluffy world." She spread her hands outwards.

"It's nice," he said. "I must have walked past here a million times and never been in."

"Yes, well — you're either the sort of person who is attracted by feathery fairy lights or you're not."

"I don't know," he said, glancing around. "I quite like some of this stuff. These cushions are great." He fingered the price tag of an ivory-sequinned cushion and winced slightly. "Oh, my God," he said, "for a *cushion*?"

"Uh-huh." Leah nodded. "You don't want to know the cost price."

"No," he agreed, "I don't suppose I do."

They both turned as the doorbell chimed and an old lady in a woollen coat walked in. Leah smiled at her.

"I hope you don't mind me turning up like this, unannounced. It's just, I'm not sure, really, but I just feel a bit strange that I haven't seen you since what happened the other day. And you mentioned that you worked in a pink gift shop and I was passing and assumed that this must be the pink gift shop you were talking about. So I thought I'd come in and say hello. And thank you. Again."

"What for?"

"For being so cool, calm and collected in a crisis."

"Ah, well. If nothing else, I am good in a crisis."

"Yes, indeed you are."

"So. Have you had the funeral yet?"

"Yes. On Tuesday."

"How was it?"

"Oh, miserable," he said, smiling. "Horrible. It rained all day and his relatives were gruesome."

"Oh, dear," Leah replied, smiling back.

"Yes, but lots of interesting things have happened since."

"They have?"

"Yes. My life's been sort of turned upside down, really."

"God, really. In what way?"

"Well . . ." Toby paused and licked his lips. Then he stroked his sideburns and squinted. Leah watched him curiously.

"Are you OK?" she said.

"Look," he said, "I hope you don't think I'm being strange, but I recall you saying that you considered yourself to be a curious person, about human beings, that is, and unfortunately curiosity is not one of my fortes, and I'm in a very strange quandary and I really need to, God, this will sound so American and so inane, but I really need to *share*. And I know we're strangers, but I don't really have anyone else whom I feel *comfortable* discussing these things with . . ."

"You want to talk to me?"

"Yes," he nodded.

"About your problems?"

"Well, yes."

"Cool," she smiled, sliding down from her stool, "let's go for a coffee."

They went to the Ruby in the Dust. Toby ordered a cappuccino and Leah had a peppermint tea and a slice of cheesecake. She glanced up at Toby. He had a foam moustache and some chocolate powder dusted across his stubble. She resisted the temptation to wipe him down with her paper napkin and smiled at him.

"So," said Toby, "this is the thing. Gus has left me some money. Posthumously."

"Well, obviously."

"Yes. And now, in a weird twist of fate, my estranged father is coming back to London to see me and, frankly, I'd given up on him for dead, never thought I'd see him again, and I'm forty next year and I just feel as if this is my last chance to, you know, make a life for myself, because I've become stuck in a terrible, terrible rut, come to a kind of grinding halt, I suppose, and now I have both the incentive and the means to do something about it, to refurbish the house and put it up for sale. But there's a snag."

"There is?"

"Yes, my tenants. I need to get rid of them."

"Right . . ."

"Yes. I need them all to move out. So that I can renovate the house and sell it before my father comes back."

"Which is when?"

"End of March. Ten weeks."

"OK. So why can't you just evict them?"

"Because . . ." Toby paused, then sighed. "Oh, God, I don't know, it's so pathetic, really, and I know that's exactly what I should do, but for some reason I just can't bring myself to do it. For some reason I feel personally responsible for them all."

"But why?"

"Because, well, because they're all so *lost*."

"Lost?"

"Yes, all of them, to varying degrees. And the only reason they're living in my house is because they have absolutely nowhere else to be. No friends, no family, no safety net. And if I evict them, then what will happen to them? What will become of them all?"

"Well, yes, but surely that's not your problem, is it?"

"Well, no, not technically, but I do feel a certain level of responsibility. It was me who invited them to live with me, after all. It was me who placed classified adverts, who selected them on the grounds that they were genuinely needy. It would be like kicking people out of a halfway house. And the funny thing is, I always thought it was just Gus who was keeping me from selling the house, from moving on, but now he's dead and I've realized that it wasn't just him. It was all of them."

"So what are you going to do?"

"Well, that's exactly it. The only way I would feel comfortable about asking them to move out is to ensure that they have somewhere else to go, someone else to be with. The only way I could ask them to leave would be if I knew that they were all . . ."

"Happy?"

"*Yes*. Exactly. That they were all happy. And I don't really know anything about the people I live with, beyond what brand of breakfast cereal they eat in the mornings. I don't like asking people questions. It makes me feel uncomfortable. But unless I can find out more about my tenants I don't stand a chance of satisfying their needs. And in your capacity as a naturally curious person, I wondered if you might be able to help me, or at least *advise* me on ways to *access* the inner workings of their minds."

"You want me to teach you how to be nosy?"

"Well, yes, I suppose . . ."

"Well, it's easy. You just have to ask loads of questions."

"Oh, God. What sort of questions?"

"I don't know. Just ask them how they are. What they're up to. What their plans are."

"Really," he winced. "But won't they just think I'm being terribly interfering?"

"No, of course they won't. People *love* being asked about themselves."

"Do they? I don't."

"No, well, not everyone. But most people. And I could help, too, if you like."

"You could?"

"Mm-hmm. I could get talking to them. Nose around. You know?"

Toby looked at her in awe. "You'd do that for me?"

"Of course I would. I told you. I'm desperately nosy.

She smiled then, as the idea caught her imagination. She'd spent three years watching these people across the road, three years wondering what they were like, who they were, what they did and why they were there, and now she was being asked to find out. Officially.

"Well, if you were really happy to do that, then, wow, that would be amazing. And in fact, it's my birthday next week, my thirty-ninth, and I'd been thinking I might invite a few people to the pub and, maybe, if I did that you might like to come along, too. Give you a chance to . . ."

"Be nosy?"

"Yes," he smiled. "And your, er, boyfriend? Husband?"

Leah threw him a questioning look.

"The doctor. The Asian chap?"

"Oh. Amitabh. My ex-boyfriend. We split up."

"Oh. Hell. Sorry. I er . . ."

"And he's a nurse, not a doctor."

"Oh. Right. I was just about to say, you must ask him along, too. But, obviously, ah . . . I really had no idea."

"Really. Honestly. It's fine. We split up last week. I suggested that we get married and he suddenly went all Indian on me. Said his parents would disown him. So, that's that."

"I'm very sorry to hear that."

"Yes, well," Leah shrugged, holding back her tears so as not to embarrass Toby. "Shit happens. I'm trying to be philosophical about it."

"Yes, yes, best way to be. Totally."

It fell silent then for a moment. Leah glanced up at Toby. He was staring wistfully out of the window, looking pensive. "OK, now," she said, smiling, "*that* was a perfect opportunity for you to practise being nosy. A curious person would want to know more about my break-up."

Toby stared at her, blankly.

"So — ask me some questions."

"What sort of questions?"

"Questions about the break-up."

"Well, yes, but you've just told me why you broke up. What else is there to ask?"

"Well, for example, you could ask me how long we'd been together."

"Right. OK. So, how long had you been together?"

"No! Not like that. You need to sound genuinely interested. Say: 'Oh, no, that's awful. How long had you been together?' "

Toby flushed and cleared his throat. "Erm, oh dear, poor you, how long had you been together?"

"Nearly three years."

Toby nodded.

"And?"

"And what?"

"Ask me more questions. Ask me how we met."

"So — how did you meet?"

"We met at his cousin's wedding."

"Right. I see."

"I was a colleague of the bride. I think she only invited me because someone else dropped out."

Toby nodded awkwardly.

"Go on," she said, encouragingly.

He cleared his throat. "And, er, was he nice?"

"Yes," she said, "he was. Very nice. But obviously not as nice as I thought he was."

"And what are your plans now?"

"Well, Am's moved into nurses' accommodation and I'll have to find somewhere else to live."

"And, er, how do you feel about that?"

"I feel very annoyed, very sad and very nervous." She paused then as her bottom lip trembled and her smile started to crack. She blinked away some tears and laughed. And then, she couldn't resist it, she picked up her napkin and brushed the chocolate off his chin. "There, you see," she said, forcing a brittle smile, "it's easy, isn't it? Being nosy."

"Yes, I suppose."

"So — do you think you can do it? Do you think you can get to know your tenants?"

Toby nodded. "Yes. I really think I can."

CHAPTER ELEVEN

Joanne was in the kitchen. She was wearing a pair of jeans that were cut slightly too high up her waist, a red jersey polo neck, small gold earrings and very sensible flat leather shoes. Her hair was cut into a short layered bob and held back on one side by a glittery hair slide which looked incongruously girlie against her prematurely middle-aged outfit. Her lipstick was slightly off-centre and a not very pretty shade of coral. She looked shocked to see Toby in the kitchen and almost turned to leave, only stopping to acknowledge his presence when he said hello to her.

"How are you?" he ventured, cautiously.

"Fine, thanks," she muttered, as she filled the kettle from the tap. He waited for her to ask him how he was, or at the very least to offer him a cup of tea, but she did neither. Instead she hummed gently under her breath and stared out of the window while the kettle boiled noisily. Toby glanced at her back. She was very small. Very narrow. Her waist looked like you could get your hands to meet around it and her shoulders were barely the width of a telephone directory.

"So, Joanne." He paused, not quite sure how to continue, but knowing that he had to. "How long have you been living here now?"

She spun round. "What —" she said, pointing at the floor, "*here*?"

"Er, yes," said Toby. "You know. In this house."

"Oh, right. God. I'm not sure." She pursed her lips and stared up at the ceiling.

Toby waited, a bag of flour suspended in his left hand, wondering whether she was working out how long she'd lived here or if she was just staring at a damp patch.

"Two years and eight months," she said finally.

"Right."

"And twenty days."

"Right," repeated Toby.

"I moved in on the fourth of May 2002. It was sunny."

"Was it?" he said, rubbing his chin, as if trying to remember the day itself.

"Yes. I moved from south-east London. They had a march. It was for marijuana. There were people dressed up as cannabis leaves walking down my road. I was glad to be leaving."

Toby laughed, relieved that Joanne had injected some levity into the stilted conversation, but she just stared at him blankly. "Why d'you ask?"

"I don't really know," he said, reaching for the sieve. "I was just wondering." The kitchen fell silent except for the sound of a teaspoon going round and round in Joanne's mug.

"And how are you finding it?"

"What?"

"The house. Living here. Are you happy?"

"Well," she shrugged, stirring her teabag slowly now, "yes. It's all fine. I have no complaints. Why?" Her eyes narrowed. "Is there a problem you wish to discuss?"

"God, no, not at all. I was just thinking that I hadn't really spoken to you for a few months and I just wanted to make sure that you were doing OK. That's all."

"Right," she nodded tersely and squeezed her teabag against the side of her mug.

"And how's work?"

"Fine." She dropped the teabag into the pedal bin.

"Are you still, you know, still doing the old acting?" Toby had broken into a light sweat.

"No," she said, dropping the teaspoon into the dishwasher basket.

"And the role? The one you were researching, did that, er . . . ?"

"No. It fell through."

"Oh, dear. That's a bit of a shame. Anything else in the pipeline?"

"There is no pipeline."

"Oh," he said. "Oh. OK. So you're just . . . ?"

"Just what?"

"I don't know. You're working, though, are you?"

"Yes." She picked up her mug. "I'm working."

Toby nodded, slightly manically. "Good," he managed, as she wafted past him and into the hallway, leaving the flowery scent of Earl Grey tea in her wake. "Good."

CHAPTER TWELVE

Toby was glad not to be a teenager in the twenty-first century — it all seemed so stifling, so conformist. Young girls all looked the same to Toby these days. They all had the same strip of stomach showing between the same jersey top and low-slung jeans, their belly buttons all studded with the same flashy gems. They all wore their long hair in the same side-parted style, their lips sticky with the same glossy gel, their complexions the same shade of Balearic brown all year round. And there was something about modern bras that rendered all young girls' bosoms into the shape of pudding tins, attached, bam-bam, to their fronts, somehow unrelated to their bodies, like they could be unscrewed at the end of the day and put in a drawer.

Toby, like most men, loved nothing more than a little light porn, a few minutes of harmless thrusting and fellating shot at close range and poured down the virtual tubes and wires of the Internet into his bedroom. But he didn't want real girls to look like that. He wanted real girls to have wobbly bits and breasts that were unexpected shapes. He liked variety in his women. He liked character. He liked PJ Harvey. He liked Willow from *Buffy the Vampire Slayer*. He liked that tall DJ girl with the DJ husband whose father was Johnny Ball. He actually thought that Cherie Blair was a very attractive woman, though he'd never yet found anyone to agree with him. And his all-time best-ever pin-up, since his teenage years, was Jamie Lee Curtis. He didn't have a type. He knew what he liked when he saw it. But kids today — it was all so generic. It was all so boring.

And that, when it was all boiled down to its essence, was the main problem with Con. He was boring. He added nothing to the mix in the house. His youth could have been a fizzing plop of seltzer into the still water of this thirty-something house; instead he lurked at the bottom like a dull penny.

"Hello, Con," Toby opened, coming upon him eating a Big Mac in the front room.

"Hiya." Con glanced up and looked at him in surprise.

"Good day at work?"

Con shrugged. "Nothing special."

"See anyone famous?"

Con had once shared the lift with Cate Blanchett. Cate Blanchett was quite high up on Toby's list of quirky, desirable women, so this fact had lodged itself firmly into his consciousness when he'd overhead Con sharing it with Ruby a few months back.

Con smiled. "Nah. Not today. Saw that gay bloke coming in the other day, though, you know?"

"Which one?"

"That posh one. Can't remember his name. He was in a film with Madonna."

The only film starring Madonna that Toby could bring to mind at that moment was *Dick Tracy*, but he was sure that Con couldn't have been referring to Warren Beatty, who was, as far as he knew, neither posh nor gay.

"So," he said after a moment, "do you think you'll stay at Condé Nast for much longer? Is there any promise of a . . . of any *career progression*, at all?"

Con laughed and wiped a fleck of ketchup off his chin. "Er . . . no. Definitely not. Unless I want to be post-room manager. Which I don't."

"But what about the publications? The magazines. Surely there must be possibilities there?"

He laughed again. "Not for the likes of me there aren't. It's like one of those fucked-up dreams, that place. On one side you've got reality — that's us lot in the post room, the caterers, the cleaners — then on the other side you've got this whole other world, these posh people, my age, live in Chelsea, don't know what day of the week it is, kind of floating round, like, you know . . . *oblivious*. They're the ones that get the proper jobs there. The careers. We're just there to make sure they get their letters and their lunch."

"Oh," said Toby, "I see. So, if you don't want to be the post-room manager and you don't think there are any other opportunities there, what's your game plan? What's next?"

"My PPL."

"Your what?"

"My private pilot's licence."

"You're going to learn to *fly*?"

"Yeah. Why not?"

"God, well, isn't that very expensive?"

"Can be," he shrugged. "But I've been looking into it. If I go to South Africa it's a third of what it would cost here. I've been saving since I started work, and I've worked out that I only need another eighteen months at Condé Nast to earn what I need. Then I'm off. Get my licence. Go to the Caribbean. Chartered flights. Island-hopping. The good life. Oh, man . . ."

"Right, so, er . . ."

"I tell you what, if it hadn't been for Nigel writing to you and me getting this room, and the, you know, the great deal on the rent, there's no way I'd have been able to think about learning to fly. I would never of been able to afford it. That was a good day that was, the day we met."

He smiled at Toby, a lovely warm smile full of gratitude and Toby felt his ribs crunching together as his chest slowly deflated. He sighed quietly. This was exactly what he'd always wanted. This is what this house was for. It was for allowing people to follow their dreams. His main criterion for choosing house mates was that they should benefit in some positive, constructive way from having tiny outgoings. The only exception to this rule had been Ruby, whom he'd offered a room to on the grounds that he wanted to have sex with her. He'd offered Con a room because he felt sorry for him, because his mum had abandoned him, because he had no fixed abode and was about to lose his job and end up on the streets. And now, a year later, Con had a dream, too. He wanted to fly planes.

And Toby should have been delighted. Instead he felt trapped.

Toby thought sadly about the wedge of magic money that had appeared from thin air to make real the dreams he'd had in the wake of Gus's death. And then he looked at Con, a boy who'd arrived here with nothing, no ambition beyond a bed to sleep in, no dreams other than to keep his job, who'd suddenly and magically found a path he wanted to follow. Toby had had his whole life to make a success of himself. He had no one to blame but himself for finding himself washed up in Nowheresville in his late thirties. Con had no readymade safety net — he'd had to knit his own. What was more important, wondered Toby, his own silly middle-aged need to prove himself to his father or a young man's future?

He sat for a moment, staring blankly at the television, listening to Con slurping his cola, letting his dreams slink away like naughty children. Then he slapped his hands against his thighs and got to his feet.

"I was thinking," he said, "that I might invest in a pair of new sofas. What do you think?"

Con looked at him in surprise, then at the aged blue sofas dressed with tatty ethnic cushions. "Yeah. Why not? Go for it."

"Cool." Toby put his hands in his pockets. "I'll go shopping tomorrow. Sales on now. Good time to go."

And for now, he mused, new sofas might just have to do.

CHAPTER THIRTEEN

Melinda McNulty was forty-five. She maintained her toned size-ten figure by going to the gym three times a week, attending two power-boxing classes a week, and doing Pilates on her bedroom floor in front of the TV. She ate Special K breakfast bars in the morning, then went off to Stansted airport where she worked as a check-in girl for Monarch. Her cupboard in the kitchen was full of things such as Snack-a-Jacks and instant noodle soups. She drank Cava ("It's better than champagne.") pretty much every day of the week, and went clubbing on Saturday nights with her friend Zoë, who was twenty-eight. She wore too much make-up, too much perfume and very tight velour tracksuits in bright colours that showed her muscled tummy.

Toby wasn't sure how he felt about muscled tummies on forty-five-year-old women. It was impressive, but a bit unsettling.

When Toby saw her get back from work that night, smart and trim in her airline uniform, he deliberately sought her out. He found her ironing in the front room. The room was humid with the aroma of damp cotton and rhythmic with a tinny beat emanating from her headphones. She smiled when she saw him and popped the earphones out.

"Hello m'Lord!" She had the penetrating, unripened voice of a fifteen-year-old girl. It was very disconcerting. Her face disappeared briefly into a cloud of steam. "How's it going?"

"Good," he said. "Excellent. How are you?"

"Yeah, I'm good, too. Just getting some ironing out of the way."

Toby glanced down at the pile of clothes growing on the arm of the sofa. They appeared to be mainly Con's clothes. "Do you want a cup of tea?" he offered.

"Ooh, yes." She pursed her strawberry pink lips into a crinkled ring. "White, one sugar. Can I have the mug with the cats on it? You know, the big one?"

He didn't know, but searched the kitchen cupboards until he found it. When he came back, Melinda was sitting cross-legged on the sofa, examining a glossy, blood-coloured toenail. "Ooh, thanks, Toby," she said, stretching her heavily ringed hands towards the mug, "just what the doctor ordered."

Toby sat next to her and rested his tea on the coffee table.

"I hear you're getting rid of these," said Melinda, stroking the fabric of the sofa.

"What . . .?"

"The sofas. Con said you're thinking of buying new ones."

"Yes," he said, "that is the plan. They've done their service, these ones."

"Yes," she agreed, "they are a bit minging."

Toby winced at the coarse lingua franca.

"How's that weird cat?" she continued.

"Boris?"

"Is that what you're calling him?" she laughed.

"Yes."

"Oh, I like that. He looks like a Boris. How's he getting on?"

"He's fine, as far as I can tell. Very low-maintenance. I'm not that keen on the whole litter tray thing, though. It's not very pleasant."

"Ooh, yes. My mum had one of those housebound cats. Bloody nuisance. But at least you know you're not going to get the dead rats on your pillow and the dismembered birds on the carpet."

Melinda turned to face him, one knee tucked up under her. Her hair was the wrong shade of blonde for her colouring, slightly yellow, as if it had been left out in the sun for too long. Her nose was small and hooked, and her lips were a strange shape, too thick in places and too thin in others. She didn't have any wrinkles at all until she smiled, and then she got a set of very dramatic crow's feet which exploded from the corners of her eyes like fireworks. But she had beautiful eyes, a clear Caribbean turquoise, fringed with heavy black lashes. "I know this sounds dreadful," she leaned towards him, conspiratorially, "and don't take this the wrong way, but I much prefer it here now that Gus's gone."

Toby glanced at her in horror.

"Not that I didn't like him. Don't get me wrong. But it was just a bit weird, wasn't it, having him around?

Didn't quite fit the image of the house. But now he's gone it just feels *perfect* here. You know something, Toby, I *love* this house, I really do. Can't imagine living anywhere else now." She glanced up towards the towering ceilings. "I couldn't move back into some pokey little purpose-built with paper walls now. I'm *ruined*." She laughed.

Toby gulped. "So you're happy, are you, sharing a room with Con?"

"Oh, it's lovely. You know, I was thinking I might ask you about Gus's room, now that he's gone. Thinking I might ask if I could move in there. But then I thought, do I really want to share a room with that horrible cat? And then I thought, do I really want to move out of Con's room? And I don't. Really don't. I love sharing with him. He's such a great boy. And after being apart from him for so many years. I missed out on a lot. But now . . . we're *so* close," she gushed. "It's like we're best mates, you know, we're equals. It's lovely now. Everything's lovely." She smiled and caressed her mug. "What about you, Toby? You've been single for a while. Anyone special in your life?"

"Er, no," he began, subconsciously filing away Melinda's suspect conversational leap from her relationship with her son to Toby's love life. "Not at the moment."

"Ah," she cooed sympathetically, squeezing his leg gently, "that's a shame. How old are you now?"

"Thirty-nine," he said, "next week."

"Yes. It's a funny age that. I remember my late thirties. You start panicking, thinking you're running out of time. Irony of it is that it takes you bloody *ages* to get old after that. I thought I'd be an old relic by the time I hit forty-five, but I didn't get a wrinkle until I was forty-one. And my boobs are still pretty OK." She put down her mug and gazed thoughtfully into the distance. "You know, every birthday I look in the mirror and think, not yet, Mel, you're still there, still looking good. Have to work at it mind, but it's so worth it. Especially in my line of work, looking good is so important."

"You mean, being an air hostess?"

"Well, no, not an air hostess exactly. Ground staff now. Keeps me closer to home, closer to Con. But image is still mega-important. You're the first contact the customer has with the airline. And if you look crap, well, that's not going to make the customer feel very confident about their flight, is it?"

Toby nodded sagely, thinking that he would be more likely to base his confidence in an upcoming flight on the condition of the aircraft than on the eyeshadow on the check-in girls.

"Well," she got to her feet, "you're a lovely fella. I'm sure someone'll come along when you're least expecting it. And you've got tons going for you."

"I have?"

"Yes, you're lovely and tall. Girls like tall men. You've got this amazing house. And you're generous and caring. I mean, look at us all, all us waifs and strays. Where would we all be without you, Toby, eh? You took my Con off the streets. You've given me a chance to be with my boy. You've looked after poor Ruby since she was a kid. And what would have become of Gus if he hadn't had you to take care of him? You're a hero, Toby, a true hero. And what woman doesn't want a hero?"

Toby picked up his mug and left the room, unable to think of one single thing to say in response.

CHAPTER FOURTEEN

Toby stood up, then sat down again, enjoying the sensation. He caressed her arms gently, then stood up again. He turned round and admired her lines. She was so beautiful, a long, lean slither of leather-clad perfection. He glanced across at her sister and sighed with pleasure.

They were the most beautiful sofas in the world.

They'd arrived half an hour ago, on a big white van with the word CONRAN on the side. Six thousand pounds' worth of midnight-blue calfskin and milk-coffee suede. He hadn't intended to blow so much of Gus's inheritance on sofas. He'd intended to spend a thousand pounds, very wisely, in the sales, on something practical and hard-wearing. He'd gone into the Conran Shop only for inspiration, in much the same way that you might decide to visit a museum or an art gallery, not actually to buy anything. And then a very nice young girl in a black suit had approached him as he browsed and she'd been so charming and so helpful that he'd felt it would have been rude not to accept her offer of assistance. And besides, it was such a novelty to know that for once in his life he could afford something expensive that he'd wanted to savour every aspect of it.

They hadn't seemed that expensive at the time, in the context of *everything* being expensive. They were in the sale, 25 per cent off. Compared to some of the other sofas they were a steal, but now he'd got them home, seen them contrasted against the tatty woven rugs and charity-shop coffee table, he was starting to feel a bit stupid. Six thousand pounds. He could have bought two whole bathroom suites for that, or a brand-new kitchen. He could have paid for someone to come in and redecorate the whole house. He could have recarpeted throughout and bought a new boiler. But then, he thought, glancing fondly at his new sofas, where was the wow factor in a cheap kitchen or a swathe of new carpet? Where was the inspiration? These sofas were going to inform the rebirth of this house, set the benchmark for style and taste. These sofas were seminal.

Toby heard the front door go and footsteps behind him. He felt suddenly embarrassed, caught red-handed with expensive sofas. He tried and failed to arrange himself into some kind of natural position, and, when Ruby walked in two seconds later, he was perched on the edge of the coffee table, looking at a copy of *Reveal*.

"Oh," he said, "it's you." He stood up and let the magazine fall to the floor.

"Oh. My. God." She'd seen the sofas. "Oh, my God," she said again, moving in for a closer look. "*What are these?*"

"New sofas," he sniffed.

"Yes, I can see that, but, Jesus Christ. I mean — they're *beautiful*." She caressed one tenderly and let her leather jacket fall to the floor.

Toby smiled grudgingly. "Thank you."

"I can't believe you bought these. They must have cost a *fortune*."

"Well, yes, but they were in the sale."

"But still. My God. Is this real suede?"

"Yes."

She sat down and ran her hands over the mocha suede. "Well, Toby Dobbs, who would have guessed that you had such great taste?"

Toby felt a surge of pride rise slowly through him like a bubble in a spirit level.

"Where are they from?"

"Conran Shop," he mumbled through his fingers.

"*Conran?!* Jesus, Toby, did you *steal* them?"

"No, of course not. I paid for them. Cash."

"But how the hell could you afford them?"

Toby sighed. He'd known he'd have to offer an explanation at some point. "Gus."

"Gus?"

"Gus left me some money. In his will."

Ruby's eyes widened. "No! How much?"

"A few thousand. Not that much. Not really enough to be buying sofas from the Conran Shop. But I just . . . I don't know . . ."

"You wanted them?"

"Yes, I wanted them."

"Oh, Tobes," Ruby rested a hand on his knee. "That's OK. That's what normal people do all the time. It's called *extravagance*. Embrace it."

Toby smiled. "So," he said, "you like them, then?"

"I *love* them."

"Good," he said.

"But, really," she said, "how much did Gus leave you? Exactly?"

"I'm not telling you!"

"Why not?"

"Because I don't want anyone else to know."

"I won't tell anyone else."

"How do I know that?"

"Because I promise and I swear."

"No," he said adamantly, folding his arms.

"Oh, Toby. I can't believe you don't trust me by now."

"It's not that I don't trust you. It's just . . ."

"That you don't trust me. God, Tobes, as if I'd steal your money."

"I'm not saying you'd steal it."

"Yeah, well, whatever. I'll find out somehow. You know me."

Toby smirked. He'd lived with Ruby for fifteen years, but he wasn't entirely sure he did know her. He knew what she sounded like when she was having sex. He knew what colour her nipples were. He knew her moods and her patterns. But did he know *her*?

"So," he said, "what's happening with Paul Fox? He hasn't been around for a while."

Ruby shrugged and fiddled with a piece of thread hanging off her jumper. "Not a lot. We had a bit of a row last week."

"Oh, right. What about?"

"Oh, you know, *Eliza*."

"Well, really, I'm not sure what you expect. I mean, the man has a girlfriend, for God's sake."

Ruby raised her eyebrows. "Oh, God, Tobes, don't start on me. I don't need you telling me what to do."

"I'm not trying to tell you what to do, but, really, this thing you have going with Paul, it's just so wrong on so many different levels. I don't understand why you have to keep underselling yourself the entire time."

"You mean you want me to settle down with a nice boy?"

"Well, yes. Isn't that what you want?"

"No. Not even slightly."

"But what's going to happen to you?"

"Happen?"

"Yes. Where will you go? What will you do?"

"I don't know what you mean."

"I just mean . . ." He was about to say, you're thirty-one, you're single, you've got no career and I'm about to kick you out of the only home you've known since you were sixteen. He was about to say, you're free-falling and you've got no one to catch you. He was about to say, *I don't want you to end up like me*. But he didn't. Instead he smiled. "I'm just worried about you, that's all."

"Well, don't be," she said. "I'm absolutely fine. I can look after myself."

"Good," he said. "Good."

CHAPTER FIFTEEN

According to Toby's observations, Joanne's current daily routine went something like this:

7.45 a.m.:	Blow-dry hair in bedroom. Emerge with unusual hairstyle.
8.00 a.m.:	Make weird coffee substitute chicory drink thing in kitchen. Take it into dining room. Drink it while reading the *Mail* and listening to Virgin FM.
8.30 a.m.:	Leave house, wearing extraordinary combinations of clothing, sometimes wearing glasses, sometimes not.
6–11 p.m.:	Return home, sometimes sober, sometimes drunk, always alone. Go straight to room (occasionally stopping to collect cutlery from kitchen if carrying a takeaway or a wine glass if carrying a bag from off-licence).
12–2 a.m.:	Turn off TV set in room. Go to sleep (presumably).

Yesterday, she had left for work wearing a black-and-white chequerboard miniskirt with a red polo neck and a pair of thick-soled leather boots with buckles. Her hair had been gelled back off her face and she was wearing a strange lipstick the colour of sediment. Today as she bustled round the kitchen, making her pretend coffee, she was wearing a massive denim dungaree-style dress which looked like maternity wear, a white cotton shirt, thick navy tights and red pumps. Her hair was parted in the middle and had taken on a peculiar kinky wave. She wasn't wearing any make-up at all and had on her red glasses (her other pair were frameless). She looked like a pregnant French schoolteacher on the verge of a nervous breakdown.

Toby poured himself a bowl of muesli from a new packet and felt somewhat surprised to see red lumps in it. He stared at them quizzically, trying to find a rational explanation for the existence of red lumps in his muesli. He picked one up and rolled it between his thumb and forefinger. It was squidgy. He put it to his lips and licked it. It was sweet. He turned and looked at Joanne.

"Here," he said, "what do you reckon these are, in my muesli?"

Joanne jumped slightly, but didn't turn round.

"Erm . . . hello?"

Toby heard her sigh. "Sorry — what?" she turned round slowly to appraise him.

"These red things in my muesli. What do you think they are?" He held the bowl out.

Joanne stared at him, then at the bowl, over the top of her red glasses. "Sorry," she said eventually, "I'm not sure I understand what it is you're asking me?"

Now it was Toby's turn to sigh. "Don't worry about it," he said. "I was just being silly."

She squinted at him.

"It's just that," he continued desperately, "I eat the same muesli every morning and this morning, for the very first time, there are red things in it and I was just wondering if you could shed any light on the matter. That's all."

She peered at Toby, curiously. "No," she said, "no. I don't think that I can."

Toby shrugged and tried to force back a smile. "Oh, well. I guess I'll just eat them and hope for the best."

Joanne smiled tightly and went back to making her coffee.

Toby tried again. "What is that stuff that you drink?" He pointed at the jar.

"Coffee," she replied.

"No, but it's not normal coffee, is it?"

"Yes, it is," sniffed Joanne.

"No, but it's not." He smiled and pointed at the jar again.

She looked at the jar. "What do you mean?"

"Look," he picked up the jar and presented it to her. It's made from chicory."

"*Chicory?*" She took it from him and peered at the label. "But I don't understand. How can coffee be made out of chicory?"

"Well, exactly. That's the whole point. It's not coffee, is it? It's a caffeine-free coffee substitute."

"Yes, but why would someone have sold it to me when I wanted coffee?"

"Well — where did you buy it?"

"From a health food shop."

"You bought coffee from a health food shop?"

"Yes — I buy as much of my food as possible from a health food shop."

"Even coffee?"

"Yes."

"Which is intrinsically unhealthy."

"Well, I suppose, I hadn't really thought. I just saw the word 'coffee' and I needed some and I thought it would be healthier than coffee from a supermarket."

"Well, it is definitely healthier." Toby smiled, but she just scowled at him and turned away. "Didn't you think it tasted a bit odd?"

"Well, a little bit. But I just put that down to it being healthy. For God's sake." She tutted loudly and stared at the label. "Look," she said crossly, "it's there. In black and white. Chicory. I thought that was the brand name. Fuck's sake . . ." She banged the bottle down on the work top and stared angrily out of the window.

"I've got some Nescafé if you want?" Toby offered after a moment.

"No," she snapped. "No. I'll drink this stupid *chicory* thing. It's fine."

"Are you sure?"

"Yes," she hissed, her back still turned to Toby.

"OK," he said, opening the fridge and pulling out some milk. "You drink your chicory thing and I'll eat my red things and we'll just chalk it up to experience."

He followed Joanne into the dining room a moment later. "They're cranberries," he said, putting his bowl down on the table. "The red things. I checked the packaging and there it was. In tiny print. They're out to get us, these food manufacturers. They keep making all these subtle changes hoping we won't notice, then suddenly we're eating cranberries and drinking chicory. And what *is* chicory anyway?"

Joanne turned the page of her newspaper and ignored him.

"Can I taste it?" he said, "your pretend coffee?"

She looked up at him and Toby watched as the muscles in her face started to twitch and contort. "I'd rather you didn't."

"Oh." He waited for a polite explanation, but Joanne just carried on reading her paper.

Joanne was not responding very well to small talk, so Toby decided to weigh in with the big question. "So, what sort of work are you doing at the moment?"

Toby saw her chest cave in then expand again as she took in a deep breath. "Look, Toby. I have to be honest. I'm not a morning person. I like to drink my coffee and read my paper and not talk to anyone until I really have to. So if you don't mind . . .?"

Toby nodded and exhaled silently. "Of course," he said, "I understand."

He picked up a seed catalogue that someone had left on the table and flicked through it mindlessly while he ate his breakfast. Part of him admired Joanne for being so forthright. Another part couldn't believe how rude and horrible she was. He glanced surreptitiously at Joanne's hands. They were very pale with raised veins. She had a ring on the index finger of her left hand, plain gold with no stones. On her left wrist she wore a thin silver watch with a blue face. Around her neck was a silver chain with a ring and a locket hanging from it. And there, on the inside of her wrist, peeping out from just under the cuff of her starchy white shirt, was the first hint that Toby had seen of the real Joanne. A tattoo. Hard to tell what it was from the small amount that was showing, but it was black and faded, as if she'd had it done a long time ago. He opened his mouth to comment on it, then shut it again.

Joanne had a tattoo. On the inside of her wrist. Like a jailbird. Or a prisoner of war. Or a delinquent schoolgirl with a fountain pen. Joanne had a past. He was just going to have to find a way to get it out of her that didn't involve normal, everyday, polite conversation.

Toby held his breath and tried to make himself as small as possible. Joanne was a few feet ahead of him, fiddling in her handbag in the middle of the pavement. She was wearing a pink tweed jacket with a black trim and a tight grey flannel skirt with pink kitten-heeled shoes and a pink suede handbag. Her hair was a shock of home-applied blonde highlights and she was wearing far too much blusher. After a few seconds she pulled something out of her handbag that looked like a credit card, then she teetered uncertainly towards a building that appeared, according to a steel plaque on the wall, to house half a dozen businesses. She swiped her credit card through a slot on the wall and pushed her way through heavy steel doors. A large man behind a curved reception desk smiled at her and asked her to sign something. She signed it, then disappeared towards the back of the reception hall. Toby sighed and sat down on a bench.

He waited a few minutes until he was sure that Joanne would be at her desk, then strolled towards the doors to examine the steel plaque:

Davies and Co Solicitors
Rodney Field Fashions
Ultralight Beauty Systems
Larkin Abdullah Legal Services
Tiarella Textiles & Fashions

He pressed the buzzer for reception and the big man behind the desk looked up.

"Which company?" he crackled into the intercom.

"I'm not sure," he said, "I'm looking for Joanne Fish."

His forehead concertinaed into sausages of skin and he fiddled with a clipboard. "Fish?" he repeated eventually.

"Yes. Joanne Fish. She just came in, about five minutes ago. The blonde woman in pink."

"Oh, that one. Right. She's up at Tiarella."

"Tiarella. Right. OK."

"Last bell down."

"Right. Thanks."

Toby smiled tightly at the man behind the desk and gave him a feeble thumbs-up. And then, much to his confusion, he walked away. Toby had followed Joanne into work today hoping to uncover something shocking and enlightening about her, and all he'd discovered was that she went to work. In an office building. In the West End. Just like a million other people.

He sighed and headed towards Oxford Circus.

CHAPTER SIXTEEN

In the past week Leah had seen a bathroom with mould growing on the carpet, a kitchen with a pet rat on the counter and a bedroom with no windows. She'd met a man whose trainers she could smell from the front door, a woman who'd just had a face lift and a guy with five Chihuahuas. She'd been told variously that she was allowed to watch television only until nine o'clock, that she would have to stay out on Friday nights and that she wasn't allowed to drink alcohol in the "common parts". If the flat was nice, then the flatmate was awful; if the flat was awful, then the flatmate was even worse.

Leah phoned Amitabh when she got home from a man called Willy's malodorous, murky basement flat on Hornsey Lane. She phoned him partly because she was missing him and wanted to hear his voice, but mainly because she was so cross with him for putting her in this position in the first place.

"Hello, it's me."

There was a split second of silence. "Hello."

"How are you?" She tugged her trainers off with her feet.

"Good," he said, "I'm good. How are you?"

"Shit. I'm shit. Actually."

"Oh." She could hear Amitabh sitting down, presumably on his bed. She could imagine him stroking his chin like he did when he was uncomfortable.

"Yes. This whole flat-hunting thing is a nightmare. I'm too old for flat shares. I'm too set in my ways. I can't live with anyone else."

Amitabh sighed. "I can't understand why you're not looking to buy."

"Because," she said crossly — they'd had this conversation a million times — "I have one hundred and two pounds in my bank account and last time I looked flats in London were going for a bit more than that."

"Get a mortgage," he said. "They're doing 100 per cent mortgages again now, you know. 110 per cent even."

"Mmm," she said, "that's a good idea. Tie myself up for the rest of my life with the mortgage from hell that I will never be able to pay off *because I work in a shop*. And of course never actually *go out again* because I won't be able to afford to."

Amitabh sighed.

"This is all your fault, you know. All of this."

He sighed again.

"I mean, what were you thinking? What were you actually *thinking*?"

"I wasn't thinking. I was just . . . *being*. You know."

"No. I don't know. All those weddings we went to, didn't you ever, you know, stop to think about what was expected of you? Didn't you sometimes lie in bed at night wondering what was going to happen to us? How it was all going to end?"

"No," he said, "I honestly never did."

"So what *did* you think about?"

"I don't know," he said. "Food. Work. Telly. I suppose that it hadn't occurred to me that I was getting so old. That we were *both* getting so old. I suppose I just thought that we had for ever."

Leah let a small silence highlight his words. "So," she said eventually, "if that old man hadn't died and I hadn't proposed we'd just have carried on, would we, carried on indefinitely, until one day we'd suddenly have woken up and realised we were fifty?"

"Yes. No. I mean, I'd have realized sooner than that that it wasn't working, but the old man dying made it happen earlier."

"Well, then, praise be to Gus for choosing his moment so well. Because it's bad enough being in this fucking predicament at thirty-five. Imagine if I'd been forty? In fact, you know something, at this precise moment I'm feeling a lot of anger towards you . . . *a lot of anger*."

"Oh, God, Leah. I'm sorry."

"Yeah, well, sorry's not going to help. Sorry's a load of bollocks frankly. *You're* a load of bollocks. A load of pathetic, immature, selfish, fat bollocks."

"Fat?"

"Yes, fat. You're fat. And hairy. But that doesn't matter because some poor woman will just have to marry you anyway because her mum and dad tell her to."

There was a stunned silence, followed two seconds later by a roar of what Leah at first assumed was indignation, but quickly realized was laughter.

"Oh, God, Leah. You're so funny. I miss you."

Leah felt her adrenalin levels drop and her muscles relax, then she smiled. "I miss you, too," she said. "Loads. I wish you weren't Indian."

"Yeah," he said, "so do I."

It fell silent for a moment, then Leah looked at her watch. "Shit," she said, "I've got to go."

"Go where?"

"To the Clissold Arms. It's Toby's birthday."

"Toby who?"

"You know, Toby, across the road. Young Skinny Guy. Except he's not that young. He's thirty-nine."

"How come you're going to the pub with him?"

"He invited me."

"What? Like on a date?"

"No. Of course not. He wants me to meet his housemates."

"What — you mean you're going to meet the Teenager? And, and the Air Hostess. And *Sybil*?!"

"Well," she said, "maybe. I'm not sure who's coming."

"And the Girl with the Guitar?"

"I told you, Am, I don't know."

"Oh, God, that's not fair. I lived there for three years, then I move out and five seconds later you're getting in with the neighbours. Can I come?"

"No, Am, you can't. We don't go out together any more, remember?"

"But we're friends, aren't we? We can still see each other?"

"I don't know. Maybe. Look, I have to go now. I'll speak to you soon, OK?"

"OK," he sniffed. "And Leah?"

"Yes?"

"I love you."

CHAPTER SEVENTEEN

Leah got home from the Clissold Arms just after eleven. She slammed the door behind her and leaned against it, heavily, her body wilting with the relief of finally being home. The evening had been a resounding failure, a disaster in fact. Only Con and Ruby had turned up and they'd spent the entire night flirting outrageously with each other before disappearing back to the house at ten o'clock, presumably, Leah imagined, to have sex with each other. Toby had watched the whole mating ritual unfurl with undisguised anguish and Leah had tried desperately to keep a jolly stream of conversation going. Which was why she'd ended up drinking so much. She'd learned nothing about Toby's housemates, other than that they had the hots for each other, and all she'd learned about Toby was that he was obviously miserably in love with Ruby, as he talked about her non-stop for the remainder of the evening and at one point had even looked like he might be about to cry.

As the silence of her empty flat descended on her she felt a buzzing in her ears and realized how drunk she was. She sighed and gazed round the flat. She hated living here without Amitabh. But then the thought of living somewhere else, of living with *someone* else, was just as depressing. She thought back to her conversation with Amitabh earlier that day, what he'd said about wishing he wasn't Indian, him saying that he loved her. And then she did something ludicrous. She picked up the phone and she called Amitabh's mother.

"Hello, Mrs Varshney. Malini. It's Leah."

"Leah?"

"Hi, how are you?"

"Leah. It's very late."

"I know. I'm sorry. I'm just . . ." She sighed, and sat on the sofa. "I'm just, I don't know. How are you?"

"I'm tired, is how I am. I'm in bed, you've just woken me up and I'm tired. Is everything all right?"

"Yes. No. It's just. You know, what Amitabh said to me when we split up. Is it true? Would you really not want to have me as a daughter-in-law?"

She heard Malini sighing loudly down the phone. "Oh, Leah, Leah, Leah. What can I say to you?"

"Say it's not true. Say he was wrong. Say that you would be proud to have a girl like me as the wife of your youngest son."

"And so I would," she replied softly, "so I would if I were someone else. If I were Mrs Smith and my parents were from Berkshire and I went to church every Sunday, then there is no other girl I would like better for my son to marry. But that isn't the case."

"But what if I converted to Hinduism? I could do that?"

"It's not about *religion*, Leah. It's about family and lineage and caste and tradition. I can't do anything about it."

"But, Malini, I love him so much."

"I know you do, my sweet girl. But there is a fact here that has to be faced."

"What's that?" she sniffed.

"The fact is that if my Amitabh loved you as much as you love him, then he would marry you and be damned. The fact is that my Amitabh hasn't finished looking yet."

CHAPTER EIGHTEEN

Con pulled open his wardrobe and leafed through his clothes. They all looked wrong this morning, for some reason. Too bright, too clean, too considered. His jeans were too new, too blue, too many fussy zips and buckles. Con took his clothes very seriously and it showed. But this morning he wanted to wear something that looked as if it had found its way into his wardrobe by stealth, the sort of thing that Toby might wear. He considered the possibility of knocking on Toby's bedroom door and asking him if he had anything he could borrow, but discounted this as a 100 per cent gay thing to do.

He flicked through a pile of jumpers. Beige. He wanted something beige. Or off-white. Something plain. He found a brown Paul Smith merino sweater with a pale lemon check, but it was way too Ivy League. And a French Connection linen shirt in pale lime. But that was too summery. Eventually he settled on his old Levi's, a white flannel shirt with a grey windowpane check, and his brown suede Pumas. It still wasn't right — the white of the shirt was too intense, the jeans had the beginning of a tear in the knee that looked a bit fake, even though it wasn't, and the Pumas were too new-looking — but it was a step towards the look he'd been going for.

Melinda watched him from her bed. "What's going on with you?" she asked suspiciously.

"What?"

"How come you're wearing your old jeans?"

"I dunno. Just fancied something a bit old school."

"Is this about Ruby?"

"*Ruby?*" he scoffed.

"Yeah. Are you trying to impress her or something?"

"What?" he said again. "Why would I do that?"

"Er! Why d'you think?!"

Con sighed and touched his hair in the mirror. "No, Mum, I am not trying to impress Ruby. I told you, what happened — it was bollocks, OK? Nothing. I'm not interested in Ruby."

"Then why . . .?" She paused mid-sentence. "Never mind, forget it. Men. You're all a mystery to me."

Con, in all honesty, was feeling like a bit of a mystery to himself in the wake of Friday night. He'd fancied Ruby for ages, but not in a specific way, just in that general way of fancying fit women. The world was full of fit women; it was like a long roll of wallpaper with a pretty print on it. They all merged into one, but sometimes a girl jumped out of the wallpaper. Sometimes you thought about a fit girl after you'd stopped looking at her; sometimes you wondered about her when she wasn't there; sometimes you just wanted to stand and stare for as long as you liked, drinking in every last bit of her so you had some to take home with you. And when that happened you knew you were on to something special. And that had never happened with Ruby.

He walked past her on the stairs, thought, she's fit, stopped thinking about her. He watched her eating a banana, thought, she's fit, stopped thinking about her. He saw her walking up the road in tight jeans and dangerous boots, thought, she's fit, stopped thinking about her. That's how it was with Ruby. No wondering, no thinking, no stopping and staring. Just vague, general fancying. So the fact that he'd slept with her on Toby's birthday was inexplicable. It was partly the drink, obviously, and the novelty. All her teasing about how he'd never had an older woman and a little voice in his head saying: got to have an older woman, tick a box, 100 things to do before you're thirty, chalk it up, pin it down, do it while you've got the chance. It had felt wrong the minute they made the decision and, by the time they left the pub, Con knew he was making a mistake, but it was too late then. He couldn't pull out; he'd have looked like an idiot. So he'd followed her into her bedroom, laid her down amongst all that girlie shit on her bed, cushions, throws, fluff and glitter, and he'd completely gone to town. Went at it like a porn star, as if he was being filmed. He had to live with this woman after, see her every day. He had to give her the best he could offer otherwise he'd never be able to look her in the eye again. So he had.

He didn't know what happened next. He didn't want to go back there, he knew that much. Once was enough. She wasn't his type and he just wasn't really that into her. Judging by the way she was with her other blokes, that shouldn't be a problem, though. He was a scratch on her bedpost. And that was fine with him.

"Is this shirt a bit spoddy?" he asked his mum.

"No," she smiled. "It's lovely. But what's the big deal? You're only going to work. Who's going to care what shirt you're wearing?"

"No one," he said. "No one."

She was sitting at her desk in the window, with a shaft of sun cutting through her at a diagonal. She was wearing a cream chiffon shirt with roses on it, a cotton waistcoat with pockets, and a tiny denim skirt with a frayed hem. Her fine hair was rolled up at the back and her shoes were flat-bottomed and pointy. She looked like a little fairy, all pale and diaphanous.

She turned at the sound of his trolley and leapt to her feet. "Oh, God," she said. "Shit, sorry. Is it three o'clock already?"

Con nodded.

"Shit. I haven't got it all together." She started scanning her desk with her hands, trying to lay them on all the relevant envelopes and bits of paper. "I'm going to be a minute or two. Is that OK?"

This happened all the time. Dippy bloody teenagers, fresh from A levels, doing a bit of work experience before university, or graduates back from a year learning to scuba dive and smoke spliff on other continents. They didn't wear watches. They never knew what time it was. Everything was always a last-minute panic. Usually it really bugged him. But not in this case. In this case he was happy for Daisy to take as long as she liked panicking prettily around him, like a distracted butterfly.

"So," she said, flicking through a pile of cream envelopes, "how are you today?"

"I'm good," he said. "Very well indeed," he added, somehow feeling a need to be a bit suave. His grandmother had always tried to get him to speak properly, to use proper manners. Then she'd sent him to the roughest comprehensive in Tottenham, where good manners and properly enunciated vowels didn't really count for much. But at home it had been all: "Don't say what, say pardon," and "Where are your manners?" and "May I have some, not can I have some," and "Take your elbows off the table." His grandmother had been a proper old-fashioned grandmother, not one of these trendy ones in tracksuits and earrings. She'd been brought up by her grandmother and was a stickler for doing things properly.

"How are you?"

"Mental," she said, looping an elastic band round the envelopes and handing them to him. "They're all off on a trip tomorrow, so of course everything has to be done, like, five minutes ago and everyone's being foul to each other and pretending that their things are way more important than anyone else's things and of course shit rolls downhill and guess who's at the bottom?" She stopped for breath and pushed some hair out of her eyes. "See — they've got me at it now. I never get stressed. Never. I don't *do* stressed. It's not in my genes. I tell you, I cannot *wait* until today's over and they're all on that plane halfway to Mauritius. Tomorrow is going to be sooo mellow."

She loaded up his trolley with squidgy packages and slippery bags of clothes as she talked. "Are you going back down to the post room now?"

"Yes," he said.

"You know," she said, glancing across the room at a clock on the wall, "I might just come down with you. They're waiting for something from Miu Miu and apparently if it doesn't get here in the next ten minutes then the entire population of the world is going to get a terrible disease and die — apparently. I might as well just sit in dispatch and wait for it. Get me out of this hell hole for a bit."

They stepped into the lift and stared at the doors, awkwardly, until Daisy broke the silence. "So," she said, "where do you live?"

"Finchley," he said.

"Finchley? Where's that? Is that north?"

"Yes. North of Hampstead. South of Barnet."

"Is it nice there?"

"Yeah. It's OK. I live in a nice house, so it's good. What about you? Where do you live?"

"Wandsworth," she said. "Just off the common. Nice area. Crappy house."

"Why — what's wrong with it?"

"Oh, it belongs to my sister's boyfriend and it's just tiny, you know, a little tiny weeny cottage with teeny tiny rooms. The kitchen is about as big as this lift. But I shouldn't really complain. It's nice of them to let me live with them and at least I've got somewhere to live, you know."

Con nodded and thought about telling her, but decided not to. Maybe she'd feel sorry for him. Or, even worse, maybe she'd think it was really cool that he'd once spent a fortnight sleeping in a shop doorway in Wood Green. Maybe she would suddenly see him as a novelty, someone she could brag about to her posh friends and her sisters with the silly flower names; oh, my new friend, Con, so tragic, used to be homeless, you know, slept on a piece of cardboard and got washed in a public toilet.

The lift flumped to the basement floor and the doors slid open. Daisy helped Con manoeuvre his trolley through the doors.

"So, who do you live with in your really nice house? Friends? A girlfriend?"

Con felt a surge of excitement then. It was the way she said it: "A girlfriend?" She was fishing; she wanted to know if he was single. And suddenly Con felt everything in his head shift along a bit to make room for this new possibility — the possibility that this girl from another place, from a world of ponies and Caribbean family holidays and parties where boys wore tuxedos might actually want to be with him, a boy from Tottenham, who'd been brought up by his grandmother in a second-floor council flat.

"No," he said encouragingly, "no girlfriend. I live with my mum."

"Oh, you're still at home?"

"No. I mean — she lives with me. In my place."

"You share a place with your mum?"

"Yes. But not just my mum. Loads of us."

"What — like a commune?"

He smiled. A girl like Daisy would like the idea of a commune. "Yeah," he said, "a bit. This poet bloke owns it and rents out rooms."

"Wow — a poet."

"Yeah. He's a bit strange, kind of like a recluse, but he's a good bloke. And the house is massive. All sorts of people have lived there. Artists and singers and actors and stuff. It's a really cool place."

The boys in the post room all glanced up curiously as Con walked in with Daisy, their eyes straying automatically to her slender legs, but she seemed completely oblivious to their attentions. Usually when people from "upstairs" had cause to come "downstairs", you could sense their need to assimilate themselves briefly in this alien environment to get what they needed before heading back in the lift to the bright lights of normality. But Daisy wasn't bothered. She hadn't noticed that she was in a noisy room full of men, Radio One blaring in the background, tabloids being read backwards.

He led her to the dispatch area to look for her parcel.

"Anything in from Miu Miu for *Vogue*?" he asked Nigel.

"Yeah," said Nigel, grabbing a big plastic bag off a rail. "Just in, two minutes ago." He handed the bag to Con and smiled at Daisy. "Hello," he said, gormlessly. "And who are you?"

Con sent Nigel a reproachful look. Daisy hadn't come down here to be flirted with by overweight men in Primark jumpers.

"Hello," she smiled back. "I'm Daisy."

"Hello, Daisy. I'm Nigel."

"Do you like Miu Miu, Nigel?"

Nigel smiled. "My favourite," he said.

"They do nice shoes, too."

"Oh, yes," he agreed, "lovely shoes. But not as nice as those Christian Louboutins. Now those are really nice shoes."

Daisy laughed, then Nigel laughed. And Con watched in wonder as they joked together, this lardy forty-something man from Hainault and an angel from the eighth floor. And he knew it then. Daisy had jumped out of the wallpaper and was within his grasp. It was just a matter of time.

CHAPTER NINETEEN

It was five in the morning and Ruby was about to creep up the stairs and head for bed when a figure appeared in the hallway. It was Melinda, groomed and polished, blonde hair scraped back into a sleek bun, all ready for work in her navy and yellow uniform.

"Oh, hello." Melinda pulled her leather coat off the coat stand and glanced icily at Ruby.

"Morning," said Ruby, suddenly conscious of the alcohol on her breath. Her hands felt clammy and dirty. She wanted to wash them.

They stood facing each other for a while. A bird outside started to sing.

Melinda spoke first. "I'm not going to talk to you now because you're drunk, but just know this — if you do anything, *anything* to hurt my boy, I'll belt you. I swear." And then she slung her coat over her arm, picked up her fake Mulberry handbag and left.

Ruby stood for a while, feeling vodka and red wine swilling round the pit of her empty stomach. Then a rush of violent indignation hit her between the ribs, impelling her towards the front door. She threw it open and stamped down the steps, towards Melinda's receding figure. “You are a sick and twisted bitch, do you know that?”

Melinda turned and stared at her, and Ruby had a sudden moment of objectivity, of seeing this tableau through somebody else’s eyes — the wild-haired, grimy-skinned brunette in tight jeans and a flimsy jersey top screaming at the cool blonde with the shower-fresh skin and crisp suit in the middle of the street, as twilight flickered round the horizon.

“Like I said,” Melinda began, pulling her car keys out of her bag, “I won’t talk to you while you’re in this state. Have a good day.” The chirrup and click of her car locks opening punctured the silence, and she slid into the driver’s seat, slipped on her seat belt and very slowly, and very deliberately, manoeuvred her Peugeot 306 out of its space.

Ruby stood on the pavement for a while, swaying slightly in the wake of this surreal collision between the end of her day and the start of Melinda’s. And then she climbed the steps to the house, made her way to her bedroom and fell asleep on top of her bed, still wearing all her clothes.

CHAPTER TWENTY

Toby's love for Ruby ebbed and flowed like the tide. When he'd first met her fifteen years ago he'd been consumed by lust for her. It had overwhelmed him to the point that he'd had to question the validity of every other feeling he'd ever experienced, the intensity of every emotion he'd ever felt, even for Karen. He had never in his life wanted so much to perform an act of sexual intercourse with another human being. He felt engorged entirely. There was excess blood in his arms, his feet, his *eyeballs*. He sweated profusely in her presence, *glowed* with the heat that emanated from his body, like infrared. He had to keep his hands in his pockets to stop himself from touching her, inappropriately.

On her second night in his house, she'd brought home a monstrous man she claimed was an "old friend" and made love to him so loudly and for so long that Toby had had to go downstairs to sleep on the sofa. The man had then hung round for the rest of the weekend, wearing Ruby's dressing gown and smoking everywhere he went, including the bathroom. Toby had imagined this episode to be some kind of aberration and breathed a sigh of relief when the man finally disappeared on Monday afternoon, but three days later Ruby arrived home in the middle of the afternoon with the bass player from her band, said something about reworking some lyrics, then disappeared into her bedroom with him for more than an hour of ear-shattering sexual activity. And so it had gone on, a succession of "old friends" and "great mates" and "best buddies" all clambering in and out of Ruby's bed — some of them once and never again; some of them on a regular basis. Some of them matched her for attractiveness; some of them were downright ugly. A couple of them had made it to the "boyfriend" stage, but these were fleeting relationships, always ended by Ruby and never cried over.

The fact of Ruby's sexual promiscuity had not, strange to say, fuelled Toby's desire for her. If anything it had flattened it like a big bum on a whoopee cushion. What happened instead was that Toby started to look beyond the physical, his body disgorged, he stopped glowing and he fell in love with her. When it was just the two of them, watching TV, watching a band, having a drink, discussing music, when it was just Toby and Ruby, it was the best thing in the world. He learned to switch off when she was keeping male company, to immerse himself in something distracting, to turn up his music and sit it out like a forecasted downpour.

Sometimes Ruby would go without sex for a month or two, and Toby would grow hopeful — maybe she was growing up, growing out of it. Maybe now she would look at Toby and see him as a sexual being. But then, eventually, a few days later, usually in the middle of the night, the front door would open and the sound of an alien male voice would float up the stairs towards Toby's bed and he'd pull a pillow over his head and try to get to sleep before the noise started.

Once, about six years ago, Ruby had come home from a gig at three in the morning with some girlfriends and stormed drunkenly into Toby's bedroom. "Can I have a cuddle, Tobes?"

"What?"

"I'm really, really drunk and I want a lovely cuddle with my lovely Toby." She'd crawled onto his bed and draped an arm over him and nestled her head into the crook of his arm. Toby had barely moved a muscle, too scared to breathe in case she changed her mind.

"Are you naked?" she'd said after a minute or two.

"Not entirely," he'd said.

Downstairs her girlfriends clattered round the wooden floors in their heels, plundered the fridge for snacks and put on music. Toby listened to Ruby breathing, the bitter alcoholic fumes of her breath filling the space between her head and his arm. "What's this all about?" he'd said eventually.

"What?"

"This," he gestured, "this."

"Nothing," she'd murmured. "Just want a cuddle, that's all."

She'd fallen asleep there, on his bed, in his arms. One of her friends had walked in a few minutes later and backed out apologetically when she'd seen Ruby in Toby's embrace. Toby's arm went numb about an hour later, but he didn't move it. He slept for about an hour and woke up with the sun at six o'clock, and stared at her for another hour until she woke up and stumbled back to her bedroom where she slept until noon.

The whole experience was never mentioned again, mainly, Toby suspected, because it hadn't meant anything to Ruby. But Toby had secretly hoped that that intimate albeit chaste interlude might have laid the foundations for something to change. But it didn't. If anything things went downhill afterwards because it was then that Ruby met Paul Fox.

Toby *hated* Paul Fox.

He hated him because he had a stupid haircut.

He hated him because he was wealthy and successful.

He hated him because he called everyone "mate" in his stupid mockney accent, even though Toby knew he was an ex-public school boy (it took one to know one).

He hated him because when he came he shouted, "Oh God oh Jesus oh fuck," in exactly the same order and with precisely the same rhythm every single time.

He hated him because he'd once overheard him referring to him as Mr Rigsby.

He hated him because he was being unfaithful to his loyal girlfriend, even though he'd never met her.

But mainly he hated him because he'd somehow managed to persuade Ruby to sleep with him at least once a week for the past five years.

All the other blokes were of little consequence to Toby. They came; they went; they were forgotten about. But Paul Fox hung round like a terrible memory, taunting Toby with the inexplicable power he seemed to exert over Ruby. Toby didn't think things could get much worse than Paul Fox.

But now they had.

Ruby had slept with Con.

This represented, as far as Toby was concerned, a dramatic slip in her standards and, as such, a seismic shift once again in the way he viewed her. It was time for her to go. And, more importantly, it was time for him to stop loving her. He just wished someone could show him how.

CHAPTER TWENTY-ONE

Ruby's handbag vibrated. She pulled out her phone and wiped some crumbs off the screen. It was Paul. She hesitated for a moment. This was the first time he'd called since the night they'd bumped into Eliza and she wasn't sure she wanted to talk to him. She stared at the screen for a moment, then pressed the accept button.

"Hello," she said, tentatively, not sure yet what tone to take.

"Hello," he replied. He sounded businesslike, but friendly. "Where are you?"

"In rehearsals with the boys."

"Are you free this afternoon? For an hour or so?"

This usually meant that he wanted to come over for sex. She took the phone into the corridor. "Erm, I'm not sure. Why?"

"I need to see you. To talk to you. I can pick you up. How about tea at the Wolseley?"

Ruby laughed. "Tea at the Wolseley?!"

"Yes. I've got a meeting in Green Park at five, so you'll have to get yourself home. I'll pick you up at three." He hung up without saying goodbye.

Ruby switched her phone off and stared absent-mindedly at a notice board on the wall opposite, at postcards appealing for lead singers and drummers, cards advertising keyboards and clarinets. She could hear someone further up the corridor tuning a piano and next door someone was battering the hell out of a drum kit. She was in her comfort zone here, surrounded by rhythm and noise and scruffy men.

Ruby liked scruffiness. She liked wading through plastic beer cups on sticky floors in claustrophobic clubs; she liked smoking and drinking too much in dingy old pubs; she liked watching films in proper old-fashioned flea pits with no leg room and tatty carpets. Ruby didn't like slick and glamorous. She didn't like the latest thing. She liked her life to feel grimy and used, like her men. Tea at the Wolseley? This was going to be very strange indeed.

The woman at the front desk appeared to know Paul. "Of course," she smiled, when he asked if they had a table available without a reservation.

They were led through the cavernous restaurant by a small girl in black and shown to a table at the back. Ruby looked round in awe. It was like a vast black-lacquered cathedral, held up by forty-foot pillars and hung with chandeliers the size of transit vans.

Paul had spent most of the journey here talking to someone called Mike on his Bluetooth, so they hadn't had a chance to talk yet, but Ruby knew that something was wrong. There'd been no fond smiles, no fingertips trailed down her inner arm, no hand clasped over her thigh — just a subtle but clear distance.

Ruby ordered half a dozen oysters and a glass of champagne, figuring that she could eat sandwiches and cake at home any time she wanted. She glanced at Paul. "So," she began, "what's up?"

"I've got something to tell you."

"Right."

"I've asked Eliza to marry me."

Ruby winced and grabbed the edge of the table to steady herself. "Excuse me?"

"Last week. I asked her to marry me. And she said yes."

"Oh, my God," she laughed, though she wasn't amused. "You're kidding."

"No. I'm not."

"But, you've only known each other for six months."

"Eight months, actually."

"Eight months. Whatever. It's not very long."

"No, it's not. But then I'm not very young. And neither is she."

"Yes, but, *Jesus*. Getting married. I mean, that's such a fucking big deal. That means . . ." And then it hit her, exactly what that meant. It meant no more her. "What about us?"

"Well, that's the thing, Rubes. That's what I wanted to talk to you about."

"Oh, God." Ruby let her head fall into her hands. The tiredness she'd been fighting all morning at rehearsals hit her directly between the eyes like a left hook.

"There's no way that this can carry on." He gestured at the two of them. "No way. It's one thing messing round in a casual relationship. But, you know, we're talking engagement rings here. We're talking a major fucking commitment."

"Yes, yes, I *know* what you're talking about." Ruby pulled her hair away from her face and glanced up at him.

"And I can't have you in my life any more."

Ruby laughed. "Don't be ridiculous. Of course you can. You're my best mate."

"No, Ruby, I'm not. 'Best mate' is just a term that you bandy about because it makes you feel better about the fact that you sleep with men without commitment. I'm not your best mate. You don't have a best mate."

"What?" Ruby sat up straight.

"Well, you don't. I'm sorry. You have friends. Lots of friends. And you have lovers. Lots of lovers. But you don't have a best mate." He stopped and appraised her for a moment, as if he was about to say something harsh. "But anyway . . . anyway," he sighed, and pulled his hands down his face. "I didn't bring you here to give you a character assassination. I brought you here because I wanted to do this properly. Because you deserve it. So here . . ."

He pulled open his jacket and removed a box from his inside pocket. He passed it to Ruby.

"What is this?" she said.

"Open it," he said, nodding at the box.

The box clicked open and something glittered at her. It was a tortoiseshell hair comb, one of those Spanish-style ones. It was decorated with tiny pink rubies set into the shape of flowers. Ruby gazed at it for a while not sure how to react. It was a beautiful gift, but what did it mean?

"Do you like it?"

"Yes," she said, "it's beautiful. But what's it for?"

"It's for your hair," he said. "A hair thing."

"No, no. I mean — why have you given it to me?"

"To say thank you. To say goodbye."

"Right." She let the box snap shut and laid it gently on the table in front of her.

"Was it a mistake?"

"No," she sighed. "No. It's stunning. It'll be nice to have something to remind me of you. Of us."

"Are you being facetious?"

"No," she said, "of course not. You don't owe me anything. This was always a, you know, an easy-come-easy-go thing. It's fine." She stopped and caught her breath as a dreadful thought occurred to her. "But, what about our arrangement?"

Paul lowered his gaze and waited while the waitress arranged their drinks on the table.

"Well," he said, after she'd gone, "obviously that's going to have to stop."

"Right," she said, panic surging through her. "So what am I going to do? How am I going to pay my rent?"

"Toby will let you off the rent, I'm sure."

"Yes," said Ruby, "but what about everything else? What about food and clothes and . . . and . . . *life*?"

"You'll find a way," he said. "You'll get a job, sell a song. It's time for you to grow up, Ruby . . ."

"Christ," she felt panic engulf her, "what's going to happen to me? I owe Kev for the rehearsal this morning. I'm overdrawn as it is. Fuck. Can't you, maybe, just lend me some money. Just to tide me over?"

"No, Ruby. I can't. This is it. This . . ." He gestured at the gift box. "And this . . ." He gestured at her oysters which had just been placed in front of her. "After this there's nothing. It has to be like this."

"What — not even fifty quid?"

Paul sighed and pulled out his wallet. He pulled out a sheaf of twenty-pound notes and slid them across the table to Ruby. She covered them with her hand. It was more than fifty, probably about a hundred. They were still warm. She slipped them into her handbag without looking at them. "Thank you," she said, then she stared at her oysters, while she tried to corral her thoughts. Who was the first person to eat an oyster, she wondered, prodding one gently with her fork? Who prised open that first shell and thought it would be interesting to put it in their mouth? She tipped a teaspoon of pink vinegar and shallots into the shell, picked it up between her thumb and forefinger, and lifted it to her nose. The smell reminded her of summer holidays, of barnacle-encrusted shipwrecks and razor clams on empty Kentish beaches, of fish and chips eaten with wooden forks, and buckets full of seaweed and tiny translucent crabs. She tipped the oyster into her mouth and bit down on it, once, twice, swallowed it. She glanced at Paul. He was watching her wistfully over tented fingers. “Aren’t you worried about me?” she said, softly. “Aren’t you scared I won’t survive?”

“No,” he said, picking up his cutlery.

“Why not?”

“Do you *want* me to be worried about you?”

“Yes,” she said.

“Seriously?” he laughed.

“Yes. I’m scared. I’m . . . I’m . . .” She felt herself dangerously close to tears and paused for a moment. “I don’t know who I am and I’m scared that without you I might just float away.” She stared at Paul with glassy eyes. Paul smiled at her apologetically and covered her hand with his.

“You’ll be fine,” he said. “I know you. You’re a strong woman and you will be absolutely fine.”

Ruby smiled stiffly and pulled her hand away. Because if that was what he thought then he really didn’t know her at all.

CHAPTER TWENTY-TWO

Con was in the kitchen, washing up a dinner plate. Toby smiled at him as he reached past him to grab a glass off the draining board. "All right?" Con said.

"Yup," he said, "just getting some water."

He was about to leave the kitchen and head back upstairs when Con turned round. "Toby?" he said.

He looked at him enquiringly.

"Would you say that you were posh?"

Toby smiled. "*Me?*"

"Yeah. What are you? I mean you're obviously not working class, but are you posh or middle class, or what?"

"God," he said, "I don't know. I've never really thought about it."

"It's just . . . it's funny, isn't it? Meeting people and they talk a certain way or look a certain way and you think you know what sort of background they've had, but then maybe you're wrong. I mean, there are people in stately homes who haven't got any money. And you — you own this huge house, but you haven't got a penny to your name. Are you still posh? Or does being poor make you common?"

Toby smiled and leaned against a chair. "Why do you ask?"

"Dunno," he shrugged. "I'm just curious."

"Well, I suppose I'm middle class in some ways. My father's a businessman. My mother was a model. I was brought up in a four-bedroom house in Dorset, nice but no land. I think we probably had a mortgage. But then I went to a pretty snazzy public school, hung out with some pretty posh people. And now, as you say, I'm penniless. I don't have a career, but I own a property." He shrugged and smiled. "I'd say I'm a bit of a mess, really."

"But you see, compared to me, you're still posh. My mum's pretty much homeless. I don't know what my dad did. I was brought up on an estate, went to a comp. It's all about the inheritance, isn't it, what you get when they're gone? Whatever happens to you, you'll have this house, maybe some more off your dad when he goes. I'll get nothing. Well, unless my dad's actually really rich and suddenly remembers that he's got a son . . ."

He stopped and stared at Toby for a moment. Toby fiddled with the glass in his hand and waited for Con to continue. He wanted to talk about Ruby, it was blindingly obvious.

"I've met this girl," he said, eventually.

Toby nodded. Here it came.

"At work. And I'm trying to work out how posh she is."

Toby blinked and tried not to show his surprise. "Ah, I see. So, tell me what you know about her."

"Well, she's about my age. She's a junior in the fashion department at *Vogue*, so she probably earns less than me. She's called Daisy and her sisters are called after flowers I've never heard of. She lives in Wandsworth with her sister and her boyfriend. He owns it. It's really small, apparently. And that's it. She talks posh and she looks posh. But she's not bothered about people not being like her. She's comfortable around normal people, you know."

"And that's it?"

"Yeah. So far."

"So, what's the problem? She sounds lovely."

"I don't know," he said. "I think she's interested, but I don't want to blow it."

"Well, what would you usually do if you liked someone?"

"I don't know," he shrugged, and sat down at the table. "Just play it cool, I guess."

"Right, so, that's exactly what you should do. Just because she's . . . *posh*, doesn't mean she's any different to other girls."

"Yeah," he said, "yeah. You're right. I should just be myself, right?"

"Yes," said Toby, trying desperately to sound as if he were a font of all emotional intelligence. "Yes. That'll do the trick. Be yourself."

"Yeah. OK." He stood up again. "Sorry about that — I didn't mean to, you know. Anyway. I'd better get on. See you later." He sidled past Toby and into the living room.

Toby went back to his room, feeling slightly bemused but touched that Con had felt able to confide in him. The fact that Con was showing an interest in a girl without (he presumed) silicone implants and without (he presumed, although, God knows, these days *everyone* seemed to want to look like a glamour model, maybe even *Vogue* girls) a fake tan gave Toby hope. Maybe Con was expanding his horizons, leaving his childhood behind. Maybe he was getting ready to move on. Maybe it wouldn't be so difficult to get him out of the house after all.

Toby smiled to himself as he climbed the stairs back to his room. He sat at his computer and gazed across the street. The lights were off in Leah's front window. He wondered where she was. Maybe she was looking at another flat share. Or maybe she was on a date. He'd watched her coming and going from his bedroom for years without giving her more than a split second of airtime in his thoughts. She had a boyfriend. Girls with boyfriends wore a kind of invisibility cloak. They didn't exist.

As he stared at her window he saw her. She was walking towards her front door. Her hair was in a ponytail and she was carrying two fat M&S carrier bags. She stopped outside her house and started feeling round in her handbag. When she was unable to find what it was she was looking for, she sighed, rested her carrier bags at her feet, balanced her handbag on the garden wall and started searching through it again, more and more impatiently. Eventually she brought out a bunch of keys, picked up her handbag and headed to her front door. A light was activated by her presence, and for a moment she was lit up like an actress on a stage. Her front door clicked open and she walked through it. And then, suddenly, she turned, as if someone had called her name, turned and looked straight up at Toby.

He almost ducked, but didn't. Instead he smiled at her and waved. She smiled, too. And she looked, for just one brief, fleeting and exhilarating second, like the most beautiful woman Toby had ever seen in his life. The thought brought a rush of simmering blood to his head. He gulped and turned his gaze back to his screen.

CHAPTER TWENTY-THREE

Ruby saw him coming home through her bedroom window. He was holding a yellow Selfridges carrier. His hair was different — softer, less spiky, less manicured. It was the first time she'd seen him since Toby's birthday and her reaction took her by surprise. A jolt of excitement, a quiver of happiness. The boy she'd shared her home with for more than a year, the boy she'd seen as nothing more than a schoolboy with a job, had turned into a man.

She glanced at her reflection in the mirror. She looked fine. She'd thought about crying when she got home after an interminable, strangely numb Tube journey back from the Wolseley, but changed her mind and decided to have a bath instead. She was glad now, as Ruby had a face that didn't recover very easily from the indignity of tears.

She pulled out her Rimmel concealer and smeared a little underneath her eyes. Then she blobbed some translucent pink gloss onto her lips and went downstairs.

Con was in the kitchen, boiling the kettle. He jumped when he heard her come in behind him.

"Hello, stranger," she said, pulling open the fridge.

"Hi," he said, turning back towards the sink.

She pulled out a carton of mango and passion fruit juice and poured herself a glass. "How are you?"

He nodded. "I'm good. I'm fine. How are you?"

"Excellent," she smiled. "It's been a long day, but it's looking up now." She smiled at him.

"Cup of tea?" he said.

"No, thanks." She pulled out a chair and sat down. "Can't believe I haven't seen you. It's weird."

"What's weird?"

"You know — after what happened last week. I haven't been avoiding you, you know. I've just been busy."

"Yeah," he said, dropping a flattened teabag into the bin, "me, too."

"Had a gig last night. Didn't get home till five."

"God, you've got more energy than me. I can't do late nights any more."

Ruby laughed. "You're nineteen!"

"Yeah, I know. I'm a growing boy. I need my sleep."

Ruby laughed again. She glanced at him. He looked as if he was about to leave the room. She stalled for time. "I like your hair," she said. "Looks better without all that stuff in it."

"You think?"

"Yeah. Softer. You look more . . . *mature*."

He snorted and looked embarrassed.

Ruby felt a wave of longing fall across her like a shadow. He was so new, so clean, so unformed. She wanted to touch him. "What are you up to tonight?"

He shrugged. "Waiting on a couple of calls. Probably heading home to meet some mates."

"Home? That's Tottenham, right?"

"Yeah. Old school mates. You know."

"And if not . . .?"

"What?"

"If you don't go to Tottenham? Any plan B?"

"No, not really. Probably just get a DVD and order some food in."

"Is your mum in tonight?

"No. She's meeting Zoë from work. Going out Stansted way."

"Right," she said, "so . . . maybe you should just knock your plans on the head. Maybe you should just . . . *stay in*." She smiled as she said this and cocked her head to one side, but he didn't seem to be reading her.

"You reckon?" he said. "Why's that?"

"Oh, I don't know. Its just, I'm in tonight. Your mum's out. Seems a shame not to, you know, make the most of it."

"Oh," he said, realization finally dawning upon him. "Oh, right. Yeah. I see what you're saying."

"So," she stood up and faced him. "What do you reckon? I've got a DVD player in my room."

"Christ. I mean —" He hooked his hand around the back of his neck. "— that sounds great. But I kind of promised my mates I'd see them tonight."

"Oh," she said, mentally untangling the past three minutes of conversation, trying to find the bit where he'd sounded ambivalent about going out. "Sorry, it sounded as if you didn't have firm plans. It was just an option, that's all."

"Yeah, yeah, I know."

"It still is, if your mates blow you out."

"Right. Thanks."

Ruby touched his arm. She hadn't meant to, but she couldn't help herself. "I'll be in my room," she said, "if you change your mind." And then she moved her hand to his cheek. His skin felt like wax under her palm, cool and smooth and pliant. "See you," she said. She picked up her glass of juice and sauntered from the kitchen, feeling suddenly and horribly as if she was barking up the wrong tree.

CHAPTER TWENTY-FOUR

Con tugged at the tail of the pale blue and white checked lawn cotton shirt that hung from underneath the beige merino jumper he was wearing over it. He glanced down at his narrow black jeans and pointy leather shoes. The whole outfit had set him back £150. He'd promised himself he wasn't going to spend any more money on clothes, that he was saving all his money for his private pilot's licence. But then his salary had been paid into his account and he'd hit Covent Garden with his Switch card on Saturday and blown half of it, just like that.

He'd bought a scarf, too. Thin, like a tie. He'd seen a picture of Brad Pitt wearing one in one of his mum's celebrity magazines, but he wasn't sure about it now. The blokes in the post room had looked at him a bit funny when he walked in this morning, so he'd whipped it off and stuffed it in his pocket. But here, upstairs, it was different. Upstairs you fitted in by looking different, by looking as if you didn't know that Brent Cross existed. He pulled the scarf from his pocket and wound it round his neck. Then he pushed open the doors to the *Vogue* fashion department and tried to look cool, calm and collected.

Daisy was walking urgently towards him, a knitted bag slung diagonally across her chest, dressed in a grey coat and scarf.

"Oh, hi," he said. "Where're you going?"

She smiled at him, then grabbed his sleeve, pulling him out of the doorway and into the hall. "I'm bunking off," she whispered. "I've just told them my aunt's dead."

He raised his eyebrows at her.

"It's fine," she said. "I don't actually have an aunt, so I'm not hexing anyone. I'm just so bored. I had to get out of there."

Con had never skived off a day's work in his life and felt slightly shocked. "So what are you going to do?"

She shrugged and stabbed at the lift button with her thumb. "Haven't decided yet. Was thinking I might just go home."

"Seems a waste," he said.

"Why — what would you do if your aunt hadn't really just died?"

"I dunno. Probably wouldn't just go home, though."

"Hmmm." She furrowed her eyebrows together. "Maybe you're right. Maybe I should be more imaginative. I know!" she said. "I know exactly what we should do."

"We?"

"Yes. Let's go to Borough Market and buy loads of yummy food."

"But I can't skive off."

"Of course you can."

"Well, what will I tell them?"

"Tell them your aunt's dead."

"No way!"

"Well, tell them your friend's really upset because her aunt's dead and you have to look after her."

"What! No way. That's what girls do."

"God, I don't know, then. Tell them you feel sick."

Daisy rubbed some lip balm over his forehead and Con told his boss that he'd just thrown up. Five minutes later he met Daisy round the corner on Bruton Street and they scurried away together towards Oxford Circus, sniggering like the schoolchildren they'd only just ceased to be.

Borough Market was another world. Con had barely set foot in a supermarket in his life, let alone a food market. Con really wasn't a food person. He had very little interest in it beyond how cheap it was and how filling it was. It helped if it tasted good which was why he liked McDonald's. It always hit the spot. He tried not to eat crisps and sweets because his nan had always told him that if he was hungry he should eat something proper. She'd got too ill to cook for him in the end; that was when he'd started with the McDonald's. He couldn't handle watching her shuffling painfully round the kitchen, so he'd turned to Ronald to sustain him.

Con knew it was crap, the stuff he put into his body, but he couldn't bring himself to care about it. His skin was good; his hair was good; he was in good shape. He'd worry about it if he started getting fat. Food was fuel, stomach lining, alcohol absorber — that was all.

But Daisy obviously thought differently.

She was dashing round this place like it was a half-price designer sample sale. She caressed jars of gooey brown onions and misshapen hunks of bread. She sniffed at wedges of pungent cheese and lumpy phalluses of cured meat. She sampled shards of fudge and oily olives. She moved from stand to stand like a distracted dog, handing over crumpled five-pound notes and arming herself with more and more droopy plastic bags.

"Do you like gravadlax?" she said at one point, pushing some hair out of her face with a fistful of carrier bags.

"Grava-what?"

"Gravadlax. It's salmon, cured with dill."

"What's dill?"

"It's a herb."

"I don't know," he said. "What's it like?"

"It's a bit like smoked salmon," she said, "but not so salty."

He shrugged. He'd heard of smoked salmon, but he'd never eaten it. "I'm not really into fish," he said.

"Well," she said decisively, handing over another five-pound note, "then you'll like this. It's not really like fish. It's more like . . . *ham*."

She bought huge cheese straws and slivers of rust-coloured salami, cylinders of chalky cheese and a box of large eggs the colour of clouds. Feeling guilty that Daisy was spending all her money on food that he probably wouldn't even like, Con slipped away for a minute to find a bottle of wine.

"What're you having it with?" said a man in a striped linen shirt.

"Erm, food," said Con.

"Chicken? Fish? Spicy? Rich?"

"I don't know. There was some fish and some oysters and some olives and stuff."

"Sounds good," he smiled. "How about a bottle of Pouilly Fuisse?"

Con parted with a twenty-pound note with a gulp and took the tissue-wrapped bottle from the man. "Make sure it's cold," he said. "But not too cold. OK?"

He found Daisy tasting organic chocolate. "Open," she said, guiding a piece towards his mouth.

He put up his hand. "Erm, no thanks, I don't really like chocolate."

"Don't be ridiculous," she said, the piece of chocolate still hovering round his lips. "Everyone likes chocolate. Now, open up."

He parted his lips and felt her fingers brush against his mouth.

"Now," she said, watching him with excitement, "tell me that that isn't the best chocolate you've ever tasted in your life?"

He closed his mouth over the chocolate and let it melt under his teeth. His first instinct was to spit it out. It tasted like mud. But as it worked its way over his tongue and through his teeth it suddenly occurred to him that it tasted not just like chocolate, but like chocolate multiplied by a hundred.

"That's really good," he said.

"See," she nodded, "I told you. I'll get you some."

* * *

Daisy's house looked like a normal house, shrunk down. It had a door on the front, and two windows, and that was it. The front door opened directly into a tiny living room with a tiny sofa and an armchair in it. At the back was a kitchen built into a conservatory that led onto a garden the size of a bus shelter. But it was all very smart, all very modern. The walls were painted a muted shade of coffee, the TV was brand-new widescreen, the curtains looked expensive and the kitchen was fitted with slate grey tongue-and-groove units lit by halogen spotlights. Through the garden doors, Con could see a chrome patio heater and tropical plants in cobalt blue pots.

"Nice house," he said.

"Thank you," she said. "Small but perfectly formed." She sounded slightly breathless and broke into a rattling cough.

"Are you OK?"

"What?" she said. "Oh, the cough. It's nothing. Just a bit of a chesty thing."

"Is that your sister?" he picked up a framed photo of a biscuity-blonde girl who looked like Daisy, but fatter.

"Yup, that's Mimi." She dropped her carrier bags on to a small antique pine table in the kitchen and started unpacking them. "And that's James, sitting behind her."

"Her boyfriend?"

"That's right. Her boyfriend. My landlord. Lovely, lovely James."

"They look nice," he said, putting it back. And they did look nice. Nice and boring.

He wandered back into the kitchen where Daisy was chopping lemons into quarters. The drizzle outside had turned into heavy rain and the glass of the built-on kitchen started to steam up. The table was starting to resemble one of the food stands at Borough Market. There was a silver tray piled high with crushed ice and murky oysters, dishes layered with meats and cheeses, and tumbling bunches of bloomy grapes. "Have an olive," said Daisy. "They're delicious." He peered into a bowl and considered what he saw. Olives, in his experience, were small, black, wrinkly and sat on top of pizzas. They were not dark green, the size of walnuts and swimming in khaki oil with red bits in. He thought about popping one into his mouth, but then he tried to imagine what he would do if it tasted as bad as it looked. He might be sick. Or spit it all out down the front of his new merino sweater. "Nah," he said, "I'm not really into olives."

She turned then and appraised him. "Do you actually like *any* food?" she asked teasingly.

He shrugged. He'd been rumbled. "I like some food. Just not . . ." — he glanced at the table — "you know?"

"Olives, chocolate and fish?"

"Yeah."

"But you like cheese?"

"Yeah, I don't mind cheese." He smiled.

"And salami?"

"Yeah, I think so."

"And bread?"

"I love bread."

"What about bread with olives in it?"

"Hmmm . . ." he smiled. "Maybe."

She laughed. "So — what do you eat, then? What's your favourite food?"

"McDonald's."

"No!" her eyes widened.

"Yeah. I love McDonald's. Really, really love it."

"But why?"

"I dunno. It just tastes good."

"No, it doesn't."

"Yes, it does."

"Well, it tastes good for the thirty seconds it takes to eat it, then it's all over."

"Yeah, I know, but it's good while it lasts."

"But apart from McDonald's. What else do you like?"

He shrugged. "Curry, sometimes. Chinese. A good fry-up."

"Oh, God." She placed her hands against her collarbones. "This is fate! You've been sent to me for a reason. I have to re-educate your palate. Now eat one of these olives immediately!" She slid it between his lips before he had a chance to protest and suddenly he found himself chewing on something with the texture of old prunes and the flavour of rancid dog food. He gagged on the thing, but kept chewing. His teeth hit something hard in the middle, like a bullet, but he kept chewing. Daisy stared at him expectantly. Eventually some other flavours started to break through — pepper, tuna, cheese, salt — and, by the time he finished chewing, he was on the cusp of enjoying it. He swallowed and beamed at Daisy triumphantly.

"Where's the stone?" said Daisy.

"What, the hard thing in the middle?"

"Yes, the hard thing in the middle."

He shrugged. "Swallowed it."

She brought her hands to her mouth and stifled a laugh. "You didn't?!"

"Yeah," he said. "Wasn't I supposed to?"

"No. You're supposed to spit it out."

"What? Really?"

"Yes."

"Oh, shit. Is it bad for me?"

"No," she shook her head, smiling. "I don't think so. You might end up with a little olive tree growing in there, though." She pointed at his belly.

He glanced down, then up, and smiled. "Well," he said, "I reckon if I can eat an olive stone and not notice, then I'll probably be all right with the rest of this stuff." He gestured at the table. "Bring it on."

For the next two hours, Con did something he'd never done before. He dined. He feasted. He repasted. He lingered over his food. And even though not everything was to his liking (particularly the goat's cheese, which tasted to him like something you might find underneath your toenails), he enjoyed the majority of it. But mainly what he enjoyed was sitting at a table, under opaque, steamy glass, sensing the slow slide of the sun behind the terraces, drinking perfectly chilled white wine and listening to Daisy talk.

Everything about Daisy intoxicated him, from the breathy way she said "fuck" like it was a term of endearment, to the way she sucked her fingers one by one after eating anything oily. He loved the way she had an opinion on everything, from feet ("Disgusting, but not as disgusting as tongues. Have you ever actually *looked* at a tongue?") to Sicily ("My favourite place in the universe, except my parents' house.") to dogs ("Once you've looked into the eyes of a Pyrenean mountain dog, you're ruined. You'll spend the rest of your life pining for one.").

"Tell me something really interesting about yourself," she said, pouring coffee from a cafetière into two white cups.

"*Really* interesting?"

"Yes. Something *mind-blowing*."

"Shit," he said, rubbing his chin. "Why?"

"Because there's something really mysterious about you and I want to know what it is."

He nodded at her slowly. "OK," he said. "Well, after my mum went off to Turkey last year, I lost the flat and had nowhere to live. So I slept on the street. In a shop doorway. For two weeks."

"What — *you*?"

"Yes."

"God, I just can't imagine that. You're so . . . *immaculate*."

"Immaculate?"

"Yes, your hair and your clothes. Not a crease or a smudge. You smell of Persil. You look as if you've just stepped off the pages of a catalogue. I mean, how was it? Was it awful? Did you wash?"

"Yes, I washed. Even changed my underwear. It wasn't that bad. I was still coming into work every day."

"Did you beg?"

He laughed again. "No! I was still earning a salary! It was only a fortnight."

"God, though. How terrible. The thought of not being able to get into a lovely warm bed at the end of the night. Not to be able to turn off the light and roll onto your side and feel all safe and secure. Awful."

He shrugged again. "So," he said, "what about you? Tell me something about yourself that's going to blow me away."

She squeezed her eyes closed briefly, then opened them. "Hmmm," she said. "Are you sure you want to know? It's a total downer."

"Yes," he said, "I want to know."

"Well, there's this thing about me and I don't usually tell anyone about it, but I'm telling you because . . . I don't know. I've got this feeling about you . . ." She stopped for a second and glanced at him. "There's this thing, this *condition*, with my lungs. They make too much of this mucousy stuff and I have to take all these pills and do all this massage so that my airways don't get blocked up. But I'm also more prone to infections and stuff. It basically turns you into a complete wuss, this condition. I once spent a week in hospital with a cold. All wired up. Life and death. Pathetic."

Con stared at her for a moment, not knowing what to say.

"I told you it was a downer."

"But you don't seem ill."

"No. I don't feel ill. But then, I've had this all my life, so I don't really know what it's like to feel healthy."

"What's it called, then, this condition?"

"It's called cystic fibrosis."

"Oh, yeah, I've heard of that."

"Yes. I have a very famous condition. A celebrity condition, in fact. My condition gets invited to film premieres every night."

"Sorry, I . . ."

"No, I wasn't being facetious. I'm not sensitive about it. It's just the way it is. And who cares about a silly old condition anyway, frankly? Life is for living. And eating. And drinking. Talking of which," she grinned, "shall I open another bottle of wine?"

Con nodded and watched as she took a bottle from the fridge. Her smallness, her *translucence*, took on a new and unsettling significance in light of what she'd just told him. The milky alabaster of her skin had a hint of blue underlying it and her fine hair looked fragile and brittle. She wasn't a fairy or a nymph. She wasn't a Condé Nast flibbertigibbet. She was ill. Seriously ill.

Con took a deep breath and tried not to ask her if she was ever going to get better.

CHAPTER TWENTY-FIVE

Ruby turned the last page of the *Barnet Times* and sighed. She couldn't be arsed. She just could not be arsed with applying for any of these stupid jobs and turning up for stupid interviews wearing stupid clothes that didn't suit her and talking crap for half an hour in a room with a stranger. She did not want to be an office administrator for a charity in Golders Green. Nor did she want to be a sales assistant in a photography shop in Finchley Central or a receptionist for a firm of accountants in Whetstone.

She wanted to be a singer/songwriter. That was all she'd ever wanted to be and while she'd had the security of Paul's monthly payments into her bank account she'd been able to fool herself that that was what she was. Now she was just unemployed and broke.

She'd even contemplated the adverts for pole dancers and lap dancers. She had a good body and she could dance, but frankly the thought of having to make sure that she was always freshly plucked, buffed, tanned and shaved was off-putting in itself, even before she tried to imagine what it would feel like having a sales rep from Chingford called Dean shove a ten-pound note into her knickers.

She was up to her overdraft limit and next month's rent was due next Monday. She didn't even have any credit cards to fall back on. She'd never been together enough to apply for one and hadn't supposed anyone would have been stupid enough to give her one even if she had.

A Conran van had pulled up outside the house that afternoon and two blokes had started unloading things into the house, loads of things, things in boxes, things in bags. She watched them in amazement from her bedroom window, waiting for them to hitch the back door of the van back and pull away before running downstairs. Toby was feverishly ripping parcel tape off things in the hallway.

"What the fuck . . .?"

"Shit," he said, clutching his heart. "You made me jump."

"What the fuck is all this stuff?"

"Just stuff," he muttered. "Things for the house."

"Wow," she said, picking up a leather wastepaper bin and examining the price tag with raised eyebrows. "Nice stuff, Tobes. Got anything useful?"

"That is useful," he hissed, snatching it off her. "It's a bin."

"It's a £95 bin."

"It's quality. It'll last for ever."

"And what's in that gigantic box?" She gestured with her eyebrows towards a box leaning against the front door.

"Coffee table."

"Ooh — let me see."

"In a minute," he said.

"God, this is like Christmas," she said. "Let me open something, will you?"

"No," snapped Toby, pulling a clear Perspex globe out of a box.

"What is that?" she pointed at it, accusingly.

"What does it *look* like?"

"It's a plastic globe. But why?"

"Because . . . because . . . *I like it*. That's why."

"Fair enough." She sat back on her heels and watched him for a while. He was peeling bubble wrap off the plastic globe, looking stressed and slightly flushed. "So," she started, "this money from Gus — how much was it, exactly?"

Toby tutted.

"No, really. I thought we were talking a couple of grand, but seriously — look at all this stuff. What was it? Twenty? Thirty? A hundred?"

Toby tutted again and glared at her. "Ruby. Please. I've told you already. It's none of your business."

"Well, actually, it is. It's my business because you're my friend. And it's my business because . . ." She drew in her breath and waited until she'd made eye contact with him. ". . . because Paul just dumped me and he's stopped my allowance and I'm completely skint."

"Paul? Paul Fox?"

"Yes. Paul Fox. He's marrying that old bat and doesn't think that married men should be subsidizing young girls' lifestyles. Which is fair enough, I guess, but

I'm fucked, Tobes, completely fucked. And this money you've got, Gus's money. I'm just thinking that if there's enough for plastic globes and leather bins, there's probably enough for a loan?"

Ruby winced slightly and waited for Toby's face to soften. Toby had never let her down. Before she'd met Paul, he'd always treat her to lunch, let her off her rent, lend her a fiver here and there. And now he actually had some money, some proper money, surely he'd spread a little her way?

He paused for a moment and Ruby watched as he chewed thoughtfully on the inside of his cheek. And then he turned to her and said, "No."

"What?"

"No. Sorry, Ruby, but no. You're thirty-one. Nearly thirty-two. You're a grown woman. It's time for you to, you know, look after yourself."

"I'm not asking you to *look after* me," she snapped. "I'm asking you to lend me some money. Just to tide me over. Just until I get myself sorted out."

"Yes, but that's the problem with you, Ruby. You won't sort yourself out. You'll never sort yourself out until you absolutely have to."

"What the fuck does that mean?"

Toby sighed. "I'm just saying that you've always had people round you to prop you up and maybe it would be good for you to, you know, take responsibility for yourself. Stand alone for a while."

Ruby looked at him in amazement. "Alone?"

"Yes."

"Excuse me. Are you Toby Dobbs?"

"What?"

"You know, Mr Caring and Sharing, Mr My-Home-Is-Your-Home. Toby 'No one should ever be alone' Dobbs?"

He tutted.

"What's happening to you, Toby? You used to be the most generous person I know."

"Yes," he muttered, "well. Look where that's got me."

Ruby sighed. Toby was feeling sorry for himself. She was wasting her time. "Fine," she said, "whatever. I'll work something out."

"Good."

"Right." She stood up and surveyed him from above. He was starting to lose his hair on top, and the skin on the back of his neck folded together like old suede. He was getting old. Because she'd first met him as a teenager she'd always thought of him as an old man, but it was slightly unsettling to see that he was finally starting to look like one. Old and alone. Old and throwing money away on stupid Perspex globes and leather bins. She brushed her hand against his hair. "See you."

"Yes," he said, tersely. "See you."

She got halfway up the stairs, then remembered something. "Tobes?"

"Yes?"

"I can't pay you any rent this month, you know?"

"That's fine."

"Are you sure?"

"Yes. Just don't tell the others." And then he turned to her and a small smile twitched the corner of his mouth and Ruby knew then that she still stood a pretty good chance of persuading Toby to part with some of his money.

CHAPTER TWENTY-SIX

A man came into the shop on Saturday morning. This was unusual in itself, unaccompanied as he was by a woman looking for a birthday gift for her best friend or seeking out tiny leather ballet shoes with rosebuds for her sister's new baby. Just a man. On his own.

He was a big man, about six foot one and broad across the back. He had very dark hair, thinning on top but thick elsewhere, probably about forty-five, maybe a well-preserved fifty. He was wearing a leather coat, jeans and slightly battered boat shoes. There was a copy of the *Guardian* folded in four and tucked under his arm. He was handsome, if you liked that kind of thing, which Leah didn't. He seemed to be taking a great interest in the furniture, particularly a small cream desk stencilled with faded amaryllis. He turned at her approach and smiled. He had a big dimple in his left cheek and very thick eyelashes. He was definitely a man with charisma and charm, but he was too self-assured for Leah's tastes.

"How much is this desk?" he asked. He had an accent, very soft. She guessed at Italian.

"Three hundred and fifty pounds," she said, smiling her best Pink Hummingbird smile. "It has a matching stool" — she pointed behind her — "with an upholstered seat. And there's a range of filing boxes to complement it. Linen-covered," she finished.

"Do you deliver?"

"Uh-huh," she nodded. "It's free within a three-mile radius."

He nodded. "How soon?"

"When would you like it?"

"Immediately."

"Monday morning?"

He beamed at her. "This is exactly why I came here. Local shops. Personal service. You go to John Lewis and it's all, please pay over there, ten days' delivery, it's not in stock, blah, blah, blah."

Leah smiled.

"Are you the owner?" he asked.

"No. I'm the manager."

"Good," he said, "good. Maybe you could help me. I've just moved into the area, post-divorce, and I want to surprise my girls — I have two daughters, thirteen and fifteen years old. They'll be staying with me every other weekend and I want to give them bedrooms to die for. You see?" He threw her another dazzling smile.

"I think so."

"I want them to wish the days away with their mother so that they can come to be with me again in Muswell Hill, in their beautiful new rooms, in my beautiful new house. I want their friends to be jealous, to think they have the best father in all the world. I want glitter, fluff, flowers, lights — all that stuff.

Everything you can offer me. Do you offer a design service?"

"Well, no, but I am happy to make recommendations within a budget."

"There is no budget."

"Right, you mean . . . ?"

"I mean, money is no object. In fact," he lowered his voice, conspiratorially, "I will give you five hundred pounds to do it."

She looked at him, slightly alarmed. "Do what?"

"Choose the furniture. Choose the accessories. Come to my house. Arrange things. Five hundred pounds. Cash."

Leah glanced round her to make sure none of the other girls had heard their conversation. Five hundred pounds. That was a month's rent.

"OK," she said. "But I can only do furnishing. No decorating."

"That's fine," he said. "The rooms are already decorated."

"Great," she beamed. "What colour are they?"

"Pink." He smiled at her.

"Perfect," she said.

Leah stayed at work until ten o'clock that night. She ordered in a pizza and spent the night pretending to be the fifteen-year-old daughter of a wealthy Italian businessman. Jack had given her brief descriptions of his girls (Lottie: thirteen, clever, outgoing, into football and music; Lucie: fifteen, clever, shy, into reading and her boyfriend). "They're no princesses, my girls, but I want their rooms to be fit for royalty," Jack had said.

Leah picked out fluffy cushions, bean bags, mirrors, stationery, lamps and bedding. She ordered a pair of miniature chaises longues in bubblegum-pink velvet and two sleigh beds in cream and lilac. She ordered red Perspex bookshelves for Lucie, a huge disco glitter ball for Lottie's ceiling and enormous pastel-coloured sheepskin rugs for both of them.

The bill came to nearly £6,000. Leah gulped and hoped that Jack would approve. And then she folded her pizza box in half, disposed of it behind the back of the shop, turned off all the lights and headed home.

Leah turned into Silversmith Road and glanced across at the Peacock House. The lights in Ruby's room and Con's room were switched off, but Toby was there, as ever, framed in his window, his face lit up by the glow of his computer screen. Leah felt a wave of warmth pass through her. Poor Toby, living in a house full of people, but always alone. He looked up from his monitor and saw Leah gazing up at him. She raised her hand to him and smiled. He waved back, then he stood up and indicated that she should wait there, that he was coming down. She waited on the pavement, watching her breath leave her mouth in ghostly ribbons. Eventually the front door opened and Toby appeared, dressed in a huge green sweater, black tracksuit bottoms and lambskin slippers. He'd had his hair cut, Leah noted. It was still a mass of brown scrub, but seemed to have more shape to it. It made him look a little less *absurd*.

"Hello! Hello!" He pranced across the street in his furry slippers. He ran like a girl, or, in fact, not like a girl, but how a man would run if he were trying to run like a girl. Leah swallowed a smile.

"Hi!" she said.

"How are you?"

"I'm fine," said Leah. "You?"

"Yes, I'm fine, too. Look. I just wanted to say, I'm really sorry about the other night."

"Oh, honestly, Toby, it's fine."

"No, it's not. It must have been miserable for you. I have no idea what those two were thinking" — he indicated his house — "and I wasn't much fun myself. I'm sure you have much better things to do with your time than sit around in pubs with an old fart like me. And I just wanted to say, well, thank you for trying, I really appreciate it. But I've decided to give up the whole idea."

"What?"

"Yes. I'm not going to sell the house. My father will just have to accept me the way I am."

"But, Toby. I got the impression that this wasn't just about your father. I thought this was about *you*, about moving on, getting out of a rut."

"Yes, well, it was. But, really, I've tried talking to those people and there's no way any of them are ready to leave yet. I mean, I can't even get a whole sentence out of Joanne. Con's saving up for flying lessons, which is just *amazing*, but it means that he really needs to stay in the house — and Melinda's not going anywhere without him. And as for Ruby — well, she's worse than ever, dumped by her boyfriend, sleeping with Con, begging me for hand-outs. She can't even afford to pay the rent. I've been trying to get quotes from builders, but they don't return my calls or they say they're going to come round, then they don't show up or they're completely exorbitant or completely dodgy and, frankly, I'm starting to remember why I found myself in this rut in the first place. Because getting anything to change is just so unbelievably difficult.

"This is my rut," he shrugged. "I made it and now I'll have to lie in it. But thank you. Thank you for trying. You're a really, really nice person." He smiled apologetically, then he turned and headed back towards his house.

Leah watched him walking across the road, climbing the steps to his front door. The plaster lions seemed almost to purr as he passed by them, the master of the house. He slipped his key into the lock and turned to look at Leah. He smiled, then he was gone.

Leah went inside, climbed into her pyjamas, climbed into her bed and dreamed about pink lions with marabou-trimmed paws.

CHAPTER TWENTY-SEVEN

Toby was listening to his crappy music. Con could hear it through his bedroom door. He didn't know what it was, but it wasn't modern. It wasn't even indie. Con hated indie music, but at least he could kind of relate to it, at least it was made by people roughly his age, people who were still alive, people who didn't take drugs with stupid hippified names and die in car crashes. But the stuff that Toby listened to — it was beyond his comprehension; whirling guitars, tinny drums, no chorus, ten minutes long sometimes. He'd seen the album covers downstairs — weird old blokes with beards and chiffon scarves, floppy hats and face paint. It made Con feel uncomfortable, just looking at them.

He knocked firmly against the door, once, twice, three times, until Toby finally appeared. He was in a thigh-length stripy jumper and black drainpipe jeans, unwittingly fashionable. He had some black ink smudged across his cheek and toast crumbs on his cuff.

"Hi, sorry to bother you."

Toby smiled. "No, not at all. I wasn't really doing anything, just, you know . . ." he trailed off, hooking his hand round the back of his neck.

"Can I ask you a favour?"

"Sure. D'you want to come in?"

"I need to borrow your computer."

"Right, of course."

"Except I don't know how to use them. Well, except the system at work. But I don't know how to use the Internet. Can you help me find something?"

"God, of course, sure."

Toby moved a plate of toast out of the way, some paperwork, notepads and textbooks. He moved things into one large pile, then pulled up a stool for Con to sit on.

"Is that all your poems and stuff?" asked Con.

Toby glanced at the pile and shook his head. "Well, sort of, I suppose. It's notes and ideas. I write my actual poetry straight onto my computer."

"Right. And what sort of stuff do you write?"

Toby grimaced. "Kind of . . . well, it's hard to say. It's all so different."

"Yeah, but are they long poems, short poems? Do they rhyme?"

Toby smiled. "No. They don't rhyme. And they're quite short. OK." He placed his huge hand over the mouse and jiggled it. His computer came to life and he brought up Google. "So, what is it you want to look up?"

"It's an illness. It's called cystic fibrosis."

"Ah, right."

"I'm not sure how it's spelled."

"That's OK. I'm pretty sure I know how to spell it." He typed it in and hit a button. A big list came up on the screen. "Now what was it that you wanted to know, exactly?"

"Well, shit, it's . . ." He ran a hand through his hair and stared at Toby. He may as well tell him. "Remember that girl I was telling you about?"

"The girl at work? The posh one?"

"Yeah. Her. Well, we've kind of been hanging out. I went to her place and she cooked for me and stuff. And then she told me that she's got this condition, this . . ."

"Cystic fibrosis."

"Yeah. And it made sense because she's really little and delicate and her skin's kind of, you know, blue. And she's got this cough. But I didn't really want to ask her too much about it, you know? In case it made her feel like a freak. And I went to a bookshop today to see if I could find anything there, but I didn't know how to spell it so I couldn't look it up in the indexes. And I just want to know what it is. What it means. Like — is she really ill? Is she going to die? That kind of thing."

"Fuck." Toby sucked in his breath and ran a hand over his chin. "Right, let's see what we can find."

Con had known, even before Toby started clicking on his list and reading stuff out. He'd known it was bad. It had been obvious from the very first moment Daisy had mentioned it to him. She'd had that tone of voice, that tone of someone who knows they've drawn the short straw and doesn't want to waste time going on about it.

According to the Internet, Daisy's life was already difficult and uncomfortable. She needed daily physiotherapy to dislodge the mucus that built up in her lungs, she had to take drugs to help her body absorb nutrients and drugs to help prevent lung infections. She needed to consume higher than average daily calories, but experienced poor weight gain and the chances of her carrying a child to full term were low.

She was also, apparently, quite likely to die in her thirties.

Con and Toby sat in a numb silence for a minute. Toby kept breathing in and out really loudly and tugging at his hair. Con could tell he was trying to think of something reassuring to say.

"God, Con, I'm really sorry," he said, in the end.

"Yeah, it's bad, isn't it?"

"Quite bad, yes, but remember, all the research they're doing, medical breakthroughs happen every day. And she could last a lot longer than the average, even without a breakthrough."

"No," Con shook his head, "it's bad. Whatever way you look at it. She can't have kids and even if she could she wouldn't be around to see them grow up. And you know, that must be why she lives with her sister. I bet her sister does all that chest shit for her every day. So she's, you know, reliant on other people, just to get out of the house in the mornings. Her life sucks."

Toby sighed again and touched Con's knee. "Do you think *she* thinks her life sucks?"

Con shrugged. He thought about her enthusiasm for food, her love of her family, her passionate views about everything, especially the truly mundane. She didn't *act* like someone who hated her life. She acted like someone who couldn't believe her luck. "No," he said, "I don't think she does."

"Well, then," said Toby, "best thing you can do is carry on as if you never saw any of this." He indicated the screen. "Best thing you can do is help her to enjoy her life."

Toby gave Con a poem before he left. "I wrote this on the morning of my mother's funeral," he said. "It might help you work out how you feel about Daisy."

"I didn't know your mum was dead."

"Yes, she died when I was thirteen. Breast cancer."

"God, I'm sorry."

"Yes, well . . ."

"It's funny, though. I've been living here for nearly a year and I never knew your mum was dead. You don't say much really, do you? Don't talk much."

"No," said Toby, "no. I don't suppose I do."

The last person Con wanted to see when he stepped out of Toby's bedroom a few minutes later, clutching the unread poem, was Ruby.

"Hello!" she beamed at him. There was a brown lump in her mouth, chewing gum. It looked like Nicorette.

"All right," he said. "What's with the gum? Are you giving up the fags?"

She laughed. "No! Don't be daft. I just keep a pack in my drawer, in case I run out of fags and can't be bothered to go out and get any. I like the taste."

"Ah," he nodded, feeling a sudden sense of sick disgust that someone blessed with a pair of healthy, functioning lungs should abuse them so wantonly. "I see." He tried to move past her, towards his room, but she positioned herself across his pathway.

"So," she said, "what are you up to tonight?"

He shrugged, his mind whizzing with potential lies. "Not sure, really."

"Your mum's out."

"Yeah, I know."

"I saw her leaving about an hour ago."

"I know," he smirked at her, sarcastically.

"Fancy sharing a bottle of wine?"

"What?"

"I was just going to get myself a glass. Fancy sharing it with me?"

Con shook his head. "No," he said. "Thanks. I've got stuff to do." He tapped Toby's poem against the palm of his hand.

"What's that?" She glanced at the typewritten sheet.

"A poem. One of Toby's. He just gave it to me to read."

Ruby laughed. "Oh, God! Not one of Toby's poems."

Con glanced at her. "What's the problem?"

"Have you ever read one of Toby's poems before?"

He shook his head.

"Right," she laughed again. "Well, you'll see what I mean when you do."

"Oh," he said, feeling a sharp pinch of annoyance in his chest. Everything about Ruby was wrong. Her brown gum, her offer of wine, her belittling of Toby.

Distasteful, and wrong. He pushed gently past her to get to his bedroom door.

He could feel Ruby's eyes boring a hole through his shoulder blades.

"Have I done something to piss you off, Con?"

"What?"

"Are you annoyed with me?"

"No!"

"Then why are you being so . . . so *cool* with me?"

"Cool?"

"Yeah. Offish."

"Sorry," he said, "I didn't realize I was."

He closed his bedroom door behind him, kicked off his trainers and sat down on his mattress, cross-legged. And then he read Toby's poem:

Young

I saw you yesterday.
You wore an old lady's nightdress, it wasn't yours.
You were young.
I saw you the day before.
You wanted to dance, but you couldn't get out of bed.
You were young.
Last Christmas you were young, in a holly-print apron and a tissue hat.
And every birthday of my life. In mini skirts and maxi skirts, hair long and short. Home-made cakes and jam tarts.
Young. And beautiful.
Soon it will be winter.

I will be older.
You will be young.
I'll look in the mirror, see a grey hair.
A boy will call to me in the street,
Hey! Old man!
Still, you will be young.
Young and beautiful.
For all your days.

Con folded up the poem, slid it onto his bedside table and cried for the first time since his grandmother's funeral.

CHAPTER TWENTY-EIGHT

Giacomo Caruso's house was the nicest house Leah had ever seen. It was an Arts and Crafts mansion on the best street in Muswell Hill, with a hallway the size of Leah's living room. All the rooms were wood panelled and all the windows were stained glass. The manicured garden wrapped itself round all four sides of the property and there was an outdoor swimming pool. With a pool bar.

Jack poured her a glass of iced water from the filtered-water dispenser in his huge stainless-steel American fridge and let her wander round while the Pink Hummingbird delivery boys unloaded the van. Downstairs there were two living rooms: one with a pitched ceiling and a chandelier; the other with an enormous oak fire surround with gargoyles carved into it. There was a billiards room, a study, a dining room and a luxury kitchen diner built into a huge conservatory at the back. Every room was decorated with antiques and fitted out with state-of-the-art audiovisual equipment, including a home cinema in a turret room off the main hall.

Upstairs were four bedrooms and five bathrooms. Leah didn't like to ask what the fifth one was for. Leah complimented Jack on his impeccable taste. He brushed away the compliment by informing her that he'd bought the house fully furnished.

"So, what do you do?" she asked him, perching herself on a Perspex barstool in the kitchen.

"Textiles," he said. "I make fabric."

"What sort of fabric?"

"Very, very pretty fabric," he smiled. "Luxury. Silk, organza, tulle, chiffon."

"Lovely."

"Yes. It is. But now I am retired. I still own the mills, but I don't have to look at them any more."

"Are they in Italy, your mills?"

"Yes. Near the lakes. I still have a home there, but I use it now only for holidays." He sighed. "I love England. I really do. But I wouldn't choose to live here. I live here for my girls. For Lottie and Lucie. And I live here because I cannot resist English women!"

Leah laughed.

"I came to London when I was twenty-one, I met a girl called Jenny, I fell in love. And that was it. My first wife was English — Elaine. Beautiful girl. Peaches and cream. The marriage lasted only a year, but by then I was addicted. And then there was Paula, my ex-wife, the girls' mother. Blonde hair, blue eyes, big bum. I love English bums. I love all those dimples. And the accent — ah! So, I am destined to be here for ever. For the love of my children and for my love of English bottoms!"

Leah laughed again, suddenly feeling conscious of her blonde hair, blue eyes and size-fourteen jeans. "How long have you been divorced?"

"A year. I've been living in a rented flat, in Hampstead, searching and searching every day for my perfect castle! I wanted something quintessentially English and this . . ." he gestured at his home — "is it. Now," he sighed, "I just need to find my queen."

The boys finished unloading the van and Leah went upstairs where she spent two hours arranging cushions, throws and picture frames, plugging in fairy lights, hanging mirrors and filling drawers with scented letter paper and pots of neon-coloured gel-filled pens. She dressed the sleigh beds with pastel polka-dot bedding and hung the windows with swathes of lilac dupion. It was starting to get dark when Jack came upstairs to see how she was getting on and the rooms looked beautiful, fairy lights twinkling in the dusk.

"Perfect," he beamed, "absolutely perfect." And then he started crying.

Leah looked at him with alarm.

"I'm sorry," he said. "I'm still very emotional. Very raw." He tapped his fist against his heart. "I didn't want it to be like this. I didn't want to live apart from my wife, my children. I didn't want to be a weekend father." He sniffed, loudly. "I wasn't meant to be alone. I'm not designed for it. But this" — he gestured at Lottie's room — "so beautiful. So perfect. She will love it. Both of them will. Thank you!" And then he threw his arms round her and squeezed her to him. His tears left a wet patch on her cheek which she brushed away as subtly as she could. “Here,” he said, “why don’t you stay? Stay. I’ll cook you dinner. What do you like to eat? Fish? I have some beautiful fresh tuna in the fridge. Tuna and capers? Or a salad niçoise?”

“Oh, God, thank you, but I can’t.”

“Something else, perhaps. Some pasta? Something simple. Aglio e olio? Please.” He put both his hands to his chest. “Let me cook for you. It would make me happy.”

“Oh, God, I’d love to, I really would,” she lied, “but I have to go back to the shop, cash up, lock up.”

“Ah, well. Maybe another time, then. But for now” — he pulled an envelope out of his back pocket and handed it to her — “for you.”

She smiled and took the envelope. It was satisfyingly plump. “Thank you,” she said.

“And any time” — he led her to the front door — “any time you’re passing, you have my card, phone me. If I’m in, come over. I’ll cook for you.”

“I will,” she said. “Thank you so much. And any time you’re passing the shop . . .”

“Oh, yes,” he smiled, “I’ll be sure to come and say hello.” He lifted her hand to his mouth and kissed the back of it. Leah felt herself flush slightly. No one had ever kissed the back of her hand before. She gave him one last look, just to check that she didn’t find him attractive. The look confirmed it. She didn’t.

She sighed and headed out into the cool night air. The moon was big and yellow, and there seemed to be more stars than usual in the sky. She turned to look at

Jack's house one more time before crunching across his gravel driveway and heading back to the shop.

CHAPTER TWENTY-NINE

Daisy and Con had lunch on a bench in Green Park. It was eight degrees, but the sun was strong. Daisy took another bite of her sandwich and smiled. "This," she said, pointing at the sandwich, "is absolutely delicious. Did you really make it yourself?"

"Uh-huh." He swallowed a mouthful and nodded. "Toby helped, but basically I made it."

"I am seriously impressed. Where did you get the bread from?"

"Toby made it."

"Is this Toby the poet?"

"Yeah. He bakes a loaf of bread every day."

"Really? That's so sweet! So, what's he like, this Toby? Is he broodingly handsome and mysterious?"

Con laughed. "Er, no. Not really. He's kind of . . . he's very big. Tall. Big hands. Big feet. Big nose. And sort of scruffy. Mad hair, big sideburns. He's really shy, and really clever. I kind of like him."

"And is he a successful poet?"

Con laughed again. "Not that I know of. I don't think he's ever had anything published and he's never got any money."

"What sort of poems does he write? Have you ever read any of them?"

"Yeah," he nodded, "yeah, actually. He showed me one last night."

"What was it like? Was it any good?"

"Yeah, it was. It made me . . ." He paused, looked at Daisy, exhaled. "It made me cry."

She gasped. "Wow!"

"It was about his mum. He wrote it the day of her funeral. It was all about . . ." He stopped. He couldn't tell her what it was really about. "It was all about how much he loved her, what a great mum she'd been. Reminded me of my gran." He shrugged and smiled.

She squeezed his forearm, gently. "You really loved her, didn't you?"

He shrugged again. "She brought me up. That's the person you really love, isn't it? The person who raised you?"

"As opposed to your mother, you mean?"

"Yeah. I suppose."

A pair of joggers ran past them, a man and a woman in matching Lycra suits. Con finished his sandwich and tucked his screwed-up paper napkin into the plastic bag. He glanced at Daisy's hands. Long fingers, a single ring in the shape of a daisy, blue veins, a smudge of butter. He reached over to hold it, before he found a reason not to. It was surprisingly warm. She squeezed his hand back and smiled at him.

"I'm really touched," she said, breaking the silence, "that you went to all this trouble with the sandwiches."

"It was nothing," he said, rubbing the tip of his thumb back and forth across her fingernails. "In fact," he smiled, "I'd go so far as to say that it was a pleasure."

"You mean you enjoyed cooking something that didn't involve a kettle or a microwave."

"Well, I wouldn't call it cooking, but it was, you know, fun. I liked it."

"Well, then," said Daisy, "in that case, I present you with a challenge, Connor McNulty."

"Oh, yeah?"

"Yeah. How about you invite me over for dinner at yours?"

"Dinner?!"

"Yes. Dinner. With a starter, a main course and a pudding. And wine."

"Are you serious?"

"Deadly."

"But my house. It's full of people."

"That's all right. I like people."

"Yes, but they're . . . *weird* people."

"I like weird people even more." She smiled.

"And it's one thing knocking together a sandwich, but a whole meal. I might poison you."

She shook her head. "You'll be fine. I've got faith in you."

"You have?"

"Yeah. Definitely. You're one of those people, I reckon, one of those people who'd be good at anything they put their mind to."

He shook his head and laughed. "What gave you that idea?"

"I don't know," she said. "I just think you are. You've got this aura. Really cool. Really capable."

"So how come I only got two GCSEs, then? And what am I doing working in a post room?"

"You're only nineteen. You were homeless, for God's sake. And your grandma died. Just you wait. One day you'll be flying a private jet across the Caribbean sea. But, oooh, wait, no, you won't just be the pilot. You'll be the *owner*. There'll be a beautiful woman by your side drinking champagne and you'll fly over your sprawling beachside estate, or, no, actually, you'll fly over your *own private island* and you'll think to yourself, just think, I used to live in a house full of weirdos in Finchley and spent my days wheeling bitchy women's letters round a big building and you'll smile and the beautiful girl will smile and you'll remember me saying this to you. You really will." She gripped his hand tightly in both of hers. "Give yourself a chance. You're special, Con, really special. And your life's only just beginning."

Con gulped. Only nineteen.

Daisy was only eighteen, but she was already two-thirds of the way through her life; halfway if she was lucky.

"You'll be that girl, though? The girl on the plane. That'll be you, right?"

She smiled. But she didn't reply.

CHAPTER THIRTY

Leah's phone rang at 7.05p.m. It was Amitabh.

"Hello," he said. "What are you doing?"

"Looking out the window. What are you doing?"

"Having a bath."

Leah found it very strange when people made phone calls from the bath. It was almost as if they were inviting the recipient of the call to imagine them naked. "What do you want?" she said, more abruptly than she'd intended.

"Nothing," he said. "I was just thinking about you. Wanted to make sure you were all right."

"Oh."

"Found anywhere to live yet?"

"No," she said, winding the cord of the phone round her wrist. "I made a bit of extra cash last week so I've decided to stay here for another month."

"What! But that's such a waste of money! Paying out all that rent for just you."

"Well, what do you suggest I do?"

"I dunno. I just think if you've got some spare cash you should put it in the bank. Start saving for a deposit."

Leah rolled her eyes. "Oh, God, Am, can you just drop the subject, please. I'm bored with it. And besides, it's nothing to do with you any more."

"Oh, don't say that, Leelee."

"And don't call me 'Leelee'."

"Why not?"

"Because it's my girlfriend name, *not* my ex-girlfriend name."

"Yeah, but you'll always be Leelee to me."

"What, even when you're married to some girl from Mumbai and you've got loads of hairy children?"

Amitabh laughed, then he sighed. "Oh, Christ, Leah. God, I don't know. Maybe this is all wrong, you know."

Leah squinted and pursed her lips simultaneously, her body instinctively drawing itself inwards. "What?"

"Maybe we shouldn't have given up so easily."

"*We?!*"

"Well, yeah, *me*. Maybe I should have . . . God, I don't know."

"Amitabh, what exactly are you saying here?"

"I don't know what I'm saying. But I miss you, that's all. I didn't think I would, but I do."

Leah noticed a shadow on the other side of the road, long and thin, cast by the street light overhead. She cupped her hand to the window and peered through. She could hear the tap-tap of hurried footsteps. It was Joanne.

"Sorry, Am," she said, oblivious to what he was saying. "I have to go now. I'll call you back. Bye."

She dropped the phone and dashed to the front door. Joanne was just about to open the garden gate.

"Joanne!" she cried. "Hi!"

Joanne turned and glared at her. She was wearing a black leather coat, black lacy knit tights and black ankle boots with furry bobbles hanging off them. Her hair was black and held back with diamanté cherries. She was wearing red lipstick and black eyeliner, and looked like Juliette Binoche on a very bad day.

"Sorry, I didn't mean to make you jump."

"You didn't," she replied stonily.

"Right. OK. I was just, er . . . I hope you don't mind me accosting you on the street like this, but I've been meaning to talk to you about something."

Joanne narrowed her eyes at Leah, regarding her as if she were trying to ascertain what species she was. "Sorry," she said, pulling her keys out of her handbag, "but who are you and how do you know my name?"

Leah looked at her in surprise. Surely she must have noticed her at least once during the past two years? "Er, I'm Leah? Toby's friend? I live there." She pointed at her front door. "Just over the road from you."

"Oh," said Joanne, "I see."

"And the reason I wanted to talk to you was, and I know this might sound a bit strange, but I've noticed that you take great care over your appearance . . ."

Joanne glanced down at her leather coat. "Well," she said, "I wouldn't say that."

"Oh, but you do. I always notice how well turned out you are, always wearing different clothes, different hair. I mean, I'm just lazy when it comes to clothes and make-up and stuff. Jeans, boots, bit of mascara — that's as far as I go. I haven't changed my image for years. And that's what I wanted to talk to you about. I run a gift shop in Muswell Hill, the Pink Hummingbird?"

"Oh, yes," she nodded. "I know it."

"Well, we're having a special open evening, on Friday night, to celebrate the launch of a new cosmetics range." She pulled a piece of pink card out of her pocket and handed it over. "It's all 100 per cent organic, imported from California. We're going to be one of the first London stockists. They're sending us over one of their make-up artists and they'll be doing free makeovers, free wine, snacks and stuff. It's quite exclusive. I'm only allowed to invite a handful of guests and I just thought it seemed like the sort of thing you might enjoy?"

Joanne turned the card over and squinted at it. "When did you say this was?"

"Friday night. Six to nine."

"Hmmm." Joanne turned it over again. "I don't know." She was feigning disinterest, but Leah could tell that Joanne had taken the bait. She would be there, without a doubt.

"Well," she said, "if you can't make it, please let me know. Numbers are tight and I'd like to pass your invitation on to someone else if you're not going to come."

"Yes," she said, slipping the card into her bag. "OK. I'll come."

"You will?"

"Yes. Count me in."

"Excellent," beamed Leah. "I'm really glad. It's going to be such a lovely evening. You'll love it."

And then something remarkable happened — Joanne smiled. "I look forward to it," she said. "Thank you for inviting me."

"My pleasure," said Leah, "my pleasure entirely."

Leah glanced at the phone when she got back inside. An image of a large, wrinkled Amitabh, lying in a cold bath, waiting for her to call him back, passed through her mind. She touched the phone briefly with her fingertips, then retracted them. She couldn't face it. She'd call him tomorrow.

Instead she went back to the front window and peered across the street again. She saw the shadowy movement of a figure, climbing the stairs, through the central window of the Peacock House. She assumed it was Joanne, on her way to her lonely, fortressed room with a pink invitation in her handbag. She glanced upwards and saw Toby, sitting as ever in his window, playing on his computer. She wondered what he was looking at. Was he in a chatroom talking to a fat girl from Maryland called Paris? Was he cogitating over his poetry? Or maybe he was just staring, vacantly, meaninglessly, into whiteness.

She wondered if he'd seen her just now, talking to Joanne on the street.

She wondered if he'd approve or if he'd think she was interfering.

A couple of minutes later he stood up, walked to the other side of the room, then came back and drew his curtains, and all at once Leah found herself staring at a dark, silent house. Feeling a bit weird, she drew her own curtains and got on with her night.

CHAPTER THIRTY-ONE

Joanne was the first guest to arrive at the Pink Hummingbird on Friday night.

She was wearing her black leather coat over a black jersey dress and bottle-green shoes with leather laces that crisscrossed up her ankles. Her hair looked as if she'd used crimpers on it and she was wearing bottle-green eye shadow. Leah removed her coat and put it in the stockroom. "I'm so glad you came," she said, handing Joanne a glass of white wine. Leah noticed for the first time that, out of her coat and in her clingy jersey dress, Joanne had a really lovely figure: a tiny waist; angular shoulders; firm, round breasts. "Did you come straight from work?"

Joanne nodded distractedly and gulped a mouthful of wine. Her eyes swivelled round the shop, taking in the detail — the lamps, the silk flowers, the mirrors.

"Where do you work?" asked Leah. "In town?"

"Yes," said Joanne. She took another gulp of wine. "Where's the make-up?"

Leah started, slightly shocked by her brusque manner. "Erm, it's through there, in the back room. But they're not quite ready yet."

Joanne glanced at her watch, an elderly Swatch with a clear plastic strap. "I thought you said six-thirty? It's six-thirty-two."

"Yes, I know. They won't be long. Just another minute or two. So, what do you do, Joanne?"

"Do?"

"Yes. For a living?"

Joanne sighed. "I'm an actress," she said.

"Oh, really. So is that what you're doing at the moment? In town?"

She shook her head. "No. I'm working on something else at the moment. There are some nice things in here."

Leah was finding it hard to keep up with the abrupt conversational leaps Joanne kept making. "Oh," she said, "yes. It's very feminine."

"Yes," said Joanne. "I like those camisole tops." She pointed at some rose-pink pointelle jersey underwear with silk ribbon trim.

"Lovely, aren't they? Come with matching knickers and trousers."

"Really?"

"Tempted?"

"Mmmm," Joanne smiled, "maybe. Do you have any other clothes?"

"No. Not really. Just a bit of lingerie, some hats, some slippers."

"Oh," she looked mildly disappointed, "never mind."

"You're really into clothes, aren't you?"

Joanne smiled again. "Clothes, to me, are like paint to an artist or words to a writer."

"I've noticed," said Leah, choosing her words carefully, "that you're quite experimental with clothes."

"Yes," said Joanne. "I am." She'd finished her wine. Leah poured her another glass. She could see Joanne was getting fidgety and that, if she didn't get what she'd come here for soon, there was a danger she would leave.

"Let me just see how they're getting on back there."

Clarice and Maya from Santa Monica were set up and waiting, brushes at the ready. The doorbell rang. Leah let in a gaggle of Muswell Hill yummy mummies in designer jeans and Joseph shearling coats. Leah asked one of her assistants to take over on the door and went to find Joanne. She was admiring a pair of ivory silk slippers with pink embroidered butterflies on them. "Cute," she said, putting them down.

"Gorgeous, aren't they? Anyway — they're ready at the back. Do you want to come through?"

Joanne seemed rapturously interested in every last detail of the blînk organic cosmetic range. She hung on Maya's every word, absorbing every reference to beeswax and nettle powder and ground blueberry essence, as if it were the truth of life itself. Leah watched as Clarice stripped Joanne's face of make-up, with soft pads of cotton wool and a liquid cleanser infused with green tea. She then gave Joanne's face a gentle massage with something called "angel oil". Devoid of make-up, Joanne looked young but tired.

"So," said Clarice, "what do you do, Joanne?"

"I'm an actress," she said.

"Oh, wow! Really? Like a real proper actress?"

"Yes, well, I trained at the Central School of Drama."

"Wow. So, have you been in anything I'd have heard of, like a movie?"

"No. I shouldn't think so. I mostly do stage work. Although I haven't worked in a while now."

"Oh, I see. Having kids?"

"I'm sorry?"

"Did you stop working to have kids?"

"Why do you ask that?"

"Oh," she said, "I don't know. I guess I just talk to so many women about your age and they all tell me what they *used* to do. I *used* to be a model, I *used* to be a marketing director. You know, I just *assumed*."

"Well," said Joanne, "that's not the case."

"So — just taking a break, huh?"

"Yes," said Joanne. "Just taking a break."

"Well, that's great. And I have to say, you have amazing skin, Joanne. It must be doing you good."

Leah waited at the front of the shop for Joanne to emerge from her makeover. The Pink Hummingbird was buzzing with women. Everyone seemed to know everyone else and there was lots of talk of Gymboree and swimming lessons and skiing in Morzine. It was hard for Leah to believe that she was the same age as these women, when their lives were so entirely different to hers. It took a lot of hard work to look as good as these women did at their age, especially after a couple of kids. It wasn't a happy accident. It was a full-time job.

Joanne walked past. "Let's see, then," said Leah.

Joanne spun round, looking slightly alarmed.

"Wow," said Leah. "You look really beautiful."

And she did. Without her own heavy-handed approach to make-up, she looked soft and pretty and warm. "Are you happy with it?"

"Yes," said Joanne. "I am. Well, thank you for inviting me. I've had a very nice night."

"Oh, you're not going already, are you?"

"Yes."

"But what about those silk slippers? Did you want to get a pair of those?"

"Oh, no. I don't think so. I may come back another day."

"But no!" Leah took a breath to calm her voice down. "No. Buy them now! I can give you them at a discount. Twenty per cent off?"

Joanne wiggled her nose and turned her head to look at the slippers. "Hmmm. How much are they?"

"Twenty. Sixteen pounds with the discount."

"What about that jersey camisole?"

"Yup. That's thirty-nine ninety-nine. I can let you have it for thirty-two?"

"OK," she said, swinging her handbag round onto the cash desk. "Do you take Switch?"

Leah sent an assistant to collect the slippers and the camisole, and hoped that she would be as slow as she usually was. "So," she said, to the side of Joanne's head, "are you going home now? Back to Toby's?"

She turned to face her. "Yes."

"He's lovely, isn't he, Toby?"

She threw Leah a strange look. "Yes," she said, "I suppose so."

"And that house is amazing."

"Yes. Rather poorly maintained, though." She turned impatiently to see what the shop assistant was doing. She returned with the slippers in a box and opened it up for Joanne's approval.

"They look a bit big," said Joanne. "What size are they?"

"Large," said the assistant. "What size are you?"

"I'm a size five."

Leah sent the assistant away to get the slippers in her right size and tried to think of a way of turning this conversation to her advantage.

"So, what's it like living with all those people?" she began.

"Which people?"

"The people? In Toby's house?"

She shrugged. "It's fine."

"Really? It's just, I've just split up with my boyfriend and now I've got to move out of our flat and I've been looking at all these flat shares and I just feel so old, so set in my ways. The thought of having to share with people I don't know is just awful. How do you do it?"

"I ignore everyone. I pretend they're not there."

Leah looked at her in amazement, then she laughed. And then, amazingly, so did Joanne. "I know," she said, "it's not very nice. But if I actually acknowledged their existence I'd go insane."

"You know what," said Leah, "I think you're got the right idea."

"I definitely have the right idea."

"So, will you be moving out soon?"

The assistant arrived with the right slippers and went off to find the camisole top.

"No. Sadly not."

"No lovely man in the background who you're secretly dying to move in with?"

"No."

"Shame."

"Not really."

"Oh, I see. Not into men at the moment?"

"I'm not really into anyone at the moment."

"Ah," said Leah. "Fair enough." Joanne was softening as they talked and she knew that given just a few more minutes she might actually start to get somewhere. "I'm starting to feel a bit the same myself," she said, taking the top from the assistant. "I thought my future was in the bag, but suddenly I'm thirty-five and I've got to start again. It does make you feel a bit . . . *bitter*."

"Bitter?" said Joanne. "I'm not bitter."

"No, no, no," said Leah. "Not bitter, but just a bit — *lost*. You know?"

Joanne pursed her lips. "There are worse things," she said, "than splitting up with someone."

"Oh," said Leah, "right, yes. I suppose there are."

"Yes."

"I'm healthy. I'm alive."

"Yes."

Leah took Joanne's card and swiped it through the terminal. "Did you split up with someone? Is that how you ended up in Toby's house?"

"No." She tapped her pin number into the terminal. "Not really."

"Not really?"

"Life is episodic. A certain passage of my life had come to a close. It was time to move on."

"That's one way of looking at it, I suppose."

"It's the *only* way of looking at it." She handed the terminal back to Leah and they both stared at it in silence for a moment.

"But even if you believe that life is episodic, surely there's a continuity between chapters?"

"Not necessarily. I'm the heroine of my story. I can go where I like and never meet the same person twice."

"Like a road movie."

"Yes, I suppose — like a road movie."

Leah placed Joanne's slippers and camisole in a carrier bag and handed it to her across the cash desk. "Ah," she said, "but the whole deal with a road movie is that the protagonist is either running away from something or in search of something."

"And who says I'm not?" Joanne slung her handbag over her shoulder and tightened the belt of her leather coat.

"Running away? Or looking for something?"

"Both."

They were just reaching the kernel of the conversation and Leah had run out of excuses to keep her in the shop. Her next question had to be a bullseye.

"And how far along the road are you?"

"What?"

"Between what you're escaping and what you're seeking?"

Joanne smiled. "About halfway," she said.

"Ah," said Leah. "The hardest place to be."

"Indeed," said Joanne. And then she turned and left, cutting a swathe through the chattering womenfolk of Muswell Hill like a small but very sharp knife.

CHAPTER THIRTY-TWO

Toby and Con were in the kitchen together. Toby was stuffing hunks of Greek cheese into raw chicken breasts and Con was wrapping them up in filmy slivers of Parma ham. In the oven was a tray of miniature new potatoes and garlic cloves, slavered in olive oil and strewn with pine nuts and rosemary needles. Some tenderstem broccoli sat in a steamer basket on the work surface and in the fridge there was a pot of home-made tuna pâté which they would have with some pumpkin and sunflower seed bread rolls that Toby had baked specially this afternoon.

Con couldn't believe how much Toby knew about food. How did he know, for example, that you could put garlic in the oven like that, whole? And that you could cut open a raw chicken breast, stuff it with whatever you fancied, then seal it shut with this ham that was like a sort of meaty cling film? He was making out that everything was really simple and really unexceptional, but to Con what he and Toby were creating in the kitchen tonight felt like magic.

"Thanks," he said to Toby. "Thanks for all of this." And then, quite unexpectedly, he found himself giving Toby a hug. Not a bear hug, but a sort of clasp. He was surprised by how solid Toby felt underneath his clothes for someone who looked like they could be blown over by a summer breeze.

"You're welcome. It's nice to have an excuse, you know, to do some proper cooking. It never seems worth it just for me. Anyway — I hope you both have a great night. And you shouldn't be disturbed. I happen to know that Joanne's out tonight and I don't suppose Ruby will be around, not on a Friday."

Toby went upstairs and Con washed his hands thoroughly with antibacterial handwash. He was being ultra vigilant about hygiene. The thought of accidentally poisoning Daisy and her ending up in hospital because of him made him feel ill.

He checked the time. Seven-twenty-five. He heard the front door go and jumped. And then he held his breath, hoping that whoever it was would just go about their business and not wonder why there was music coming from the dining room and the smell of baked rosemary coming from the kitchen.

Footsteps creaked across the hallway floor towards the kitchen, then they stopped. Slowly the door opened and there was Ruby. Con exhaled.

"What the . . .?" Ruby looked round the dimly lit room in wonderment. "What the fuck is going on here?"

Con sighed. "Just dinner," he said.

"Who for?"

"For me," he said, "and a friend."

"A friend, eh?" She smirked and pulled out a dining chair.

Con sighed. "Yes. A friend from work."

She sat down and pulled a packet of cigarettes from her handbag.

"No!" he said. "Don't."

"Don't what?"

"Don't smoke in here. In fact, don't smoke anywhere tonight."

"Er . . . excuse me?"

"My friend. She's not very well. She's got a lung thing, condition. So please don't smoke."

"Oh, my God, have I walked into some weird freaking parallel universe? Spooky old music, candlelight, ill girl-friends."

"Just don't smoke, that's all. Please."

Ruby nodded, tersely, once, and put the cigarettes back in her bag. "Just for you," she said, "just this once. So — who's the lucky girl?"

"She's no one," said Con. "Just a girl." He watched the clock on the TV click from 7:29 to 7:30. "Look, Ruby," he said, "I'm not being funny or anything, but she's going to be here in a minute and I kind of made out we'd have the house to ourselves tonight. So . . ."

"You want me to fuck off?"

"Yeah, well. Yeah."

She sighed and stood up. "Fair enough," she said, "fair enough. But don't expect me to lock myself away in my room all night, OK?"

She picked up her bag and turned to leave the room. "What's she got then, this girl? Asthma or something?"

"Yes," nodded Con, "she's got asthma." And then the doorbell rang.

CHAPTER THIRTY-THREE

Ruby could hear them chatting through the gaps between her floorboards. She couldn't distinguish any words, just a symphonic series of bass rumbles, mid-tone gurgles and the occasional cymbal crash of laughter. As far as she could ascertain there hadn't been an awkward silence yet, and Con's "friend" had been here for nearly two hours.

She headed downstairs, her third spurious visit to the kitchen of the evening. She'd caught only a fleeting glimpse of the girl as Con had ushered her through the front door and straight into the dining room. She was very small, thinner than Ruby, with that sort of very fine, very blonde hair that Ruby thought of as "chalet girl" hair. She got a whiff of flowery perfume and a flash of silver ballet pump and crocheted shawl.

She poured herself a glass of water in the kitchen and picked at some leftover bread and pâté. Con and the girl were talking about someone called Nigel and laughing a lot. Ruby wanted to light up a cigarette and blow smoke through the keyhole, straight at the back of the girl's head. She wanted to go and sit down at the table with them and say, "So, little girl, tell me about your incredibly short life. Tell me about the five minutes that have elapsed since you ceased being a child. Tell me all about how little you have achieved and experienced. And then she would tell her all about her own life, about the men and the pain and the nights that should never have happened. She'd show her her tattoos and her scars and describe in great detail the night she fucked Con. Because even though Ruby was eleven years older than Con she had more in common with him than any fresh-faced little overgrown school-girl of his own age. He'd lived, at least a little. He knew what it was like to have nothing and no one, to function on your own.

The sound of a chair being scraped across the wooden floor next door disturbed her train of thought.

"No, leave those," she heard Con saying.

"No, no, no," said the girl. "Let me. You've done everything."

Before Ruby could think about whether to stay or leave, the girl was standing in front of her, carrying a pile of dirty plates.

"Oh," she said, "hello."

"Hi." Ruby took a second to consider her own appearance. She was in jeans and a grey T-shirt, hair moderately clean, face moderately made up, drinking a glass of water and minding her own business. There was no reason for the girl to think that there was anything untoward about Ruby or her presence in the kitchen. She brought herself up tall and smiled. "I'm Ruby," she said.

"Oh, hi. Yes. Con's mentioned you." She put down her pile of plates and offered Ruby her hand to shake. "I'm Daisy."

Daisy.

Yes, she would be a Daisy.

She was pretty, in that undefined way that these sorts of girls often were. Small, straight nose, fine eyebrows, little chin. She had small hollows under her cheekbones, which saved her from plainness. Pretty enough, thought Ruby, but not as good-looking as her. And she looked painfully young, younger, possibly, than Con himself.

"Nice to meet you," she said, her eyes taking in the rest of her. Fitted cream blouse, grey woollen shorts to just below her knee, flat shoes, a black waistcoat, a strange necklace with leathery things hanging off it. Kind of a mess, but she carried it off.

"So," she said, "you work with Con?"

"Yes. I'm at *Vogue*."

"Ah," Ruby nodded. Of course. A fashion girl. It made sense. "And I believe he cooked for you. How was it?"

"Delicious," Daisy smiled. She had slightly crooked teeth, but they suited her.

"Really?" Ruby grimaced. "Are you sure?"

"Honestly! I promise. I'm so impressed with him. Considering when I first met him he wouldn't eat anything except McDonald's."

"Oh, yes. His beloved McMeals."

"I know! He's my project. I'm determined to get him to eat healthily."

"Well, sounds like you're doing a pretty good job already."

"Con tells me you're a singer?"

"Yes. That's right."

"What sort of singer are you?"

"Oh, you know, kind of rocky, bluesy, soully. Depends what kind of mood I'm in, really."

"Wow. That must be amazing. Getting up on stage and singing in front of all those people. How do you do it?"

"Vodka," said Ruby, suddenly feeling the need to embellish her rock-chick credentials. "Lots of it. I never go on stage sober."

"God, I don't blame you."

Daisy stooped to scrape some leftovers into the bin. Ruby could see her shoulder blades through her blouse, sharp and angular as scythes. "So, Daisy. How old are you?"

"Nineteen," she said, "well, nearly. It's my birthday in February."

"Young," she said.

"Yes."

"God. I can't imagine I was ever that young."

"Well, surely you're not that much older than me?"

"I'm thirty-one," she said, bracing herself for the customary blast of disbelief.

"No!" said Daisy, right on cue. "God. I thought you were much younger than that."

"Oh, yes. How old did you think I was?"

"God, I don't know, about twenty-three."

Ruby smiled. "Yeah," she said, "you're not the first person to think that."

The door opened then and Con appeared. He looked at Daisy, then at Ruby. A coldness passed across his face. "Oh," he said, "I didn't realize you were down here."

"Just came down for a glass of water." She waved it at him.

"Right."

"Me and Daisy have been chatting."

"Right," he said again.

"I hear your cooking skills are quite impressive?"

He shrugged. "Well, yeah. Toby helped. But it was pretty good."

"Wow. You'll have to cook something for me some time. See if I'm as kind about your efforts in the kitchen as Daisy here."

"Yeah. Right. Anyway, we're going back now." He put a hand gently around Daisy's waist to guide her towards him. Ruby felt something bitter and acidic rise up in the back of her throat.

"Nice to meet you," said Daisy.

"Yes," said Ruby, "likewise."

The door began to close behind them. "Have fun," she called after them. But they didn't hear. Ruby listened at the door for a moment, to see if they were talking about her, but the conversation passed seamlessly back to themselves, as if the encounter with Ruby had never happened. She saw Con's hand on Daisy's back like an imprint left on her retina by a flash of light. She heard them laughing together — Con's rough estuary snigger; Daisy's crystalline Chelsea chime. She caught sight of her reflection in the blackened glass of the kitchen window and stopped for a moment. Who was she? What was happening to her? She had now been rejected twice in a fortnight, in both instances for someone diametrically different to her. It wasn't as if she wanted commitment; it wasn't as if she was making any demands beyond sex and a bit of a laugh. What was wrong with men today? What did they want with flat-chested asthmatic girls and forty-two-year-old divorcées with stretch marks?

Ruby poured herself a large glass of Toby's vodka and took it to her bedroom, "accidentally" spilling some on Daisy's crocheted shawl on the way.

CHAPTER THIRTY-FOUR

Con stared at the top of Daisy's head. She had a double crown, her fine blonde hair spiralling out of two separate whorls, like horns. A spray of hair had fallen from her hairline across her cheek. He'd been resisting the temptation to move it for the past ten minutes, concerned that he might awaken her. She started to stir and Con quickly rearranged himself, to look a little less like he'd been staring at her while she slept.

She looked around the room as her eyes opened. Con could see her checking out her surroundings, reminding herself where she was.

"Morning," he said.

She turned and smiled. "Morning." She pushed herself up onto her elbow and looked at him. "God, you're handsome in the mornings," she said.

He blushed. "Thanks," he said. "You look pretty good yourself."

"I doubt it," she said, pulling her hair away from her face. "Mornings are not my best time of day. What time is it, anyway?"

He glanced at his radio alarm. "Nine-fifteen."

"Oh, God, really?"

"Uh-huh."

"Oh, shit. I'd better get going."

"Really?"

"Yeah. Chest stuff." She tapped her collarbone and began to cough. "Sorry," she said, turning away from him. "Mornings are worst. Mimi usually gets to work on me first thing. In fact, I'd better call her, let her know I'm on my way back." She pulled her handbag towards her, her thin back arching away from him as she lent across the floor, knuckles of bone protruding through her milky skin, a triangle of white down covering the base of her spine. She coughed again as she pulled her mobile from her bag. Her breathing was becoming laboured and heavy.

She spoke to her sister. Con could hear the concern in Mimi's voice from the other end of the line. It was clear that Daisy didn't do this sort of thing very often. "It's not that late!" protested Daisy. "Yes. I'm leaving now. I don't know. The Tube. OK, then, a cab. No, he hasn't got a car. I don't know, OK. Look, Meems, I'm really sorry, OK. I didn't realize you were going out today. I'll be there as soon as possible. I'll call you when I'm in a cab." She switched off her phone and smiled apologetically. "Not impressed," she said.

"I could tell."

"I don't blame her. It's a real bind for her, you know, having to do my physio every morning. It's not fun and it means she can't go away without arranging a nurse for me or do anything, you know, *spontaneous*. She always has to think about me."

"The physio," he said, "what your sister does for you? Is it difficult? I mean, could someone else do it for you?"

She shrugged. "I suppose so. It's just lots of hitting me on the back, hitting me on the chest, moving me round in different positions."

"For how long?"

"As long as it takes to loosen me up."

"Could I do it for you?"

Daisy turned and gazed at him.

"That way you wouldn't have to rush off. That way you could stay. If you wanted." He gulped.

She smiled and brought the crown of his head to her lips. She kissed his head deeply. Con could hear the machinations of her broken lungs through her ribcage. "You are so lovely, Connor McNulty. You are so good. I knew you were, the first time I saw you. But it's not that simple. You'd have to be trained. Mimi would have to show you what to do. And besides," she said, "it's a bit like going to the loo with the door open, isn't it? Not very romantic."

Con smiled and kissed her on the mouth. And then he picked up his own mobile phone and switched it on.

"I'll call you a cab," he said.

"Thank you," said Daisy. "Thank you."

CHAPTER THIRTY-FIVE

Leah pulled open the Yellow Pages and flicked through it until she found the number for the Central School of Speech and Drama. She dialled the number and spoke to three different people before she was finally put through to someone who was able to help her.

"I'm looking for information," she said, "about an ex-alumni. Her name is Joanne Fish."

"What exactly did you want to know?"

"Well, I'm a casting assistant and we're thinking of calling her in for an audition, but we wanted a bit of background on her first. So, you know, anything really, anything you're allowed to tell me."

"Well," she said, "that would really depend on how much information she let us have, whether she kept in touch. Hold on and I'll see if I can find her file."

Leah stared through the window while she waited, feeling her heart racing under her ribcage with the excitement of lying.

"Right," said the woman on the other end of the line, "I've got her file. Let's have a look. Aah, yes, well, she graduated in 1993."

"What about marital status, family? Any information like that?"

"No, but her emergency contact is given as a man called Nicholas Sturgess."

"Oh, great, do you have a telephone number for him?"

"Well, yes, but bear in mind this is out-of-date information. The number still has the old code."

"Can I have it?"

"I don't see why not. Have you got a pen?"

"Uh-huh."

"OK — the number is 081 334 9090."

"Great, thank you. Anything else?"

"Not really," said the woman. "There's no record of any work after graduation. But that could be because she didn't stay in touch. A lot of students just disappear. But, ahm, she does seem to have given us some information about, well, I hope this doesn't have a negative impact on your casting decisions, but according to my records she got her first acting qualification at, er, Holloway."

"Holloway?"

"Yes, HM's Prison."

"She was in prison?!"

"Well, yes, it would appear so. She took a foundation course there, in acting. I assume that that must have been while she was, er, incarcerated."

"God, does it say what she was in for?"

"No. That's all it says. Gosh, how fascinating."

"Yes," said Leah, "that really, really is. Thank you so much. You've been incredibly helpful."

CHAPTER THIRTY-SIX

Damian Ridgeley was a medium-sized man, about thirty years old, with hair the colour of Lucozade and a grey French Connection T-shirt on. He had an accent of some description, a lazy Hicksville twang, could have been West Country, could have been East Anglian, flattened out, either way, by a few years in London. He wore a ring on his wedding finger and a chain round his neck. On his forearm there was a tattoo of a mermaid. He was standing on Toby's doorstep, but Toby had no idea why.

"Leah sent me," he said.

"Leah?"

"Yes, you know, Leah. From over the road. She said you had a job for me."

"She did?"

"Yes. Didn't she tell you?"

"Well, no. But then I haven't seen her for a few days."

"Well," he said, "do you? Have a job?"

"Well, that depends, really. What sort of job are you qualified to do?"

"I'm a project manager. I renovate old houses."

"And you're a friend of Leah's?"

"I'm her second cousin. Or her half cousin. Or something like that."

"Oh, I see. Right, well, then, why don't you come in?"

Damian perched himself on the edge of the Conran sofa and sipped a cup of peppermint tea (Toby liked that he'd asked for peppermint tea).

"So," he said. "What do you think? Is it the sort of job you'd want to take on?"

Damian nodded, slowly. Damian did everything slowly. There was something a bit Zen about him, Toby thought. It wouldn't have surprised him to find that he meditated in his spare time, did a spot of Tai Chi in the mornings. "Yeah," he said. "Sure. There's no restructuring, no building work. I mean, essentially you're just looking for a facelift, yeah?"

"Yeah."

"Cool." He pulled a notebook and an expensive-looking pen from the inside pocket of his denim jacket and made some notes. "I've just had a cancellation, a pretty big job, so I've got some guys at a loose end. I could get some people in next week. When are the bathrooms and kitchen coming?"

"Well, I haven't actually bought them yet."

"Cool. No worries. We can crack on with the plumbing, the roof. Get on with the kitchen and stuff once you've chosen them. I can get you what you want at trade if you'd like."

"You can?"

"Sure. You go shopping, tell me what you want and I'll get it for you."

"Seriously?"

"Yeah, of course. I can get you all your white goods, too. Whatever it is you need, just let me know. I'll charge you for my time, but it'll still work out much cheaper."

"God, that would be great. I seem to have got into a bit of a habit of overspending on things for the house, so it would be great to save a bit of money."

"Make up for the extra you'll be spending on me, then." Damian smiled and Toby breathed a sigh of relief. Damian was clearly from a different school of tradesmanship. Damian was clearly a professional.

"Will you require a deposit? Something up front before you start?"

"I'll put a quote together, put it through your door later on today. If you approve, I'll let you have a schedule of works. Once the boys are in and we're all happy, I'll ask for 20 per cent of the invoice. Total payable at the end of the project. Simple. Easy. No room for complications. Just how I like it."

He took Damian's hand at the door a few minutes later and shook it warmly and strongly, and perhaps for a split second too long. He felt like a man who'd just met the girl of his dreams and was already feeling paranoid that she wasn't really interested and that he'd never see her again. He carried Damian's mug through to the kitchen, tenderly, trying to prolong the sense of connection to him. He balanced Damian's beautifully designed business card against the kettle and stared at it, wistfully. Then he went upstairs and slowly, deliberately and, he hoped, not prematurely ran a line through items 7, 8 and 9 on his to-do list.

CHAPTER THIRTY-SEVEN

Toby saw Leah come home a few hours later. He gave her half an hour to make herself at home, get into her pyjamas, do whatever it was she usually did when she got home from work, then he headed downstairs. He stopped in the hallway to check his reflection. He had a bit of cobweb attached to his hair. He didn't know where it had come from or how it had got there, but he was glad that he'd thought to check before he left the house.

He felt a sudden surge of nerves as he stepped across the road to Leah's house and stood outside her front door for a full five minutes, trying to work up the courage to ring on her doorbell, but she looked happy to see him when she came to the door. She was wearing faded jeans with an embossed nubuck belt and a black cashmere sweater. Her hair was down and she was wearing glasses.

She took them off as she led him inside and placed them on top of an open paperback. He tried to see what book she was reading, but didn't recognize the name of the author.

Leah's flat was very neat, very modern. She had a big grey sofa, a black coffee table and a TV in a cabinet.

There were a few Pink Hummingbird-style lamps and mirrors around the place to soften it up, but essentially it was a masculine flat.

"I'm so glad you came over," she said, hooking a shank of blonde hair behind her ear. "I've been meaning to come and see you, actually, but then I see you up there, in your window and you always look so . . . *engrossed*. I hate the thought that I might accidentally disturb you in the middle of writing a poem and ruin the whole thing."

"Oh, no, you must never worry about that. I am eminently disturbable, I can assure you. Any excuse to get away from my computer. The two of us spend *far* too much time together as it is." He grinned and put his hands in his pockets.

"Can I get you a coffee? A tea?"

"Tea would be great. Thank you." He watched her move to the kitchen and fill the kettle. "I saw Damian today."

"You did. Excellent. I'm so glad. How did it go?"

"I think I'm in love."

"He's brilliant, isn't he?"

"He is. And he's starting work next week."

"Fantastic!"

"Thank you so much, for organizing that for me. I'm incredibly grateful."

"Oh, I'm so relieved. I was really worried that you might think I was being a bit meddlesome."

"Meddlesome? No, why would I think that?"

"Well, you said you'd changed your mind about selling the house."

"Well, yes, but that was mainly because I couldn't stomach finding someone to do the work when everyone I came into contact with was a complete cowboy. But now I've met the venerable Damian . . ."

"You've changed your mind?"

"Well, yes, I suppose I have. Although the problem of extracting my deep-rooted tenants is still no closer to a resolution."

"Ah, right. That's another thing I have to confess to having taken into my own hands."

"It is?"

"Uh-huh. I invited Joanne to a party at the shop last week."

"You did?! My God — did she come?"

"Yes."

"Well, that's quite remarkable. You obviously have great powers of persuasion. Did you manage to uncover any interesting facts about her?"

"I found out that she trained at the Central School of Drama. So I phoned them and asked them loads of questions about her and guess what?"

"What?"

"She's been in prison."

"No way! What for?"

Leah shrugged. "I don't know. But it was years ago, when she was young. And guess what else?"

"What?"

"I have a phone number for her next of kin. A man called Nicholas."

"Wow! And who is he?"

"I don't know. I've tried calling about fifty times, but there's never a reply and there's no answer phone, so I'm just going to keep trying. But he's obviously someone significant. And that's not all."

"It isn't?"

"No. I've found a man. For Melinda. A big, handsome Italian with a huge house in Muswell Hill who's sweet and lonely and loves English blondes. They're made for each other. We'll have to set them up on a blind date."

"My God, Leah. You're a marvel."

"I know!" she smiled.

"You know something," he said as he took a mug of tea from her outstretched hand, "I'm so glad it was you who found Gus on the pavement. I don't know you very well — in fact, I don't really know you at all — but it's obvious that you're a good person and not just a good person but a truly special person."

"Oh, well . . ." Leah shrugged, awkwardly.

"No, really. You're so confident and uncomplicated. You're the sort of person who one might look at and think, what would it be like to be someone like that just for a day, to see life in such a clear and intelligent way, to know who you are, to understand other people, what makes them tick, how to make them happy? And frankly, your boyfriend, that nurse chap, I mean, I'm not sure what he was thinking. I can only imagine he must have been threatened by your overall . . . *greatness*, and that's why he didn't want to marry you, but really, by any measure, you are entirely eligible and really very . . . *desirable*."

He stopped. A police siren started up in the background. Leah laughed.

"Oh, God. Did I just say desirable?"

"Leah nodded.

"Oh, dear Lord. Oh, God. I really didn't mean . . . that sounds awful. I just meant, in the same way as a piece of antique glass or a certain outcome to a situation might be desirable, not that I desire you, sexually, though you are, sexually desirable, but that's not what I was trying to say. Oh, God . . ."

"Oh, Toby," Leah laughed, "it's OK. I'm flattered."

"You are?"

"Well, yes. I'm thirty-five, I've just been dumped, I'm not the slim thing I used to be. I feel a hugely long way away from desirable. So thank you. And I'm really glad that I found Gus on the pavement, too, because if I hadn't I'd have moved out of this flat without ever having had a conversation with you and that would have been very sad. Because you're great, too. So . . . there you go . . ." She trailed off and Toby noticed that she'd turned rather pink.

"Well," he said, "thank you very much." He grabbed his mug off the coffee table and took a big gulp, slightly too big it turned out, as it hit the back of his throat and started trickling down the wrong way. He tried to redirect the tea down the right side of his throat, but the harder he tried to stop himself choking the more the choke built up until finally with eyes streaming and bulging and his mouth full of tea he could control it no longer. He tried to direct the regurgitated tea into his mug, but such was the force behind the explosion that he wasn't able to. Instead the tea sprayed all over Leah's coffee table, all over her wooden floor and all over himself.

Leah got to her feet. "God, Toby, are you all right?"

Toby couldn't reply; he was coughing too hard, the sort of harsh, painful hacking cough that feels as if you might actually die of it.

"Here, let me get you some water." She ran into the kitchen and emerged with a glass of water and a roll of kitchen towel. She pulled off a piece and started patting at Toby's shirt and jeans while he continued to cough like a horse. She passed him the water and helped him tip it to his lips. But it was too soon. His throat muscles were still in revolt and he sprayed water all over the front of her black sweater.

Toby finally stopped coughing and Leah looked at him with concern.

"Are you OK?"

He nodded, found his voice. "I sprayed your glasses. And your book. I'm really, really sorry."

"Well," she said, smiling, "that's the last time I give you a compliment."

He grinned. "It's been so long since anyone said anything nice to me that I actually almost die when someone does!"

Leah laughed and sat down. "Well," she said, "how about we get together again, some time soon, and if you like I'll say some more nice things to you, just for the practice?"

"That would be great," he said, "but go easy on me. I'm a compliment novice."

"Oh," she smiled, "I'll be gentle, I promise."

* * *

Toby loved going to bed. It was the highlight of his day. He loved, particularly, the moment when he folded down the corner of his book, pulled his second pillow from under his head, dropped it on the floor and switched off his bedside lamp. He loved the sense that the day was done and now he could surrender himself to the vagaries and randomness of his other life — his dream life. Toby loved to dream. In his dreams the sun shone and he travelled the world. In his dreams he made lasting, intimate connections with strangers and with friends. In his dreams he always had on exactly the right clothes and said exactly the right thing. He occasionally had an anxiety dream, a dream, for example, of being ignored by everyone at a party, or having a row with someone he loved, but they were still infinitely preferable to the reality of his existence, which was without parties at which to be ignored or loved ones with whom to row.

When he came to bed that night, however, he felt strangely indifferent to the prospect of sleep. He dropped his pillow to the floor, felt for the nub of his light switch and threw his room into darkness. But he wasn't ready for sleep. The friends of his nether world waited like shadows in the wings of his mind, but he didn't want to meet them yet. For now, he wanted to dwell in reality.

Because, for the first time in fifteen years, the reality of his day had been far, far better than anything his tired, confused, fragmenting brain could come up with.

Because, for once, something good had happened to him. He'd spent time with a woman. They'd shared a bottle of wine and their conversation hadn't come close to drying up. They'd made an arrangement to meet on Saturday afternoon, for a walk across the Heath. And then they'd stood outside the woman's house and they'd both stopped and smiled and, even though they hadn't kissed, a current had passed between the two of them, an invisible crackle of something meaningful, something entirely possible, something that made the prospect of tomorrow thrilling and terrifying. And that was why Toby finally succumbed to sleep that night. Not to escape his present, but to hasten the arrival of his future.

CHAPTER THIRTY-EIGHT

Boris seemed, if anything, to be getting even thinner. His fur looked even stragglier and his eyes looked even bulgier. Toby was concerned that this was more than just a weird-looking cat, that this was a cat preparing to meet its maker, so he made an appointment for him at the nearest vet.

He was staring out of his bedroom window, pondering the logistics of getting a cat from Silversmith Road to the surgery, which was a ten-minute walk away, without a cat box, when it occurred to him.

Melinda's car.

He was staring right at it.

It was red and shiny and parked outside. Which meant that Melinda was at home, as she never went anywhere by foot or public transport. Before he'd given himself a chance to think of a dozen reasons why he shouldn't do it, Toby was knocking on Con and Melinda's bedroom door.

Melinda came to the door. She was wearing a pink towelling dressing gown. Without her make-up, Toby noted, she looked much younger, much more approachable. She smiled when she saw him, making no attempt to bring her dressing gown together over her cleavage. "Hello!"

"Hi, there!" Toby smiled and wondered briefly, not for the first time, how this pink, blonde, overly genial woman had ended up living in his home.

"This is a rare privilege."

"It is?"

"A visit from the lord of the manor! I *am* honoured! What can I do for you, love?"

"Are you busy today?"

"No, not particularly. Did you want me to do some ironing for you? Or a spot of dusting? I don't mind if you do. Keeps me busy!"

"No, no, no. Nothing like that. It's just, I'm a bit worried about Boris. And I've made an appointment for him at the vet's later and I was wondering, if it's not too much hassle for you, if you'd mind taking us there? In your car?"

"What time?"

"One o'clock?"

She smiled. "No worries. I'd love to. I'll see you downstairs at one."

Toby couldn't remember the last time he'd been in a woman's car. Women's cars were strange, alien places. They were a funny shape, round, bulbous. They had tissues in them and, in Melinda's case, soft toys. And they smelled strange, not like cars at all. More like cakes. Melinda's car smelled of peaches. Not lovely fragrant peaches, straight off a tree, but sickly sweet peaches, steeped in syrup. The root of the smell was a small plastic peach hanging from her rear-view mirror.

She was restored to her usual state of casual glamour in bleached frayed jeans, pink hooded top, pink trainers and a Burberry visor. She tapped her foot pedals gently and methodically, as if they were driving a church organ. And she talked. And she talked. And she talked.

Toby sat in the back with Boris on his lap in a cardboard box trying to find an opportunity to start the conversation he'd been hoping to engineer since he'd first set eyes on Melinda's car this morning. He waited until they approached a roundabout, as he'd noticed that she tended to stop talking for a moment when she was concentrating, then he said the first thing that came into his head.

"So, are you . . . *seeing* anyone at the moment, Melinda?"

She turned round and grinned at him. "Why? Are you interested?"

"Good Lord, no. I mean. No, not at all. Not that I wouldn't . . . not that I don't . . . but no. I was just wondering."

"No," she said, turning back to the road, "no. I'm young, free and single. And that's the way I like it."

"It is?"

"Yes. Bloody men. I've had it up to here with them all. They're all losers."

"Oh, surely not all of them."

She smiled at him again. "Well, not you obviously, Toby. You're different. But generally speaking, in my opinion, men are just liars and losers and idiots."

Toby drew in his breath, about to do something that was so out of character for him that he felt like his head might fall off. "So," he said, "then you wouldn't be interested in meeting my friend Jack?"

She laughed. He couldn't blame her. "Your friend Jack?"

"Yes, well, not *my* friend, exactly. A friend's friend. A friend. Of a friend. She's been raving about him. Says he's amazing. Apparently." He breathed out, feeling quite dizzy with embarrassment.

"Oh, yeah?" Her head turned from side to side as she approached a junction to turn right. "Well, if he's that great, then why doesn't she want him for herself?"

He shrugged, then winced as one of Boris's claws pierced first the cardboard, then his jeans and then his skin. "I don't know," he said. "Maybe she doesn't fancy him."

"Well, then, he's obviously a minger."

"No, no, no. Not at all. Apparently he's very handsome. And very rich."

"That's what your friend's told you, is it?" She laughed again, somewhat patronizingly. Toby began to feel that maybe he'd gone about this all the wrong way.

"Yes," he said, sliding the wriggling, scratching box off his lap and onto the seat next to him. There was a small freckle of blood on his jeans which he dabbed at with a fingertip. "I have to admit, I've never met this man, but he does sound like quite a catch."

"Oh, bless you, Toby, and your way with words. Quite a catch, eh?!"

"Well, apparently."

Melinda pulled in to the car park behind the veterinarian's and turned off the ignition. "What are you trying to say here, my love? You want to fix me up with this rich old guy who your mate don't fancy?"

"Well, I wouldn't say he's old . . ."

"Well, what sort of age is he, then?"

"I'm not sure. Your age, I think. Maybe a little older. And he's Italian."

He felt her go still in the driver's seat, like a child hearing the distant tone of an ice-cream van. "Italian?" she said.

"Yes. Jack. Short for Giacomo."

"*Giacomo*." She let the name run across her tongue and over her lips. "Is he dark?"

"I don't know. I assume so. I mean, I could find out for you if you'd like."

"And when you say rich, how rich exactly?"

"I don't know exactly, but he's got a four-bedroom house on Cranmore Gardens. With a swimming pool."

"And he's not married?"

"No. Recently divorced. Two teenage daughters. Desperately lonely, according to my friend."

"Nah," she said, "sounds too good to be true. Sounds dodgy." She pulled her keys out of the ignition, slung her handbag over her shoulder and headed towards the vet's.

The vet was unable to find any medical reason for Boris's deteriorating condition. "Boris is very old," he said, sympathetically. "I would imagine that he's pining for his late owner and, being a runt, he probably isn't able to deal with the degradations of ageing as well as a more robust feline. Leave him be, see how it goes and, if it gets much worse than it is now, bring him in and we'll put him to sleep."

"How long do you think he's got?" Melinda asked as if she were playing a bit part in a daytime soap.

"That's hard to say." The vet patted Boris's head. "Could be a few days, could be a few weeks."

"So basically, he's dying?" said Toby.

"Basically, yes."

Melinda started to cry then, thick rivers of mascara running down her cheeks.

But Toby felt a curious sense of unburdening, of a loosening of the straps tying him into his rut. Boris was dying, but slowly, day by day, Toby was being reborn.

CHAPTER THIRTY-NINE

The sun came out that afternoon, just as Toby left the house. It matched his mood. He hadn't been for a walk across the Heath in a very long time. He hadn't, now he thought about it, been out on a Saturday afternoon for a very long time. Saturday afternoons were for other people, Toby felt, for people with children and people with partners and people who'd been in bed all morning because they'd been out all night. Saturday afternoons involved partaking in activities of which Toby had no experience — playing sports, doing the weekly shop, seeing friends. People did things on Saturday afternoons that they couldn't do during the week because they were at work. Toby, being without gainful employment, had no need to venture out on a Saturday afternoon. But now Toby had a friend, and Toby had somewhere to go. He felt strangely euphoric as he walked down the High Road towards the Tube.

He met Leah outside East Finchley station and they walked down the Bishops Avenue together, playing the "Which house is most disgusting?" game. It always disturbed Toby somewhat that people with so much money were allowed to spend it on such horrible houses. Toby had seen one for sale once, in one of the property magazines that got hefted through his letterbox occasionally, a low-built Southfork monstrosity with pillars and red bricks and cathedral windows. It had a gold-plated entrance hall, a cinema, a gym and two swimming pools. It was priced at £35,000,000.

Toby and Leah weren't the only people to decide that it was a nice afternoon for a walk around Kenwood. The grounds around the house were thronging with designer prams, big dogs, and toddlers in fleecy hats. The sky was a brilliant shade of blue and the sun was a blinding white orb behind the leafless trees.

They were ascending a small slope and Toby felt his lungs begin to strain against the amount of breathing he was having to do.

Leah stopped and turned to look at him. "Are you OK?"

"Yes," he said, holding his hand to his chest and squinting slightly. "Just a bit . . . *breathless*."

Leah smiled. "Are you really that unfit?"

Toby nodded. "Too much time . . . in front . . . of my . . . computer."

"Oh, dear Lord, that's terrible. You know, I've seen you up there at your desk, every day, every night, for three years. It never occurred to me that I was actually *watching you die*."

"Oh, God, it's not that bad."

"But it is. Look." She pointed at the hill they'd just climbed. "It's barely a slope. Terrible," she said. "Terrible. You should start exercising."

"No, no, no." Toby shook his head and they started walking again. "I'm not that kind of person. I don't do sports."

"It doesn't have to be sports."

"I don't do gyms."

"Swimming," she said, "try swimming. It's the best all-round exercise."

"Oh, I don't know. I have a slight phobia of swimming baths. The smell of chlorine, the eerie echo, women in rubber hats. And I get claustrophobic in goggles."

Leah laughed. "Come with me," she said. "I go every week. And I don't wear a rubber hat."

"You don't?"

"No. I promise."

"Well, then, maybe I will. Though I must warn you, I don't have entirely the correct physique for swimming trunks."

"And what exactly is the correct physique for swimming trunks?"

"Oh, you know, muscles, shoulders, buttocks — all that business."

"Well, I've got muscles, shoulders and buttocks, so we should sort of balance each other out."

Toby envisaged Leah in a damp swimsuit, her muscles, shoulders and buttocks shiny and wet. "OK," he said. "Yes. Why not? Let's go swimming."

"Good," said Leah. "It's a deal."

They headed back to the main house and queued for tea and cake in the café. It was mild enough to sit outside, so they took their trays into the courtyard and found themselves a table.

"Con's girl stayed the night," said Toby, stirring the bag round his teapot.

"What, the posh one?"

"Yup. He cooked her dinner. Well, *we* cooked her dinner. Her coat was still in the hallway the next morning."

"Well, that's brilliant."

"You know, I'm starting to feel rather fond of Con. In a kind of paternal way. There's more to him than I originally thought. In fact, I'm starting to feel more warmly disposed towards all my tenants. And you know, in a strange way, I'm quite enjoying this project. I'm quite enjoying being . . ."

"Nosy?"

"Yes," he smiled, and poured his tea into his cup. "Yes, being nosy. It's fun."

"Well, I *am* having a good influence on you, aren't I?"

"Yes," said Toby, "I'd say you are." He glanced up at Leah. She was scraping whipped cream off the top of her hot chocolate and licking it off her spoon. Her cheeks were the colour of strawberry sauce. She looked divine. He stared at his hand for a while where it rested against his teacup. He could feel it twitching. It wanted to move; it wanted to slide across the wooden table top and lie on top of Leah's hand. Toby talked to his hand. "Don't do it, hand. She'll freak out. It'll spoil everything." But the hand seemed intent on disobeying Toby's instructions. He watched as it moved across the table, slowly, disembodied from him, like something out of a zombie movie. It was halfway across the table when someone suddenly boomed in Toby's ear, "Leah! Leah!", and his hand came scuttling back to him like a nervous cat.

There was a large man standing behind him, in a fur-lined parka and trendy jeans.

"Am!" said Leah. "My God!"

"Hello," said Amitabh.

"Am — you know Toby, from across the road?"

Amitabh smiled at Toby. He had a lovely face. "Well, I don't *know* Toby, but I recognize you from through the window. Good to meet you." They shook hands. Amitabh's hand was warm and fleshy.

"Who are you here with?" said Leah.

"No one," Amitabh shrugged. "Just me. I was supposed to be studying this afternoon, but I couldn't face it. Thought I'd get some fresh air."

"Right," said Leah. "So, just got here? Just leaving?"

"Just got here." He pointed at a table behind them with his tea and cake on it. "Mind if I . . . ?" He pointed at their table.

"No," said Leah. "Why not?"

She grimaced at Toby while Amitabh went to get his food and mouthed a "Sorry."

Toby shrugged, trying to look as if he didn't care much one way or the other about Leah's ex-boyfriend crashing headlong into the nicest afternoon he'd had in fifteen years.

Amitabh put down his cheesecake and cappuccino, and sat next to Leah. He was very solid and very healthy-looking. His skin was clear and his hair was abundant and shiny. He had very white teeth and a high-octane personality. "You look good," he said to Leah. "You're wearing make-up."

"Yeah, well, us single girls have to make an effort."

He smiled. "So — what have you two been up to?"

"Nothing much," said Leah. "Just walking. Just chatting."

"I've got to say, mate, and don't take this the wrong way, but it's kind of unnerving seeing you like this . . ."

"Like . . . ?"

"You know — *out*. I've only ever seen you through the window. Me and Lee — we thought you were agoraphobic, to be honest."

"You did?"

"Am!"

"What?! I'm just saying. Yeah. It's good to see you out. Good to know you've got legs. You have got legs, haven't you?" he grinned and glanced underneath the table. "Phew," he said, wiping his brow, "imagine if you hadn't, if you'd been in a wheelchair. Shit."

Toby smiled and tried to look as if he was amused by the idea of having no legs. He stared at Amitabh's mouth, at the way it moved when he talked, which he did, non-stop. He watched it receiving large forkloads of cheesecake and being relieved of a cappuccino moustache by the back of his large, dark hand. He was very intense, robust, alive, full of news and chat and blather. He was slightly immature, seemed young for his thirty years and, to Toby's mind, a bit silly. He could kind of see how he and Leah would have worked together. They were both youthful for their years, teenage in their style of dressing, with a fresh-faced, puppyish approach to the world. But he could also see why they'd split up. Leah was ready for phase two of her adulthood. Amitabh was stuck firmly in phase one.

Toby finished his tea and buttoned up his overcoat. "Look," he said, "I think I'm going to head off, leave you two to catch up."

"What? No," said Leah, "don't go."

"No, really. I better had. I've got some stuff I need to get on with and you two haven't seen each other for a while. I'll see you soon, Leah. And nice to meet you, Amitabh."

"Oh, Toby." Leah got to her feet. "I don't want you to go. What about our pint at the Spaniards?"

"Another day, maybe." He smiled and gave her a perfunctory kiss on the cheek. "See you soon."

He walked away then, towards the entrance. He tried not to look back, but he couldn't resist it. He saw two people, perfectly matched in levels of attractiveness, in style and outlook, sitting together in the early dusk, laughing and at ease with each other. He wondered how different a tableau had been painted by the two of them before Amitabh's arrival; a preternaturally tall man with unruly hair, ungainly mannerisms, an old coat and a large nose, sitting with someone as fresh, normal and wholesome as Leah.

For a moment, for an hour, Toby had felt like just another man, out on a Saturday afternoon, out with a friend, inhabiting a world he usually only viewed as a spectator. Until a large, jovial man in a parka had crashed into his moment of normality and reminded him that he really didn't belong out here at all.

He headed back down the Bishops Avenue, the soulless, ugly spine of road that connected his world with this world, alone. And then it started to rain.

CHAPTER FORTY

Ruby faced the door of the small terraced house. It had been repainted since her last visit, five years ago. The whole house looked improved. There were new curtains in the windows and a couple of glossy pot plants. She smoothed her hair behind her ears, adjusted the strap of her handbag on her shoulder and rang the doorbell.

A woman came to the door, small, dark-haired, busty. She was wearing a nurse's uniform and was bare-footed. She looked tired.

"Hello, Mum."

"Hello, Tracey. What are you doing here?"

Ruby shrugged. "I don't know. I hadn't been in touch for a while. Wanted to say Happy New Year. See how you were."

Her mother narrowed her eyes at her. "What do you want?"

Ruby tutted. "Nothing, Mum. I don't want anything."

Her mother sighed and swung the door open. "I suppose you'd better come in, then. We'll have to sit in the kitchen. The boys are on the X-Box in there." She pointed at the living room door. Ruby could just make out three teenage boys sprawled across a brand-new sofa. Her half-brothers. They'd been children last time she'd seen them, full of pent-up energy, in a state of perpetual motion. Now they were adolescents, heavy-limbed, static, draped across the furniture like tendrils of wet seaweed.

Her mother filled a shiny new kettle with water from a brand-new tap on a brand-new sink.

"Tea?"

Ruby nodded. "House looks nice," she said.

"Yeah. Well, we've done a lot of work on it. It was either that or buy a new one."

"So you're still with him, then?"

"Eddie? Yes."

"Where is he?"

"Where d'you think he is?"

"I don't know. The pub?"

"Correct. Do you take sugar? I can never remember."

Ruby shook her head. She glanced round the kitchen. There was a chicken wrapped in cling film on the work surface, a bag of potatoes, some sprouts sitting in a colander in the sink. "So, what's new?"

Her mother shrugged, and poured water into two mugs. "Nothing much. We've done the house, got Christmas out the way, the boys are back at school. Just getting back into the rhythm of things, you know."

"How's work?"

"It's OK."

"Are you still at the nursing home?"

"No. I'm working private now, for Mrs Scott."

"Mrs Scott at the church?"

"Yes. Reverend Scott passed away a few years back. She's living alone now. I'm there five days a week, plus Saturday and Sunday mornings."

"She must be paying you well?"

She passed Ruby her mug. It had the golden castle and hammers of West Ham United on it.

"Not especially," she said.

"Better than the nursing home, though?"

"Just about."

"*Mum!*" A gruff boy's voice floated up the hallway.

"*What?*"

"*Can I have a cup of tea?*"

Ruby's mother tutted and raised her eyebrows. Then she filled the kettle again and put it on to boil. A slave to her men, thought Ruby. Nothing new there, then.

"So — what's new with you, then? Still living in that weird house?"

"Yup. Still there."

"Got a job yet?"

"Still singing, if that's what you mean."

"God, how old are you now?"

"Thirty-one."

"Yeah, that's right, of course you are. Isn't it about time you gave up on that? If you haven't made it by the time you're thirty, you can forget it, can't you? Isn't that how it works?"

Ruby sighed and sipped her tea. She'd known it was going to be like this. It was always like this. That was why she never came back. That, and Eddie.

"*Tommy! Your tea's ready!*"

Tommy came to the kitchen door. He looked like Eddie, small and stocky with sandy hair and a tiny nose. He gave Ruby a once-up-and-down. "All right?" he said. "What are you doing here?"

"Just visiting," she said.

"But I thought you said you were never coming back ever again."

"Yeah, well. I changed my mind."

"Are you staying for lunch?"

"I don't know." She glanced at her mother. "That depends . . ."

"You're welcome to stay. I've got plenty for everyone. But Eddie'll be home for lunch. And he's been in the pub. It's up to you."

"No," she turned to Tommy. "I'll stay till your dad gets back. Then I'll hit the road."

Tommy shrugged and took his tea back to the living room.

"Look," said Ruby, turning back to her mother, "I'll tell you the truth. I'm in trouble. I'm broke."

"Oh, right. Here we go."

"Here we go what?"

"Well, I knew there was more to this visit than just a friendly chat."

"Mum — when have I ever asked you for money? I've been out of your hair since I was sixteen years old. I've made my way in the world without any help from you. All I'm asking for is a few hundred, just to pay off my debts."

"Get a job."

"I can't get a job."

"Why not?"

"Because I can't do anything. Who the hell's going to give me a job?"

"Jesus, Tracey, you think 99.9 per cent of the population of this country can actually *do* anything? You think I can *do* anything? You think if I had the choice I'd be round at Mrs Scott's seven days a week? Cleaning her bum, washing her underwear? You think I wouldn't rather be good at something, have a talent, be special? Everyone wants to be special, Tracey, but the key to growing up is *realizing* that you're *not*."

Ruby sighed and pinched the bridge of her nose. That could be the family motto. "You're nothing special." Her childhood had been full of expressions like that: airs and graces, little madam, too big for your boots, la-di-da. She'd put up with it until her sixteenth birthday, then she'd packed a bag and gone, moved to London with the first person to tell her that she was every bit as special as she felt. He'd only said it to get her into bed, but it didn't matter. She'd escaped. She changed her name from Tracey to Ruby by deed poll and got on with the business of being herself.

"Anyway, look. I didn't come here to be reminded of my miserable ordinariness. I came here because I'm your daughter and I need help. Badly."

"How badly?"

"Put it this way. My bank has made me cut up my Switch card and send it back and I owe money to other people, too."

"What other people?"

"Friends, colleagues."

"No one dodgy, then?"

"No."

"So you're not in danger?"

"Well, no. I'm not in danger of being mutilated by hard men, no. But I am in danger of losing a lot of friends and being kicked out of my home."

Her mother turned her back to her and stared through the window, her hands in the pockets of her nurse's dress. Ruby watched her. Her hair was turning grey. Her shoulders were rounder than they'd been. She had hard skin on the soles of her bare feet. Her middle was wider. She'd become middle-aged and it had happened so quickly.

"No," she said. "I can't help you, love. I'm sorry."

"What?"

"I can't let you have any money. It's not fair on the boys and it's not fair on me."

"Fair?"

"Yes. I work hard for what I've got. Really hard. I do things you can't imagine doing. You do nothing but flounce around like you're something special and ponce off other people. Well, you're not poncing off me. You'll have to find another way."

"Oh, so your hard-earned money — it's all right for Eddie to take it down the pub and drink it away, but you can't spare a few quid for your own daughter?"

Her mother shrugged, raised her eyebrows, as if it was out of her hands.

"I don't owe you anything, Tracey."

"My God, you do owe me something. You brought that man into our home. You brought him in and you let him ruin everything. You watched him destroy my childhood, you let him belittle me and beat me and humiliate me, and you did nothing. You owe me, Mum. You owe me *big time*."

Her mother sniffed, picked at the film wrapping of the chicken, sniffed again.

"You know," Ruby got to her feet and picked up her bag, "I wasn't going to come. I really wasn't. I thought this would be a waste of time. But there was this little voice in the back of my mind going, 'She's your mother, she's your mother, she's your mother.' Like that actually meant anything. Like being a mother was something important, something *special*. But obviously, like everything else in your tiny, ordinary, sad little life, it isn't."

She left the kitchen and passed by the living room. She flung open the door and regarded her brothers. "Don't listen to them," she shouted. "Don't let them make you believe you're nothing special. Everyone's special. Even you lot." Three pairs of blinking, uncomprehending eyes stared back at her. "I'll see you when you're adults," she said, "when you're ready to get out of here."

And then she left, slamming the front door behind her.

CHAPTER FORTY-ONE

By Monday evening Damian's men had removed one bathroom and fitted a new one. By Tuesday evening they'd removed and refitted the second bathroom. On Wednesday morning, Damian came round to check their work.

"Nice suites," he said in the bathroom. "They look good." He peered into a box of limestone tiles on the floor. "These for the walls?"

"Yes. And the floors."

"Lovely," he said. "Smart."

"You know about the market, don't you, Damian? You know about the sort of people who would want to buy a big house like this. Do you think I've got it right? Are these the right sort of bathrooms?"

"Spot on," said Damian. "Yeah. Just right. You can't go wrong with limestone these days."

"And what about decorating? I was thinking grey walls, white woodwork, occasional flashes of blue?"

"Occasional flashes of blue, eh?" Toby and Damian turned round at the sound of a female voice. It was Ruby. She was wearing a slash-necked T-shirt and a tiny slither of faded denim that Toby assumed was a skirt.

Her legs were pale and very thin, with a large bruise above her right knee.

"Oh," said Toby, "hello."

"Hello yourself. What's going on?"

"This is Damian. He's running this project."

"Project?"

"Well, not project, but he's in charge of the works. The, you know, the bathrooms and kitchen."

"Hello, Damian!" She threw Damian one of her smiles and flipped her pelvis out at an angle. She was so obvious, so shameless. Toby felt a flutter of embarrassment for her. "I have to say," she peered into the bathroom, "I'm amazed you think we deserve such luxury, Tobes. Limestone tiles, power shower. We're not worthy."

"Yes, well, if you're going to do something, why not do it properly?"

"God, I'm not complaining. I think they're beautiful. I'm just a bit surprised you've thrown so much money at them, that's all."

"They weren't that much."

"Ha!" She snorted, incredulously. "Right." She turned to Damian. "He inherited a load of money from his sitting tenant and he's turned into the last of the great big spenders. Have you *seen* our living-room furniture?"

"The sofas?"

"Yes, the sofas. Six grand's worth. Ridiculous."

"Well, they're very nice."

"I know, but in the big scheme of things, it just seems so *wrong*. I mean — it's wasted on us, really."

"Well," said Damian, "it's what the market wants."

"Yes, but who cares what the market wants. We're not the market. We're just a bunch of scallies."

Toby had stopped breathing. Damian looked confused. "But the people who live here after you, they'll want to see a well-presented house, they'll want to see high-quality bathrooms."

Ruby laughed. "The people who live here after us? Nobody's going to live here after us! Toby would never sell this place."

Damian glanced from Toby to Ruby and back again. "Oh," he said, "right."

"Toby's not allowed to sell this house," she continued. "What would happen to all his waifs and strays? What would happen to me?" She rubbed herself up against Toby and squeezed his arm. She glanced at Damian and saw the confusion on his face. "Did you think Toby was doing all this work so that he could sell the house?"

"Well," he said "yeah. That was kind of the impression I'd got, but, obviously . . ."

"Toby — *are* you selling this place?"

"No," he said, "no way."

"Are you sure?" she said. "Because I couldn't stand it if you did. I'd be devastated."

"No," he said, "I realize that. That's why I'm not selling it."

"Good," she stroked his cheek and smiled at him. "Good." Then she turned to smile at Damian. "I've lived here since I was sixteen, you know. It's the only real home I've ever known."

Damian nodded, uncertainly. Ruby went back to her room.

"Oh, dear," said Damian.

"Indeed," said Toby.

CHAPTER FORTY-TWO

Toby counted his money on Wednesday night.

He had £32,650 left. Enough to pay for a kitchen, to pay Damian, to buy new curtains, new carpets, get a gardener in, then maybe still have some left over for a new PC and a widescreen telly. He entered the sums into a spreadsheet, and smiled. Everything was on track. He was on top of it. He was in control.

There was a knock at the door and Toby quickly shut the drawer and flicked his computer screen. "Hello?"

"It's Con. Can I come in?"

"Of course."

Con walked in. "Those bathrooms —" He gestured behind him with his thumb. "They're a bit smart."

"Do you like them?"

"They're amazing. Like something in a hotel."

"Glad you approve."

Con edged into the room and looked at Toby's screen. "I'm not disturbing anything, am I?"

"No. Far from it. What can I do for you?"

"Right." He sat on the corner of Toby's bed. "It's a bit embarrassing, actually. But I was wondering if you could help me with something."

"OK."

"I wondered if you'd be able to show me how to . . . do a poem."

"Do a poem?"

"Yeah. I want to give something special to Daisy. And she's not the sort of girl who'd go for jewellery and that kind of thing. So I thought I might, you know, write something for her. Something nice."

"A love poem?"

"Yeah, that kind of thing. But nothing too gay."

Toby smiled. "Right," he said. "Well, I can't necessarily show you *how* to do it, but I could certainly help you. You just need to think about what sort of feelings you're trying to express."

"Yeah," he said, "I knew you were going to say that. And I kind of know what it is I want to say. I just need to know how to make it into a poem."

"Right, then. OK." He pulled a notepad from his desk and a pen from his pen pot and passed them to Con. "Write down some words, phrases. You don't even have to write in straight lines, just scribble them down."

Con took the notepad from him and furrowed his brow.

Toby turned back to his computer.

"Do they have to be rhyming words?"

Toby smiled at him. "No. Just *feeling* words."

"Right," he said, tapping the Biro against the page. "OK."

A few minutes passed. Toby pretended to be researching important things on the Internet, while Con scratched away with the Biro.

"I've finished," he said, handing Toby the notebook.

Toby looked at the page. Con's writing was very small and messy.

"Can you read it OK?"

"Yes," said Toby. "Perfectly. OK. Let's have a look." He read out loud: '"changed my world' 'perfect' 'precious' 'different to anyone else' 'real' 'special' 'I feel like I've found my way' 'better than me' 'an angel' 'magic' 'inspiring' 'more than I ever thought I'd get'."

Con laughed, a tight, nervous laugh. "This is a bit embarrassing," he said.

"No, no. Not at all," he said reassuringly. "This is wonderful stuff. Really."

"Will I be able to make a poem out of it?"

"Yes," he said, "definitely. Now — what is your intent?"

"My what?"

"What is this poem for? To tell her that you love her?"

"Yeah," he said, "I guess. I just want her to know how I feel about her. But I also want her to think I'm, you know, clever."

"Clever," Toby smiled. "I see."

"Well, *creative*. I think she probably knows I'm not clever."

"OK, well, let's start, shall we?"

"What, now?"

"Yeah. Why not? OK, first of all we need to give it a title. Any ideas?"

"Yes," said Con. "Yeah. I know exactly what I want to call it. I want to call it: 'My Sunshine Girl'."

* * *

Con left Toby's room two hours later, clutching his ode to Daisy close to his chest.

Toby sighed, feeling gentle waves of happiness undulate through his body.

Con's poem hadn't been particularly brilliant or even particularly poetic, but it had been honest and true and sweet and raw. And it had moved Toby, deeply. He gazed across the street now, to Leah's flat. The lights were on; the curtains were drawn. He tried to envisage her, in pyjama bottoms, her hair in a bun, her reading glasses on, a glass of wine on the coffee table, a book in her hand. She hadn't been in touch since their afternoon at Kenwood, but then, Toby hadn't really made himself available for contact. He'd kept his curtains drawn at night and himself to himself. But as he peered through his curtains, he felt a surge of positive energy ripple through him. If Con could walk so fearlessly into a love affair with someone so completely different to him, then why couldn't he? People didn't need to match to be together. Leah and Amitabh matched in every way except skin colour, and that one simple factor had been their undoing. Just because Leah was sporty, organized, tidy, fresh, easy-going and gregarious, there was no reason why she shouldn't want to spend time with someone lazy, messy, scruffy, neurotic and antisocial. She'd made it very clear that she found Toby's company enjoyable. It was she, after all, who had instigated their weekend meeting and it was she who had suggested swimming. The onus, therefore, was on Toby to accept her offer.

The next move was his. By sitting in his room thinking of reasons not to pursue his friendship with Leah, he was creating a self-fulfilling prophecy. By assuming that he was unlovable he was ensuring that he would remain unloved. By assuming that he was unwanted he was ensuring that he would remain alone.

He opened his wardrobe door and looked at his list, at points 11 and 12.

Stop being in love with Ruby.

Find someone else to be in love with.

And that was when it hit him. He *had* stopped being in love with Ruby. He'd stopped days ago and he hadn't even noticed. After fifteen years of stultifying obsession and pointless devotion, he was free. And it was all thanks to Leah Pilgrim, his very own sunshine girl.

CHAPTER FORTY-THREE

Paul Fox had stopped answering his private number. It was the number that only the people closest to him were allowed to use. A special number, for special people. She knew he was ignoring her calls on purpose and it was pissing her off. All she wanted to do was say hello, talk to him. She missed him. It wasn't as if she wanted to marry him or anything.

Hailey Brown was playing on Wednesday night, at a club in Soho. Hailey was one of Paul's acts and he would definitely be there. Ruby put on a blue silk jersey dress with tight sleeves and a ragged hem, fish-net tights and oxblood ankle boots. She drank five shots of Toby's vodka, in the space of five minutes, over the kitchen sink. Then she painted her mouth red and her eyes charcoal and left the house in her vintage fake-fur coat. She used Con's Oyster card, taken without his permission from the pocket of his jacket, to get into town and, within five minutes of walking into the club on Dean Street, she'd been bought a drink by a stranger.

She took her drink and headed for the backstage area. A girl in a staff uniform smoking a cigarette looked at her, but didn't question her as she headed for the dressing room. She found him outside Hailey's room, talking to someone on his phone. Her heart lurched slightly when she saw him. He looked the same, if slightly bigger round the girth. Eliza's home cooking no doubt.

She pulled in her stomach, touched her hair and moved towards him. "Hello, Paul."

He turned at her voice and looked at her in surprise. "Erm, Lizy, darling, sorry, can I, er, call you back in a minute?" He snapped his phone shut and stared at her. "Ruby. What are you doing here?"

"Came to see Hailey, of course. Why d'you think?" She pulled a packet of cigarettes out of her bag and offered one to Paul. He took one and let her light it for him. She lit hers and they both inhaled in unison. "So. How are you?" she started.

"I'm fine. Great."

"You've put on weight," she patted his belly.

"Yes," he said, flinching from her touch, "probably. How are you?"

"I'm OK," she said. "A bit . . . *unsettled*."

"Right. Why's that?"

"I don't know," she said. "Just a vibe in the air. I think Toby's planning on selling the house. He's spending all this money on it. And I don't know — he's acting all *different*. He's been going out a lot, changed his hair. There's just something weird going on and I can't put my finger on it."

"Why don't you ask him?"

"I did. He said he's not selling, but I don't believe him. He lied to me about this money he got from Gus.

Told me it was just a few thousand and it's obviously a hell of a lot more than that."

Paul shrugged, looked distracted. "Well," he said, "it's his house. If he wants to sell it, that's his business."

"Yes, but where does that leave me? No job. No income. Nowhere to live. I'll literally be out on the streets."

Paul glanced at his watch and at the door behind him. "Look, Ruby. Hailey's due on in five minutes. I'm not sure what you expect me to do about this. I mean — what do you want?"

"Christ, why does everyone always think I *want* something? I don't *want* anything."

"Then why are you here?"

"I told you. To see Hailey."

"But you don't even like Hailey."

"I do like Hailey."

"You hate her music."

"That doesn't mean I don't want to come and support her."

Paul sighed. "I have to go now, Ruby. I'll see you later, OK."

"No!" Ruby clutched the sleeve of his jacket. "No! Don't go. I miss you. I want to talk to you."

Paul pulled her fingers from his sleeve. "Ruby. I told you. This can't happen. I said, no more."

"But Paul — I'm scared. I'm scared and I'm broke and I'm . . ."

"You're what?"

"I'm *lonely*." And then she started to cry. Real tears. Because she'd just realized that, without Paul and without Toby, she had absolutely no one in the world she could call her own.

"Oh, God." Paul sighed and rolled his eyes. "Come here." He allowed her into the circle of his arms and kissed her head and soothed her with quiet words. "It's OK," he said, "it's OK."

"It's not OK," sniffed Ruby. "It's not."

"You'll find your way. You'll find your place. You will."

"But what if my way and my place — what if it's the gutter? What if that's my destiny?"

"You? Ruby Lewis? In the gutter? I don't think so."

"But I'm not Ruby, am I? I'm Tracey."

"Tracey, Ruby. You're all one person."

"Yes," she sniffed. "And that's what scares me. Ruby can do anything. Tracey just drags me down."

"Well, don't let her, then. Show her what you're made of." He took his arms from round her and placed his hands on her shoulders. "Look," he said, "I really have to go now. I'm sorry."

Ruby could hear in his voice that this really was the end of the road. She took a deep breath. "Have you got any cash? Anything at all. I'm so . . . God, this sounds pathetic, but I'm so broke, Paul. So broke it hurts."

"Oh, God, Ruby."

"I can . . . *earn* it."

He narrowed his eyes at her. "What?"

"If it makes it easier for you, I could do something for it. Do . . . God, Paul, *don't make me say it*."

"Do you mean . . .?"

"Yes. Anything you want. Any time you want."

"Oh, Ruby, don't."

"Why not? I'm desperate."

"Well, I'm not." Paul pulled his wallet from his pocket and peeled off three twenty-pound notes. "Here." He handed them roughly to Ruby. "To stop you offering yourself to the next man you pass. But that . . . *is it*. No more, Ruby, no more."

He forced his wallet back into his pocket, ground his cigarette beneath his shoe and slammed the door of Hailey's dressing room closed behind him.

Ruby stood in the corridor, feeling the silkiness of the notes between her fingertips. Sixty pounds. Enough to live for a week, maybe two. She tucked them into her coat pocket and then turned, her body tingling with numb humiliation. She headed straight to the bar and ordered three straight shots of vodka, which she drank in quick succession. A man in a tight black shirt lit her cigarette for her and tried to talk to her, but she wasn't listening. The lights went down and Paul emerged from the backstage shadows. He saw her at the bar, saw the man in the tight black shirt talking to her and threw her a look of sad disdain. Ruby left the man, mid sentence, and pushed her way through the club, against the grain of the crowd rushing to the stage to see Hailey sing. Outside on Dean Street she realized how drunk she was. Soho looked like a kaleidoscopic mess of flashing lights and high heels and car tyres and teeth.

A pinched-faced man sitting on the pavement glanced up at her imploringly. His knees were wrapped in a brown blanket. An Alsatian-mix dog lay across his feet. "Spare any change, love?" She put her hand into the pocket of her leopard-skin coat and felt the two remaining twenty-pound notes and a handful of coins. She pulled out the notes and handed them to him. He looked at her in amazement. "Thank you," he said, "thank you. God bless you. God bless." He called after her as she walked away. "Have a good night. Have a good life. God bless you. *God bless you!*"

Ruby carried on walking, blindly. She didn't want to go home. She needed something to happen, something to take her mind off her conversation with Paul, something to move her life on from this current point of rancid nothingness. She needed to meet someone. Someone new.

She stepped off the curb and crossed the road, heading into some unknown corner of Soho with a heavy heart.

CHAPTER FORTY-FOUR

Con tucked the poem into the inside pocket of his jacket and was about to leave the house when he heard loud footsteps coming down the stairs. He went to investigate and saw Ruby, in a dressing gown, pinioned against a wall by an overweight man in a suit. Her dressing gown had come apart and her right breast was exposed. The other breast was covered by the man's hand. The man was kissing her throat and Ruby was staring at the ceiling.

This was the man that had woken him up last night at three-thirty, slamming doors and singing. This was the man who'd fucked Ruby loudly and mulishly until 4.30a.m. This was the man, if Ruby's cries of unbridled passion were accurate, called Tim.

Tim pulled away from Ruby and turned to look down at Con. He had one of those faces, fleshy, smug, spoiled. His hair was very thick and his suit was very expensive. He was about thirty-five and he was wearing a wedding ring.

"Morning," he said.

"Morning," said Con.

Ruby pulled her dressing gown together and avoided Con's gaze.

“This is Tim,” she said.

“Yes,” said Con, “I know.”

“Tim — this is my housemate, Con.”

“Con?” Tim boomed. “What sort of con exactly? A con artist? Or an ex-con?”

Con tried to smile, but failed. He left them there, on the stairs, Ruby in her old make-up, her fat banker in a wedding ring, and headed towards Hanover Square, to Daisy.

CHAPTER FORTY-FIVE

Leah unglued her eyelids and waited a moment while her retinas accustomed themselves to the daylight. She craned her neck to the right to peer at her alarm clock. It said eight-thirty. She blinked. It couldn't be eight-thirty — she'd set the alarm for 7.45a.m. But then — small doors in her mind started opening, memories emerged — she *hadn't* set it last night, had she, because last night she'd . . .

Her head swivelled to the left.

Amitabh.

In her bed.

She let her head drop back onto her pillow and sighed.

They'd gone to the pub last night. He'd suggested it at Kenwood on Saturday afternoon. "It just seems a shame," he'd said, "not to be friends. We've always been such good mates, you and I — and I miss you."

Given that she missed him, too, she'd agreed to meet up with him on Wednesday night. Ending up in bed with him hadn't been part of the plan. In fact, ending up in bed with him had been the thing that wasn't going to happen under any circumstances. But after a few beers it was so easy just to slip back to the flat, order a curry from their favourite takeaway, open a bottle of their favourite wine, look at each other and realize that nothing had changed, that she was still Leah and he was still Amitabh and that neither of them had ever stopped loving each other, not really, and that there was no one else involved and nobody to be hurt and that it felt good to hold someone familiar and warm and it felt good to kiss someone you've known for so long and that sex is even better when you've been apart for a while and that what happened next wasn't really important because it was all about the here and now and making each other feel better, just for a night. Just for old times' sake.

"Am." She shoved his shoulder. "Am. Wake up. It's eight-thirty."

"It's OK. I don't have to be at work until three," he mumbled, his eyes still closed.

"Yes, well I have to be at work in half an hour, so get moving."

He groaned and turned onto his side, pulling the duvet up round him.

Leah sighed and pulled herself out of bed. "Come on, Am, I'm serious. I need you to get ready."

"Oh, Lee, let me sleep. Please. I've still got my key. I can let myself out."

Leah paused for a moment, regarding Amitabh's slumbering mass, considering the consequences of letting Amitabh stay here without her. "OK. But don't make a mess."

"I won't."

"I'm going to have a shower. D'you want a cup of tea?"

"Mmmm, yes, please. I miss your tea, Leelee. Your tea rocks . . ." And then he tucked his hands under his cheek and fell asleep with a very contented smile on his face.

Leah gulped and headed for the kitchen.

CHAPTER FORTY-SIX

Ruby was having breakfast with a fat man in a suit when Toby came down to collect the mail. They were sitting together at the dining-room table, Ruby in a dressing gown, on the man's lap, watching him eat toast.

She turned and smiled at Toby when he walked in the room.

"Morning, Tobes."

"Morning, Ruby."

"This is Tim."

"Morning, Tim."

"God, I have to say, this is very weird," said Tim. "This set-up. This house."

"What's weird about it?" said Ruby.

"I don't know. All these people. It's strange. Not that I'm saying you're strange," he addressed Toby, "just — aren't you all a bit old to be flat-sharing?"

"We're not flat-sharing."

"Well, whatever this is. A commune, or whatever. I mean — I just saw an air hostess. In the full get-up. What's that all about? I mean, what is an air hostess doing living in a hippy commune?"

Toby shrugged and smiled. "That's a very good question."

Ruby pulled herself off Tim's lap and ruffled his hair. Her dressing gown gaped open slightly at the front and Toby got a view of her entire left breast. Toby had had many inadvertent views of Ruby's breasts over the years, which had served only to fuel his desire for her, but glancing at her breast now he felt curiously unmoved. He could see her perfect rubbery brown nipple, but he had no desire to touch it. He could see Tim's fat hand caressing the backs of her thighs, but he felt not a jot of jealousy. The air was full of the smell of them, of their stale union, but it didn't offend him in the slightest. He was cured. He was unafflicted. He was free. And with that thought he pulled on his brand-new overcoat and headed across the road to Leah's flat.

Toby didn't notice Leah's receding figure as he crossed the road towards her flat. He didn't see her rushing towards Fortis Green, her hair uncombed, a slice of toast in her hand. He was aware that he may have missed her, that she may already be on her way to work, but he had a handwritten note ready to drop through her letterbox, as a contingency measure.

He examined the front of his T-shirt as he waited at Leah's door and was pleasantly surprised to find no stains or encrustations of any description. He ran his tongue across his teeth to ferret out any errant morsels of cereal, then he counted to ten. If she hadn't answered the door by the time he'd finished counting, he'd assume she was out and leave the note.

At the number eight a figure appeared in the hallway.

The door opened and Toby prepared his face, arranging his features into an expression of warmth and good intentions. The door opened and Toby's face collapsed. It was him, the man, the nurse. It was Amitabh.

He was wearing a very small towelling dressing gown that barely met across his girth. His face was puffed up with sleep and his chin was covered in thick stubble. He was halfway through a yawn when he opened the door and Toby could see all his fillings.

"Oh," he said, "I thought you'd be the postman."

"No," said Toby. "Though I do have a letter. For Leah. Is she in?"

"No, sorry, mate. You've just missed her. She left about two minutes ago."

"Oh," said Toby, "bad timing. Never mind. Well, do you think maybe you could pass this on to her." He passed the envelope to Amitabh.

"Sure. No problem. I'll make sure she gets it." He yawned again and began to close the door.

Toby paused. "So, are you, have you . . . moved back in?"

Amitabh scratched his head. "No," he said, "not yet. But watch this space." He smiled and he winked, and then he closed the door.

Toby stood for a while, staring at the stained glass of Leah's front door.

What an idiot he was. What a complete and utter fool. Why hadn't he seen that coming? Why hadn't he considered the possibility that Leah's unexpected encounter with her ex-love on Saturday afternoon might have led to some form of reconciliation? Why hadn't he remembered how messy and unruly life could be, how unmanageable an emotion love was. He called himself a poet, yet he consistently proved himself to be completely out of touch with even the most basic tenets of human nature. He was a novice in this world, a naïf.

When Karen had left him fifteen years ago he'd filled his house with people from all walks of life, people with stories to tell and journeys to share, but instead of learning from them he'd used them to insulate himself from the world. And now that he was finally unpeeling all the layers and revealing himself, it was very disappointing to see that he wasn't an eccentric struggling artist with a fondness for unusual people, that he was just plain old Toby Dobbs, the tallest boy at school, the disappointment to his father, the man whose own wife hadn't wanted to live with him for more than a month.

He sighed and he turned and he headed back to his house. He made himself a cup of tea and, instead of taking it to his room, he took it up to Gus's. He lay down on Gus's shaggy carpet and he stroked Gus's dying cat and he wondered, really and truly, what *was* the fucking point of it all.

CHAPTER FORTY-SEVEN

"Daisy's not in today," said a girl whose vowels were so twisted with poshness that Con could barely understand a word she was saying.

"Oh," he said, "right. Do you know what's wrong with her?"

"No idea," she said. "I didn't ask."

Con felt an icy sense of dread. He took the lift back down to the post room and pulled his mobile phone out of his pocket. She didn't answer her mobile, so he took a deep breath and called her home number. Again, there was no reply. He tried both numbers every ten minutes until finally, at half past two, someone answered her mobile. It was a man's voice, impatient and gruff.

"Hello. Is that Daisy's phone?"

"Yes. Who is this?"

"It's Con. I'm a friend of hers. Who's this?"

"I'm Daisy's father."

"Oh." Con stopped slouching against the wall and brought himself up straight. "Hello. Is Daisy all right?"

"Sorry, what did you say your name was?"

"Con. Connor. I'm a friend of Daisy's from work."

"I see. Well — we're all at the hospital right now . . ."

"The hospital. Shit. I mean, God. Is it serious? Is she OK?"

Daisy's father sighed. "Well, we're waiting for some X-rays. It looks like another pneumothorax."

"What . . . what's that?"

"It means she's got air around her lungs."

"Shit. Sorry. Will she be OK?"

"Look. I'm terribly sorry, but I have to go now. Maybe you should come to see her."

"Would that be OK?"

"Of course. She'd love to see a friend. She's at St Mary's. Bring her something nice to eat. The food here is terrible."

Con followed the signs to Daisy's ward, clutching a bag of sandwiches and a bunch of roses. A man sat on a plastic chair in a dressing gown, his hand attached by clear plastic tubing to a drip on a stand. A porter pushed a grey-faced woman in a wheelchair towards a lift. Con shuddered. It was wrong to think of Daisy in this environment, amongst all this greyness and decay.

Her bed was at the furthest end of the small ward, underneath a window. Mimi sat at one side of her bed; a small woman with silver hair sat at the other side. Mimi was reading a magazine and the other woman was laughing at something she'd just said.

He edged towards the bed nervously. He was about to be confronted by both Daisy's illness and her family. He felt overwhelmed.

The small woman turned as Con approached and smiled. She had a dimple and crooked teeth. "Connor!"

she cried, getting immediately to her feet to greet him. "I'm Helen, Daisy's mother."

"Hello," he said, accepting a coffee-scented kiss to his cheek.

"Daisy," she said, touching her knee, "look who's here. It's your friend Connor."

Daisy was held up by a thick wedge of pillows and had a tube coming out of her chest, attached to a jar of water. She was clutching an oxygen mask in her right hand which was attached to a tank. Her skin was very blue and her hair was lying in lank strands on her pillow. She smiled wanly at him. "Sexy, huh?" she said.

He rested the roses on the bed and smiled at her. "You look lovely," he said. "A bit pale . . ."

"You mean a bit blue," she croaked. "Not to mention a bit tubey and a bit ill."

"Here." Daisy's mother moved her plastic chair towards him. "Sit down, Connor."

"No," he said. "No, honestly."

"No. I insist. I've been sitting down for so long my bum's gone totally numb. I think I might just go and stretch my legs, actually. Meems — are you coming?"

"Yes," said Mimi, getting to her feet. "I could do with a wander. See you in a minute."

Con waited until the two women had left the ward, then he kissed Daisy on the lips. "Your mum's really nice," he said.

"Yes. I told you I had fantastic parents, didn't I?"

"I brought you some sandwiches," he said, showing her the bag.

"Ooh, yum. What have we got today?"

"Tuna and capers."

"Ooh, lovely. I love capers."

He unwrapped the sandwiches for her and passed her a square. Then he poured some water for her, from a clear plastic jug into a plastic cup.

"So," he said, "what's this pneumo . . . pneumo . . .?"

"Pneumothorax. It's air around the lungs. It's horrible. I've had it before, but not this badly. I thought I was dying, I really did."

"And is it to do with your cystic fibrosis?"

"Of course. Isn't everything? Yes, so, I've got to lie here with this thing sticking into my ribs for at least three days . . ."

"And then what — then you can come home?"

"Then I can come home."

"So it's not, you know, not something that might . . ."

"No. It's not going to kill me. Just ruin my social life for a few days."

"Oh," said Con, "oh, that's good, then, that's . . . oh . . . God . . ." And then Con felt all the pent-up anxiety he'd been carrying round all day suddenly leave his body in an enormous *whoosh* of emotion and he started to cry. "Oh, God," he sniffed, "I'm really sorry. Shit. I just thought . . . when your dad said you were in the hospital I just panicked. And then he wouldn't tell me if you were going to be OK and I just thought that you were going to . . . that you might . . . and I couldn't, I really couldn't handle it if anything happened. I couldn't deal with it . . ."

Con pressed his eye sockets into the heels of his hands, trying to stem the flow of tears. Daisy passed him a paper tissue from a box on her trolley. He took it silently and breathed in deeply, in and out, in and out, trying to bring himself under control. "I'm sorry," he said, "I'm being really pathetic. You must think I'm psycho."

"Of course I don't," said Daisy, clutching his fisted-up hands with hers. "I think it's really sweet."

"Oh, God," he laughed, and wiped his face with the tissue, "that's even worse."

"I can't believe you were that worried about me."

"Of course! I mean, I know we've only known each other a few weeks, but you're really important to me. You're, you know, special." He gulped.

Daisy squeezed his hand. "You're very special to me, too."

"I am?"

"Of course you are. You're up there, you know, up there with my mother and my father, my sisters, my best friend. You really matter to me. You . . ." She stopped and tried to catch her breath. She brought the oxygen mask to her mouth and took a few deep breaths. Her blue eyes peered at him from over the mask, pale and scared and young. "Sorry," she said, a moment later. "I should stop talking for a while . . . it's . . . hard . . ."

"No. Don't talk. You don't have to say anything. Look — here. I've got you something else." He pulled the poem from his jacket pocket and handed it to her.

She unfolded it and started to read. Con watched her intently as she read, trying to gauge her reaction. She folded up the poem, rested it on her lap and smiled.

"Con?" she said.

"Yes?"

"I love you, too."

Mimi and Helen came back a few minutes later with plastic cups of coffee and a packet of Fruit Pastilles. Then Daisy's father returned and shook Con warmly and firmly by the hand. They were a noisy family, talkative and open and full of swearwords and booming laughter. They wanted to know all about Con and acted as if many of their friends were teenage boys from Tottenham. They didn't seem at all fazed or desperate about Daisy's situation or about the fact that she was dating someone like him. They weren't like anyone Con had ever met before. They were so confident in themselves, in their unity, in their *themness*, that there was no room for doubt or fear or awkwardness.

There was talk of Daisy taking some time off work, of Daisy spending a week at home recuperating. "And of course," said Helen, touching Con's knee with her birdlike hand, "you must come to visit. You must come to stay, for as long as you like."

"Oh, yes," said Daisy's father. "We've already got one fellow in the house."

Con looked at him questioningly.

"Camellia's at home at the moment and of course her fellow couldn't bear to be separated from her for a minute, so he's staying at the house. Nice chap. He's a bassoonist, plays with the LPO. I think you'd like him . . ."

Con left the hospital at eight o'clock that night, letting the cold night air swallow him up. He walked quickly through the streets of Paddington, following signs to the Tube station. His breathing was hard and fast, his heart full of the euphoria of escape. He'd just seen reality, the very basic truth of Daisy and him, of what they were doing and where they were going. And he couldn't handle any of it. He couldn't handle her closeknit family, their talk of "the house", of bassoon-playing boyfriends and invitations to stay. He couldn't handle their unquestioning acceptance of him because he knew it was borne out of nothing more than middle-class politesse. But more than anything, he couldn't handle the fact that the first woman he'd ever loved was going to keep getting ill and that one day she was going to die and that there was absolutely nothing he could do about it.

CHAPTER FORTY-EIGHT

Toby spent the whole of Thursday looking out of the window. He saw Amitabh leaving Leah's flat at two o'clock, wrapped against the cold in his cosy parka and a knitted hat. He saw the builders passing in and out of the house, taking stuff out of their van, putting stuff back in their van, throwing things onto the skip, sitting on the wall eating sandwiches. He saw people, dozens of people, coming and going, children being piled in and out of cars, estate agents doing viewings, cats patrolling their territory. He saw a Tesco delivery van unloading, a woman across the street throwing a sack of rubbish into her wheelie bin, a man with a fluorescent bag dropping restaurant leaflets through people's front doors. He saw the sun start to fall and the moon start to rise and he watched the two of them share the indigo sky for half an hour as they changed shifts. He saw Melinda park her car and climb the front steps, chatting to someone on her mobile phone. He saw Ruby going out with her guitar. And, at eight o'clock, he saw Leah come home. He watched her open her front door, lean down to pick up some letters, then disappear. He saw her switch on her lights, draw her curtains. He wondered if she'd seen his note yet. He wondered what she'd think of his jauntily worded little message, expressing his desire to join her at Crouch End Public Swimming Baths one day this week (if he promised not to try out his butterfly stroke). He wondered if Amitabh would be coming back tonight.

He was about to go downstairs, to get himself something to eat, when he saw something else through his window. He saw Joanne, looking flustered and panicky in dungarees and a leather flying jacket. She was walking very fast and kept looking behind her. Toby saw a man, following behind. He was tall and slim with fine shoulder-length hair. He was shouting to her. Toby couldn't hear what he was saying. He saw Joanne turn to the man and shout something back. And then he saw Joanne start to run towards the house. He heard her footsteps up the front stairs and he saw the man chase after her. He heard the front door slam shut and he heard the man's fist beating against the door. He got to his feet and ran down the stairs, two at a time. Joanne was standing breathlessly at the foot of the stairs.

"Jesus. Joanne. What's going on? Are you OK?"

"I'm fine," she said, pushing past him to get up the stairs.

"But who's that man at the door. Why is he following you?"

The man beat at the door again. Toby could hear his muted shouts from the entrance hall.

"I don't know," she said. "He's no one."

"My God. Shall I call the police?"

"No," she said, "don't do anything. He's just mad, that's all. He'll go in a minute."

"But, Joanne. He looks really dangerous. What shall I do?"

"Nothing," she said, disappearing up the stairs, "don't do anything."

Toby glanced round the empty hallway. The man was still banging on the door. He fell to his hands and knees, and crawled to the entrance hall. He slowly lifted the letterbox and brought his mouth to it. "Go away," he said, "or I'll call the police."

A pair of eyes peered at him through the letterbox and Toby let it slam shut. He stood up straight. "Go away," he shouted through the door. "Go away. I'm calling the police."

"I want to see Joanne."

"Well, she doesn't want to see you. You're scaring her."

"I just want to talk to her."

"I told you. Whoever you are, she doesn't want to talk to you."

"Please," said the man, "please. Just let me see her. I have to see her."

The man's voice had softened now and it sounded to Toby as if he might even be about to cry.

"Who are you? What do you want?"

"My name's Nick," he said. "I'm Joanne's husband."

CHAPTER FORTY-NINE

The third week of February dawned clear-skied and sunny, and a few degrees warmer than it had been. Toby no longer needed to wear a hat while he prepared his dough in the early morning and he didn't wince when he sat down on the loo.

Things were progressing. The house was growing up. The bathrooms were tiled and the lights were fitted. Toby had taken one look at the finished bathrooms and immediately gone out and spent £300 on fat bath towels in shades of taupe and chocolate. There were tilers on the roof and a plumber had replaced the water tank and all the radiators. A clearance firm had taken the last of Gus's furniture and his carpet had been ripped out, rolled up and thrown on the skip. Boris now lived in Toby's room, where he pined and moped and refused to eat, slowly mutating into a small black skeleton.

The decorators were starting next week and Toby had been staring at colour cards for days on end, trying to decide between a hundred different shades of beige and grey. His room was full of test pots and his walls were covered in brushstrokes with pencilled annotations: *Labrador Sands 12*. He had a box of carpet swatches under his desk (Sisal or seagrass? Or should he just strip the floorboards?). Two young men called Liam and Guy were currently replacing the kitchen, so the fridge was in the hallway and everyone was using a two-ring electric hob in the dining room. There were boxes stacked along the walls, filled with food and crockery and pots and pans. The place was a mess, but it was being transformed.

By the time Toby's father arrived at the end of March, the house would be complete and on the market. But it would still be full of people. The velvet-gloved eviction of Toby's tenants had come to a grinding halt.

Ruby was still sleeping with her married man and surviving on handouts and the occasional poorly paid gig. The wheels appeared to have come off Con's fledgling love affair with the posh girl from *Vogue*. Melinda was revelling in the luxurious transformation of the house and more determined than ever to stay. And Joanne had disappeared. Literally. She'd left for work the morning after her "husband" had followed her home and not been seen since. She'd put an envelope under Toby's door containing a cheque for the next month's rent and a note suggesting that she'd gone on holiday.

And Leah — Leah was cohabiting once more with her nurse.

She never did respond to Toby's note about the swimming baths and their paths hadn't crossed since. She was, once more, simply the woman across the road with the Asian nurse boyfriend. And without Leah,

Toby was lost. He couldn't deal with the nuances and foibles of his tenants' emotional lives. He couldn't organize fortuitous meetings and think about what they needed. The list taped onto the inside of his wardrobe remained untouched, paused at number 10, like a freeze-framed video. So he sat, in his room, in his window, pretending to write poems and waiting for something to happen again. Toby was back at square one.

CHAPTER FIFTY

Leah felt all wrong. Amitabh had moved back in and she really didn't know why. It had been nice at first having him there, where he belonged, on their sofa, in their bed; being able to walk past a pub and not have to worry about whether he was in there with another woman, just to know where he was and what he was doing. That had been the worst thing about him moving out — losing track of him. Having to invent scenarios and imagine situations. But two weeks on and the novelty of knowing where Amitabh was all the time had already worn off and now Leah was just left with a big list of questions: What are we doing? Where are we going? Are you going to go against your family and marry me? Do you love me? Do I love you? *Is this what I want?* It had been exactly what she wanted for so long that the possibility that maybe it actually wasn't hadn't ever really crossed her mind before, and it was an unsettling realization. If she didn't want Amitabh, then what exactly did she want? She was thirty-five. Surely she should know by now.

She pondered her situation during a quiet morning in the shop. They'd just had a big delivery of alphabet cookie cutters and she was unpacking them in the stockroom, wondering at the concept of having either the time or the inclination to bake biscuits in the shape of names.

She fiddled with them on the floor, arranging them absent-mindedly into words. LEAH. AMITABH. And then, weirdly, TOBY. She scuffed them together, hurriedly, into a puddle of letters, and took them upstairs. She was alone in the shop. Her assistant wasn't due in until eleven. She looked round the shop, and sighed. What was she doing here? Why was she arranging cookie cutters on shelves? Something was wrong. Something was missing. She felt overwhelmed by a sudden need to escape, to shut the shop and to run away somewhere for the day. It was as if a parallel world had veered into her real world just for a moment, as if she'd caught a fleeting, fuzzy glimpse of another life — and she liked it more than this one. And if she stayed here, if she followed the pre-ordained pattern of her day, she'd be missing her chance to jump across the parallel lines and see what else life had to offer.

But she had to stay here. It wasn't her shop to shut.

She sighed and unlocked the door, turned the sign from "closed" to "open", and hoped that maybe today her destiny would come and find *her*.

CHAPTER FIFTY-ONE

I am thinking bout u, my ruby-chews I am thinking that I luv u! I need u. can't breath without u. c u tonight. T xxxx

Ruby smiled tightly and switched off her phone. She was in a laundrette on the High Road, watching her underwear swirl slowly back and forth inside a gigantic tumble drier. The tumble drier at home was out of commission while the kitchen was being replaced and she'd been forced to bring her washing here. Not that she minded. She liked laundrettes. She liked the people who used laundrettes. She could relate to them. People who didn't have washing machines tended not to have mortgages or children or jobs. They were students or OAPs or immigrants living in temporary accommodation. She liked the smell of laundrettes, the dry heat, the feeling of having nothing better to do than read a magazine for an hour. She liked the old-fashioned signage, the washing-powder machine; she liked being somewhere that was exactly the same today as it had been twenty years ago.

She opened her in-box and read Tim's message again. She should reply, but she didn't know what to say. She'd never told a man that she loved him before, even when she had. The thought of using those words fraudulently made her cringe. Once those words were uttered, everything changed. She would lose her power; he would expect more of her. But worse than that, Tim Kennedy would probably leave his wife.

Ruby had slept with married men before; she'd heard all the clichés about problematic marriages and unempathetic wives. A dozen men had told her how unhappy they were at home, how they only stayed for the children. But Tim was different. He really was unhappy. And he really would leave his wife. He'd leave her tonight. He'd leave her now. All Ruby needed to do was say the word. Tim Kennedy was in love, like no one had ever been in love with her before. He sent her text messages twenty times a day. He sent her flowers; he bought her jewellery. He'd offered her his heart on a cushion.

Tim was a stockbroker. He lived with Sophie, his wife, in a Georgian cottage in Hammersmith, a one-minute walk from the river. He'd been married only a year. They'd been together for five years before that. They had no children, but they had a bulldog called Mojo over which they'd signed a pre-nup. They'd just got back from a skiing holiday in Austria or Switzerland or somewhere like that, and they played a lot of tennis — in couples. Tim drank red wine and played squash and worried about his weight. Sophie, apparently, was very thin and went to the gym five nights a week, when she got home from her job as a retail director for a chain of furniture shops.

It was all too, too tedious for words. It was no wonder he was crazy about her. He'd never met anyone like her before in his life, and if it hadn't been for the chain of events that had led to Ruby walking into the same Soho bar as him that night, and if she hadn't been in the very particular state of mind that she'd been in that night, he never would have. They were from two different worlds.

He'd turned up at a club on the Holloway Road last week, fresh from work in his suit and tie, wedged himself between sweaty men in thin T-shirts and women with tattoos, a plastic cup of beer clutched in his hand, just to see her play. When she came off stage he'd looked at her in awe, eyes blinking, mouth unable to form the words he wanted to utter. "You're brilliant," he'd managed eventually, "completely brilliant."

He adored her. And Ruby had to admit, she quite liked it. It had been a long time since anyone had felt so strongly about her and it couldn't have come at a better time. But she didn't love him. She didn't even particularly like him. She could just about stomach having sex with him. But right now, with everyone else in her life letting her down, with Toby selling the house, her mother fobbing her off, Con ignoring her and Paul abandoning her, Tim was all she had left, and Ruby needed him, more than she could bear to think.

She pressed reply and started to type:

thinking I might love you too. See you tonight xxx

CHAPTER FIFTY-TWO

"It's time," said Melinda, peering over Toby's shoulder at the cat, which was curled up against the wall, body expanding and contracting like a set of poorly maintained bagpipes.

Toby nodded his agreement. "Shall we go?"

Toby picked up the cat and wrapped him in an old bath towel. He placed him carefully in a cardboard box and they took him down to the car.

They sat next to each other in silence in the waiting room at the vet's. Toby tickled the top of Boris's head absent-mindedly with his index finger. Melinda flicked through a flimsy gossip magazine.

"Boris Veldtman?"

Toby looked up. The receptionist smiled at them. "You can go through now."

"Ah, yes," said the vet, peering into the box at Boris, "yes. He's very close to the end now. Very close. I would recommend a shot. End it for him."

"So you don't think it would be better to wait, to let him go naturally?"

The vet put his finger to his lips and considered the question. "You could take him home now and he might last out another few hours, another day, maybe two.

But I would say that right now Boris is experiencing a fairly high level of discomfort. It's up to you, but most people tend towards ending things sooner rather than later."

Toby and Melinda exchanged a look. Melinda nodded. "OK," said Toby, "let's do it."

The vet nodded sombrely. A nurse brought through a hypodermic syringe and Toby and Melinda patted Boris's bony back while the injection was administered. Boris didn't even flinch when the needle punctured his skin and his bloodstream was flooded with cold chemicals.

Toby and Melinda watched the cat, rapt. His breathing continued, long and heavy, up and down, for a few minutes, until finally it started to slow. Melinda grabbed Toby's hand and squeezed it hard. He squeezed it back, surprised by the sense of emotional tranquillity the touch of another human being brought to him so quickly. A minute later, Boris stopped breathing. Toby turned to the vet. "Is he . . . ?"

The vet put his stethoscope to Boris's ribcage. He nodded. "Yes," he said, "he's gone. Would you like me to leave you alone for a moment, just to say goodbye?"

"Yes," said Toby, "if that's OK?"

The vet and the nurse left the room and Toby and Melinda stood over Boris, stroking his warm, lifeless body and squeezing each other's hands. Melinda sniffed. Toby glanced at her. There were tears rolling down her heavily made-up cheeks. "Poor old Boris," she said. "It's so sad."

"I know," soothed Toby, "I know."

"But at least they're together now. Him and Gus. Up there," she said, casting her eyes upwards.

"Do you think?" said Toby, who tended towards an unromanticized view of death.

"Of course," said Melinda. "He's an angel now, too. A beautiful little angel cat with wings, flying off to find his daddy. That's all he ever wanted. His daddy. Isn't that right, little one?" She tickled Boris's dead head and wiped some tears from her cheek.

"Come on," said Toby, who was starting to feel a little bit uncomfortable himself, "let's go home."

"But what about Boris? What shall we do with Boris?"

"I don't know," said Toby. "I assume that they sort of deal with that."

"Oh, no," she cried, "we can't leave him here. We need to give him a proper burial. A proper farewell. See him on his way."

"We do?"

"Of course," she said. "It's the decent thing to do."

It was raining by the time they returned that afternoon with Boris, now cold and somewhat stiff, in his box. Toby ventured into the garden shed, and rifled round for a while, searching through piles of compost sacks, wheelbarrows, old furniture, bicycle tyres and flower pots for a spade. He emerged five minutes later covered in cobwebs and clutching a trowel.

"Couldn't find a spade," he said breathlessly to Melinda. "I don't think, in retrospect, that I ever actually had one."

"I'll get you one for Christmas, love."

Toby smiled, grimly, and started to dig, in a spot selected by Melinda at the bottom of the garden. The earth was wet and smelled like old dogs. Melinda stood above him for a while, holding an umbrella, but soon retreated inside when she realized how long it was going to take. A mouse scampered past at one point, tiny and brown and utterly petrified. Toby clutched his heart, but carried on digging. His hands were icy cold and his knees were wet and muddy. Life didn't get much bleaker than this.

Melinda brought Boris outside, once the hole was dug, and Toby gently lowered the towel-wrapped corpse into the hole. Melinda threw a handful of wet mud on top of the towel and immediately went inside to wash her hands. Toby covered the hole as quickly as he could, then went indoors. He wanted a bath, a big hot steaming bath in his beautiful new bathroom. He wanted to lie in his bath for an hour and get warm to the core and contemplate his existence, maybe even start a poem. But Melinda was standing in the doorway when he walked in, with a bottle of Cava in one hand and two glasses in the other.

"Oh," he said, "What's this in aid of?"

"We're having a wake."

"Oh, God. Really?"

"Yes. We've just buried someone. We have to have a wake."

"But I was just going to . . ."

"Come on," she said, pulling him by the elbow into the dining room, "take your coat off. Sit down. We're going to get pissed."

CHAPTER FIFTY-THREE

Leah had just noticed with some pleasure that it was nearly five o'clock and it still wasn't dark. It was the same realization that she had every single year at around this time and it was always a good moment. It meant she'd broken the back of winter, that the long hard slog of it was over. She opened her handbag, searching around for a packet of mints. Her hand passed over a note. She pulled it out and opened it up. It was Toby's note about swimming:

Dearest Leah, today I did three press-ups. I feel I am now ready to tackle swimming. If I promise not to attempt my butterfly stroke, would you permit me to join you next time you visit the baths? Yours, with affection, Toby x

She smiled and refolded the note. It was about the fortieth time she'd read it and every time it made her smile. She loved his old-fashioned turn of phrase and the fact that he signed the note with a kiss, like a girl. The doorbell tinkled and she glanced up. It was Jack. She had the curious sensation of two good moments blending into one another and doubling in size. She smiled widely.

"Jack! Hello!"

"Good afternoon, Leah. You look very happy!"

"Oh, don't be fooled. It's just a momentary lapse."

Jack pulled a concerned face. "You aren't happy?"

She smiled. "I'm fine. How are you?"

"Excellent. I've been on a diet and I've lost nearly a half a stone."

She eyed him up and down. He looked exactly the same. "Well done!" she said. "You look great."

"Thank you. And I have to say, Leah, that you are looking more scrumptious than ever."

"Scrumptious?!"

"Yes. Like a delicious pudding. Something rich and creamy, with whipped cream on top. *Scrumptious!*"

"Right," she laughed uncertainly. "I'm not sure how to take that, but thank you, anyway."

"A compliment!" he smiled. "Take it as a compliment. But I did not come here today to give you compliments. I came here to invite you to dinner."

"Oh!"

"Yes. I have a professional kitchen, a spectacular dining hall and no one to cook for. I have been waiting and waiting for you to knock on my door, but you never came. And now my wife has taken my girls away for a whole week! Taken them skiing! So — here I am, all alone in my big house. Imploring you to join me for dinner. Bring your special friend, if you like?"

"My special friend?"

"Yes, I assume a woman as beautiful as you must have a boyfriend?"

"Yes. I do, actually."

"Ah," Jack sighed.

"But, if it's OK, I'd love to bring my friend Toby. And maybe another friend of mine. A woman?"

"A woman! Yes. Please. A woman, for Jack. You are so kind, lovely Leah. So kind."

Leah smiled.

"Is she pretty, this woman? In fact, no, no, don't tell me. Let it be a surprise. I will imagine a very ugly woman with yellow teeth and stringy hair and tattoos all over her, and then I can only be pleased."

"She doesn't have yellow teeth. She's —"

"Shhh," Jack put his finger to his lips. "No more. No more. I will see you and Toby and your ugly woman at eight o'clock, on Saturday. Come hungry. I will cook enough for a dozen."

CHAPTER FIFTY-FOUR

The sun had gone for the day, the windows of the dining room were black mirrors and Toby and Melinda had been drinking for two hours.

"You're a funny old sod, Toby, you know that?"

Toby shrugged. "Am I?"

"Yes. I've never met anyone like you before." Melinda poured the last of their second bottle of Cava into her glass and let the empty bottle bang onto the table top.

"Oh," said Toby. "Is that a good thing or a bad thing?"

"Good, of course. You're a good person. But it's taken me a while to realize that."

"Oh, God, has it?"

"Yeah. I thought you were a bit up yourself when I first moved in. You know, a bit stand-offish. You kept yourself to yourself, didn't stop for a chat. But the past few weeks, you seem to have come out of yourself a bit. And you're lovely, you know that? Really lovely. You've got so much going for yourself, you really have. But you don't half make life difficult for yourself."

"What do you mean?"

"I mean — you should get out more, make more of yourself. You know, you're not a bad-looking fella. Got a bit of a schnozz on you, but you've got a lovely face. Beautiful brown eyes. And yet . . ."

"And yet what?"

"Well, your hair, those . . . *things* growing out of your cheeks, the way you dress. You're not doing yourself any favours."

Toby blinked incredulously at Melinda, sure that at any minute now she would start cackling and say, "Only joking, love. You look gorgeous." But she didn't.

"You know what would suit you, Toby? A shaved head. You know, like Justin Timberlake. A pair of clippers. Number one. The whole lot — off."

"My head is rather a strange shape. I'm not exactly sure that would be the best look for . . ."

"And you should probably take the time for a trip to a dental hygienist."

"Oh, my God — are you suggesting that I have halitosis?"

"Oh, Lord, *no*. I wouldn't be so rude. I just mean, for a bit of a polish, a bit of a sparkle. Nothing ages a person more than uncared-for teeth, you know."

"Really?"

"Yes. I mean, you've got a lot going for you, really. You've got this beautiful house; you've obviously got a bit of money coming in judging from what you've been spending lately; you're a *poet*. What woman can resist a poet? But you really need a serious image overhaul. I mean — what's with all the second-hand clothes?"

"What's wrong with second-hand clothes?"

"Well, they *smell*, don't they? I mean — *other people* have worn them." She shuddered delicately and got to her feet. "There's enough good cheap clothes out there. You don't need to buy other people's cast-offs."

"But I've bought a couple of things, lately. I mean — a jacket, some shoes, a coat."

"Yes. I saw. And very nice they are, too. But you need to start from scratch, Toby, love. Start all over again." She threw him a look of deep sympathy and reached into a cardboard box on the floor for a bottle of tequila. "Shots?" she said, waving it at him.

Toby winced. He was already more drunk than seemed reasonable for a Monday night.

"Ooh, go on. We're having such a nice time. Let's just go for it."

He smiled. "Go on, then. But just a little one."

"I'll come shopping with you, if you like. Steer you in the right direction."

Toby stared at Melinda for a moment, in stasis, unable to think or breathe or move. She was wearing a cropped cream jumper, knitted out of what looked like old bath mats, tight pink cotton trousers, brown pixie boots and hoop earrings. Her hair was in a frizzy ponytail and her nails were painted brown. Even if Toby could bear to admit to himself that he might be in need of an image overhaul, Melinda was the last person on God's earth whom he would allow to assist him.

"That's very sweet of you," he said, "really. But I've pretty much spent all my money now, on the house."

"Ah, well. The offer's there, if you need it. It's lovely of you, you know, making the house so nice for us all. I mean, don't get me wrong, I liked it before, but what you've done — it's stunning. I would never have had you down as having such good taste. Would have thought you'd have gone for all that sort of antiquey, junk-shoppy stuff. You know — second-hand!"

"Yes, well," he smiled, and accepted a teacup full of tequila. "I surprised myself."

She held her teacup aloft. "A toast," she said, "to you. For all your kindness. God bless you, Toby, for looking after me and my boy. God knows where we'd be without you. Cheers."

They banged their cups together and downed the drinks.

"Toby — can I ask you a personal question?"

"Er, OK."

"When was the last time you had sex?"

"God, er, um, well, it must have been, probably about, fifteen years ago?"

"No! Oh, my God, that makes me feel better!"

"Why — when was the last time you, er . . .?"

"Last summer. In Turkey. Just before I moved back here."

"Oh, I see. And that, I assume, was the man with whom you were living."

"Living with? *Engaged* to."

"Oh, right."

"Yes. I should have been married by now. I should have been Mrs Akhun Erbakan. Then the fucker hit me."

"Ooh," Toby recoiled.

"Yes. I know. Managed to get to forty-four years of age without a man ever laying a finger on me and then, *bam*."

"God, did he hurt you?"

"No, not really. It wasn't a *beating*, as such. But I was out of there faster than you could say one-way ticket to Luton airport. No man hits Melinda McNulty. Nuh-uh." She shook her head defiantly and poured two more shots of tequila. "Never been so happy to see English soil. Nearly kissed the tarmac when we hit the runway. And then to find that my beautiful boy was living in this gorgeous house in such a nice part of London. Kind of killed my travel bug off for good."

"So, Melinda, you know, I've always wondered and I've never really wanted to ask before, but why . . . why did you leave Con? Why didn't you bring him up?"

"Ah, yes," Melinda took a sip of tequila. "Bad mother. Naughty girl. *Slapped wrists*." She slapped her own wrists. "I don't know. I've asked myself that question so many times, and I think what it all boiled down to was *confidence*, you know? I was twenty-six, but a *young* twenty-six. Con's father didn't want to know. And I tried, I really did try. I gave up work and spent six months at home being a full-time mum, but I just felt like I was so *crap* at it. Like I couldn't do anything right. He kept getting ill and he wouldn't feed properly and all the women at the clinic made me feel like it was my fault. And then my mum would walk in and Con's little face would light up and he'd stop crying and he'd feed like an angel and I just thought, you know what, what am I doing here in this miserable fucking country with this baby who hates me? He's not happy; I'm not happy. And I knew my mum would do a better job of bringing him up than me. So I got this rep job based in Spain. I came home every couple of weeks at first, to see Con, but in the end I couldn't handle it any more. The coming and going, the emotional stress of it all. And they had such a unit, Con and my mum. They were such a little team. I felt kind of sidelined. So, in the end, I just stopped. Just tried to forget about him . . ." She sniffed and dabbed her eyes with a piece of kitchen roll. "Not that I ever did. You can't forget your own child, can you? Not when you're a mother."

"So, when did you see him next? After the last time?"

"At mum's funeral. Oh, God, that was dreadful. It really was. Can you imagine? The harlot mother with the Spanish tan turning up after twelve years, in some miserable fucking crematorium in Seven Sisters. And then seeing Con, for the first time, this big lad, so handsome, so sad, so good. And everyone looking at me, pointing, that's her, that's Con's mum, that's Edie's girl, the one who ran away to Spain and didn't give a fuck." She shuddered. "Worst day of my life. But then" — a small smile lit her face — "after that, once my mum was buried and gone and everyone had stopped staring, when it was just me and Con sitting in the pub after, you know what? It was perfect. He didn't judge me. He didn't guilt-trip me. He just comforted me, you know, because my mum was dead. He blew me away, just totally blew me away."

"So, why did you leave again? Why did you go to Turkey?"

She shrugged and sighed. "Shit. I don't know. We'd just got this flat together, me and Con, a really fancy place in Leyton. I went for the most expensive place I could find, no expense spared. I really wanted to show Con that I was serious about us, about our relationship. I was stupid, really. I thought that we were going to have this *amazing* experience, that we were going to go out together all the time, get to know each other, just kind of lose ourselves in each other, really. And then when I realized that he had his own life, his own friends, that he wasn't going to make me the centre of his world, I got the hump, I suppose. Thought fuck you. And did what I always did. Ran away. It was only supposed to be a holiday, but then I met Akhun and suddenly I was the centre of someone's world and I thought, well, Con doesn't need me, nobody needs me. So I stayed. I didn't think he'd miss me. It didn't occur to me that he'd be kicked out of that flat. I just thought he'd be fine. So when I came back and found out that he'd been living rough — oh, my God, I wanted to slit my own wrists. I've never felt so awful in my life, just thinking of my poor beautiful boy, in a doorway, nowhere to call home. I keep myself awake at night a lot over that, I can tell you. And I will never, ever leave him again, that's for sure."

"Well, yes, I can see how you feel, but surely at some point a mother has to let their child . . . *do their own thing*."

"Well, if Con wants to get rid of me, he'll have to ask. Otherwise, I'm stuck like glue. Me and men —

we're done. There's only one man in my life now, and that's Con."

"Oh," said Toby. "I'm not entirely sure . . ."

"What?"

"Well, you're very young still. And you're very good-looking. It seems a shame to cut yourself off from the, you know, the possibility of . . . *love*."

"Nah," she shook her head, "I've tried love and it sucks. Big time. The only love that counts is the love you have for your children. Anything else is just hot air."

They downed the rest of their tequilas and sat in contemplative silence for a moment. And then the door bell rang.

Toby pulled himself heavily to his feet. He was horribly drunk. The floor felt like sponge beneath his feet and cardboard boxes kept veering away from the walls and into his path. He banged his toe against the corner of the stairs and couldn't remember which way to turn the handle to open the front door. It took him a minute or two to place the man standing on his doorstep with a suitcase and bleeding nose. He knew he looked familiar, but he needed more information to identify him.

"Hello, Toby," said the man.

"Hello, er . . ."

"Tim. Remember? Ruby's friend. Is she here?"

"God. I don't know. I've been . . . I haven't really been paying attention. She might be. Let me check." He stood at the foot of the stairs. "RUBY! RUBY!"

She appeared on the landing, clutching a cigarette and looking annoyed.

"What?"

"Your friend's here."

"What friend?"

"Er . . ." Toby sighed. He'd forgotten already. "Sorry, what's your name again?"

"Tim," hissed the man, dabbing some blood from his nose.

"TIM!"

"What?!" cried Ruby. "Oh, God."

Toby smiled apologetically at Tim. "She's just coming. Do you want to . . .?" He held the door open for him. "I'm drunk, I'm afraid. I hasten to add that I rarely get drunk. Particularly not on a Monday night. But we've just buried the cat, you know, and one thing led to another and, aaaah, here she is . . ."

"Oh, my God, Tim. What happened to your nose?"

"Sophie."

"What?"

"Sophie hit me."

"She *hit* you? Jesus. Why?"

"Because I told her about you."

"Oh, fuck. Tim."

"And I've left her. Look." He pointed at his silver Samsonite. "I've left her, Ruby. I'm free."

CHAPTER FIFTY-FIVE

As Leah approached her front door that night, a taxi stopped in the road and a man got out. He hauled a large suitcase out behind him and wheeled it along the pavement and up the stairs of the Peacock House. Leah watched from the other side of the road, wondering who he was and what he was doing. It occurred to her that maybe it was Toby's father, but he looked too young. And, besides, Toby's father wasn't due until next month. She stood and waited for someone to come to the door of the house. It was Toby. He looked flushed and a bit unsteady. She couldn't hear what was being said, but it seemed that the man was a stranger to Toby. Eventually, Toby held open the door, and the man walked in. And then the door closed again.

Leah stared at the house for a moment or two. Her skin was crawling with curiosity. Who was that man? Why did he have a suitcase? Whose friend was he? She'd completely lost touch with the comings and goings in the Peacock House since Amitabh had moved back in. But now she had the perfect reason to catch up. Jack's invitation.

She crossed the road and knocked on the door. Toby opened it. It was clear, now that she was in close proximity to him, that he was extremely drunk.

"Oh, my goodness," he said, "Leah. How totally lovely to see you."

"It's been a while."

"I know. It has. Entirely my fault."

"No. Mine. I'm sorry. I've been meaning to come over for days now . . ."

"Well," Toby smiled, "you're here now. And you find me somewhat drunk, I'm afraid. Melinda and I have been having a wake."

"Oh, no. Who for?"

"For Boris. Little Borissy Boris. No longer with us, sadly. But happily, too. If you believe in angels. Do you believe in angels, Leah?"

Leah smiled. Toby was funny when he was drunk. "No," she said, "I don't. But apparently you only start believing in angels when someone you love has died. Do you believe in angels?"

Toby shook his head. "No," he said, "no. Especially not cat angels."

"What about spirits?"

"No. No spirits. Except, maybe tequila. Would you like one?"

Leah blinked at him.

"No. I suppose that's not really a particularly tempting offer, at seven o'clock on a Monday night."

Toby leaned against the doorframe and smiled at Leah. She smiled back at him. "Do you think I should shave off all my hair?" he said, rubbing his hands over his unruly mass of curls.

Leah laughed. "What?"

"Melinda reckons my hair's a state. Said I should shave it all off, like some pop-star fellow. What do you think, Leah?"

"No," she shook her head and laughed again. "You've got the wrong-shaped head for shaved hair."

"That's exactly what I said." He straightened himself up. "*Exactly*. You're very observant, Leah. It's remarkable, what you pick up about people. I wish I was more like you."

Leah shrugged and smiled. "You're more observant than you think."

"I think not. For example, if I were more observant, I might have guessed that you and your ex-boyfriend would be reunited. And if I were really observant I'd have predicted that Ruby's new boyfriend would arrive on my doorstep on a Monday night, having left his wife. But I am not. I see nothing. I hear nothing. I sit alone, disconnected. An island . . ."

"No man is an island, Toby."

"Well, then I am a headland and you, Leah, are the causeway."

He smiled weakly at her and let himself fall against the doorpost again. "Oh, God," he groaned, letting his head fall onto his fist. "Listen to me. Just listen to me. What a drunken, pretentious idiot. And I am absolutely sure you didn't come here to listen to my pitiful blatherings. What can I do for you, lovely, lovely Leah? Would you like to come in?"

She turned to glance at her flat, where the lit-up windows showed signs of life. "No," she said. "No. I'd better get back . . ."

"Yes, yes, yes. Of course, of course, of course." Toby nodded emphatically.

"But I just wanted to let you know, Jack came into the shop today, Italian Jack?"

"Oh, yes?"

"And guess what? He's invited me over for dinner on Saturday night. And he said I could bring whoever I wanted."

"Well, well, well."

"So? Are you free? Saturday night?"

"What? Me?"

"Yes. You and Melinda."

"Oh, my God. You mean, this is it? The big set-up?"

"Yes," said Leah. "That's exactly what I mean."

"Oh, God. How exciting. I mean, yes, I'm free. And I'm sure Melinda will be. *Melinda!*" he called over his shoulder.

"*Yes?*"

"*Are you free for dinner on Saturday night?*"

"*Depends. Who's asking?*"

"*Me. I'm asking.*"

"*Then, yes.*"

Toby smiled. "Excellent," he said. "So, who'll be there?"

"You, me, Jack and Melinda."

"And what about Am . . . Ama . . . ?"

"No. Not Amitabh. He'd hate it."

"Well, that's wonderful. Just great."

"And also — isn't it about time we went for that swim?"

"Oh, so you did get my note, then?"

"Yes. Amitabh gave it to me. I've just been, you know . . . ?"

"Yes, I do know. I know, I know, I know. I am *knowing*."

"So, shall we go?"

"Go where, lovely Leah?"

"Shall we go swimming? This week, maybe?"

"Yes. We shall. Definitely. When would you like to go?"

"Thursday afternoon? It's my day off."

"Thursday afternoon, it is. I will invest in some new trunks. And maybe a St Tropez Spray Tan."

"I'm going out on Saturday night," she said to Amitabh a few moments later.

"Oh, right," he said, untangling the wires on his headphones. "Where to?"

"Out with Toby."

"What — him over the road?"

"Yes."

He threw her a look.

"Why?" she said, defensively. "What's wrong with that?"

"There's nothing *wrong* with it," he said. "It's just a bit weird, that's all."

"Weird?"

"Yeah. Weird. I mean — he's strange. He's not the usual sort of person you'd be friends with."

"He's not strange at all. He's completely charming, as a matter of fact."

"OK, OK. No need to be so defensive. I'm just not sure about him, that's all. Do you think maybe he fancies you?"

Leah spilled farfalle into a pan of boiling water and sighed. "No, of course he doesn't fancy me."

"Is he gay?"

"No. Don't be stupid. He used to be married."

"We both know that means nothing . . ."

"Well, anyway. He's just not. He's in love with that dark-haired girl, Ruby, so he can't be."

"How the hell do you know that? Did he tell you?"

"No. It's just . . . *obvious*."

Leah stirred a fork through the pasta and pulled a jar of pesto sauce out of the fridge. She was finding this conversation very annoying. She was finding Amitabh very annoying. This whole scenario was putting her in mind of *Truly Madly Deeply*, where the dead lover comes back to the grieving woman as a ghost and completely pisses her off. Amitabh was, without a doubt, a warm and lovely person. But he was also incredibly passive and annoyingly flaccid. He existed in a bubble of here and now-ness. He didn't look at big pictures or ask himself big questions. It was all about cosiness and comfort and general ease of passage through life. He had no nooks or crannies, no interesting little corners of intriguing mystery. Where Toby was like an old Victorian bureau, full of tiny drawers and cubby holes and secret compartments, Amitabh was more of a blanket box.

"Where's he taking you, then, the old charmer?"

"We're going for dinner," she said.

"Very nice," said Amitabh, plugging his earphones into his hi-fi, "very nice indeed."

Leah forked some pesto out of the jar and into a bowl and ground her teeth together, very gently.

CHAPTER FIFTY-SIX

Ruby opened her eyes.

Her gaze alighted upon a large aluminium suitcase.

She shut them again.

She took a deep breath and turned her head to the left. Tim was lying facing her, staring at her. She jumped.

"Sorry," he said, pulling her hair away from her eyes. "Sorry. I just . . . it's so amazing, waking up with you."

"Oh, Jesus, Tim. God, I've only just woken up. Give me a chance to, you know . . ."

She rolled onto her side away from him.

"This is a bit fucking mega, isn't it?" said Tim.

"You could say that."

He rolled towards her and kissed her shoulder. "It'll be fine, Ruby-chews. you'll see. I'll make sure everything is fine."

He got out of bed and started to dress himself. Ruby glanced at him from the corner of her eye, at his large, white body, at the ski tan that stopped under his chin, like he'd been dunked in a can of creosote, at the black fur that sprouted from his chest in the shape of angel wings and the soft penis that hung from beneath his belly like a naked abseiler, trapped beneath an overhang. She sighed and rolled onto her back. "Where are you going?" she said.

"To the office. I've just got back from holiday. I can't take any time off. But — on Saturday, you and I are going flat-hunting."

"We are?"

"Yes. Where do you fancy? I've always fancied living in Clerkenwell. How about that? A warehouse apartment. Or what about Soho? A nice little penthouse in the middle of town?"

"What — you're going to buy me a flat?"

"No. Not buy. Rent. For now."

"But I can't afford to pay the rent here, let alone in the West End."

"Don't be silly," he said, smiling at her, indulgently. "You don't have to pay anything. That's what I'm here for. I tell you what . . ." He looped a Thomas Pink tie around his neck and folded his shirt collar down over it. ". . . you think about it. Make a list of places you'd like to live. We'll talk about it tonight."

"OK," said Ruby, whose mood had improved rapidly at the thought of quirky little one-bedroom flats above sex shops in Soho, "let's."

CHAPTER FIFTY-SEVEN

Con opened the yellow carton and pulled out his Big Mac. He considered it for a moment before he brought it to his mouth, stared at the pale flecks of sesame, the tongue of sludge-coloured meat emerging from the lips of the bun. He peeled it open and gazed at the road accident of relish, the damp lettuce, the smear of glistening mayonnaise. He closed it and put it back in the carton.

He was sitting in the tea room at work, surrounded by men and newspapers, half-eaten sandwiches and plastic cups. He picked up the paper carton of french fries and ate them rhythmically, robotically, while he flicked through the *Evening Standard*.

"Connor McNulty, I don't believe it! I turn my back for five minutes and you're back on the McDonald's!"

Con looked up. So did everyone else in the break room. It was Daisy. She was wearing brown leather shorts with a cream blouse and grey waistcoat. Her hair was in a thin plait and she was clutching a big paper bag from the deli round the corner.

"Daisy," he said. "You're back. I didn't realize."

"Yes." She put the paper bag down on the table and took the seat next to him. "It was my first day back yesterday, actually."

"God, how are you? You look . . . *great*."

"Yes," she nodded. "I feel pretty good. It was great to have some time at home. Some good old-fashioned parental TLC. How are you?"

"Yeah. I'm good."

"Good," she smiled, and pulled the paper bag towards her. "Well, I've got us panini. Tuna and cheese, or ham and cheese. Which do you fancy? If you've got any room after all those *McDonald's chips*, that is."

Con took the tuna panini and grinned. "Our kitchen's being replaced," he said. "Nowhere to make sandwiches."

"That's no excuse." Daisy licked some grease off her thumb. "That's what delis are for."

"You know what, though?" He pointed at his Big Mac. "I couldn't eat it. Honestly, I just looked at, I mean *really* looked at it. And that was that. Had to shut the lid on it."

"Hoo-rah!" she cried. "You are cured! My work here is done."

Con smiled and bit into his panini.

"So," she said, carefully. "I missed you."

Con glanced at her. He tried to think of something to say that wasn't reciprocal, but wasn't heartless either. He couldn't. He smiled wanly at her instead.

"I kind of . . . I don't know," she said, "I'd kind of thought you might visit. Or phone."

"Yeah," he said, staring at his sandwich. "Yeah. I know. I just . . . it was . . ."

"It's OK," she said. "I wasn't expecting you to explain yourself. I mean, I know, illness can be quite scary. Especially at our age. I know it's not something everyone can deal with. But, a phone call might have been nice."

"Yeah," he said. "You're right. I'm sorry."

"Mimi said . . ." she paused.

"What?"

"She said you might have been a bit freaked out by our parents. All that stuff about coming to stay at the house."

"Nah," he shook his head. "Why would I be freaked out by that?"

"I don't know. Maybe it was a bit much? A bit soon."

"No. I told you. Your parents are cool."

"Then why?" she said.

"Why what?"

"Why . . ." — her eyes filled with tears — "why haven't I heard anything from you for nearly two weeks?"

He stared at her, desperately trying to find an explanation that wouldn't make her cry even more. "Oh, God, Daisy . . ."

"Is it me? Is it actually nothing to do with me being ill or my family? Is it actually just that you're not interested?" A tear fell from her eye and landed on her cheek. It rolled down towards the corner of her mouth where she wiped it away. "Because if that's the case then I'd really like to know."

“No,” he said, “of course not.”

“Then what is it? Because, really, it’s just not entirely normal, is it, to write someone a poem, tell them that you love them, then leave them in hospital, seriously ill, and not get in touch again?”

The room fell silent, except for the tinny sound of Rachel Stevens on Capital radio and Daisy’s voice.

“It doesn’t make any sense, to me,” she continued. “None at all. And I came in here, I’d made all these excuses for you — that you were intimidated by my illness, my family. And I was going to be so cool and everything was going to get resolved and be OK. But it’s not, is it?”

Con glanced at the other blokes in the room, out of the corner of his eye. They were all watching, listening. He shrugged, “Everything’s cool,” he said.

“Is it?”

“Yeah. I’m just. It’s just, not . . . *God*.”

“No. It’s fine.” Daisy dropped her panini onto the table top and stood up. “Really. It’s absolutely fine. Don’t bother trying to explain. It’ll only make things worse.” She gripped the straps of her handbag with one chalky-white hand, stared at Con for a moment and then she left.

The room fell silent. Con listened to his heart throbbing under his ribcage. He let his sandwich fall out of his hand.

“Jesus, Con,” said someone, at the back of the room, “you total fucking bastard.”

CHAPTER FIFTY-EIGHT

Melinda came to Toby's room on Tuesday evening. She was holding a box.

"Now," she said, sailing past him and towards his bed. "Don't freak out, but I've come to sort you out."

"Sort me out what?"

She opened the box and pulled out a black contraption with a cord coming out of it. It was about the size of a mobile phone. She looked round the skirting boards to locate an electricity socket, then she plugged the contraption in. "Now," she said, wheeling his office chair away from his PC and towards his bed, "come over here." She patted the seat. "Sit down."

"Er, Melinda, what . . . ?"

"Trust me Toby. This is for your own good. You will never, ever regret this, not for a minute. Now — sit — down."

He followed her instructions and glanced at the black contraption in her hand, nervously. He stood up again, sharply, when she switched it on and it started vibrating very, very loudly.

"Oh, Jesus," he said, staring at it in horror, "What are you going to do to me?"

"Just sit down," she said, "and you'll see."

Toby tried to relax. He assumed that the vibrating black thing was some kind of massage device, and prepared himself for a pleasant sensation between his shoulder blades. Instead Melinda started rubbing it against his cheekbones. She brought it back and forth across the left side of his face and, he had to admit, it wasn't an entirely unpleasant feeling.

"Is that nice?" she said.

"Well, it's not awful, but . . ." He stopped when his gaze fell upon the empty box sitting on his bed. It had a photograph of the contraption on the lid and the words "Hair styling kit" and "clippers". He looked at the floor. Tiny tumbleweeds of his hair lay on the carpet. He slapped his hand against his cheek, where for nearly half his life there had been hair. He felt skin, soft and smooth, like the underbelly of a kitten. "Oh, my God! Melinda! No!"

He got to his feet and felt the contraption skidding through his hair.

"Shit, Toby, will you sit still?"

"Oh, God," he grabbed the side of his head and felt a channel of baldness. "Oh, Jesus!"

"Toby, just sit down."

"No! I won't. Oh, God, what have you done?! *What have you done?!*" He raced to the mirror and gazed at his reflection. He had one sideburn and a section of hair missing. He looked like he had a terrible, terrible illness.

"Toby, don't panic. Come over here and I'll sort it out for you."

"I can't believe you've shaved my sideburn off."

"Well, what did you think I was going to do with a pair of clippers?"

"I didn't know they were clippers."

"Well, what on earth did you think they were?"

"I don't know, some kind of massage device. I thought you were going to give me a massage."

Melinda slapped her hands over her mouth and let out a snort of laughter. "Oh, shit," she said. "Oh, fuck a duck, Toby. I'm sorry. I thought everyone knew what clippers look like."

"Yes, well, apparently not." Toby looked at himself in the mirror again. He looked away, in horror. "Oh, Christ, Melinda. What are we going to do?"

CHAPTER FIFTY-NINE

Con breathed in. He touched his hair and peered into a blackened window at his blurred reflection. He breathed out again. Then he pushed open the door to the fashion department, with an air that he hoped was breezy and businesslike. The first thing he saw was the back of Daisy's head. She was standing over the fax machine, watching a document ooze through the mechanism, page by page. She was wearing a blue thighlength sweater over a cream lace petticoat with tan boots, and her hair was in a bun. Con moved his trolley quickly to the post tray near Daisy's desk, hoping that she wouldn't turn round and see him. A girl in hornrimmed glasses passed him a Jiffy bag, unsmilingly. He dropped it into his trolley and kept moving. Just as he reached the post tray, Daisy's phone started ringing. She tutted and sighed and turned round. When she saw Con hovering near her desk, she went stiff, momentarily, before looking away. She returned to her desk and picked up her phone.

"*Hello. Daisy Beens.*"

Con turned and started loading his trolley from the tray. Daisy was chatting to someone. It sounded like a friend.

A minute later she hung up and walked towards him. "I've got a few more letters," she said, coldly. "Can you wait a sec."

He nodded, tersely, and waited while she sorted through her mail. He stared through the window at the blotchy, drizzle-laden sky outside. Someone a few desks along squealed with laughter. "No!" she breathed down the phone. "That's the most outrageous thing I've ever heard!"

A middle-aged woman came out of an office, followed by a harassed young minion clutching a pile of notes. Daisy turned and handed Con a small wedge of cream envelopes. "First class," she said, "please." And then she walked back to the fax machine and picked up the paper document.

Con pushed his trolley back into the corridor and exhaled, his flesh crawling with embarrassment, guilt and sadness.

CHAPTER SIXTY

Toby glanced at the time on his PC.

11.23a.m.

He sighed and pulled his boots from underneath his bed.

He wound a scarf round his neck and picked up an old mug.

He paused before he left his room, and glanced at himself in the mirror. He still couldn't countenance the more or less hairless man who stared back at him. They'd been forced to take the whole lot off. Melinda had tried a short-back-and-sides, but Toby had looked like a neo-Nazi, so she'd just kept going with clippers until he was left with a smattering of stubble. The sideburns, of course, were beyond rescuing. She'd taken the second one off and Toby had watched it fall to the floor in tufts with a sad, heartbroken gulp.

Seeing so much of his face alarmed him. He constantly felt like he had his flies undone, or his underwear showing. He stroked his cheeks continually, feeling for stuff that used to be there. His scalp was bizarre, pink and unaired, like a testicle. He wore hats pretty much all the time now. Melinda had insisted that he looked gorgeous, "like that bloke in *Doctor Who*".

But to his eyes he just looked bald — and slightly alarming. He bared his teeth at his reflection, and gulped.

In half an hour he would be at the dentist. He'd phoned to book an appointment with the hygienist and they'd somehow, by some kind of dental stealth, booked him in for a standard appointment, too. He hadn't been to the dentist in years. They would, he knew it, insist on pulling out half his teeth and then on drilling holes in the rest of them. He would be in there for at least three hours and would leave feeling as if he'd been chewing a pint glass. If he was lucky.

Toby wasn't scared of dentists — just annoyed by them. *Doctors* didn't make you show up twice a year just to check that you were OK. Doctors waited until you felt ill enough to show up of your own volition. Why couldn't dentists do the same? Why did they make you feel guilty if you didn't see them for a while? Surely it was a good thing if you didn't come, as it meant that you weren't in any pain, that things were ticking along nicely.

He took his boots and his mug downstairs. He put the mug on the black granite work surface of his new kitchen and pulled on his boots. The kitchen fitters had finished last night and it was, of course, the most beautiful kitchen Toby had ever seen. It had aubergine-coloured cabinets and a six-ring hob and a barbecue and a breakfast bar and an American fridge with a water dispenser. The kitchen floors had been stripped and stained to look like American walnut and there were a dozen twinkling halogen lights hanging from tracks on the ceiling. And, thanks to Damian's canny buying, the whole thing had come in at only £5,000 more than he'd meant to spend.

Melinda's food boxes were piled up by the back door, waiting to be unpacked tonight. Sticking out of the top was her tequila. Before he'd had a chance to question what he was doing, Toby had removed the cap and swallowed three large slugs. He didn't trust anaesthetics. If some dentist was going to start slicing his mouth open, he wanted to be sure he wasn't going to feel anything. He tipped the bottle to his lips again and swallowed some more. He glanced at the bottle in his hands. It was nearly empty. He finished it.

CHAPTER SIXTY-ONE

It was three-twenty. Leah had arranged to meet Toby outside Park Road Baths at three o'clock. She glanced up and down the road once more before giving up and making her way inside.

The pool was quiet. She liked coming on her day off. She padded barefoot to the end of the pool and slid into the water. It was lukewarm, viscous, immediately calming. She ploughed up and down the pool, feeling the tension leave her shoulder blades, her neck, her hips. After four lengths, she stopped and hugged the edge of the pool for a moment. And that was when she saw him.

She wasn't sure it was him at first, the tall, thin man in the tiny schoolboy Speedos that clung film-like to every lump and bump of his genitals. He had no hair and a very strange lopsided face. But as he approached and began to smile, she knew without a doubt. It was Toby.

"Oh, my God," she said, "Toby. You look so . . . what happened to your . . .? Oh, my God."

"I'm a monster," he said. "Melinda attacked me with a pair of clippers, then a man called Mr Shiyarayagan pulled out one of my teeth." He opened his mouth to show her the gap. "Now I am virtually naked in a public place for the first time since my school days. Bits of me are just falling off. I am being slowly disassembled. By next week, I will be bereft of any covering at all. I'll just be bones."

The left side of his face was slightly swollen and palsied with anaesthetic. His voice was muffled. "And I'm sorry I'm so late. It all took so long at the dentist's. I saw the hygienist, too, who felt that my teeth needed nearly an hour's worth of her attention." He shook his head, disbelievingly. "It's been a very strange week."

"Well," said Leah, "you may as well continue the theme. Jump in!"

"Oh, God." Toby peered at the water. "I really . . . this is just so . . . I haven't been in a pool for so long. I mean, maybe I can't even swim any more?"

"Of course you can. Come on. Jump in."

Toby was looking a little bit wobbly. He stood on the side of the pool contemplating the water, swaying slightly.

"Are you OK?"

"Yes," he said distractedly. "I am. It's just the air in here, it's so . . . *blue*, isn't it? Doesn't it make you feel light-headed?"

"No," laughed Leah.

"You're probably used to it. It must be the chlorine. Or something. I have to say, I'm feeling really a bit odd." He took a step closer to the edge and closed his eyes. He swayed unsteadily to the left, then he swayed unsteadily to the right. Then his entire being, all six foot something of it, swayed forwards, poker straight and head first into the shallow end of the pool.

"Oh, my God, Toby!" Leah watched in horror as a thin plume of red ribboned its way up to the surface of the pool. Toby's body lay motionless on the bottom of the pool. The lifeguard blew a whistle and people started running towards them. Leah hooked her arms under Toby's armpits and brought him to the surface. "Oh, shit, Toby, are you OK?"

His eyes were closed and he had a large gash above his right eye. An elderly man appeared at Leah's side and helped her pull him from the pool. Leah scrambled out of the water and pushed her way to Toby through a cluster of people. "It's OK," she said, pushing past the lifeguard. "I'm a qualified first-aider." Toby was unconscious and bleeding profusely. She tipped his head backward and pinched his nose. Then she pulled his lips apart and brought her mouth down over his, to apply the kiss of life. Someone had pressed a towel to his forehead and someone else was calling an ambulance. Leah pushed her hands against Toby's chest, then blew into his mouth again. Still he didn't breathe. Still he didn't open his eyes.

"Here," said the lifeguard, pulling her back by the shoulder, "please get out of the way."

"No!" Leah pulled away from him and continued pumping. Finally, as she took her mouth away from his for the fourth time, Toby coughed. Leah rocked back onto her heels and exhaled, heavily. There was an audible sigh of relief from the crowd of onlookers. Toby coughed again and this time a fountain of chlorinated water left his mouth. The third time he coughed, he vomited, copiously, all down his chest and onto the tiled floor. The crowd of onlookers inched back.

Toby opened his eyes and looked straight at Leah. Then he looked round at the sea of faces. Then he sat up. "Leah," he croaked, looking at her in awe. "Did I just drown?"

"Yes," she nodded.

"But you saved me?"

She nodded again.

He touched his fingertips to his temple. "Am I bleeding?"

"Uh-huh. There's an ambulance coming."

"Oh, God, what's going on, Leah? What's happening to me?"

"It's fine," she soothed. "You'll be fine. Do you think you can stand up?"

"Yes," he said. "No. I don't know. Do you think I should try?"

"Yes."

"Oh, God," he said, glancing at the floor. "Oh, God. There's sick everywhere. Did I do that?"

"Yup."

"Oh, how disgusting. I'm so sorry. Did you have to kiss me, with, you know, *sick* on me?"

She smiled and helped him to his feet. "No," she said, "you did that after I kissed you."

"Oh, thank God." He took the bloodied towel from the man who'd been holding it against his head. "Thank you," he said. "Thank you, everybody. And I'm really sorry," he said to the lifeguard, "about the mess."

His foot hit a slippery patch of sick and he skidded slightly as they moved towards the changing rooms. He clung on to Leah, his bare skin against hers. She pulled him towards her by the waist and was struck by the feel of his flesh under her hands. It felt so hard, so vital, compared to Amitabh's softly upholstered body. She thought fleetingly of the hundreds of times she'd glimpsed Toby's backlit form in the window of his bedroom, of the occasional sightings of him on the street, bundled up in peculiar clothes, strange hats, an abundance of hair and layers and coverings. Even in the summer he covered his legs, his arms, his head. It was oddly gratifying, almost *thrilling*, to see him unwrapped, stripped bare of his hair, his clothes, his dignity. It made him real, not just another character in her own personal soap opera, but a *man*.

Someone retrieved Toby's clothes from the changing rooms and they sat together in reception, waiting for the ambulance.

"You'll need stitches in that," said Leah, peering underneath the bloodstained towel.

"Ah, well," said Toby wryly, "that just caps off my week, I suppose."

"I'm really sorry," said Leah. "I feel really guilty."

"Oh, no." He looked at her in concern. "Really, you mustn't feel guilty."

"Well, I do. It was my idea for you to come swimming. And now you're injured. You could have *died* in there, Toby."

"No," he said, "it's entirely my fault. I had tequila for breakfast . . ."

"You didn't?!"

"Yes. I'm ashamed to admit that I did. Not because I have a drink problem because, really, if I have any drink problem at all, it's that I don't drink *enough*. Although from my recent appearances you'd probably find that hard to believe. And then God knows what they gave me at the dentist. Gas and air and drugs and . . ." He shuddered. "I was a fool to come. But I've just been looking forward so much to seeing you . . ."

"Really?"

"Yes, it's all that's got me through the week. The light at the end of the tunnel."

"Oh, no. And look how it ended up."

He smiled at her. "It's ended up fine," he said. "I have a scar to add character to my face. And I've been kissed by a beautiful woman. Not that I can really remember much about it."

Leah smiled, feeling strangely delighted by his description of her as a beautiful woman. "It was very nice," she said. "You're a very good kisser."

"Even when I'm comatose?"

"Absolutely."

"Well, that's good to know," he said, "for the next time I'm kissing somebody in an unconscious state. And I'm so grateful to you for not letting that man save my life."

"The lifeguard?"

"Yes. I would have been horrified if I'd come to, with his greasy chops all over me."

Leah laughed. "That's why I didn't let him. I knew you'd be appalled."

He smiled at her and Leah was suddenly struck by how incredibly different he looked without his hair and muttonchops.

"You know something," she said, "I was wrong. You've got a very nice-shaped head. In fact, I prefer you without your hair."

"You do?"

"Yes," she said. "You used to look like Tom Baker. Now you look like Christopher Ecclestone."

"Oh," he said, "that's exactly what Melinda said. Is that a good thing, then?"

"Yes," she said, "it is. It's a very good thing indeed."

The ambulance pulled up outside the baths and Leah got into the back with Toby.

"You know you don't have to come with me, don't you?"

"Yes," she said. "I know. But I want to."

"Good," said Toby. He took hold of her hand. "Good."

They were still holding hands when the ambulance pulled up outside casualty ten minutes later.

CHAPTER SIXTY-TWO

Toby now resembled a Gorbals hard nut on a Sunday morning. They'd closed his gashed forehead with eight stitches and his eye had swollen up and taken on the colouration of the late stages of a Caribbean sunset. People kept their distance from him when he walked down the street, even in his brand-new Agnès B jacket and suede desert boots. He was a towering skinhead with a black eye, stitches and a missing tooth. He'd toyed with the idea of having a T-shirt printed up with the words "I am a poet" on the front and "I went to a very good public school" on the back. Everyone he came into contact with recoiled at the sight of him. In some ways it freaked him out; in other ways it liberated him.

It was like being in fancy dress, being at once conspicuous and anonymous. He felt he could take people by surprise, subvert the course of his day-to-day life just by leaving the house without a hat on.

And maybe that was why he suddenly found himself able to take the reins, to take control of his house. He had until next week to break the news to his housemates that he was selling the house and that they had to move out. After that he had three weeks to redecorate their rooms (regardless of whether or not they were still in them) and finish off the house. He couldn't afford to mess around any more. The longer he left it, the tougher it was going to be for everyone.

He headed for Con and Melinda's room first. The old Toby would have felt impolite and awkward knocking on his tenants' doors in the middle of the evening. The new Toby didn't give a shit.

Con opened the door to him. Melinda wasn't in the room.

"Hello, Con. D'you mind if I come in?"

"No. Sure." He was watching something with very loud shouty people in a studio. He reached for the remote control and turned down the volume. Toby glanced round the room, quickly making mental notes for his decorating scheme. "Do you mind if I . . . ?" He pointed at the edge of the carpet and fell to his knees. "I just need to see if you've got floorboards under here." He pulled back the green patterned carpet and peered underneath. "Um-hmm." He nodded to himself and pushed the carpet back down. "Very good."

Con looked at him. "What are you doing that for?"

"Oh, just thinking about taking up all the carpets, you know, stripping all the floorboards. Just wanted to check yours were sound."

Con nodded and sat on his mum's bed.

Toby passed his palm over the velvety crown of his head and smiled. "So, Con. How are things? I feel we haven't spoken for a while. All going well with Daisy?"

Con shrugged and fiddled with Melinda's hairbrush.

"Ah, dear, that sounds a bit . . . unpromising. Is it not working out?"

"Yeah, well, the whole thing was a joke, really."

"Oh," said Toby, "why's that?"

"I dunno. Her family, you know — they were just so . . ."

"Condescending? Arrogant? Unwelcoming?"

"No. None of that. They were really nice to me when I met them, but it seemed a bit . . ."

"Fake?"

"Yes. Well, no. It just didn't make any sense, that's all. They've got this beautiful girl, they've sent her to the best schools, looked after her, watched her going in and out of hospital since she was a kid. I mean, surely they'd want the best for her?"

"Well, yes, but I don't see your point."

"Well, it's obvious, isn't it? Why would they want someone like me hanging around their girl? I mean, they even invited me to stay at their house."

"And why wouldn't they?"

"Because, fuck, I don't know — what would we talk about? I mean, just imagine it, all sitting round the dining table eating breakfast, they'd all be reading their big newspapers, talking about politics and world affairs, and classical fucking music. I'd feel like a right spanner. I just feel like they're only being nice to me because they think I'm some kind of, you know, passing phase. Like I'm nothing serious. Like they may as well be polite because I'll only be around for a while. I think if they knew how I really felt about their daughter and how she really feels about me they'd run a mile."

Toby sighed. "Have you talked to Daisy about this, about how you feel?"

He shook his head, pulled a hair out of Melinda's hairbrush and twisted it round his little finger. "Nah," he said. "We're not really talking any more."

"You mean, it's over?"

He shrugged. "Yeah. I guess so."

"But, Con, that's ridiculous. You're in love with this girl . . ."

He shrugged again.

"You've cooked for her, written her poetry. This girl was all set to change your life."

"Yes!" Con slapped the hairbrush against his thigh. "Yes! Exactly. She was all set to change my life. And I didn't fucking want her to. I don't want some girlfriend who spends half her life in hospital, whose parents expect me to hang out with them all, like a big happy family, who'll be watching me all the time, making sure I'm good enough for their girl. I like my life, you know. I've got plans. Things I want to do."

"You can do those things with Daisy, surely?"

"What — go off and live in the Caribbean? And what happens next time she gets a lung infection, or a chest infection or, fuck, you know, something even more serious? What happens then, when we're a boat ride and a plane ride away from the nearest decent hospital? What do you think mummy and daddy dearest will think about that? No, man — it's just too . . . I can't do it. I can't."

"Well, couldn't you tailor your plans a bit? Maybe you could, I don't know, island hop in the Channel.

Guernsey, Jersey, Sark, the Scillies. Or around the Med, the Greek islands?"

"No," said Con, "no. I had a plan. Eighteen more months at Condé Nast. Get my licence in South Africa. Head to the Caribbean. I'm sorry, Toby, I know you were really into the whole me and Daisy thing, and I really appreciate everything you did. But it's just not going to happen. OK?"

Toby sighed. "Well," he said. "I think that's a shame, I really do. Real love, it doesn't just pop up when it's convenient, you know? It doesn't just turn up and fit in with everything. Real love is a pain in the arse. You have to make compromises for it."

"Yeah, well. I've made enough compromises in my life already, you know?"

"What sort of compromises?"

"Looking after my Gran, feeling too guilty to go out and leave her on her own. Working in a shitty job. Sharing a room with my fucking mum."

"I thought you *liked* sharing with your mum?"

"No. Of course I don't. It's all right when she's working nights, but when she's on days it sucks."

"Then why don't you tell her it's time to move on?"

"No way! I can't kick my own mum out."

"Why not? She's done it to you."

"Yeah, but that's different."

"Why is it different?"

"I don't know. It just is."

Toby sighed. This called for drastic measures. "Look," he said, "how much does it cost to get your pilot's licence?"

Con sniffed. "About twelve grand."

"And how much have you saved up?"

"About five."

"Right, so you need another seven grand. And you reckon you can save that up in eighteen months?"

"Yeah. If I'm good. If I keep away from the clothes shops, you know."

"I think that would be pushing it. I think it'll take you more like two years, on your salary. So here's a deal. I lend you the seven grand, you go off and get your licence, pay me back when you get a job. But there are two things I need you to do in return . . ."

Toby's next stop was Joanne's room.

He'd barely seen her since the night the man claiming to be her husband had turned up out of the blue. She'd disappeared for a fortnight and returned three days ago, her hair cut short and bleached white, with a pink nose stud in her nostril. Nobody, of course, had asked her where she'd been. Curiosity was futile; everyone in the house knew that.

Toby had a plan. It was a simple plan, and one he only now felt able to put into action. His plan was to play her at her own game. He would be as brusque, rigid and inhuman as Joanne, and it took a man with a skinhead and a black eye to pull it off. Toby breathed in and patted her door with his knuckles.

"Yes?"

"Joanne. It's Toby. Could I have a quick word, please?"

It took a full minute for Joanne to come to her door and when she did she opened it an inch and a half, revealing just a slice of her face to Toby.

"Yes?" she said again.

"Could I come in?"

Her eyes flashed at him in alarm. "No," she said, "I'd prefer it if you didn't."

"Right," said Toby, "well, then would you mind coming to my room?"

Joanne narrowed her eyes at Toby. She breathed in deeply and then exhaled, loudly. "OK," she said, "when?"

"Well, now would be good."

"Fine. Give me a moment."

She was wearing pyjamas when she slid through the door of Toby's bedroom a minute later — red tartan pyjamas and her red-framed spectacles. The pyjamas were far too big for her and her hair was a mess. She slid across the room attached to the wall as if by some magnetic force. "What happened to your face?" she said.

"I fell into the shallow end of a swimming pool, head first."

"Oh, dear," she said. "Did it hurt?"

"Yes," he said, "it did."

"And is that why you've got no hair?"

"No," he said, "that was Melinda. She decided I had too much hair and took matters into her own hands."

Joanne nodded and inched a bit nearer. "It looks better," she said, "I agree. You did have too much hair before. It didn't look hygienic."

"Oh," said Toby, "right. I'd never thought about it like that before." He paused for a moment, absorbing the fact that he'd been walking round with unhygienic-looking hair for years. The thought saddened him. "Anyway. The reason I wanted to see you was to find out how you're getting on."

"Getting on with what?"

"Oh, you know, just generally. Are you happy with the situation here?"

She nodded tersely, wrapped her arms round herself. "Yes," she said, "on the whole. I like the new bathrooms and the kitchen."

"Good," he said, "good."

She slanted her eyes and pursed her lips. "What's the matter with you?"

"Sorry?"

"You. You're different. You're all . . . spiky. What's going on?"

"Spiky?"

"Yes. You're being all pushy."

"Am I?"

"Yes. You're different."

"Well," he said, "I suppose that could just be your perception of me having changed due to my new image."

"Hmmmm."

"Anyway. What I really wanted to talk to you about was what happened here last month."

"I don't understand."

"Nick. Your husband."

"I told you. I don't have a husband. He was just some lunatic — a druggie, probably."

"Well, how did he know your name?"

She shrugged. "I have no idea."

"And if you don't know him, then why did you disappear for two weeks?"

"I told you. I was on holiday. Have we finished now?"

"No. We haven't. Here." He passed her a can of lager. She took it silently and opened it. "You wrote to me two years ago. You told me that you were an actress at an interesting juncture in your life. You told me you'd be acting in a film and that you wanted a room here to give you the freedom to research your role before filming started. That was 2003. It is now 2005 and all I have seen you do is go to work and return home most days with some shopping bag or other. Which leads me to conclude that you have a lot of expendable cash. Which makes me wonder what you're doing here?"

Joanne flushed, the first time Toby had ever seen any colour pass through her face. "Well," she said, "you don't know anything about me . . ."

"Indeed I don't. And that's what I'm concerned about. All I know is that you have lots of money, lots of clothes, an attitude problem and a very unhappy husband called Nick. Now, if I knew more about you I might be able to muster up some sympathy for you, but, as it is, I'm finding it harder and harder to feel anything for you at all."

"I'm not asking you to feel anything for me."

"No. You're not. But you are asking me to live with you, when you could afford to live pretty much anywhere."

"I don't have to live here."

"Then why do you?"

"Because . . ." She paused. "Because this is where I live."

"But you don't even like it here."

"Who said that I don't like it here?"

"My friend Leah."

"From across the road?"

"Yes. She said that you said that you found it hard living with us, that you dealt with us by pretending we weren't here."

"Oh, for God's sake."

"But it's true?"

"Well, yes, to a certain extent. Sharing a house with people is difficult."

"Which brings me back to my original question. Why do you live here, when you could afford not to?"

"I don't know."

"Right, well, I think I know the answer. I think you live here because it means that you don't exist because your signature isn't on anything. I think you live here because you're hiding from something or running from something. And I think that something is Nick. Your husband."

Toby paused, waiting for Joanne to deny once more that Nick was her husband. But she didn't. Instead she stared at him for a moment, then let her head drop dramatically onto her hands. "He's not my husband," she said, softly.

"Then who is he?"

"He's my fiancé. Was. He was."

"Right." He paused again.

"Did he come back again? While I was away?"

Toby nodded.

"Fuck," she said. "What did he say?"

"Nothing. He said absolutely nothing. But he asked me to give you this."

She looked up at him. Toby reached behind him into his drawer and pulled out a letter. He passed it to her.

She held the envelope in her hands for a moment, running it across her fingertips, staring at the handwriting on the front. Leah had almost persuaded him to steam it open yesterday, to read it. He'd only just resisted the temptation. Now he held his breath, wondering if she would open it now or take it to her room.

"Did he say anything else?" she said.

"No. Just to give you that letter."

She nodded. "Right."

"Well," he said, "will you open it?"

She nodded again. "Would you mind," she said, "if I opened it here?"

Toby gulped. "No. Of course not."

"Good." Her hands were trembling slightly as she opened the envelope. She slid the paper out slowly and unfolded it. Her bottom lip was caught under her top teeth as she read.

After a moment, she refolded the letter, and slid it back into the envelope.

"Well," he said, "is it what you expected?"

"Mm-hmm," she nodded.

"Are you OK, Joanne?"

"Yes." She stood up. "I think so. I, er . . ."

Toby waited for her to continue. Her lips were moving strangely, trying to form words and control tears at the same time. "I think, if it's OK with you, that I might, erm, go back to my room now."

"Yes," said Toby, "of course. Will you be all right?"

"Yes," she said, "and thank you for the beer. And the talk. It's been good. I need to go now, and think. Bye." She threw him a tight smile and left the room, the over-long sleeves of her tartan pyjamas bunched up over her hands, the letter clutched tightly in her fist.

Toby turned back to his computer and sighed.

Two down, two to go.

CHAPTER SIXTY-THREE

The first place Ruby and Tim looked at on Saturday morning was a tiny two-bedroom flat in Meard Street. It had wood-panelled rooms, an ornate marble fireplace and a kitchen the size of a Smart Car. It was very small and very beautiful.

The next place they saw was a one-bedroom flat on Brewer Street, above the organic supermarket. It was modern and slick, with an aluminium kitchen and a tiny terrace. By the time they'd seen a one-bedroom flat on Wardour Street with a hot tub on the roof terrace and a two-bedroom flat on Neal Street with a built-in dressing room, Ruby's head was spinning.

Living in Soho was the fulfilment of a lifetime's dream for Ruby, something she'd fantasized about since she was sixteen years old and first finding her way round London. The thought that in a week or two she'd be packing her bags and moving out of Toby's miserable house and away from all those miserable people was all she could focus on right now.

At one o'clock they went for lunch at Bam-Bou on Percy Street. They were given a cosy table overlooking the street on the first floor. Tim was in his weekend attire — blue chinos, a rugby shirt, a cream jumper with some kind of logo stitched on the left breast. He looked out of place here, amongst the retro opulence of the surroundings, with his skinny, tousle-haired girlfriend in drainpipe jeans. He'd suggested Bertorelli's for lunch. He'd have been happier there, in the slightly 1980s whitewashed environment. It was Ruby's idea to come here, where it was edgier, darker, quirkier. Tim was bending himself into unusual shapes just to keep Ruby happy. He didn't want to live in a tiny flat in Soho. He wanted to live in a huge Clerkenwell loft with white walls. He didn't want to eat Vietnamese food. He wanted Italian.

"So," he said, "what do you recommend?"

"I don't know," she said. "I've never been here before."

"Oh," he said, "right. I just assumed . . ."

"An ex of mine used to come here. He was always going on about it." She pulled a cigarette out of her handbag and lit it.

Tim's face assumed the sad kitten expression it always took on whenever she made any allusion to her sexual history. She did it on purpose. It amused her.

She ordered lightly, but expensively, and asked for a glass of champagne. "So," she said, "what do you think, so far?"

He shrugged and smiled. "I like all of them."

"Yes, but you must have a preference."

"Well," he said, "on a purely practical note I'd have to say the one on Neal Street. It was the biggest and we'll need the room for when Mojo comes to stay."

Ruby tutted. "Yes," she said, pouting very slightly, "but it's in Covent Garden. And I really, really want to live in Soho."

"Well, then we'll just have to find a bigger flat in Soho, won't we?" He smiled at her and pulled her hand towards him. His hands were one of the things that Ruby found the most unappealing about Tim. They were very fleshy, which she didn't mind in itself, but it was the length of his fingers that alarmed her. Very short. Out of proportion to the size of his palms. And his fingernails were tiny. She forced a smile and squeezed his hand back.

"Yes," she said, "we will."

CHAPTER SIXTY-FOUR

Melinda got back from work at five o'clock on Saturday afternoon. Con followed her into the kitchen, "Cup of tea?"

"Oh, yes, please." She pulled off her shoes and rubbed her feet. "What a bloody day. I was going to go to the gym, but I really don't think I can face it."

"Good," said Con. "Stay here. We'll have a nice chat."

Melinda threw him a questioning look.

"What?" he said, his hands upturned. "You're my mum. I like you. I like talking to you."

Her face softened and she smiled.

"So," he said, dropping an English Breakfast teabag into a mug, "how's everything?"

"Blimey," she laughed.

"No. Really. How are you? How's your life?"

"I'm fine, thank you, Connor. How are you?"

"Don't take the piss, mum."

"Sorry, love. I'm sorry." She reorganized her face and considered his question. "I'm pretty good, actually," she said.

"Yeah?"

"Yes. It's nice just to be *here*. You know, in one place. Not on the move. And it's so nice hanging round with you."

Con smiled tightly. "Even though you have to share a room with me?"

"I *love* sharing a room with you, Con." She paused and glanced at him. "Are you trying to tell me something?"

"No." Con shook his head and filled the kettle from the tap. "No. It's just, I was talking to Toby last night and he said he'd invited you out for dinner tonight at some bloke's house."

"Oh, Gawd." She raised her eyebrows. "Yeah. Can you believe it?! He told me about this bloke weeks ago, said he thought I'd like him. Next thing I know he's set us up on a blind date."

"I think you should go."

"What?! No way."

"But why not? He sounds great."

"I don't care how great he sounds. The last thing I need in my life right now is a bloke."

"Why not? What's wrong with blokes?"

"It's not the blokes that are wrong. It's me. I go funny when I've got a bloke. I forget what's important. Like you."

Con flicked on the kettle. "Mum," he said, "I'm nineteen. I'll be twenty in July. I don't need you by my side to know that you care."

"I know you don't, but . . ."

"You know I don't hold it against you, don't you, that you weren't around? You know it's not a big deal to me?"

"Well, you say that, Con, and I've always appreciated that you haven't made me feel bad about what happened, but, really, how can you not hate me? I mean, I was your mother and I abandoned you."

"You didn't abandon me, Mum. It's not like you left me outside an orphanage, is it? You left me with a truly great woman."

"Is that really how you feel?"

"Yeah. Definitely. Where I grew up, it's not like it was when you grew up there. It's changed. It's heavy. It's tough, you know. And the reason I survived, why I didn't get, you know, sucked up in all that shit, was Gran. And, don't get me wrong, I'm not saying you wouldn't have been a great mum, but maybe if you'd brought me up, as a single mother, it mightn't have worked out like that. You might have hooked up with some bloke who didn't want me on the scene, you know. You might have had more kids. I might have got sidelined, tried to find my identity outside the home. But with Gran, I always had something solid to come back to, something real. She didn't have any shit, any issues. She knew what was what. She knew the shit out there on the street and she knew how to keep me away from it. She was the right person to bring me up. And leaving me with her — you did the right thing, Mum. Totally."

Con exhaled. His body flooded with adrenalin. He'd wanted to say that to his mum for so long, since that very first time he'd seen her at Gran's funeral, but he'd never been able to find the words before. He hadn't even really realized that that was how he felt before. But he knew it now. There were no "mistakes" in life — just a series of random decisions that led to a series of random outcomes, good and bad. How could he blame his mother for doing something that had caused him no harm, for making a decision that had hurt her more than it had hurt him?

Melinda looked up at him. Her eyes were brimming with tears. "Do you really mean that?" she said.

"Yes," he said, "totally."

"Oh, Con." She got to her feet and embraced him. "That means so much to me, to hear you say that. So much. I've hated myself for so long, for being so weak."

"Well, stop it." He squeezed her back, his nose buried in her shoulder. She smelled of Gucci Rush and Fairy fabric conditioner. She smelled like his mum. "I love you, Mum."

"I love you, too, Con."

"But you know we can't live like this any more?"

"Like what?"

"Together."

"Well, no, obviously we can't. I mean, that would just be . . ."

"I'm going to South Africa."

"Yes," she said, "I know you are."

"No," he turned his back to her and pulled the teabag out of her mug. "I mean I'm going soon. Next month."

"What?! But how can you . . ."

"Toby's lending me the money."

"Toby?"

"Yes, look, I think Toby's up to something."

"Why, what did he say?"

"He didn't say anything. It was just . . . I don't know, something in the air. And why would he be doing all this work to the house, just for our benefit? He asked to look under our carpet yesterday. Said something about doing up the floorboards. I think this whole scene's about to crash. I think he's going to sell the house. I think it's time to move on."

"Oh, God, but *where*? Where will I go? Maybe I could come to South Africa with you?"

Con laughed. "No, Mum! South Africa's about me. It's about finding myself. It's time for you to find yourself now."

"I'm a bit old for finding myself, aren't I?"

"Well, you know what I mean. I mean — you hate your job. You could go back to air hostessing."

"I'm too old for that, too. I'm too old for all those jobs I used to love, repping and stuff. Let's face it, I'm too old for adventures. I'll be fifty before I know it."

"Well, then, how about settling down with a nice man."

"Oh, I see. You mean, *Toby's* nice man?"

"Well, yeah. Why not? Come on, it's a Saturday night, you can have a few drinks, something nice to eat. And the worst thing that can happen is that you don't fancy the bloke. You'll have had a nice night out with Toby and it won't cost you a penny. Go on."

Melinda looked at him suspiciously. "Are you trying to get rid of me?"

"Yes," he said, "I am. But only because I love you. Only because I want you to be happy. Nobody should be alone . . ."

Melinda smiled. "All right, then, I'll go."

Con beamed. "Excellent!" he said. Then he kissed his mother on the cheek and took the stairs two at a time to Toby's room to tell him that he'd completed the first half of their bargain.

CHAPTER SIXTY-FIVE

Melinda had pulled out all the stops for her blind date at Jack's house. She was wearing a turquoise satin dress with sequins around the neckline and contrasting green satin stilettos. Her hair was swept back and held in place with a bejewelled comb and she was clutching a tiny gem-encrusted handbag. Toby met her at the bottom of the stairs and gasped. "Wow, Melinda, you look quite superb."

She beamed at him. "You don't look too bad yourself."

"Why, thank you." Toby smiled and glanced down at his new black trousers and black stripy shirt, bought that morning, in a sale at a menswear boutique on the Broadway. It was a shop he'd walked past a dozen times and never been into, mainly because he'd had no money, but also due to the strangely angular mannequins in the window, who were all bald and hollow-cheeked and looked as if they might come to life and take over the world given half a chance. But being now bald and hollow-cheeked himself, it had occurred to him that the clothes on sale therein might be just the ticket.

"I'm really glad you changed your mind," he said.

"Yes," she said, "well. Me and Con had a good chat about stuff earlier."

"Oh, you did?" Toby feigned surprise.

"Yes. He's not a kid any more. He's got his life. It's time I got mine."

Toby smiled. "Good," he said, "very good."

The door bell rang and Toby spun round. He could see Leah's outline through the stained glass. He bounded to the door to let her in.

She was wearing a purple silk shalwar kameez and jeans. Her hair was down and wavy with a small diamanté clip holding it back at one side. It was the most feminine Toby had seen her look. "You look lovely," he said, holding the door open for her. "That top is stunning."

"Thank you," she said. "I haven't got any proper evening clothes, but I've got piles of these things. Amitabh's mum was always bringing them back for me from Mumbai."

"Well, I must say, they really suit you."

"Thank you," she said again. "And you look amazing." She stroked the sleeve of Toby's shirt. "New outfit?"

"Yes. I went into a menswear boutique. On my own."

"Ooh," she said, "well done."

She smiled at Melinda. "You look beautiful," she said.

"Thank you very much. So do you."

The three of them stood a moment in the hallway, beaming at each other.

"Well," said Toby, "shall we go?"

* * *

The chemistry between Melinda and Jack was instantaneous and overwhelming.

"Oh, but, Leah, you have brought me a goddess!" said Jack, holding Melinda's outstretched hand in his and gazing at her in awe and wonder.

Whether Melinda's reaction to Jack was influenced in any way by the guided tour of his house that he insisted on giving her within moments of her stepping through the front door was impossible to gauge.

Jack and Melinda returned, looking smiley and delighted.

"Isn't this place *gorgeous*?" said Melinda, smoothing her skirt and seating herself on the edge of the sofa. "And I love what you did to Jack's girls' rooms, Leah. They're stunning."

Jack offered everyone aperitifs. Toby wriggled slightly, feeling a small squirm of discomfort. This place was so plush. Jack, for all his childlike charm, was a proper grown-up man, probably only five or ten years older than Toby, but different in every way. He had children, a business, a fleshy middle-aged body. He'd paid for his house himself, not been bought it by an emotionally deficient father. Jack's ex-wife was still a part of his life, not a vague, dream-like memory. He'd used his own money to decorate his home, not the life savings of an elderly homosexual Dutchman. And now he was about to serve up immaculate Bloody Marys in proper glasses with all the trimmings.

"So, Toby." Jack passed him his glass, replete with celery stick and crushed black peppercorns. "What have you done to yourself? A sporting injury?"

"Oh, my eye? I fell into a swimming pool . . ."

"He was drunk . . ." chipped in Leah.

"Well, only a little bit. It was the drugs, really . . ."

"The *drugs*?" Jack raised an alarmed eyebrow.

"Not those sort of drugs. Dentists' drugs. I had a tooth removed . . ." He opened his mouth to show Jack the gap. "I shouldn't have gone swimming, really."

"It was my fault," said Leah. "We went for a walk in Kenwood and he nearly passed out walking up a slope and I was so horrified by how unfit he was that I made him come swimming with me —"

"Even though I haven't swum since I was sixteen —"

"And to prove it he wore his school trunks —"

"Yes. It's true. They still have my name label in the back."

"I am impressed that they still fit you," said Jack, patting his own girth. "I would be happy to get my school trunks on to one thigh these days."

"Don't put yourself down," said Melinda. "You've got a lovely physique."

"You think so?" said Jack.

"Yes," she said, "you're in good shape."

"For an old man, you mean?" He smiled. "I work out," he said, "at the gym, three times a week."

"Oh, really, which gym are you at?"

"Esporta," he said. "You know, the posh one in the old mental hospital in Friern Barnet."

"Oh, yes," said Melinda, "I know the one. Very smart. I'm at the Manor on Fortis Road. Plus I do Pilates twice a week and kick boxing on a Wednesday."

"Yes," said Jack, his eyes skimming appreciatively up and down her body. "It is clear that you look after yourself. But, not too well, I hope."

"What do you mean?" she giggled.

"Well, it's not good for a woman to exercise away all her . . . softness. It's not good for a woman to feel like a man. Like that Madonna," he shuddered. "What must he think, that man of hers, an English man? When they are in bed together and the lights are off, he must feel he is fucking a small boy."

Melinda laughed and Jack smiled. "Excuse my language," he said. "And now, I must go and stir something."

"Need a hand?" said Melinda.

"That would be lovely."

Toby waited until they'd left the room, then nudged Leah gently with his elbow. "You are so good at this," he whispered.

"What?"

"You really do know people. I mean, Jack and Melinda — genius."

Leah smiled and rubbed her fingernails against her collarbone. "I can't deny I have a certain knack."

"And this house is extraordinary, isn't it?" He looked round the living room. It made his plans for his own house pale into insignificance.

"I know," she said. "It's hard to imagine, isn't it, just exactly how rich you'd have to be to live somewhere like this."

"*So* rich," said Toby, "so *extraordinarily* rich. Tell me again why you rejected Jack's advances."

"I am a woman of unimpeachable moral fibre."

"Well," said Toby, "let's hope the same is true of Melinda."

"She's a good woman."

"Yes," said Toby, "you know what — I think she is? I've got quite close to her over the past couple of weeks. She's really very well meaning, if a bit misguided."

"Aren't we all?" said Leah, sucking tomato juice off her celery. "Aren't we all?"

"He's got a maid in there!" said Melinda, bursting into the living room a moment later. "Some little Asian girl — wearing an *apron*!"

"Oh, my God," said Leah. "That's dreadful."

"Why is that dreadful?" asked Melinda. "He can afford it. I'm sure he pays her well. And you can't expect a man like Jack to look after a big house like this all by himself."

Leah shrugged. "So," she said, "what do you think?"

"What do I think? I think he's gorgeous. Totally. And such a nice man."

Leah smiled. "He's lovely, isn't he?"

"He's a sweetheart. So funny. And that accent . . ."

"Look," said Leah. "We need a secret code. A special thing that you say when you want to get rid of us."

"Yes," said Toby, "we'd hate to outstay our welcome."

"OK," whispered Melinda, "when I want you to go, I'll say . . . *Can you two fuck off now because me and Jack want to shag*." She let out a loud burst of laughter and put her hands over her mouth. "I'm not that sort of girl," she said primly, "but if I say *ai carumba*, then scarper."

Over the course of the next three hours Jack and his Filipino maid, Marietta, served up five courses of superb Italian food. Platters of aged Parma ham and cornichons, truffle and wild mushroom soup, sea bass with lemon and parsley, and Amaretto-soaked pears with cloves and vanilla cream. He poured bottle after bottle of expensive wine into huge glasses and served them home-made almond biscotti with tiny cups of coffee from a proper Gaggia espresso machine. Then, once they'd finally started to digest the first four courses, Jack brought out a groaning cheese board and a bottle of pudding wine the colour of early morning pee.

"Ai carumba," said Melinda, caressing her distended belly. "I've never been so stuffed in my life."

Toby and Leah folded their napkins, made their excuses, collected their coats and left.

"Well," said Toby, pulling on a knitted hat outside Jack's house. "I think we can safely call that a success."

"Wow. What do you think will happen? Do you think he's already having her, on the cheeseboard, as we speak?"

Toby smiled. "I doubt it. They'll have to wait for the maid to go home first." They both turned then at the sound of Jack's front door. A small figure crunched across the gravel driveway and turned onto the road. It was Marietta. "Good night!" she smiled, before disappearing towards the Broadway, in a black puffa jacket and a baseball cap. Leah and Toby looked at each other and laughed.

"Well," said Leah, "I guess there's nothing stopping them now."

"Christ," said Toby, "can you imagine those two in bed? I bet they'll both talk the whole way through."

"Oh, yes, *dirty* talk."

"Oh, definitely. And role playing. And dressing up. They'll be at it all night, with whipped cream and leather dildos."

"Ooh, stop it!" They smiled at each other.

"Walk me home?" said Leah.

"Yes," said Toby, "why not? Although it is, of course, a little out of my way."

They headed towards the Broadway. The pubs had just closed and the streets were full of drunk people looking for cabs. They passed a group of rowdy men in their early twenties and Toby instinctively brought his arm round Leah's waist to protect her. He didn't even realize he'd done it until they turned into Silversmith Road and it was still there. "So," he said, "swimming again on Thursday?"

She laughed. "Only if you're sure you can face it."

"Absolutely," he said. "What doesn't kill me makes me stronger."

"Great," she said. "It's a date. But you might want to buy yourself some new trunks."

"Oh, dear. Were they terribly embarrassing?"

"Well. They weren't the best look."

"New trunks it is, then," he said. "And if you're free, afterwards, I'd like to take you for a drink. Just to say thank you. For saving my life."

"I didn't save your life!"

"Yes, Leah, you really did. And in so many ways." He sighed and looked at her. He couldn't believe that he had to deposit her at a house that she shared with another man, a man who she hadn't even been living with when he first got to know her, a man she'd been getting over, a man who'd somehow managed to inveigle himself back into her life as a direct result of a meeting that *he'd* inadvertently engineered. "So — what's going to happen with you and your nurse? Is he going to marry you now?"

Leah shrugged. "I don't suppose so. But then, I never really wanted to marry him in the first place. I just wanted some sort of confirmation, I suppose, that my life was going somewhere. That I wasn't going to end up like Gus."

Toby nodded. "So is it — going somewhere?"

"No," she sniffed, "not really." She laughed wryly.

"Then why . . .?"

"Why did I take him back?"

"Well, yes."

"Because he asked. And because . . . because I was lonely."

"Oh, Leah," Toby stopped and turned her towards him. "How could a girl like you ever be *lonely*? Someone as vital and good and clever as you."

She shrugged again. "I don't know. Maybe I'm not as clever as you think."

"But you are. You're a hundred times cleverer than I think."

"Well, if I'm so clever, then why have I let this man back in my life when I know I'm just a temporary arrangement? When I know that any day now his mother will present him with some twenty-year-old from Mumbai with eyes like coals and he'll be gone in a flash."

"Oh, God, is that the situation?"

"Uh-huh. Yes. I had no idea until two months ago, thought his parents were all trendy and westernized. But it turns out that they were just letting their little boy have some fun until he turned thirty."

"So, if that's the case, then why has he moved back in?"

"Because it's better than living at the nurses' home. Because I'm a nice girl. Because he's in denial that he's actually thirty and he can't cope with the reality of what's expected of him. Basically because he's in some sort of state of arrested development."

"So, you're back at square one?"

"Totally. All I know is that as long as Amitabh's living with me I don't have to hand in notice on the flat, therefore I don't have to look at any more shitty flat shares and I can pretend that I'm still a grown-up."

"Can't you find somewhere on your own?"

She shook her head. "Can't afford it."

"What about your parents? Can't they lend you some money?"

"No. If they'd had money to lend they'd have offered it to me by now."

"Leah — this is crazy."

"I know. I know it is." She sighed and lowered her eyes. "I've really fucked up."

"Just tell him to go!"

"I can't."

"You can! I'll lend you some money."

"Oh, Toby, I can't. I . . ."

"Yes. You can. I've got no mortgage on my house, you know? Once I sell it I'll have, God, hundreds of thousands of pounds. I'll have more money than I'll know what to do with."

"Yes, but you'll need that, to buy a new house, start your new life."

"I'll need some of it, but not all of it."

"No way, Toby. Absolutely not. You've spent the past fifteen years subsidizing other people. It's time to let go, let people take responsibility for themselves. But thank you. Thank you for offering. You are a very generous man."

Toby smiled, wanly. "To a fault, it seems."

She squeezed his hand and smiled. "Yes, well, maybe."

Toby squeezed her hand back and then, because it seemed like it wouldn't be entirely the wrong thing to do, because she wasn't in love with her nurse, because she was lonely and lost just like him, he reached out with his other hand and stroked her cheek. Her skin was cold and smooth under his palm. She lowered her eyes briefly, then smiled. "You've got cold hands," she said.

"And you've got cold cheeks."

"Time to go home," she said.

"Yes," he said, "let's go home."

He draped his arm across her shoulders and pulled her towards him, and they walked down Silversmith Road in a warm and companionable silence.

CHAPTER SIXTY-SIX

Con completed the second half of his bargain with Toby on Monday. At lunchtime, instead of hiding in the break room as he'd been doing every day since Daisy had been back at work, he went upstairs to the fashion department.

She was sitting on the edge of another girl's desk, looking at some photographs. She was wearing a brown polo neck and a pale denim mini skirt, with a long knitted waistcoat. She glanced at him as he walked in, then glanced away again, muttering something to the girl.

"Daisy," he started.

She looked up at him again, in surprise. "Yes?"

"Are you busy?"

Daisy looked at the girl, then back at Con. She shrugged. "No," she said, "not really."

"Fancy lunch?" He held the plastic bag aloft. "I made the bread myself."

Daisy sighed, frowned, looked at the bag, looked at him. "OK," she said. "Give me a minute."

They took the sandwiches into Hanover Square and sat awkwardly side by side on a bench. Con passed a sandwich to Daisy. She took it, silently.

"Crab and cucumber," said Con. "Home-made bread and organic butter."

She handled the sandwich sadly. "I'm leaving," she said after a moment.

"What?"

"*Vogue*. I'm leaving *Vogue*. Leaving London."

"Why? It's not because of . . . ?"

"No. It's not because of you. Though what happened, it didn't really help. No, it's just not working out. I hate my job. I hate London. I miss all my friends back home. And it's not fair on Mimi, having to look after me. So I'm going home."

"When?"

"I'm working out my notice. Three weeks, then I'll be gone."

Con stared at his sandwich. He didn't know what to say. "What will you do?" he said eventually.

Daisy shrugged. "I don't know. I might go to college. Or I've got a friend who owns a restaurant in the village. I could see if he's got anything for me there. Maybe waitressing. I don't know. All I know is that me and London didn't click and I need to go home. I gave it my best shot. At least I tried."

"That's fair enough, I guess."

"Yes," she said, "it's the right thing. I feel happier already."

"I'll miss you," he said.

"Will you?"

"Of course I will. Look, Daisy. I'm sorry," he said, "I'm really fucking sorry about how things were. I've been a fucking idiot."

She shrugged.

"I don't really know what happened."

"It's OK," she said. "It's done. You don't need to say anything else."

"No, but I do." He turned to face her. "Look, you were right. I freaked out, at the hospital. I lost the plot, completely. Seeing you like that, thinking you might be, you know, *dying*, and your family, they're so different to mine. You know, fucking bassoon players with the fucking philharmonic whatever. I left that hospital feeling like I'd been on another *planet*."

"So, why didn't you just say? I would have understood."

"I don't know." He shook his head. "We were in the tea room, all those blokes in there. And I hadn't worked out how I felt yet. I didn't know myself what I wanted to do. But then, seeing you the next day, up there —" He pointed at her floor of the Condé Nast building. "And you were so cold. We were like strangers. It just tore me apart. And I realized then that I have to give this a chance. Because, you know, love's not always *convenient*, is it? Sometimes it's just a pain in the arse. But if you don't try, then you don't know. And I want to try. And I want to know. Because otherwise I'll spend the rest of my life wondering what happened to the first girl I ever cared about, what happened to you. And that would tear me up, totally."

It was silent for a moment. Con put his untouched sandwich back in the bag.

Daisy sighed. "I don't really understand. What exactly are you saying?"

"I'm saying that I love you and that I'm sorry for what I did and that I want to be with you."

"Oh, Con. Christ. It's too late now. I'm moving away. It's all too late."

"No" he said, "it's not. Toby's offered to pay for my flying lessons. I've spoken to a couple of schools in South Africa that have got places, where I could start next month. But if you say that you'll forgive me, if you say that you'll let me into your life, let me be there for you, look after you, I'll wave goodbye to South Africa in a flash. There are flying schools in this country. They're more expensive, but Toby's said he'll lend me the money. As much as it takes. I could be anywhere. Anywhere that you are."

Daisy sighed again. "But I'll still be ill. My parents will still be my parents. My sister's boyfriend will still be a bassoonist."

"Yeah, I know all that. But I won't be *me*. I won't be a post boy who shares a room with his mum in a jumped-up squat. I'll be a trainee pilot. I'll have my own place. I'll be, you know, *going somewhere*. Being someone. I'll be good enough for you."

"But, Con," she said, "that's the whole stupid bloody point. You already were."

"No," he shook his head. "I wasn't. I really wasn't. But meeting you and knowing you, you make me want to be everything. I want to look after you. I want to make you proud."

Daisy smiled then, and picked up his hand. "There's a flight school two miles up the road from my parents' place," she said. "I hear it's a good one."

"Oh, yeah?"

"Yeah. I'll pick you up a brochure, if you like."

"Cool."

Con nodded and smiled. Then they both picked up their sandwiches and ate them in silence, their hands firmly grasped together on the bench between them.

CHAPTER SIXTY-SEVEN

Toby put a bowl of tortilla chips on the coffee table and glanced at the time. It was just before eight, two minutes until the house meeting was supposed to start. Ruby was the first to appear. She was due to play a set at a pub in Tufnell Park at ten o'clock and was all dressed up in her stage gear — pointy boots, sheer black sleeveless shirt, tight pinstripe jeans and a diamond choker.

"Nice necklace," he said.

She collapsed on the sofa and scooped up a handful of tortilla chips. "Tim gave me it," she said, biting the tip off a chip. "Gorgeous, isn't it?" She ate the rest of the chips in quick succession, licked the crumbs off the palm of her hands, then grabbed another handful.

"Don't eat them all," said Toby. "Save some for the others."

She tutted. "Look, I'm the only person who bothered to get here on time. I get snack privileges." She munched on yet another chip. "So — this is all very mysterious. *House meeting*. Hmmm . . ." She put her index finger to her lip and adopted a sarcastic tone. "*I wonder what it could possibly be about?*"

Footsteps on the staircase behind them heralded the arrival of Melinda and Con. They both sat down on the other sofa and Con helped himself to a handful of chips. "Oh, look," said Ruby, "it's the happy couple. How's married life?"

Con raised his eyebrows. Melinda shot her a look, then ignored her.

The last person to arrive was Joanne, fresh from work and clutching a Jane Norman carrier bag. She popped her head round the door. "Sorry," she said, "I just need to go to the loo. Start without me if you have to."

Toby perched himself on the edge of the coffee table and tapped his fingers against his knee. Nobody talked. The only sound was the crunching of chips. Joanne came back and Toby stood up. He glanced round the room. Four pairs of eyes gazed back at him. This was it, the moment he never thought would come, the scenario he'd never been able to envisage. "Thanks for coming," he began. "I know you've all got busy lives."

Ruby snorted, like a teenage girl in the back row of the classroom.

"Anyway, the reason I've brought you all together tonight is because I have an important announcement to make, one that will impact on all of you. As you know, my father bought me this house fifteen years ago, as a place for me to live with my wife. As you also know, my wife left me three weeks later and I haven't seen her since. Since then I have used this house as a place for people to stay for a while, when life isn't on their side, a place for people to work out their dreams and hopes, and hopefully find a way to move on. I would probably have gone on using the house for those aims indefinitely, but for two events that occurred within two days of each other. First Gus, my sitting tenant, died, then I received a letter from my father, announcing that he was coming back to the country and wanted to see how I was doing. Three days later I was left a sum of money by Gus, with specific instructions that I use it to refurbish this house. And to, er . . . well — to get on with my life. Because Gus felt, as I now feel, that I've got rather stuck in a rut, rather *lost* my way. So I will be putting the house on the market as soon as the renovations are complete. And, I'm afraid, I will have to now give you all four weeks' notice, as of today."

Toby stopped and lifted his gaze from a stain on the carpet he'd been addressing.

"Ooh," said Ruby, her hand against her chest, "what a *shock*."

The other three just stared at him blankly.

"Well," said Con, eventually. "I think that's cool. I do."

"Yes," said Melinda, "good on you, Toby. You deserve it."

Toby looked at Joanne. Her face was blank. She placed her hands slowly on her kneecaps, then rose slowly to her feet. Then she left the room, her footsteps silent and unfathomable.

"Joanne, it's Toby."

The door opened and Joanne's face appeared. She'd been crying.

"What?" she said.

"I want to talk to you."

"What about?"

"About what happened just now. About moving out."

"It's fine," she said.

"Well, no, it's clearly not fine."

"It is," she said, starting to close the door.

Toby stuck his foot in the gap and waved a bottle of white wine at her. "Here," he said, "share it with me. Let's have a drink and a talk."

"No," she said, "but thank you." She squeezed the door against his shoe. He pushed his shoulder against the door.

"I'm not going anywhere," he said, "until you let me in."

"Oh, for fuck's sake." She pulled open the door and regarded him. Her eyes were red and swollen. "I really don't want to talk. It's your house. You can do what you want with it. It just would have been nice if you'd given us all a bit more notice. Evidently you've known about this plan of yours for a while. I assume since Gus died. I don't understand why you're only telling us now."

Toby smiled. "Well," he said, "perhaps if you let me in, I could explain."

She shook her head. "It's a tip in here," she said. "Let's go to your room."

Joanne looked like a small, rather unwell child with her white-blonde hair, her red eyes and pinched nose.

Toby handed her a glass of wine and she took it gratefully.

"I understand," he said, "that it might seem strange that I've only just given you all notice, but there's a reason why I didn't tell you sooner."

She nodded wanly and sipped her wine.

"I felt as if you were all my responsibility and that therefore I couldn't just kick you out without ensuring that you were all ready to go. So I've been trying to get to know you all a bit better. Which, I have to say, I've found rather hard. It's not in my nature to snoop or interfere. You and I are quite similar in that respect. We like to keep ourselves to ourselves, keep the world at bay. But I've also found it strangely exhilarating at times, the journey over the past few weeks, the things I've learned about the people with whom I live. I really feel as if I've made an impression, as if they've moved on in some way. But you, Joanne, I don't know. You're . . . *impossible*."

A small wry smile cracked her deadpan face. "Yes," she said, "I know."

"I haven't a clue who you are, where you're from, what you want, why you're here. So I'm resigned to having to let you go out into the world as I found you. A mystery. An enigma. A lost soul . . ."

"I am not lost."

"Oh, Joanne. Of course you are. You're nearly middle-aged, yet you have no profession, no home, no friends. You change your image with the frequency of an immature teenage girl, you spend all your money on clothes and cosmetics, and yet you never go anywhere. And then this man arrives, this sad man with tears in his eyes, a man you used to love, who still, it seems, loves you. He leaves you a letter that makes you cry, yet you ignore it. You carry on as if it never happened. I mean, Joanne, what is it that you left behind when you came here? What could be so bad that living with strangers is preferable? Why have you allowed yourself to become a peculiar, unlovable *ghoul* when clearly you have known love in your life, when clearly you have known more?"

"Oh, Toby," she said, "do you hear yourself? Do you hear?"

He threw her a questioning look.

"Turn that question round. Ask it of yourself."

He sighed. "But that is the point, Joanne. I have asked that question of myself. And I now know the answer. I allowed myself to become a peculiar, unlovable ghoul because first my mother left me, to be raised primarily by the public school system and secondarily by my father, who hated me. Then my father left me, to start another, I assume *better*, family abroad. But I didn't mind because I had love, a beautiful new wife, a beautiful new home. And then my wife left me and I decided that I no longer wanted to be left. I wanted to stay in one place and keep my soul safe. I shut my door; I kept the world out. I grew my hair; I made myself physically unappealing. I stayed in my room and on the odd occasion that I needed to venture down the street I knew that I was safe, that no one would try to know me because I was the strange bloke with the hair and the hats and the boots full of holes. I made a freak of myself, Joanne, to keep everyone away.

"I saw a documentary once, about Siamese twins, and these women, these twins, were discussing their love lives with their boyfriends, as if it was the most normal thing in the world. Like the sort of bloke who wants to have sex with a woman who has another woman attached to her by the head was just a regular bloke. And I just thought, how sad that these women will only ever get to have relationships with sick fucks and weirdos. And that's how I've felt about myself for years — that anyone who'd want to be with me, the way I am, the way I *was*, the way I'm trying not to be any more, was, by definition, a weirdo. And it's only now, it's only because of this house, that I've begun to leave the little hole I'd dug for myself. It's only now that I can acknowledge my freakdom and move on. But what about you, Joanne? When will you acknowledge what you've allowed yourself to become?"

Joanne gulped and rolled her wine glass between her hands, disconsolately. "Is that what I am?" she asked, her eyes brimming with tears. "A freak?"

Toby nodded. "Yes."

She sighed and let her head fall into her chest. "I just, I don't know what else to be. I can't remember how to be *me* any more."

"You?" said Toby. "What was you?"

"Me was . . ." she sniffed. "Me was someone who'd lost their way in life, then found it again. Me was in love. Me was happy. Me was . . ." She paused, stared into her wine glass then looked up at Toby, her eyes luminescent with sorrow, "a *mother*."

CHAPTER SIXTY-EIGHT

Joanne Fish was born in Ipswich in 1968. Her parents split up when she was five years old and she moved with her mother to Norwich. Her mother died in a car crash when Joanne was ten and she moved to London to live with her father and his girlfriend in Lewisham. Her father was an actor, an alcoholic, always out of work and spending his dole money in the pub. He loved Joanne. She was his only child and the only child he would ever have after a vasectomy went wrong and resulted in the removal of both his testicles. His girlfriend was called Drew. She was twenty-one and a drug user. Joanne's father left the two of them alone most nights when he went to the pub. Joanne would watch Drew in fascination, fixing up her drugs, tying off a vein, flicking the needle, sticking it in. She'd been living with her father and Drew for nearly two years before the inevitable happened and Drew offered to let her try it for herself. Joanne had just turned twelve.

Drew moved out when Joanne was thirteen and took her drugs with her. That was when Joanne started stealing. She stole clothes mainly, which she sold to girls at school. Then she started stealing from girls at school because it was easier. She was expelled six months later and put into care shortly afterwards. Between her fourteenth birthday and her eighteenth birthday she spent a total of eighteen months in juvenile detention centres and she was given her first proper prison sentence a week after her eighteenth birthday — three years for aggravated burglary. It was at Holloway that she finally found something she loved to do. Acting. Her teacher was a tall, thin man called Nicholas Sturgess, ten years her senior. He proposed to her the day she was released and she moved straight into his house, a three-bedroom terrace in New Cross.

She got a place at the Central School of Speech and Drama, completed a BA in Acting in Film and graduated when she was twenty-five. Her father died of liver failure two years later and Joanne nursed him until the end. Shortly afterwards, she and Nick started talking about having a family. They tried for three years without success, then embarked on a course of fertility treatment. Joanne's years of drug abuse had damaged her reproductive organs, but finally, six months after starting treatment, Joanne's period was late and a test revealed that she was indeed pregnant. Her pregnancy went smoothly and she delivered an eight-pound baby girl on New Year's Day, the first girl to be born that year in the borough. They called her Maisie and took her home. Joanne had never felt so happy in her life. For once she hadn't made a mess of things. For once she had everything a person was supposed to have. A career. A home. A lover. A family. Maisie was a good baby. She fed and she gained weight and she slept as well as could be expected. But Joanne was tired. Very tired. The labour had taken her through two nights of sleep and she still hadn't recovered. So Joanne slept when she could, snatched moments, here and there. She slept when Maisie slept, either next to her on the double bed or on the sofa while she fed.

One Thursday afternoon, when Maisie was three weeks old, Joanne put her to her breast, her small soft body resting on a pillow on her lap. She switched on the television and she flicked until she found a programme she wanted to watch. It was *Bargain Hunt*. She watched for a while. Two married couples who'd met on holiday dashed round an antique fair, with one hour to find three antiques. The last thing she remembered was a woman looking at a cut-crystal decanter, buying it for twenty-five pounds. She adjusted Maisie's head slightly, angling her nipple back into her baby's warm mouth. And then she fell asleep.

When she woke up, *Bargain Hunt* had finished and Maisie was still and cool on the pillow. She put her hand to her cheek, gently, not wanting to wake her. Her skin felt icy. She looked blue. Joanne picked her up, and held her to her chest. Maisie flopped from side to side. She patted her back. She laid her back on the pillow and stared at her. Her heart pounded in her chest. What had been only a faint sense of discomfort had grown into a sickening certainty. Her baby wasn't breathing. She rested the pillow on the sofa and got to her knees on the floor. She opened Maisie's mouth and tipped back her head. She breathed into the sweet milk-scented cave of her mouth, once, twice, three times. She put her ear to her baby's tiny ribcage and listened for her heartbeat, that sound that she'd listened to every month at the antenatal clinic while she was pregnant. She couldn't hear it. A sob caught in her throat and she choked. She opened her mouth to scream, but no sound came.

She called the ambulance. She told them what had happened; she told them where she lived. She put down the phone, then she rested her cheek on her dead baby's stomach until they came and took her baby away.

Nick met her at the hospital. Asphyxiation. Her baby had been suffocated to death, by her. She'd crushed her against the pillow, with the weight of her tiredness and the depth of her sleep.

They buried her the following week, just the two of them. Joanne couldn't deal with anyone else. She couldn't deal with anything. Nick said, "It's not your fault, it's not anyone's fault." Then Nick said, "It's my fault. I should have taken more paternity leave. I should have been there for you both. I knew how tired you were." Nick said, "We will get over this. We will." Nick said, "I love you, Joanne. I love you. Please, don't cut me out." Nick said, "Maybe you should think about therapy." Nick said, "I can't go on like this."

And then, one day, five months after Maisie's death, sitting in the waiting room at the doctor's surgery, hoping to be prescribed some antidepressants strong enough to block out all the pain, Joanne saw Toby's advert in *Private Eye*. She picked up her pills from the chemist, she went home and she composed a letter full of lies. When Toby wrote back and offered her the room, she packed a bag and she left. It was a Saturday morning. Nick was at the barber's. She left him a note that said, "Don't try to find me." There was a march down her street in support of the legalization of cannabis. A man dressed up as a cannabis leaf smiled at her as she loaded her suitcase into the boot of a taxi. "Peace, man," he said. "Peace." He pressed a small unlit spliff into the palm of her hand and he carried on his way.

She settled into Toby's house and started temping. Every week a different company, a different role. Everyone seemed to want to employ an out-of-work actress. People seemed happier to think that someone creative was filing their paperwork or entering their data or answering their phone. And Joanne loved the freedom that the anonymity of temping gave her. She could be anyone she wanted. She made up stories. I live in Chelsea. My husband's an art dealer. I live in Chiswick with my sister — she's a hairdresser. I lived in LA when I was twenty-one, slept with Christian Slater. She took each job as if it were a role in a film. She planned her costumes, researched her part, learned her lines. Every day when she left Toby's house she became a different person and, every time a temp job finished, so did the person she'd created. The clothes she'd worn would be laundered, ironed, folded up and put away and a new wardrobe would be purchased. Sometimes a job didn't last long enough to wear everything she'd bought, and clothes would stay unworn in carrier bags, cosmetics unopened in drawers.

And then, one day, she'd been walking home from the Tube station and a tall, fair man had grabbed her elbow. It was Nick. "I thought you were dead," he said. "I thought you were dead." She packed a bag and she checked herself into a small hotel in Bloomsbury. She stayed there for two weeks, until she ran out of money, then she came back to Toby's house. Toby had changed. His hair was cut brutally short. He had a black eye. He seemed harder, more substantial. He made her talk to him. It was the first time she'd talked to anyone, as herself, as Joanne Fish, in more than two years. It was very strange. Toby gave her a note from Nick. It said, "Please come home. I haven't moved on and I can't until you're back where you belong. Nothing in this world makes any sense without you. I love you."

She didn't know what to do, what to think. She'd put Nick in a box when she moved into Toby's house and she'd imagined that he'd have done the same with her. She thought about him occasionally, imagined him with a new wife, a new baby, getting on with his life. And who could blame him? She couldn't imagine why he'd ever have wanted to be with someone like her in the first place, someone whose body was raddled and old before its time, whose arms were scarred by years of drug abuse and stained with the ink scribbles she'd endured to prove her worth in prison. She'd failed as an actress. She'd failed as a mother. She'd failed as a human being. But for some reason he still wanted her in his life.

She kept the note close to her at all times. She pulled it out of her handbag and read it at work. She absorbed its meaning word by word, day by day. And every time she read it, she let a little bit more of her old self trickle back into her soul. And then Toby called a meeting, told her something she'd never thought possible. He was selling the house, kicking her out. He talked to her in his room, told her she was turning into a freak. She'd suspected as much, but to hear it put so frankly, so directly, was like having a bucket of iced water poured over her head. She went to bed at midnight that night, full of wine and thoughts and feelings. She glanced round her room, at the shadowy lumps of unworn clothes and the ghostly images of her dead mother and father in the frame next to her bed. She picked up the picture and peeled off the back cover. Then she pulled out a picture of Maisie and held it to her heart, hot, steady tears flowing down her cheeks.

CHAPTER SIXTY-NINE

Ruby started packing on Tuesday. Tim had signed a contract on a two-bedroom penthouse flat off Carnaby Street and they were moving in on Thursday.

She pulled a box off the top of her wardrobe and blew a thick layer of dust off it. That box had been there since she'd moved in. She couldn't even remember what was in it. Ruby's possessions didn't circulate. She didn't have clear-outs or spring cleans. Ruby put things down and they stayed there. The box was full of school books and report cards. She opened one, randomly:

Tracey Lewis. Class 3A.

Tracey has had a challenging term. Her levels of attention in class and general attitude remain uneven, but she is showing a pronounced improvement in other areas, such as music studies and English literature.

She smirked and put the card back in the box. She'd been a troublesome student. Lazy, insolent and too clever by half. None of her teachers had known what to do with her and she'd left school with three O levels and a bad reputation.

She looked round the room, taking in all the detail, the cornicing, the layers of dust, the tendrils of old cobweb, the boxes covered over with pieces of cloth, the cheap furniture buried under layers of her possessions. She'd been here, in this room, since she was sixteen. She'd written countless songs, practised countless chords, slept with countless men. She'd eaten her supper up here, she'd cried up here, she'd got drunk with her friends. She'd sat on the balcony in her bikini on hot summer days, buried herself under her duvet with a bottle of Benilyn when she had the flu. She'd lived here longer than she'd lived at home. This *was* her home. It had never really occurred to her that she'd leave. She'd never imagined that Gus would die, that Toby would change, that she'd be packing away the contents of her room and leaving here for ever.

There was a gentle knock on the door. She sighed.

"Yes?"

"Ruby, it's me. Can I come in?"

"Sure."

The door opened and Toby walked in. He was wearing a really quite nice grey crew-necked sweater with really quite nice jeans. With his short hair and his clean-shaven face he looked strangely, almost unnervingly good. Ruby didn't like it. Toby changing his image had stripped yet another layer off her sense of normality. Toby wasn't supposed to look good. He was supposed to look like Toby. This house wasn't supposed to have sexy bathrooms and a designer kitchen. It was supposed to be tatty and unkempt. And Ruby — well, Ruby wasn't supposed to be moving into a flat with a nice but fundamentally dull banker called Tim. She was supposed to be unconventional. She was supposed to live on the edge. But right now her options had dried up. Right now Tim was all she had.

"I brought you a cup of tea," said Toby, handing her a steaming mug.

"Oh," she said, "thank you."

"So," he said, "how's it going?"

She shrugged. "Only just started," she said. "It's going to be a big job, I reckon."

He nodded and smiled. "I am not looking forward to doing my room."

"It's tempting just to throw it all away," she said. "Start afresh."

"Well, then, why don't you?"

"No," she said. "I can't. I've got nothing else to call my own. If I throw this lot away, I might just evaporate." She tried for a smile, but didn't quite make it. Toby threw her a concerned frown.

"Are you sure about this?" he said. "About moving in with Tim?"

She nodded, defensively.

"Because you don't have to move out right now, you know? You've got a couple of weeks. You don't have to rush into anything."

"A couple of weeks?!" she said. "Oh, well, why didn't you say?! A couple of weeks? That's *plenty* of time for me to get a job and earn enough money to put down a deposit on a flat and sort my entire life out, isn't it?"

"Ruby, I've been trying to encourage you for weeks now, ever since you and Paul split up. I've been saying to you that you must take responsibility, grow up. You could have gone out and found a job, but instead you went out and did what you always do — found a man."

"Yeah, well, it's all right for you. Your rich *daddy* bought you a big house and now you're cashing in. You'll be fine. But what have I got? Nothing. Nothing but a nice body and a good voice. And if I can't earn a living from my voice, then I have to fall back on the only other thing I'm any good at."

"No, Ruby. You're wrong. You don't know what you're capable of because you've never tried. You've never pushed yourself. You came here sixteen years ago as a talented singer/songwriter with a penchant for booze and seedy men. And nothing's changed. You haven't changed. Because you're too scared to see what else you can do in life."

"Bollocks," she said. "I'm not scared. I'm not scared of anything. You're the one who's sat in his room for fifteen years, wasting your life. I've been out there. I've been living. It's not my fault things haven't worked out."

Toby sighed, dragged his hand down his face. "No. It's not. It's not your fault. It's my fault."

She looked at him, questioningly.

"I made life too easy for you. I made excuses for you. I should have been tougher. I should have seen what was happening and done something to stop it."

"What was happening?! Christ — you make it sound as if I'm some kind of failure."

"No," he shook his head sadly. "I don't think you're a failure. I think you're incredible. I've always thought you were incredible. I just wish you believed that, too, instead of just pretending to."

Toby crossed the room, and kissed the top of her head, before turning and leaving, closing the door silently behind him. Ruby sat for a moment, thoughts going round her head like a cyclone. Then she picked up a book and hurled it at the back of the door.

On Thursday morning, Ruby and Tim filled a hire van with Ruby's accumulated clutter. Tim bought a magnum of Bollinger which he left in the fridge as a thank you to the house and they left. Nobody saw them off. As the van pulled away from the house, Ruby glanced up towards Toby's window and saw him there, a pensive figure, staring sadly down into the road.

Ruby swallowed the lump in her throat and concentrated instead on the road ahead, on her new life in Soho, on the man by her side, on the future.

CHAPTER SEVENTY

Toby met Leah outside Park Road baths on Thursday afternoon. It was a blustery, wet, miserable day with the nasty bite of a chill north wind. Toby's cheeks felt raw and exposed without their furry covering and he brought the collar of his coat up high round his face to protect himself.

In his carrier bag he had a brand-new pair of trunks, purchased that very morning from his new favourite menswear shop. They were black with a grey stripe down the sides and made of a very unembarrassing cotton fabric that didn't cling to anything at all. Leah looked windswept and dishevelled when she arrived a moment later, but she was smiling widely and greeted Toby with a kiss on the cheek.

"Nasty day," said Toby, following her towards the entrance.

"Vile," she said, smiling at him over her shoulder. "Perfect day for a swim."

Leah was already in the pool when Toby emerged from the changing rooms a few moments later, clutching his towel to his chest. He watched her for a minute or two, moving effortlessly up and down the pool with strong, languid movements. She smiled when she saw him watching her and patted the edge of the pool. "Are you coming in?"

He nodded, marvelling at the solid slope of her bare shoulders, the domed sheen of her wet hair.

"Just be careful," she teased. "No stunt dives this time."

He put the towel down on the side of the pool and carefully picked his way to the shallow end. He lowered himself onto his bottom and let his legs dangle in the lukewarm water. He heard a distant memory echo in his head, a teacher calling to him, "*Dobbs! I want to see ten lengths, breast stroke. Get that gangling body in the water now!*" Toby shuddered slightly and let himself slide into the pool. Leah swam to him and got to her feet. Water cascaded off her body. She was wearing a black swimming costume that gleamed in the fluorescent light. Toby tried not to let his gaze wander too freely around her impressive form, tried not to let it linger too long on her firm round breasts, on her strong thighs, her armpits, her knees, her collarbones, her groin . . . but it was impossible. She looked astounding. She looked so good that he wanted to throw her over his shoulder in the manner of a caveman and make love to her in the undergrowth. He gulped and tried to turn his attention to the matter in hand. To the matter of getting his whole body under the water and afloat in some mode that wouldn't humiliate either himself or Leah.

He started off on his back, having some vague recollection that that was easier than swimming on your front. Leah smiled encouragingly at him. "Are you

OK?" she mouthed. He nodded, causing water to flood over his brow and into his mouth. He flung himself over onto his front and choked. He really wasn't designed for this. If the optimum aerodynamic design for swimming was, say, the dolphin, then Toby was more of a newborn giraffe. Leah, on the other hand, was sleek and solid and built for the water. She smiled as she swam back towards him. "Why don't you just splash around in the shallow end for a while, wait until you've got your fins back."

"My fins?"

"Yes, everybody's got fins. They're invisible. You just have to work out how to operate them."

"Right," Toby nodded, unconvinced, and flipped himself over onto his back again. His ears filled with water and he closed his eyes, enjoying the sensation of being partially cut off from reality. He floated there for a while, his hands and feet rotating gently under the water, listening to the gurgle of underwater movements, the muted echoes of shouting children, and considered his next move. Because he hadn't come to the swimming baths today with Leah to *swim*. He had much grander plans for the afternoon than a bit of splashing around inelegantly in piss-filled municipal water. Today he was going to take another big step towards his future. Today he was going to shape his destiny. Today he was going to do something utterly amazing, but potentially devastating.

He drifted across the pool, his head full of plans, his eyes closed, oblivious to the existence of anybody else until his head his something hard and he realized that somehow or other, without even really trying, he'd reached the other end of the pool.

Toby had a lot of news to fill Leah in on in the pub over the road. She listened rapt as he told her all about Con and Daisy getting back together and Ruby moving out with Tim. She was moved to tears when he told her Joanne's story and delighted when she heard that Jack had invited Melinda out for dinner and that Melinda was bouncing round the house like a lovesick teenage girl.

"So it's nearly all come together?" she said.

"Yes," he nodded. "Just got to get the house finished and I'll be ready to move on."

"To Cornwall?"

"Yes," he said, "or maybe Devon. Look." He pulled open his carrier bag and took out a sheaf of papers. "I printed these off today, for you to see." He handed her the papers and watched her while she flicked through them. They were properties he'd found on the Internet. Fishermen's cottages and Georgian townhouses and windswept bungalows and barn conversions. They had landscaped gardens tumbling towards the sea, courtyards filled with hanging baskets, manicured lawns that stretched to the horizon, paddocks, outbuildings, driveways, workshops. They were small; they were large; they were compact; they were rambling. Each one represented a dream of some kind or another, a suggestion of a lifestyle, of an existence.

"What do you think?" he said.

"I think," she said, "that living in London is the biggest rip-off known to man. I mean, look at this one —" She pulled out the details for a double-fronted cottage facing the sea in a fishing village in Devon. "That's probably what my flat's worth. A piddling little one-bedroom flat in Finchley? Or a gorgeous three-bedroom cottage *facing the sea*?" She shook her head. "These are amazing. Completely. I could happily live in any one of them."

"You could?" he said, his heart starting to race lightly beneath his ribcage.

"God, yes. Oh, wow, look at this one. Look at the garden. And that kitchen. And it's even got a shop . . ."

Toby smiled and pulled the page from her hand. "Do you like that one, then?"

"It's amazing. Imagine living there, running your own little shop. How lovely would that be?"

"I think it would be the loveliest thing imaginable," he said. "Completely perfect."

"So, wow, which one are you going to buy?"

"I'm going to buy," he said, "the one that you like the best."

"No," she laughed, "it's your dream. You have to decide."

Toby glanced down at his beer, then back up at Leah. Her hair was still damp from the swimming pool. Her face was clear of make-up. She was so vital, so healthy, so alive. He could imagine her throwing sticks for dogs on beaches, cycling up a hill to get the papers, going for a bracing dip in the sea in the middle of winter. He could see her running stewed fruit through a muslin cloth into an empty jam jar, collecting apples in a basket, sitting in a low-beamed pub drinking something local. She was a country girl trapped in an urban existence. She would thrive in the country. She would blossom. And so would he.

Toby took Leah's hand in his and breathed in deeply. "I think you should come with me," he said.

"What?" she smiled. "To look at places with you, you mean?"

He breathed out. For a moment he said nothing. He knew exactly what he'd intended to say, what he *wanted* to say. He wanted to say, No, come with me and *live with me*. I'll be lost without you. I need you in my life. I need you to feel normal. But as he listened to the words in his head, another voice started whispering in his ear, saying, This is mad. Completely mad. I mean, why would you leave everything behind to come and live with me? You didn't even *know* me two months ago. And you've got a boyfriend and a job and I'm just some weird bloke who lives over the road. You know, some bloke who's still married, for God's sake, married to some woman who's probably dead for all I know, some bloke who's managed to be in love with a selfish, silly, horrible cow for fifteen years even though he knew it was pathetic, some bloke who *claims* to be a poet though he's written nothing worth even *looking* at for years, some bloke who's sitting here wearing *second-hand underpants*. I mean, if you ever wondered who it was that went into charity shops and actually bought other people's underwear, well now you know, you're looking at him. And for some reason, Christ knows why, I'd got it into my head that you and I had some kind of future together, that you and I made sense. I thought I was going to make this wild, random, *utterly insane* suggestion and that you would actually give it serious consideration.

"Ha!" he said, loudly and unexpectedly.

"What?" said Leah.

"Nothing," said Toby. "Just, er, I was going to say, but, now, I don't know. And, I just . . . *shit*," he punched the table. "I'm such an idiot." He pulled on his overcoat and began stuffing the property details back into his carrier bag. Leah gazed at him. "I'm sorry," he said, "I have to go. I have to, er . . ."

"Toby," she said, "what's the matter? Don't go."

"Sorry," he said, "I have to. Goodbye."

He grabbed his carrier bag and left the pub without looking back, striding through the early evening gloom and drizzle, each drop of rain burning against the raw surface of his skin.

Leah tried to catch up with him. He could hear her calling out to him. He started to run, his feet hitting the wet streets of Crouch End with heavy, rhythmic thumps, until he couldn't hear her voice any more.

CHAPTER SEVENTY-ONE

Leah and Amitabh waited outside the station at Ascot for his father to collect them. Malina had invited them over for lunch, just the two of them. Amitabh had been in a strange mood all weekend and Leah knew that something was afoot, as Malina usually invited them over only for family dos with brothers and sisters and cousins and aunts in attendance.

A gigantic Mercedes SUV swooped to a halt in front of them and Hari got out. He greeted his son with a firm hug and Leah with kisses on either cheek. Leah sat in the back as they headed through the countryside towards their well-ordered cul de sac of executive new-build houses. Hari and Amitabh sat in the front discussing Chelsea's performance in the Champion's League.

Malina was her usual delighted, charming self and met them at the door with squeezes and strokes and kisses. She brought them beer and asked Leah a million questions about her health and her family and her life. She stood over the hob in their immaculate kitchen, stirring big pans of fragrant-smelling curries and basmati rice.

They had lunch round the dining table, surrounded by framed photographs of Amitabh and his sisters and his brother, in their graduation gowns, clutching rolls of paper, looking gauche and proud. Above the fireplace was a family portrait, Hari, Malina and their four children, posed together in a studio in bland early 1990s clothes with too-long hair. On the mantelpiece was a brass carriage clock, an invitation to a gala dinner at the Royal Ascot Golf Club and an ornate statue of Ganesha.

Leah helped herself to another serving of spinach and lentils, and tore off a strip of roti. Amitabh was sweating slightly, rivulets running down his temples, which he mopped up at intervals with a linen napkin.

"Are you OK?" Leah asked, nudging him gently.

"Yeah," he said, "I'm fine. Just a bit, you know . . ."

"What — too spicy for you?" teased his father.

"No," he said. "It's nothing. I'm just feeling a bit . . . it's nothing."

Amitabh didn't speak again for the duration of the meal, just grunted in response to questions and shovelled food into his mouth. He was fidgety and distracted, as if he were planning to do a runner.

"What on earth is the matter with you?" Malina finally snapped as she cleared away pudding bowls. "Are you ill or something?"

"No, I'm not ill. I'm . . . I've got to do something."

"You need to go to the toilet?"

"No, I don't need to go to the toilet, Mum. I need to . . . God, I need to do *this*."

He launched himself from his chair and suddenly he was on his knees, on the floor, at Leah's feet. He grabbed her hands with his sweaty ones and he gazed into her eyes. "Leah," he said, "two weeks ago Mum and Dad offered me a bride. A girl. I saw her picture; she was really pretty. And I spoke to her on the phone. She's really nice. A trainee barrister, twenty-six years old. And . . . and I thought about it. I really did. I wanted to want it. I wanted to do the right thing. But all I could think about was us, about how happy we are and how much I love you and how much I want to be with you. And then it hit me, like a bullet, in the head. I can't live without you. I tried it and it was horrible. And I want you to know how serious I am about you, about us. So . . ."

He put his hand into the back pocket of his trousers and pulled out a small velvet-covered box. With clumsy, sweaty fingers he snapped it open and presented it to her. "Leah, I love you. I've always loved you. Will you marry me, please, and be my wife?"

Leah stared at the ring, then at Amitabh. His brown eyes were moist with emotion. The ring was lovely — a plain silver band with a round-cut diamond in it. She watched as he pulled the ring out of its crevice and started guiding it towards the third finger of her left hand. Then she looked up and saw Hari and Malina and pulled her hand away. "But," she said, "but what about your parents?"

Amitabh looked at them. "I'm really sorry, Mum, Dad," he said. "I know you wanted different things for me, but I'm nearly thirty-one and I'm too old to compromise, too old to do what I'm told. And that girl, she was great. You chose well for me and I appreciate that, but she's not . . . *she's not my Leah*."

Leah caught her breath and stared at Hari and Malina. Hari was nodding, inscrutably; Malina was crying. Nobody said anything for a moment. Leah could hear her blood pulsing through her temples.

"Well," said Amitabh, taking hold of Leah's hands again, "will you? Will you marry me?"

Leah closed her eyes, tightly. When she opened them again, Amitabh was still staring at her. "I don't know," she sighed eventually. "I really don't know."

"But — I thought this was what you wanted."

"It was," she said. "It is. It's just. It's a bit sudden, that's all. A bit unexpected. I need time to think. I need . . ."

"Give the girl time to think," said Malina, stroking her son's shoulder.

"Yes," agreed Hari. "This is a big question you have just asked her. Let her breathe."

"Yes," said Malina, "let her breathe."

Leah smiled wanly and hooped her arms round Amitabh's downcast shoulders. She pressed her face into his thick hair and breathed in his smell, her favourite smell in the world. "I'll go home," she whispered. "You stay here."

His head nodded faintly underneath her lips. She kissed his crown, then his cheeks, and then Hari drove her back to the station.

"If you were to be our daughter-in-law, you know that we would accept that, don't you?"

"Really?" said Leah, watching the wipers arc backwards and forwards across the rain-dimpled windscreen.

"It is not what we would ask, not what we would hope, but the bigger hope for us is our children's happiness. Always."

"Amitabh thought you'd cut him off. That you'd ostracize him."

Hari shook his head. "No," he said. "It is always good to allow your children to believe that the punishments for their sins will be greater than they are, but my son's sin would have to be great indeed for me to remove him from my life. My son is my joy and my sunshine and my past and my future. My son is everything to me, everything."

Leah smiled tightly and dug her fingernails gently into the palm of her hand.

"But, Leah, just because my son was prepared to make such a sacrifice for you, that does not mean that you must accept his proposal. He would not want you to marry him out of a sense of guilt or duty. And neither would we. Think long on it. Think hard. Follow your heart, Leah. Follow your heart."

CHAPTER SEVENTY-TWO

All the structural work had been completed now. The balconies were fixed, the windows had been reglazed, the kitchen and bathrooms were done, the front path had been relaid, the plumber had been, the electrician had been and the plasterers had been. All that was left now was the fun stuff. Painting, carpets, gardening, curtains.

Toby decided that some retail therapy was needed. He'd been in his bedroom pretty much continuously since Thursday evening, nursing the open sores of his self-orchestrated humiliation. He couldn't bear even to peer through his curtains in case he saw her or, worse still, in case she saw him. But it was Monday morning now. She would be at work. The streets were safe. He pulled open the bottom drawer of his desk to get out some cash and gasped.

The drawer was empty.

He pulled open the drawer above, hoping that in some bizarre lost moment, some forgotten corner of time, he'd decided to put it somewhere else.

Over the course of the next ten minutes he applied this theory to every single corner of his room, to every drawer, box, tray, corner, nook and cranny. He upturned everything, looked on top of everything, behind everything, underneath everything. It couldn't be. It was impossible. Inconceivable. The fact of the nonexistence of £30,000 of his own money could be explained away by only one possibility. Someone he lived with had taken it. He sat on the edge of his ransacked bed and tried to make sense of things. It couldn't be Con. He'd already promised to lend him all the money he needed. There was no reason for him to steal from him. Equally he was sure it couldn't be Melinda. She just wasn't the type. Air hostesses didn't *steal*. That just left Joanne, a convicted burglar, an ex-drug addict about to be made homeless, or Ruby, a penniless, self-centred musician who'd left the house on Thursday morning without a forwarding address. It could be either of them. "*Shit*," he hissed at himself, "*shit, shit*, SHIT."

CHAPTER SEVENTY-THREE

Leah had her lunch at a café across the road on Monday afternoon. Ruth was back in the country for a few days and was in the shop looking strangely shiny and taut, and being incredibly annoying. Judging by her demeanour and her appearance, Leah suspected that Ruth's time in LA may have involved a surgical procedure or two, and the possible dissolution of her fledgling relationship with a young man called Rex.

She ordered a bagel and a fizzy water and breathed a sigh of relief. It was good to be alone. She had so much stuff swirling round inside her head that she thought she might be sick. She rested her head on her hands and glanced around the café. Immediately she saw three couples, surrounding her on three sides, seemingly planted by fate to help her consider her situation. On her left sat an Asian couple; young, smart, trendy, sharing a newspaper over two cappuccinos. On her right was a mixed couple: him, Asian; her, white and pregnant. In front of her sat a white couple, with a small baby in a sling. The white couple with the baby wore no wedding rings, the mixed couple with the pregnant bump wore an engagement ring, the Asian couple both wore bands. Every possible permutation of her destiny surrounded her. Mixed marriage, arranged marriage, pregnancy, parenthood. And then she saw herself, reflected in a mirror on the other side of the café, a person, not quite a woman, but no longer a girl, sitting alone with a huge decision to make and no one to help her make it.

She made a mental pros-and-cons list in her head.

Reasons to marry Amitabh

- She loved him.
- They were compatible.
- She wouldn't have to be single and go on dates and show other men her body and shave her legs every day and get to know someone else's parents/friends/siblings.
- She wouldn't have to move out of her flat and move in with strangers and end up like one of those lost souls in Toby's house.
- She could have a baby now rather than waiting until she met someone else, got to know them, committed to them, waited a couple of years, got married and then had a baby, by which time she'd be nearly a hundred.
- She would still be a relatively young bride and could get away with a proper full-on wedding dress. If she wanted. Which she probably didn't, but it was nice to have the option.
- Her parents would be happy.

Reasons not to marry Amitabh

- He was really annoying.
- They'd end up living in that flat for ever because Amitabh didn't like change.
- He was marrying her only because he thought it was what she wanted and if they stayed together then nothing would have to change.
- He probably didn't even want babies, given that he was still one himself.
- The love she felt for him was more sisterly than carnal.
- He would be convinced that by marrying her he'd completed his side of some imaginary deal and would make absolutely no effort with anything else ever again.
- His parents would be philosophical, but always slightly disappointed.

Two months ago she'd been ready to settle down, but now, oddly, she wasn't. Her time away from Amitabh had given her space to see that there might be other things in store for her.

She lifted her handbag onto her lap and pulled out a piece of paper. It was the details of the cottage in Devon, the one with the vacant shop at the front that Toby had given her to look at on Thursday. She sighed, imagining herself there, in that snug, simple place. She thought about what she might sell, from that tiny bowfronted shop. Cakes? Underwear? Hardware?

Records? Things that people actually needed, instead of overpriced frippery and froth? And then, unexpectedly and magically, she imagined Toby there, too, standing with her at the shop counter, his big hands unpacking boxes, smiling shyly at a customer.

She folded the particulars into four, slipped them back into her handbag and headed back for work, feeling only marginally less confused.

CHAPTER SEVENTY-FOUR

Within two minutes of his phone call to Damian explaining his unfortunate situation, three men in overalls had switched off their radio, collapsed their ladders, put their empty mugs back in the kitchen, loaded their van and left. Toby watched them from his window, reversing their van out of its parking space, disappearing up the road, going somewhere to paint walls for someone who could actually afford to pay them. He sighed, feeling vaguely nauseous. Half an hour later Damian arrived, looking very serious, his customary air of philosophical acceptance somehow not in evidence.

"This is bad," he said.

Toby nodded and handed him a cup of Japanese green tea.

"Very bad," he continued.

"I know," said Toby, "it is truly the epitome of bad. And I just wish there was something I could say to you that would make it less bad than it is. But there isn't. I had £30,000 and someone has taken it and I have absolutely no way of getting it back. You're not going to take me to court, are you?"

Damian pondered the question. He took a sip of his tea and smacked his lips together. He pondered the question further. "No," he said, eventually. "No. You're a friend of Leah's. You're a good bloke. But my men need to be paid and we need to work something out." He got to his feet and started pacing the room. Toby watched him anxiously.

"I tell you what," he said, "how about this? I've got a development going on in Mill Hill. I need to furnish it. And this stuff," he gestured round the room, "would look the part."

"What — my furniture?" Toby asked in horror.

"Yeah. These sofas, the coffee table, any other stuff you've got. Conran, you said it was?"

"Yes, but . . ."

"How much would you say it was all worth?"

"Christ. I don't know. Six grand for the sofas, three for the coffee table."

"Cool. Nine grand. OK, so I'll take this lot now and then, as a favour, because you're Leah's mate, I'll take the rest of the money when you've sold the house."

"What, really?"

"Yeah. I don't like spreading bad karma around. I like keeping things simple and fair. Uncomplicated, you know?"

Toby nodded, furiously, desperately wanting to keep Damian as happy as possible in case he changed his mind and decided to summon up the gods of bad karma after all. He shook his hand, firmly and gratefully, at the door five minutes later.

"I'll let you know about picking up the stuff," said Damian. "Probably be early next week, I'd have thought."

"Excellent," said Toby, attempting to make the prospect of having no furniture sound like a real treat. "Excellent. And the men? They'll be here tomorrow morning, will they?"

Damian gave him a quizzical look. "The men?"

"Yes. Your men. To finish the job."

A slow smile of understanding dawned across Damian's face. "Oh, I see. No," he said, "they won't be coming back."

"They won't?"

"No. Sorry, mate, but you can't expect people like that to work for nothing. I've pulled the job."

"You have?"

"Sorry, mate. No choice in the matter. But, look, good luck, yeah? And I'll be in touch."

Toby watched Damian walk down the street, climb into his battered old Land Rover and drive away. Then he turned round and headed inside. The house was a shell. There were approximately sixty walls, fifteen doors, twenty radiators and eighteen window frames to paint, six flights of stairs to carpet and two and a half thousand square feet of floorboards to strip and stain. In two weeks. With one paintbrush, one ladder and one pair of hands. Toby dropped to his haunches in the hallway and considered the magnitude of the task that confronted him. Even if he painted all day from dawn till dusk he wouldn't get the house finished by the end of March.

He had only one option. He had to put it on the market as it was, unfinished, half-baked. He had no choice.

CHAPTER SEVENTY-FIVE

Leah watched Toby materialize, foot by foot, first his big feet in thick socks, then his calves, his knees, his hips, his stomach, his shoulders, his head, as he descended the stairs. She felt a surge of pleasure and smiled.

He led her into the kitchen and she gasped. "Oh, my God. What an absolutely amazing kitchen."

"Thank you," he said, caressing the granite work surface. "It's beautiful, isn't it?"

"Stunning," she agreed. "Must have cost a fortune."

"Not as much as you might think. Damian got it for me at trade."

"Ah," she smiled, "good old Damian."

"Yes," said Toby, "indeed. And luckily for me he is good old Damian. Otherwise I'd be on my way to court by now."

Leah threw him a questioning look.

"Someone's stolen Gus's money. My money. All of it. Every last penny."

"No!" Leah slapped a hand over her mouth. "Who?"

He shrugged. "I don't know," he said. "I thought it might be Joanne, but I confronted her about it just now, when she got back from work, and she would have to be an extraordinarily good liar to have pulled off such a convincing denial. And then I thought maybe it was Ruby, that she'd taken it before she left. But then I remembered that I'd seen the money on Saturday, that it was still there after she moved out. And besides, why would she need to steal my money when she's got Tim to pay for everything? So now I've got no idea. There was no sign of forced entry and nothing else has gone missing."

"Could it have been one of the builders, perhaps?"

"No," he shook his head. "No. The money was still there on Saturday and I realized it had gone on Monday morning before I'd been out of my room. No — whoever it was took it sometime between Saturday afternoon and Sunday night. It has to have been someone in the house. But I can't think who."

"What are you going to do?"

"Nothing," he said. "There's nothing I can do. Damian's taking my furniture in lieu of a third of what I owe him and he's taking the rest when I've sold the house. And in the meantime I'm left, stranded, in this bare shell of a house, without a penny to my name."

"Aren't you going to finish it?"

"No," he said, "I'll have to put it on the market as it is, half-finished. I shouldn't imagine it will affect the value . . ."

"No, but that's not the point, is it? It's about the house. About knowing that you did it justice. You can't just leave it like this. Where's your closure?"

"My closure?"

"Yes. This house has been your best friend for the past fifteen years. You can't just abandon it, half done. You need a proper ending."

"Well, yes. I agree. I do. But how? I can't afford to pay anyone and it's too big a job to take on by myself."

"Well, then, ask the others."

"No. They've all got full-time jobs. I can't expect them to take time off work."

"Well, then, do it over the weekend. You could have a painting party."

"A what?"

"A painting party. Invite everyone you know, give them a paintbrush, a beer and some pizza. The place'll be done by Monday morning."

"I'm afraid I don't know quite enough people to pull that one off."

"Oh, surely you must. What about all the people who've lived here over the years. You must have stayed in touch with some of them?"

"No," said Toby, "not really. I'm not really a staying-in-touch kind of person."

"But you must know where they are?"

"Well, most people left forwarding addresses, yes."

"And phone numbers?"

"In some cases."

"Well, then phone them up!"

"And say what? Say, hello, remember me, well, I'd like you to come to paint my house?"

"Yes! Tell them you're in trouble. Remind them how you helped them out when they were in trouble. Tell them that they owe you."

Toby shook his head. "No," he said, "I can't. Absolutely not. I would rather die. I mean, I hate the phone as it is. The thought of phoning all those people, all the questions, the how are yous and the what are you doings and the catching up and the . . . the . . . *chatting*. It just . . . urgh, no, I cannot do it. I'm sorry."

"Well, then, I'll do it. Give me your address book and I'll do it."

"Really?"

"Yes. Really. I want to see this house finished every bit as much as you do. Tell me who to call, and I'll call them."

"Half of them probably don't have the same number any more, you realize. I mean, I don't suppose you'll really be able to track any of them down."

"Stop being so negative."

"Well, really, I just don't want you to waste your time. It's so nice of you to offer and I'd hate you to go to so much trouble for nothing."

"It's not trouble. It really isn't. I'll enjoy it. It'll take my mind off . . . things."

"Things? What sort of things?"

Leah paused, wondering whether or not to tell Toby about Amitabh's proposal. She shook her head and smiled. "Nothing," she said, "nothing. Just, you know, work and stuff. Here," she said, reaching into her handbag for the cottage details, "I brought this back. You left it at the pub, the other day when you, er . . ."

"Stormed out inexplicably?"

"Yes," she smiled, "when you stormed out inexplicably."

"Hmmm." He rubbed his chin and smiled. "Yes. I'm very sorry about that. And I'm afraid I can't really offer you a particularly satisfying explanation for it. I was just, er, feeling a bit *overwhelmed*."

"Overwhelmed?"

"Yes. It's been a strange year so far. So much has happened, so much has changed. I think something just sort of *combusted* in my head." He took the paper from her hand and gazed at it for a while. "This is the one that you liked, isn't it?"

"Mm-hmm," she nodded. "I've become a bit obsessed by it, actually. Thought I'd better give it back to you before I did something stupid like *buy* it." She flashed her eyes at him and laughed.

"That wouldn't be stupid," said Toby.

"Well, yes," she said, "it would, actually. I haven't got any money, for a start. Let alone the two hundred and twenty-five other reasons I could give you for not moving to the country."

"Like what?"

"Oh," she said, "like not having a job and not being able to get a decent curry and not being near my parents and Amitabh . . ." She paused. "Well, he would rather gouge out his own eyeballs than live in the country. So . . ."

Toby nodded. "Yes. I see."

It fell silent for a moment. Then Toby sighed. "Ah, well" — he folded the paper back into four — "maybe I'll buy it and then you can come and visit."

She smiled. "Good plan," she said. "And I would like to stay in touch, you know. Once you've gone. It would be a shame not to."

"I agree," he nodded, "whole-heartedly. Utterly. Whatever happens. Let's stay in touch."

"Yes," said Leah. "Let's."

CHAPTER SEVENTY-SIX

Joanne bought herself a glass of red wine and took it to a table by the fire. She glanced at her watch. It was nearly eight o'clock. She took a sip of wine and waited, her heart beating quickly under her sweater. Getting dressed for this meeting had been strange. She'd forgotten what sort of clothes she liked to wear when she was just being herself. She'd had to force snapshot images into her mind of herself at various points in the past, imagine what she was wearing. She'd settled on jeans and a cashmere sweater with ankle boots and a nice belt. Her hair was still very blonde, but she'd styled it softly onto her face and worn subtle make-up in shades of brown and pink. She wanted to look nice for him, like the girl he remembered, not the peculiar person she'd become.

At exactly eight o'clock the door opened and Nick walked in.

Joanne gulped. He still looked the same. The fine, shoulder-length hair, the slight physique under a sensible jacket and scuffed old boots. He smiled at her, shyly, and headed towards her. They greeted each other with barely there kisses and gently squeezed arms.

"How are you?" she said.

"I'm fine," he said. "You look nice. I like your hair."

"You do? I'm going to dye it back. Its just, you know, temporary."

He smiled and nodded. "So," he said, "I'll just get myself a drink. Are you all right?" he pointed at her wine glass.

"Mm-hmm," she nodded.

She watched him at the bar, remembering the shape of him, his lines, the way he looked at bars in pubs. He came back with a pint of something and put it on the table.

"So, you got my note, then?" he said.

"Yes. Toby — that's my landlord — he gave it to me a couple of weeks ago. I've been, er . . ."

"Thinking about it?"

"Yes," she smiled tightly. "And we've been busy at the house. Decorating it. Toby's selling it and someone stole all his money and he couldn't afford to pay the, you know, painters and decorators, so we did it ourselves. I've been sanding floors all the hours, day and night. Look, I've got blisters . . ." She showed him the palms of her hands.

He winced.

"Yes, so. It's been a busy few days, so, er . . ."

"No, that's fine. I wasn't expecting you to reply immediately. I mean, it's been two years."

"It has."

"So, how are you?"

"Yes. Fine. Tired. But, you know. How are you?"

"Well," he said, "like the note said. Pretty crap. I've had you down as a missing person, you know?"

"God. Really?"

"Yeah. Of course. I thought you were dead. Thought you might have thrown yourself off a bridge. God, I've just thought and thought and thought. I just never thought you might be, Christ, just *living*. Just getting on with stuff."

She smiled tightly. "I wouldn't call it getting on with stuff."

"You wouldn't? What would you call it?"

"Existing. I've been existing. I've been pretending and acting and fooling myself and everyone else around me. I've been . . ." Her voice caught. "I've been the unhappiest girl in the whole wide world."

She started to cry then, aching, primal tears that came from the deepest wells of her being. Nick moved his chair nearer to hers and held her in his arms. "It's OK, Jo," he soothed, stroking her soft hair and kissing her juddering shoulders. "It's OK. I'm here now. I'm here."

Joanne sobbed and let Nick soothe her, his familiar hands on her hair, his warm breath on her skin, the only man she'd ever loved.

"Come home," he said. "Please, come home."

She thought of "home", that distant place, the place she'd left behind all those months before. She thought about the front door, the number six in beaten iron, the worn-out mat inside the door, her feet wiping back and forth, the little wooden table where she dropped her keys, the brass hook on the wall where she hung her coat. She suddenly remembered everything, every detail, every smell, every picture, mirror, cushion. She suddenly remembered her home.

She turned then and buried her face in Nick's chest, breathing in his smell, the smell of Saturday nights curled up on the sofa watching DVDs, of climbing into bed at night, the smell of his clothes before she put them in the washing machine and of impromptu hugs in the kitchen, the smell of her life before Maisie had died and taken everything good with her.

"Yes," she said, "yes. I want to come home."

CHAPTER SEVENTY-SEVEN

Leah's painting party turned into a painting week. A dozen people turned up at various points throughout the following ten days, bearing brushes, ladders and floor sanders; curtains, carpets and plants. It was bizarre, emotional, nostalgic and moving. Ex-tenants who Toby hadn't seen in more than ten years arrived at the front door, sometimes with wives and husbands and children in tow. Artists and actors and architects and singers gave up their free time to help finish the house. Leah herself came over every evening after work, sometimes alone, sometimes with Amitabh. Con and Daisy did the garden. Melinda risked her vinyl-tipped nails to help and even brought Jack along one night to finish painting her room. And Joanne — Joanne was a revelation, forgoing a week's temping to work full time on the house. She was surprisingly strong for such a small person, hefting large pieces of furniture out of the way and sanding all the downstairs floors.

Toby had never spent so much time out of his bedroom and found the entire experience utterly exhilarating. Catching up with old friends, meeting new people, the constant hum and chatter of lively conversation, loud music, ring pulls snapped on cans of lager, sanders buzzing, lawn mowers growling, nails being knocked into walls, curtains being hung. It was like living inside a huge stage set. The house felt thrilling and alive, a triumph of teamwork born of goodwill and humanity.

And then, finally, one Thursday afternoon, when everyone else had gone, Leah and Toby slid to the floor in the living room, opened a can of lager each, looked round and declared the house complete. Every floor was sanded and polished; the stairs and landing were carpeted; the walls were pristine and hung with carefully selected pieces of art.

"It's beautiful," said Leah.

"It is, isn't it?" said Toby. "Wonderful."

"You clever man."

"Clever." He looked at her and shook his head. "Not a bit of it. This is all down to you, all of it. I couldn't have done any of this without you."

"Oh," she said, "I'm sure you'd have found a way."

"No," he said, "I wouldn't. I'm fundamentally useless, you know?"

She laughed and he smirked. "So," she said, "what now?"

"Well," he said, "Joanne's moving out tomorrow, back to New Cross. Back to Nick. Con's going to stay with Daisy at her folks' place. Melinda's going to stay with Jack."

"And your dad?"

"He's due on Monday. I haven't heard from him, but . . ." He shrugged.

"Oh, he'll come. He's bound to."

Toby felt strangely numb about the prospect. Not excited; not nervous — just slightly sceptical. He couldn't remember enough detail about his father to be able to truly imagine what it would be like for him to be there, in front of him. He could remember a kind of tarragon-y aftershave, a thick slick of silk tie, a puff of silver hair and chinks of ice-blue iris. He could remember a Home Counties accent, tinted with a hint of estuary left over from his childhood years in Rainham, and he could just about envisage tan leather shoes and a large pockmark on his chin, just inside the crease. But he couldn't remember the whole person. He couldn't remember what his father *felt* like.

"Are you nervous?" said Leah.

Toby shrugged. "No, not really. Just . . . a bit wary, I suppose."

"What time's he coming?"

"Afternoon," said Toby. "Teatime. About four."

"Are you going to bake a cake?"

"Of course," Toby smiled. "If I can't show him anything else that I've achieved over the past fifteen years, if I can't show him a wife or grandchildren or a reasonable income, the least I can do is make him a bloody good cake."

Leah smiled. "You could show him a girlfriend."

He looked at her and frowned. "And how exactly would I do that?"

"I'll be her."

"Sorry?"

"I'll come along and pretend to be your girlfriend."

"Oh, God, Leah, but that's lying. I'm terrible at lying. He'd know immediately that something fishy was going on."

"But, really, when you think about it, it's not that much of a leap from the truth. I am a girl. I am your friend. And we do have . . . well, we have a bond. Don't we?"

Toby gulped. "Well, yes," he said. "I think we do."

"And we are affectionate. I mean, we've held hands, we've hugged. I've kissed you. Sort of . . ." she laughed.

He gulped again. "That's true," he said.

"So, really, it wouldn't take much to convince your father that I was your girlfriend. We could just — be ourselves."

Toby shrugged and nodded and tried to look nonchalant. "Yes, well," he said. "When you put it like that."

"You don't even have to say I'm your girlfriend. You could just leave it to your father to *assume*, based on our . . . *chemistry*."

He nodded again and swallowed some lager. "Good plan," he said. "Really good plan."

"That is, of course, if you don't mind your father thinking that I'm your girlfriend."

"Oh, God. Why on earth would I mind my father thinking that you're my girlfriend?"

"I don't know. Maybe I'm not your . . . type?"

"My *type*? Good grief, Leah. You would be any man's type."

"Well, that's not strictly true."

"Oh, but it is. Any sane man would be proud to present you as a girlfriend. You're the archetypal girl next door."

"Or girl over the road, in this case."

Toby smiled. "Well, yes. Indeed."

"So, is that a plan, then? I'll come over, Monday afternoon, give you a few kisses and cuddles? Charm your father. Eat some cake?"

"That sounds like a *glorious* plan."

"Good," said Leah, raising her can of lager to his. "But there's just one condition."

"Oh, yes?"

"It has to be a chocolate cake. With chocolate icing."

"It's a deal."

CHAPTER SEVENTY-EIGHT

"Well, hello!" Daisy's father strode across the driveway. "Welcome to Beens Acres!" He shook Con by the hand and took his small case from him. "Is this all you've got?"

Con nodded. "Yeah," he said, "I travel light."

He looked up at the house. It wasn't as big as it had been in his head, probably about the same size as Toby's house, except built from a different colour brick and surrounded on all four sides by fields.

"This is really good of you," he said to Daisy's dad as they climbed the pocked sandstone steps to the front door.

"Oh, it's nothing at all," he said. "We're used to it. All the girls have their boys to stay at some point. We call this the Beens Hostelry for Lovesick Boys."

Con smiled. "It's only temporary," he said, "just until I get accommodation sorted out."

"Yes, yes, of course. Spend as long as you like. As long as you like."

There was a very big dog in the hallway. Its tail beat loudly against the tiled floor and its ears flattened against its head with repressed excitement. "This is Rory," said Mr Beens. "There's a small one somewhere, too, called, variously, depending upon whom you ask, Smarties, Arthur or Bongo. You'll meet him soon, I'm sure."

The hallway was large and cluttered, full of books and lamps and piles of outdoor clothing. Through a door to the left, Con could see a big dusty sitting room, furnished with pastel-hued antiques, sage walls and yet more books.

Daisy appeared at the doorway. She was wearing a huge anorak and furry boots. She beamed and ran towards him. "You're here," she said, wrapping her arms round him.

"I am," he said.

"I didn't hear your cab."

"No," he said, "I walked from the station."

"Oh, no! Why didn't you phone? We could have picked you up."

"No," he said, "honestly. It was fine. I've never been to the country before. I wanted to see it."

"Never been to the country?" said Mr Beens, incredulously.

"No," he said. "Never. Went somewhere on a school trip once, but all I can remember is the coach journey."

"Well," said Mr Beens, "a double welcome to you, then, from us, *and* from the country."

Daisy looped her arms round Con and kissed him on the cheek. "I can't believe you're here," she said. "This is so great."

He kissed her on the lips and smiled.

"Come on. Let me show you round."

Con followed her through the house and the dog followed them, stopping every time they stopped and sitting down patiently, as if it was the first time he'd seen the house, too. The house was a weird mix of tasteful antiques and random garish pieces of furniture from the 1960s and 1970s. A small semi-glazed room at the back of the house was wallpapered with an iridescent lime-green bamboo print and the walls of the downstairs toilet were painted orange and covered in badly framed cartoons torn from newspapers. It was a house that didn't take itself seriously, that didn't care too much what anyone thought of it, a house that was comfortable in its own skin and Con could immediately sense that he would be fine here.

A small fat pony grazed thoughtfully in the back garden and a large hairy cat dozed on the kitchen counter in a circle of sunlight. The small dog that Daisy's dad had mentioned was found eating toilet paper in the bathroom.

"Oh, God, Bongo, not again." Daisy pulled the roll from his mouth and gathered up the pink shreds that lay scattered across the tiled floor. "You stupid, stupid dog."

The big dog looked disdainfully at the small dog before getting to his feet to continue the tour of the house.

"And this," said Daisy, opening a door on the attic floor, "is your room."

It was a large room, with a low sloping ceiling and a rather cheap-looking Velux window in the roof. A tiny dormer window looked out over the driveway and the main road. The bed was a single, clothed in a bright duvet and a fat pillow. There was a small pine wardrobe at the other end of the room and a Victorian washbasin and jug on a wrought-metal stand, with a lilac hand towel. "Is this OK?" said Daisy.

Con looked round. It wasn't the most characterful room in the house, but it was warm, it was dry and it had a bed in it, and as long as Con lived he would always consider that to be the most that any man could ask for.

"It's perfect," he said. "Really perfect."

"Good." She smiled. "You do know, though, don't you, that they wouldn't have the slightest problem with you being in my room?"

"I know," he said, "but it just doesn't feel right. It feels . . . *disrespectful*."

"Oh, Con. You're so old-fashioned."

"I know," he said. "I'm a gent. And I want to give your parents something," he said. "Some money. For letting me stay."

"No way," said Daisy. "Dad would be insulted."

"He would?"

"Yes. He doesn't consider this house to be his house. As far as he's concerned it's *our* house. Us girls. And he and my mother are just house-sitting for us until they die. He wouldn't dream of taking money from you."

"Well, then, let me buy them something. A gift."

"No," she said. "Don't do anything. Just relax. Just be."

"Be what?"

"Be yourself. My parents don't expect fancy presents and best behaviour. They just expect good company. Oh — and maybe a hand in the kitchen. I've told them all about your culinary prowess."

"Oh, God, you haven't, have you?"

"Of course. They're dying to try your home-baked bread."

"Oh, shit."

"What?!"

"I don't know if I can make bread on my own, without Toby there to tell me what to do."

"Of course you can. We'll do it together. You and me." She took his hand.

"You and me?"

She nodded and smiled. "Come on," she said, "let's get started."

CHAPTER SEVENTY-NINE

Ruby peeled the foil wrapper off the meal in front of her and peered cautiously underneath it. A slither of grey chicken breast with something brown and lumpy buried inside it, a smattering of tiny peas, a cluster of oily potatoes, all coated in a viscous tan-coloured sauce. She resealed the container and reached for the crackers instead.

"Pretty gross, huh?" The man next to her pointed at her tray and smiled.

"Mmm," she nodded, "not really what I fancy." She'd been aware of the man sitting next to her since she'd first taken her seat on the plane three hours ago. She'd been expecting him to strike up a conversation at some point; he'd had that air about him. He'd been reading a book, but it didn't grip him — he kept putting it down, looking away from it. He'd flicked through the in-flight magazines without reading any of the articles. He wasn't self-contained. He was bored. Ruby had tried to give off her "don't talk to me" vibes, but he'd obviously decided to override them.

"Troy," he said, offering her his hand to shake.

"Ruby," she said.

"Ruby? That's a beautiful name."

"Thank you."

"So, what takes you to New York, Ruby? Vacation?"

She shook her head. "No," she said, hoping that, if she didn't feed him any extraneous information, he might just give up.

"Right," he said, "just visiting, huh?"

"Yeah," she said, "kind of."

"I'm not from New York, myself. I live in Pittsburgh. I'll be getting a connecting flight."

She nodded and smiled and smoothed cream cheese onto a cracker.

"So, I notice that you're wearing a wedding ring. Are you meeting your husband in New York?"

"No," she said, "I'm not married."

"Oh, right. Boyfriend, then?"

"No. I don't have a boyfriend. I just wear this ring to stop people hitting on me."

"Oh," he said, "whoah. I get it. But don't worry. I'm not hitting on you. Happily married man." He tapped his wedding band and winked at her. "But if you'd like me to back off . . ."

She sighed, then softened. "No," she said, "it's fine. But when I pick up my book" — she pointed at it — "that's a sign to stop talking, OK?"

He laughed, throwing his head back. The woman across the aisle glanced at them. "Righty-ho," he said. "I hear you, I hear you. So," he said, "Ruby, what do you do?"

"I'm a singer," she said, "singer/songwriter."

"Wow." He pulled back from her and regarded her with admiration. "What sort of singer? Are you famous? Should I have heard of you?"

She laughed. "No," she said, "not unless you've been hanging out in dingy clubs in North London."

"Ah, no," he conceded. "Not quite my scene."

"No, I didn't think it would be," she smiled.

"But you're good, huh? A good singer."

"I'm bloody brilliant," she said.

He laughed again. "I bet you are," he said. "Waiting for your big break?"

"Waiting and waiting and waiting. This is my last-ditch attempt."

"Oh, right. New York or bust?"

"Yeah," she said, "that kind of thing."

"Well, hey, look, in the meantime, I should give you my card. My sister's getting married next month, been looking for a singer. Something unusual, something a bit . . . *edgy*, you know. If your luck doesn't come up, give me a ring."

Ruby shook her head. "No," she said, "not my thing. But thanks for the offer."

"Well, I tell you what, she knows some people, my sister. Big people up at Sony, up at Geffen. Might be a good opportunity to meet some people, make an impression."

Ruby turned and smiled at Troy. "Now that," she said, "sounds very interesting." She took the card from between his fingers and slipped it into her handbag. And then she let Troy F. Shultzberg buy her a bottle of champagne.

CHAPTER EIGHTY

FAIRLIGHTS, SILVERSMITH ROAD, N2
£995,000

Six double bedrooms, two bathrooms,
three receptions,
kitchen/diner,
45ft south-facing garden

A beautiful and unique residence on this ever-popular road just off the High Street. Fairlights is a fully detached double-fronted villa full of period features and brimming with character. Subject to a recent sympathetic refurbishment, this extraordinary house would make an ideal family home and an early viewing is recommended.

CHAPTER EIGHTY-ONE

Toby had grown used to waking up alone in his big, empty house. He celebrated his aloneness by tuning the radio to Radio Three and letting classical music flood every room in the house. His kitchen was as clean and uncluttered as it had been before he went to bed the previous night and the five hooks in the hallway bore only his own coat, his own jacket and his own scarf. He'd taken to having a paper delivered daily, now he knew that nobody would get to it before him, and he hadn't switched on the television since Melinda had moved out the week before. He performed a strange but very enjoyable dance as he prepared his breakfast in his pyjamas. And then he broke wind, very loudly, delighted by the absence of anyone to offend.

He considered his plans for the day ahead. He would walk down to the High Road and buy some fresh flowers for the house. Then he would go to Budgens and pick up the ingredients for his cake. Somewhere in his dusty collection of memories of his father he had an inkling of a fondness for fig rolls (or was it garibaldis?), so he would pick up a pack or two of those. And then he'd get a new teapot from the pound shop, as he'd just discovered that the teapot he'd always assumed was his was actually Ruby's and had disappeared with her two weeks ago.

When he got home, he'd put some real coffee on to brew and bake a loaf of bread, not because he wanted either coffee or bread, but because he had two more viewings that morning and he wanted the house to smell delicious. He'd done six viewings over the weekend and the house had been on the market for only three days. He enjoyed showing people round the house. Half the time he knew they couldn't afford it, that they'd only come to nose round, to see what the weird house on Silversmith Road actually looked like, but he didn't care. He was so proud of it that he saw his role more as that of a curator than a home owner. He wanted as many people as possible to see his beautiful house before it was sold and locked up against the world again.

After the viewings he'd make his cake (he didn't want to mess up the kitchen beforehand) and while it was in the oven he'd have a bath and a shave, then he'd put on some clean clothes and some new shoes, and go downstairs to await the arrival of his father.

His day was carefully constructed to leave no time at all for milling about, faffing around or thinking. He focused on the precise nature of the icing he'd make for his cake and the exact hue of the lilies he'd buy. His father's arrival was something so vague and unthinkable that he couldn't bring himself to contemplate it, until his father was actually standing right in front of him, on his door step. Until he really, really had to.

CHAPTER EIGHTY-TWO

"Does that include service?" Reggie eyed the waiter through slanted eyes.

"No, sir," said the waiter. "It doesn't."

Reggie sighed and pulled a handful of coins out of his pocket which he dropped onto the tray disdainfully. He didn't bother counting them. He didn't care. A few quid was enough.

He glanced at his watch. Three-thirty. He patted his belly and downed the last of his coffee. Disgusting coffee. You couldn't get a decent cup in London. He looked out of the window at the street outside. It was raining. Of course it was raining. This was London. He'd had enough of London, only been here two weeks and he was fed up with the place already. Admittedly March wasn't the best time of year to be here, but, still, he remembered now exactly why he'd left in the first place. Bad coffee, overpriced food, never-ending rain, and all these miserable, whey-faced people wandering about, grumpy and dissatisfied, as if all the troubles of the world were on their shoulders.

Talking of which, it occurred to him that he'd arranged to see his son this afternoon. Well, he hadn't arranged it; Peter had arranged it. Reggie hated talking to people on the phone. It was bad enough talking to people you knew well; the thought of phoning up his son was unbearable.

He pulled a piece of paper out of his wallet and looked at it.

31 Silversmith Road, London N2. Where the hell was London N2? And how was he going to get there? He sighed and put the paper back in his wallet. He thought of his big peculiar son, his strange haunted eyes, his mass of unkempt hair. Could that much have changed? Was it really worth trekking all the way out to some godforsaken part of North London to find out that they still had nothing in common, that he still didn't like him very much?

But then, he'd like to see this house, the house he'd bought him all those years ago. And he'd like to see Karen and any children they may have had together. His grandchildren. He had no other plans for this afternoon. Sod it, he thought, sod it. He'd go.

He allowed a man by the front desk to fold him into his overcoat, then he unfurled his small umbrella and left the restaurant. He waited awhile on the corner of Dover Street and Bond Street, for a cab to appear. When one failed to materialize he began to walk, feeling the legs of his trousers soaking up the rain with every step. People barged towards him, forcing him into puddles and almost into the kerb. This was what it was to get old. No respect. No acknowledgement of the person you were or the person you had been. A strident gust of wind forced the spokes of his umbrella into rigor-mortised angles and he battled to bring it back under control. He zigzagged through the streets of Mayfair, his eyes scanning the street constantly for that welcoming amber glow. Finally he saw a cab, across the road, just dropping off a fare. He skipped across the road, feeling his rich meal slopping about in the pit of his belly.

"London N2," he said, breathlessly.

"Sorry, mate," said the driver. "I'm on a call. Pre-booked."

"*Shit*," hissed Reggie, under his breath. "Well, where are you going, then?"

"South Ken."

Reggie thought briefly of his son, waiting for him on the other side of London. And then he thought of his warm flat in Chelsea, where he would be alone, required to talk to no one, to do nothing.

"Fuck it," he said, "fuck it. Take me there. Take me to South Ken."

He closed his umbrella, slipped into the back of the cab, and looked forward to getting home.

CHAPTER EIGHTY-THREE

"Oh, God, Toby," said Leah, stroking his back, "I'm really sorry. I can't believe he didn't come."

Toby stared though the window at the street outside. He'd watched dusk come and go, and now it was dark. There'd been no phone call, no word from his father or from Peter. They were sitting side by side at the dining table. The chocolate cake sat on the table in front of them, a forty-five-degree wedge missing. A plate of garibaldis and fig rolls sat untouched next to a brand-new white china teapot. Toby tried to feel sad about this poignant arrangement of objects, tried to be hurt by the non-appearance of his father. But he couldn't.

"You know what?" he said. "I don't care that he didn't come. I really don't. This isn't about him any more. And I'm not sure it ever was. This" — he indicated the house — "this is about me. About . . . God, I don't know, about *growing up*, I suppose." He laughed wryly and wiped some icing off the edge of the cake plate with his fingertip.

"Are you suggesting that you weren't a grown-up before?"

"No. I was a very nearly forty-year-old teenager. Wearing the same clothes, writing the same crappy poems, in love with the same woman . . ."

"Ruby?"

"Yes, Ruby. How did you know?"

"Blatantly obvious."

He raised his eyebrows and sighed. "Ah, well. There you go. Wearing my schoolboy crush on my sleeve like an adolescent. I made a list, you know, after Gus left me his money, after my father wrote to me. A list of things I needed to do. It started off with buying new sofas and it ended with this." He cast his arm round the room. "I've achieved nearly everything I set out to achieve."

"You should feel very pleased with yourself."

"I do," he said. "Now I just need to write some publishable poetry, finalize the divorce and marry someone, and my list will be done and dusted."

"Marry someone?" she smiled. "You put that on your list?!"

"Well, not marry someone, necessarily. Just, you know, meet someone. Someone special. God, that sounds so naff."

"No, it doesn't. It sounds absolutely right. Everyone should have someone special."

Toby nodded and a silence followed. "What about you and Amitabh? You seem to be getting on well."

"Do we?"

"Yes. Well, from what I could see."

She sighed and laughed. "Well, that's funny because we're not. Not at all."

"Oh, dear. Why's that?"

"Because," she said, sighing and flicking her thumbnail against the ring pull on her lager, "because he asked me to marry him . . ."

Toby turned to gaze at her, in amazement. "Oh, my God. *Really*?"

"Uh-huh. A couple of weeks ago. And I still haven't given him an answer."

"You haven't?"

"No. I just keep changing my mind. The pros and cons are so evenly weighted and I don't know what to do."

"But you told me you didn't want to marry him."

"I know. I know I did. But it's all about options, isn't it? It's all about where I go next. And really and truly, where do I go next? If there was a sign somewhere, something to guide me on to the next place, the next turn in the road, then . . ."

"Then you'd turn him down?"

She nodded and smiled ruefully.

"Oh, Leah . . ."

"I know," she said. "I know. Pathetic, isn't it? I'm sure life wasn't supposed to be like this. I'm sure the idea was that you met someone and you knew, that it was one thing or another, that it was black or it was white. But life — it's so stupidly *grey* half the time, isn't it? So vague and so silly and . . . *nothing*."

"Oh, but, Leah. It doesn't have to be."

"Well, I know that. But sometimes it just *is*. And there's nothing you can do about it."

"But of course there is. I mean, look at me. My life was as grey as it gets. As grey as clouds, as grey as pigeons, as grey as concrete. And then, well, *you* came along. And made everything Technicolor."

Leah laughed. "I did? How?"

"Just by being you. By being so alive and fresh. By seeing beyond my strange demeanour and finding a perfectly nice, normal bloke underneath there whom I never knew existed. And when I say that I owe all of this to you, I'm not just talking about the house, my tenants, all of this, I'm talking about this man, sitting next to you, who goes out to shops and chats with old friends, and solves problems for people and buys his underwear from Marks and Spencer's. I owe this man to you. Completely. You've transformed me, Leah, and I can't bear to think that, having made my world kaleidoscopic with new and wonderful things, you'd compromise your own right to a proper, satisfying ending." He turned his chair to face her properly. "I've spent my entire life letting the world wash over me. But not any more. It's my turn now. And I want you to know that I'm here for you. One hundred per cent. Whatever you decide to do. But I also want you to know without a scintilla of uncertainty that I could be happy with you for ever. I want you to know . . ." — he stopped, blinked, looked at Leah — "that I am completely in love with you . . ."

She stared back at him, breathlessly.

"Does that surprise you?" he said.

She nodded, mutely.

"I've been wanting to tell you for ages. That was why I ran out of that pub the other day. Because I was about to tell you, then I lost my nerve and freaked. Completely. But now, well, I've realized. I've only got one stab at this. And I'll be off soon and we won't be neighbours any more and you'll get married to someone who you're not sure about and it'll all be way too late."

"Toby, I . . ."

"Leah. It's fine. You don't have to say anything. I only want you to know this. Not to act on it. If you're going to marry Amitabh, which I don't think you should, then I want you to be armed with the knowledge that someone else loved you, too. That you had options, even if it was only me, a big, skinny old freak from over the road. I know that someone like you would never love someone like me . . ."

"Why not?"

"I don't know. Because I'm me, because I'm . . ."

"Tall, dark and handsome? Clever, charming and funny?"

Toby frowned. "Come on, now," he said. "Don't be facetious."

"Who's being facetious?"

"Well, you are, obviously."

"No," said Leah, "I'm not. I'm being completely and utterly sincere. You and me. We fit." And then, to prove her point, she turned her chair towards Toby's, brought Toby's face towards hers with her hands, and said, "I'm going to kiss you now. Is that OK?"

Toby nodded, harder and more fervently than he'd ever nodded before, and when her lips met his he felt the whole blurry, fuzzy, silly and incomprehensible nonsense of his being suddenly click into focus. He felt everything suddenly fall into place and make clear and perfect sense for the first time in his whole ridiculous life.

"I can't believe you just did that," he said.

"Neither can I," laughed Leah.

"That was amazing," said Toby.

"It was, wasn't it."

"Can I take it that you're not going to marry Amitabh?"

"Of course I'm not going to marry bloody Amitabh."

"Well, then," said Toby, "in that case, I think you should kiss me again."

CHAPTER EIGHTY-FOUR

DIDCOT WALSH

312 High Road London N2 1AG

2 April 2005

Dear Toby,

I am writing to confirm the offer received this morning for the asking price of £995,000. The buyer is chain-free and hoping to exchange within six weeks. Hopefully it should be a smooth process. I don't foresee any problems. I will be in touch shortly.

Yours faithfully,

W. F. Didcot

Walter Didcot

....

"Oh, hello, this is a message for Toby Dobbs. It's Susan here from Tixall's in Penzance. Just to let you know that

I've spoken to the owners of Chyandour House and they've accepted your offer of £289,000. They've also agreed to take it off the market for a week, pending the sale of your own property. Hope this is OK and I'll speak to you soon . . ."

....

In the BARNET County Court,
between TOBY BERTRAND DOBBS the Petitioner
and KAREN JANE DOBBS the Respondent

referring to the decree made in this cause on the 4th day of MARCH 2005 whereby it was decreed that the marriage solemnized on the 7th day of AUGUST 1990 at LAMBETH REGISTER OFFICE, THE TOWN HALL, BRIXTON HILL SW2 1RW between
TOBY BERTRAND DOBBS the Petitioner
and
KAREN JANE DOBBS the Respondent

be dissolved unless sufficient cause be shown to the court within (six) weeks from the making thereof why the said decree should not be made absolute, and no such cause having been shown, it is hereby certified that the said decree was on the 22nd day of APRIL 2005 made final and absolute and that the said marriage was thereby dissolved.

2 June 2005

Dear Toby,

Wow! Thanks! I've just got my balance and the money's gone in! Fuck — I thought it was a typo at first. Couldn't believe all those zeros! Thanks a lot, mate. It's the most decent thing anyone's ever done for me and I won't let you down. I promise not a penny of it will go on beer (or clothes!).

Sorry I haven't been in touch much. I've been really busy. Flight school starts next week and I've been looking for somewhere to live. I'll be sharing with some other guys, students from the school. The flat's not that great (I miss number 31!), but it'll be fine for a year or so. I'll be glad to move out of Daisy's place, too. It was really nice and everything, but I don't like to freeload. It's good to be paying rent again and I won't miss their stupid dog breaking into my room every night to eat my socks! They had to take him to the vet's the other day with half a flannel in his stomach!

Things are going great with Daisy. She's on really good form and you can tell just by looking at her that the country air is better for her than being in London. She's waitressing at her mate's restaurant in the village. I've been helping out there, too, washing dishes and stuff, just to tide me over. She's thinking about doing a cookery course, setting up a catering thing. I reckon she'll be brilliant. And cooking's something you can do anywhere, isn't it, anywhere in the world.

Her mum taught me how to do her physio. It's really easy, actually. And she's doing so well at the moment that it doesn't even take that long. I won't be able to do it any more when I move out, but at least I know how to do it now, if we ever end up living together. As for how I feel about her illness, I'm doing what you said, just acting like I don't know the truth, just having fun with her. I'm a strong bloke. Whatever happens in the future, I can take it. Well, I'll have to . . .

I quite like it out here, in the sticks. I miss my mates, of course, and my mum, but I don't really miss London. How are you, anyway? Have you moved yet? Maybe you're in the country, too. Weird, eh?!

Anyway, I just wanted to say thanks a lot for the money. And for everything. I'll write again when I'm settled at the school. And watch your post. You'll be getting an unexpected invitation any day now!

All the best,

Con

<table>
<tr>
<td>
5 June 2005
Dearest Toby,
Well, here I am in Kathmandu! Nick's taken a year's sabbatical from work and we're going to travel the world. Well, as much of it as possible. We started in Islamabad, came down India through New Delhi and then up the hills to Nepal. Next stop Malaysia. Having an amazing time. I'll send you postcards whenever I can. Hope you're happy. I am! Love,
Jo xxxx
</td>
<td>
Toby Dobbs
Fairlights
31 Silversmith Road
London
N2 8AS
</td>
</tr>
</table>

Dear Toby

Melinda and Jack are engaged!
Please come and help us celebrate at
41 Cranmore Gardens, London, N10 5TY
on Saturday 23rd June 2005

....

VISSER SCHOENMAKER SMIT
Literary Agency

The Estate of Augustus Veldtman
c/o Toby Dobbs

Dear Mr Dobbs,

Please allow me to introduce myself. My name is Lucia Schoenmaker and I represent Mr Veldtman at his agency. I was very saddened to hear of his death. Although I never met him, I feel he is someone close to me, having personally represented his wonderful book for so many years (more than I care to admit!).

I am writing for two reasons. First, I enclose Mr Veldtman's royalty statement and payment for the period covering June 2004 to December 2004. This amounts to the princely sum of £3.78, which is about standard.

My second reason for writing is to tell you about an interesting proposal we have had from a TV production company here in Holland. Mr Veldtman was in the habit of posting us his personal journals with the instructions that they be kept untouched until his death, at which time we could use them however we saw fit. This company is interested in making a documentary about Mr Veldtman, about his extraordinary life, his career as a film actor, his love affairs and, of course, his marvellous book. They have offered us an option of €6,000 for the rights to the journals, which they will extend to €60,000 should the project proceed to production.

I think this is a very generous offer and I would suggest that we accept it.

There is one other point, however. The last journal Mr Veldtman sent us is from 1992 and I wondered if you had come upon any further journals after his death. If so, the production company would love to have them, just to complete the picture. I understand that Mr Veldtman lived in your house for the final years of his life and this was a very interesting period in his life, I'm sure.

Please let me know what you think about these matters. I will look forward to hearing from you in due course. And maybe if you were ever to find yourself in The Hague we could meet for a coffee and a chat.

Yours, most sincerely,

Lucia Schoenmaker

CHAPTER EIGHTY-FIVE

Toby watched the removals van pull out of Silversmith Road and headed back inside. The house was completely empty now. Not a stick of furniture; not a picture or a plant. The sun streamed through the front windows, highlighting the house's natural beauty. He wandered for a while, from room to room, just as he'd done the very first time he'd seen the house. This was exactly how he'd wanted the house to look that day, all those years ago. Leah had been right to persuade him to finish the job. Leaving would have been much harder if he hadn't.

He took the stairs slowly towards the upper floors, as he'd done a thousand times before. The thud of his footsteps reminded him of Gus's slow rhythmic steps, up and down the stairs, day in, day out. He peered into Joanne's room, Ruby's room, Con's room. And then he took the next flight of stairs and went into his own room. There was a roll of packing tape on the floor and an empty box. And there, on the floor, where his wardrobe had been, was a piece of paper:

Things To Do

~~1. Buy new sofas~~
~~2. Get builder in to quote on works~~
~~3. Get plumber in to quote on works~~
~~4. Get decorator in to quote on works~~
~~5. Get tenants to move out~~
6. Get a publishing deal (?)
~~7. Get divorced~~
~~8. Sell house~~
~~9. Move to Cornwall (?)~~
~~10. Stop being in love with Ruby~~
~~11. Find someone proper to be in love with~~
12. **START LIVING**

He smiled and pulled a pen out of his jacket pocket and with a flourish of intent and satisfaction he drew a thick black line through the last two words.

CHAPTER EIGHTY-SIX

A seagull regarded Leah from the windowsill with tiny pinprick eyes. She stared back at it, until it heard a cry from above and glided away, into the clear blue sky. She peered through the tiny dormer window, to the beach across the road. The boats were out already, with their crab pots. Solitary anglers lined the shore, casting for the whiting which were back for the autumn. Leah had only been here for three months, but already she knew about the seasonal variations of aquatic life around the headland, about the tidal patterns, about the likelihood of a good catch, or a bad one. She also knew about the problems with the new headmistress at the primary school, that Mrs Wendle had been taken to the hospice on Friday night and that the beer served at the Plough up the road was watered down. It wasn't difficult to pick up local knowledge. All you had to do was keep your ears open as you walked round the village. All you had to do was talk to people.

She headed downstairs, bowing to avoid the low ceiling halfway down and stooping to collect some mail from the door mat.

Toby smiled at her as she walked towards him.

"Tea?" he said.

"Lovely," she said.

She leaned down and kissed him on the lips, then dropped the mail on the table in front of him.

"Oh, look." She pulled a newspaper from the bottom of the pile. "The paper's here."

"Oh, fantastic. Let's have a look."

Leah leafed through the pages, urgently. "Look!" she announced. "There it is!"

Sea-Bay Auction Services

Leave it with us — we'll sell it for you!

12 Bayview Parade
The Seafront
Portscatho
(right next to Prowse the Grocer)

Want to find a home for your old heirlooms, clutter and bric-a-brac? Haven't got the time or the inclination to sell it yourself? We'll take all the hassle out of it for you. Just bring us your unwanted possessions and we'll market them for you on eBay. If we don't sell it, you don't pay us a penny.
WHAT HAVE YOU GOT TO LOSE?!

**GRAND OPENING TODAY,
SATURDAY 13TH AUGUST**

"Bring this flyer and claim a free cup of tea and a slice of cake. We look forward to seeing you!"
Toby Dobbs & Leah Pilgrim

"It looks great, doesn't it?"

Toby nodded and smiled. And then he stopped and stared at an envelope on top of the pile. The writing looked strangely familiar. It had an American stamp on it and had been addressed to Silversmith Road and redirected. Slowly he sliced the envelope open with a knife and pulled out a handwritten letter, three sheets long.

Dear Toby,

What can I say? Sorry doesn't really seem sufficient. I can't really explain why I did what I did. I was scared, I suppose, and angry. I realized immediately that I'd made a mistake moving in with Tim and I freaked out. I came back to the house. I was going to ask if I could stay for a few days, but you were out. And then I saw that cash in your room and something took me over. I felt like you'd let me down, abandoned me when I needed you most. So I took the lot and went straight to the airport and bought a one-way ticket to the States.

It's been a real trip. I stayed at the Chelsea at first. That was a blast, being where all those incredible people had been, where Sid killed Nancy. Then I found a room in a flat on the Lower East Side. I played at someone's wedding a few weeks later, mainly cover versions, but I threw in a couple of my new songs. And what do you know — someone liked them and bought them off me for $5,000! Some girl band is going to use them. Apparently they're really famous, but I've never heard of them.

I tried to persuade the guy to let me record them, but guess what he said? He said, "Beautiful girl, the world does not need another chick with an attitude and a guitar." Pah! That kind of took the shine off selling my songs. I went into a bit of a decline after that. I know, I know — I never appreciate what I've got. It's never enough, is it?

I started drinking quite heavily. Got through a lot of your cash that way. Pissed off my flatmates. And it was when they threatened to kick me out that I realized I needed to take control of my life. So I joined AA.

Yeah, yeah — I can hear you laughing from here! I know, it's hard to imagine. But it's been great. I'm on the 12-Step Program (only one "m"!) and part of that is that I have to redress any imbalances in my life, undo wrongdoings, make amends and apologize. I've written to Tim and his wife, to say sorry for fucking them around. And now here's my apology to you:

Toby, you are one of the greatest people I've ever known. It's taken being away from you for me to be able to see that. You took me in when I had nobody else and you took care of me and all I ever did was belittle you and take advantage. You're a better person than I could ever hope to be and I am so sorry to have broken your trust and let you down. You didn't deserve it. I really hope you managed to sell the house and that you have moved on and found happiness. No one deserves a happy ending more than you. I hope you can find it in your heart to forgive me, but if you don't that's fine.

As for me, well, there's no happy ending in sight just yet. I've written some more songs, but they didn't go for them. To pay the rent I'm working as a waitress in some trendy Vietnamese place in Greenwich Village. I haven't had a drink for five weeks and that, for now, is enough. I'll get there in the end, I know I will. When I do, I'll let you know. And maybe one day I'll be able to buy you that Lamborghini!

With love and respect,

Ruby xxxx

Toby passed the letter to Leah and sighed. He felt something in his heart loosen, untwist itself. Ruby was alive. Ruby was safe. Tonight, for the first time since she'd moved out of his house, Toby could fall asleep without wondering, without worrying. After nearly sixteen years, the last residual traces of Ruby had finally been expunged from the soft, sticky corners of his consciousness.

"That's good, isn't it?" said Leah, passing the letter back to him a moment later. "Good news?"

Toby nodded and smiled. "Very good news indeed."

"So," said Leah, "are you ready to go to work?"

Toby nodded, and together they headed towards the front of the cottage, towards their shop.

TERRY O'DONNELL and GAY GRAY

The health-promoting college

First published 1993

Published by the Health Education Authority
Hamilton House
Mabledon Place
London WC1H 9TX

ISBN 1 85448 540 7

Typeset by Alacrity Computer Typesetting Limited

Printed in Great Britain by Biddles Ltd, Guildford